To Becky,

Legend of the Lullabyer

By Ross C Hughes

Happy reading!

ISBN: 9798849892191
First Printing 2022
www.rosshughes.biz

Legend of the Lullabyer

A Fantasy Novel

By Ross C Hughes

Cover Design by Whitney Lynn Hayes

Published 2022

Also by Ross C Hughes

A Dead Wizard's Dream, Book 1 of the Convent Series

Secrets of the Ashlands, Book 2 of the Convent Series

The Man Who Sank An Island, Book 3 of the Convent Series

Into the Madlands, Book 4 of the Convent Series

Lord of Demons, Book 5 of the Convent Series

City of Peace, Book 6 of the Convent Series

Chronicles of Maradoum Volume 1

Chronicles of Maradoum Volume 2

Chronicles of Maradoum Volume 3

Chronicles of Maradoum Volume 4

Chronicles of Maradoum Volume 5

Chronicles of Maradoum Volume 6

Chronicles of Maradoum Volume 7

The Night Comes Alive: A Gothic Fantasy Novel

Space-Crazed: The Tragedy of Billy Cull

Dedicated to Bumble

Acknowledgements

A huge thank you to my friends and family and my readers, to everyone I meet at conventions and to my fellow authors. Y'all keep me going. A big thank you to Caribbean folklore for all the inspiration and much appreciation to Whitney Lynn Hayes for her fantastic cover design and map design and everything else.

Monastery Calliope
Oldport
Pog's End
Bessaroc
Blueschist Mountains
Dos Rios
N
The Belt
CHILPAEA
Nirby
Witchwood
Blueschist Mountains
Hatbrim
Maawu Palace
Cogoba Bay
Dragon Sea

1

Smuggler's Cove

All Jamba Klach wanted was sleep. Fate, however, had conspired against him. Trapped by a summer monsoon for days, he had found little time for sleep, needed on the rudder at all hours. He had smuggled the boxes of witch-spice out of Chilpaea without a hitch. It was the return journey that was proving troublesome. Following the currents sweeping south and east around the east coast of Quing Tzu had brought him south of the island of Chilpaea, and now his homeland blotted a shadowy lump on the dim northeast horizon.

Lightning cast a spell of daylight for a breath, before the world plunged once more into black bedlam. For that salty breath, his bloodshot eyes beheld rain like a cavalcade of duppy sheeting a mammoth headland rearing up out of the cantankerous ocean far ahead of *The Somnambulant's* bobbing bowsprit. Only a few seagulls and pelicans dared risk the elements that night, most having sought shelter as any sane creature would.

"Land ahoy!" the lookout called from the prow.

"Chilpaea," Jamba murmured, rain pitter-pattering his cocoa-skinned face, close-cropped salt-and-pepper hair and arrow-shaped beard. "Home sweet home."

Fog cushioned the craggy cliff face, softening the rough edges of certain death that awaited. The tireless tempest jarred the sea awake with caustic applause, making Jamba jump now and then as he wrestled with the rudder, loose pale shirt and tight dark breeches soaked. The wind was a banshee wailing into the fully battened fan-shaped sail, bellying it so that the junk skimmed along the top of the bawling breakers as if she had wings. The mast creaked worryingly, bending like a coconut palm, and waves slapped the side of the ship, splashing water over the junk's deck.

"Good work, Lug!" Jamba yelled to the lookout, a brainless lagahoo with more brawn than a bear who always went barefoot.

Lug Thorm waved at him with an arm whose muscles tested the limits of the plain shirt he wore, a simple smile cracking his hairless egg-like head. He had slit his breeches to give his tree-trunk legs greater mobility.

"What's the first thing you're going to do when we get home, Ruffle?" Jamba asked, leaning into the rudder.

Glyphs spelled in flame, letters of the Kwi patois spoken by the Chilapeans, materialised in mid-air above the deck before Jamba's eyes. He read them without batting an eye.

'Refill my baui pouch. I underestimated how long this trip would take.'

As the sigils faded away, Jamba's gaze shifted down to the old man in a faded red robe on deck who had cast the spell and he chuckled. Ruffle Feathers' star-shine dreadlocks sagged on his bony shoulders like a mass of tangled ropes in the rain and his long braided beard dripped, but the twinkle in his eyes the colour of the moon was as spry as ever. Crow's feet formed from a broad and often used smile patterned his leathery, nut-brown face. He smiled without opening his mouth.

"Aye," agreed Jamba in Kwi, "I drank the last of the rum a few days ago. It's this damned storm what's slowed us down."

'What about you?' Ruffle Feathers asked in letters of fire that hovered before Jamba's eyes for a second before disappearing.

"What will I do when we get home?" Jamba wondered aloud, puffing out his cheeks. "Sleep. Then, women and wine, I reckon. Not necessarily in that order. In fact, definitely not. After that, it's time for the next shipment."

Ruffle Feathers rolled his eyes and waved a hand. Words glimmered in the air like strands of straw set alight. 'You won't give us a break, will you?'

Jamba grinned. "Not till we're rich, Ruffle, not till we're rich!"

A thunderbolt sword slashed the shrouded sky, and by its split-second glow Jamba bore witness to sail-shaped shadows in the distance ahead of them.

"A Gods-damned patrol!" he roared in a hoarse baritone, dark eyes dilating.

"We should turn back, find another place to dock!" keened a beardless young man, wiry as a weasel with a face to match framed by lank locks.

Jamba tutted. "Tch, we are not turning back or finding another place to dock, Wevan, you yellow-bellied toad! The cove is the only way to get back to the growers' village in good time, and I'll not be put off by a few soldiers!"

"But the patrol!" Wevan whined. "And how will you even find the cove in this cursed mist and darkness?"

"By touch, if I must," Jamba snapped. "Now, be quiet so I can think."

"But if the seneschal's men catch us, all we'll see is iron bars for the rest of our lives!"

Another faux day flashed before their eyes for a heartbeat, revealing the square-cut sails of the line of ships ahead before the night claimed rulership once more.

"I think the seneschal is the last person we need to worry about right now," Jamba replied, straining against both the rudder and despair. "Our countrymen sail lateen-rigged ghanjahs. That's not a Chilpaean patrol, after all. It's a blockade around Cocoba Bay. If my guess is right, those are crusaders from Justiqua."

"What are you saying?" Wevan demanded over the seething elements.

"Well, lads," shouted Jamba, "it appears that while we were gone, Chilpaea was invaded. Those galleys will likely sink us on sight."

Jaws hung slack in the wake of the revelation.

"We have to turn back!" Wevan cried again, throwing up his arms in resignation.

"No!" shouted Jamba, tugging the rudder until *The Somnambulist* was sailing directly towards the line of towering warships. "Batten the hatches and douse the lanterns, gentlemen! Full sail ahead! We are running the blockade!"

"If those truly are Justiquan galleys, they will be far faster than us!" Wevan wailed. "How do you expect to outrun them in this weather?"

"The weather may help," Jamba shot back. "We're well hidden in this storm. And besides, the galleys have a far deeper keel than we have. If we can win past them, we can sail closer to the cliffs than they can. They'll scupper their hulls if they try to chase us!"

"Aye," agreed Wevan, "but only because they're twice the size of us, cap'n! They'll swallow us whole like a shark does a fish!"

Jamba snarled as he fought against the wind, trying to keep *The Somnambulist* on her northeast course. "Just loose the jib, damn your eyes!"

"This is madness!" Wevan railed, but he did as bidden, letting the jib sail fly in an effort to coax every ounce of speed from the junk.

Sinking into darkness as the lanterns winked out one by one, *The Somnambulist* picked up her pace even more, though still the choppy crests and troughs slapped her this way and that. The sky split open for an instant, and by the lightning's radiance Jamba estimated the distance between the ships at about two hundred yards. The galleys could cover that distance in seconds under full sail with rowers at their posts, but fortunately for him they had their sails furled in an attempt to hold their positions. That would give him a little extra time – he hoped. Still, it would be close.

"El Vandu, blind their eyes," Jamba whispered to the God of Luck. He spat into the ocean a moment later in disgust as another flash in the firmament disclosed that the two closest warships had begun to lower their sails, clearly having noticed the smugglers' small vessel. "Why piss on my parade, El Vandu?" Louder, he shouted, "Hold your nerve, men! We'll be past them before you can say Waddi-waddi three times!"

"And why would you ever want to do that?" Wevan shrieked in horror, making Jamba chortle.

Waddi-waddi was a legendary necromancer said to have lived hundreds of years ago before the Time of Witches, a tale of terror with which parents frightened their children. Saying his name three times was said to call him forth from the underworld.

The Somnambulist skimmed over the waves fast as a dragonfly, but the galleys were turning now and sailing towards one another to block the smugglers off.

"We're not going to make it!" Wevan yowled.

"Yes, we are!" Jamba growled.

Faint clunks and twangs pre-empted the boulders flung by catapults, the giant ballista bolts and a volley of arrows splashing down into the surf just beyond *The Somnambulist's* prow. One arrow slammed into the hull and quivered.

"We're about to come into range," Jamba realised. "Everybody down behind the gunwales!"

Wevan huddled into a ball in a corner, and Jamba suddenly felt very exposed standing in the middle of the deck, hands clamped to the rudder. He glanced down to see that Ruffle Feathers was still sat by his side, eyes closed, sliding this way and that on the damp deck as the ship tilted from side to side. Jamba shook his head in amazement. Lug looked ridiculous hiding behind the gunwale, like a gorilla hiding behind a picket fence.

A moment later, boulders, bolts and arrows were raining down all around them, most disappearing into the surf but some crashing down on *The Somnambulist.* The junk bucked as a boulder hit her and juddered under the impact of arrows before being knocked sharply to one side by a ballista bolt in her flank. Jamba cried out at the sight of the giant metal bolt piercing the hull, and again when Wevan toppled overboard with an arrow in his forehead. He wondered how the Justiquan archers had managed to miss Lug; the man was a mountain. *The Somnambulist* slowed thanks to her injury, and the galleys surged through the sea to intercept her.

"We're not going to make it," Jamba whispered, eyes wide as the gap between the galleys rapidly dwindled.

He caught movement out of the corner of his eye and turned to see Ruffle Feathers facing the galleys now, still sitting cross-legged but somehow anchored in place so that he no longer slid from side to side with the boat's movement. The old man was forming arcane patterns in the air with his gnarly hands, fingers flicking dextrously while his wide sleeves hung down like wings. As if gashed by an invisible sword, the night ripped asunder then, the very fabric of reality between different realms of being tearing wide open in the form of a red rift like a ghastly maw breathing out sulphuric smoke and incarnadine flames. From the rift poured forth a pair of demonic entities that would have made Jamba think he was hallucinating if he had not seen them before.

What looked like two three-foot-long snakes slithered out, both consumed by flames from head to tail. They curled back on themselves, floating in the air, to stare the obeahman who had summoned them in the eye.

"What would you have of us, master?" they hissed in unison in

Traveller's in sibilant tones, forked tongues flickering in and out.

Ruffle pointed to the galleys, and the two blazing serpents bobbed their heads.

"They will burn in our fire!" the demons hissed, before spinning around and shooting through the air like burning arrows straight towards the Justiquan ships.

The galleys were ablaze and sinking within seconds, and Jamba watched in horror as the demonic snakes roamed around the ships' decks, punching holes in sailors' chests and throats and hollowing them out from the inside. *The Somnambulist* sailed unhindered between the two sinking ships, the desperate pleas of sailors clinging to debris in the water echoing in Jamba's ears.

"Full sail ahead!" he shouted over the lump in his throat. "We stop for no one."

Ruffle held up his hands once more, and Jamba noticed a red aurora swimming around them. The demonic serpents were hauled against their will as if by an invisible leash back into the rift, disappearing from sight. The dimensional tear glued itself shut with a *pop,* vanishing as swiftly as it had appeared. The glow around Ruffle's hands faded away, and he slumped back to lie flat on the deck with a sigh.

"Good work, Ruffle," Jamba yelled, the words sticking in his craw for a moment as he once more considered that he was in league with demons.

Hobbling and wounded, *The Somnambulist* won past the twin galleys, but others had seen them, witnessed what they had done, and were rapidly closing in from east and west to catch the junk before it could enter Cocoba Bay, an ancient caldera, and the eponymous capital city of Chilpaea. *The Somnambulist* had no intention of sailing into Cocoba Bay, however, where Jamba could faintly make out a fleet of Justiquan schooners out in the open water ahead of him, along with the expected dhows and ghanjahs of his people, all of which were docked. Instead, Jamba threw his weight onto the rudder, grunting and spitting with effort. *The Somnambulist* bobbed and slowly began to crane her head around, as if curious to see what lay west of the bay.

Lug cried out in dismay as the craggy cliffs rearing up on the bay's west shoulder loomed out of the mist before them; the foundation for Maawu Palace, the seat of the ruler of Chilpaea, the Lullabyer. He cried out again as *The Somnambulist* barely turned in time to avoid shipwreck and sail past the jagged rocks. Jamba winced as he felt the hull scrape against rock on the starboard side. Fortunately, the horrible grating sensation lasted only a second, and Jamba was confident no lasting damage had been done. That was what he told himself anyway, as a lifeline to sanity.

The turn brought *The Somnambulist* closer to the galley closing in from the west, and rocks and arrows started to pock the junk's deck once more as the crusaders came in range. The galley could not close the final distance between them now, however, for *The Somnambulist* had slipped into the sweet spot between the razor-sharp reef and the unyielding cliffs, where its shallower keel allowed it to carefully navigate between the myriad treacheries hidden just beneath the surface. The galley had no hope of crossing the reef with its deeper keel; it would sink the second it tried, and its captain knew it. All the Justiquans could do now was pray to bring down the junk from afar. They almost succeeded.

Jamba cried out as *The Somnambulist* lurched to the right under the booming impact of a boulder, almost smashing to pieces on the rocks. Jamba frantically tugged the rudder, and the junk lived to sail another few minutes. It was all the smuggler needed.

"If we can get into that mist, we'll lose them!" he yelled as an arrow splintered the deck barely a foot away, straining against the rudder to keep the junk in the pocket between reef and rocks. "The cove is close by! We can make it, lads!"

Every muscle taut, he watched the fog inch closer while the closest galley paralleled the junk's course like a hunter. He prayed to every God he knew then that the mist would hold. Just before the fog engulfed her, a boulder crashed down on *The Somnambulist's* deck, a volley of arrows tore through the rust-coloured, fan-shaped sail and two ballista bolts punctured the hull on the port side.

"No!" Jamba roared as the junk limped into the mist, already starting to sink.

The galleys disappeared behind the swirling grey curtain, and their aim was scuppered as surely as their hulls would be by the reef. Their projectiles landed harmlessly in the water after that. It did not matter, Jamba thought morosely; the damage was done.

His heart ached as he whisper-shouted, "Grab everything! Abandon ship!"

As the sun started to rise on the far side of the pearlescent phantomscape, Jamba Klach, Ruffle Feathers and Lug Thorm hauled themselves up out of the Dragon Sea and into the smugglers' cove at the foot of the cliffs, far beneath Maawu Palace.

Lying flat on the rock, shivering and gasping for breath, Jamba saw words of fire flash before his eyes.

'It seems we are at war.'

2

The Lullabyer's Fate

Maawu Palace was built as a statement, a response to all the lavish palaces of gold, marble and jade in Zamphia. The only one of its kind in all of Chilpaea, the palace did not represent one man's greed and ego, but an entire nation's. Not reserved purely for the ruler of the land and his family, with no guards or watchmen at the entrance, the jade-dome-topped palace swung its gilded doors open wide to all and sundry as a place of peace and relaxation, of barter and mingling, of contest and sport. And so, naturally, it had rapidly descended from an elegant architectural marvel to a raucous bazaar full of the poor and homeless, grateful just to have a roof over their heads. At night, folk with nowhere else to sleep congregated in the airy, marble-built palace in their hundreds until it more resembled a stacked out slaughterhouse – which was what it became the night the Justiquans invaded.

Though no guards were posted at the entry to the palace, a few stood to attention inside to protect the upper levels where the chambers of the Lullabyer and his family and officials could be found. As Jeremias Colcott, Seneschal of Chilpaea, was yanked roughly out of bed by his curly cloud-grey hair, he realised those guards must already be dead. He clawed, kicked and punched at his captors as panic bubbled up in his belly, but to no avail. He recalled the days he had wielded the sword with consummate strength and skill; those days were gone. The summer of his life was over. His autumn had begun. Old and weak, he was easily borne forth by the burly warriors in steel plate armour who came for him. Clad in loose blue nightclothes, he was dragged along the carpeted corridors of the palace, past stacks of dead bodies with familiar faces – all minor officials of the Lullabyer's court.

He bounced painfully on his rear end down the wide, curving marble stairs to the open-roofed atrium, where flickering light from the raging storm illuminated in transient flashes the sculpted pillars hiding a shadowed walkway ringing the central court. Terror fogged his mind. Knights clogged his view. He screamed as he was hauled limply over bloodied, dark-skinned bodies piled high in the atrium and had enough breath left only to whimper by the time his captors threw him unceremoniously to the mosaic floor at the feet of a towering blonde, pale-skinned warrior in steel plate armour, his hand resting on the hilt of the broadsword at his belt. A moment later, Jeremias was joined on his knees by his brother, the Lullabyer's steward, Berkley Colcott, and a few other high-ranking officials.

"What do you want from us?" he asked one of the Justiquan knights tentatively.

"Shut up!" the man growled, cuffing him with a gauntleted hand.

Not long later, the severed heads of the Lullabyer and his eldest son were brought to the blonde man, swinging in the gauntleted grip of two knights by their long hair, the dark-skinned faces slack, eyes glassy, necks still dripping gore. Jeremias closed his eyes and felt tears trickle down his cheeks. Magnuz and Dajuan Opherio had not deserved such a fate. The Lullabyer had been a good man, a friend, and no truer example of kindness and charity had existed than his son. More than that, though, the Lullabyer and his heir had held Chilpaea together with their song. Without them, the country was doomed.

"The Sleepers must not awaken," Jeremias whispered, barely aware of doing so and trembling violently.

"Just as you asked, Knight-Commander Saint-Marcente," said one of the knights in soft, sibilant tones, pale as a duppy and scrawny as a skeleton with a shock of bone-white hair.

He held up the Lullabyer's head so that the Knight-Commander, the tall blonde warrior with silver stubble, could stare into its eyes.

Doing so, the man said softly in a deep resonant voice, "Very good, Marshal Clauss, thank you. They gave you no trouble, then?"

"We killed them in their sleep, just like you said," said the other knight in an even baritone, his pink face piggish beneath a bowl-cut. "They never got a chance to make a sound."

The Knight-Commander nodded. "Good, good. You never fail me, Major Ortega. Mount the heads on spikes out in front of the palace as soon as you can. And what of the wife and child?"

Major Ortega gestured, and two of his men escorted a dark-skinned woman bearing a babe forward, a hand on each of her arms. Like the seneschal, she had clearly been torn from her bed in only a creamy nightgown. Jeremias' heart panged as he recognised the Lullabyer's second wife, Annja. He knew the babe must be her new-born daughter, Patma.

"Greetings from another land, Annja Opherio," said the blonde man, bowing mockingly. He held out his hands calmly. "Let me see the child."

Annja clutched the babe closer to her breast and shook her head vehemently.

The Knight-Commander sighed impatiently. "Come, come now, let me see the child. I will not harm her, I swear it by the Prophet."

Jeremias frowned as goosebumps prickled his flesh, feeling a strange current surge through the room like an arcane undertow. Annja's eyes glazed over as if she had been hypnotised and, to the seneschal's horror, she handed over the child without a word. Knight-Commander Saint-Marcente took the babe gently, rocked her in his armoured arms and hummed to her, waving the blanket in which she was wrapped before her face like a toy. The baby gurgled.

"No, I will never hurt her," the Justiquan cooed. "What's her name?"

"Patma," Aanja said like an automaton.

"Patma." Knight-Commander Saint-Marcente met Aanja's eyes. "I will raise her as if she were my own."

He nodded to the major, who had passed the severed head of Dajuan Opherio to Marshal Clauss. As Aanja lurched forward to snatch back her baby with an outcry, whatever spell that had transfixed her clearly dissipating, Major Ortega backhanded her in the back of the skull, sending her sprawling to the ground alongside so many other bodies. Before she could rise, Ortega plunged his broadsword into her heart and she gasped and fell back, blood bubbling up on her lips.

"Patma," she whispered in terror, before her soul set sail for the Sunset Isles.

"Thank you, major," the Knight-Commander said softly, still rocking the babe. "Carry on."

The major thumped his breastplate with a gauntlet, took the severed heads of Magnuz and Dajuan Opherio from Marshal Clauss and marched stiffly away with the skulls swinging by his sides, like the visage of death itself. A rotund dark-skinned fellow with wavy umber hair strode into the seneschal's view then, approaching the Knight-Commander to whisper in his ear. Jeremias growled low in the back of his throat unconsciously at the sight of Councillor Chup Morton, a fellow Chilpaean in the Lullabyer's court, speaking so freely and easily with the enemy.

"Traitor!" snapped Berkley, struggling to rise, only to be smacked back down by a knight's gauntlet.

Morton smirked at the Colcotts as he departed, and Jeremias wanted to rip his moustache from his lip and his eyes from his skull.

"Seneschal Jeremias Colcott," said the Knight-Commander loudly then, "identify yourself."

As Seneschal, Jeremias ranked second only to the Lullabyer as most influential person in the land. While the Lullabyer performed his nightly duties of song as a spiritual figurehead, the seneschal took care of the more pragmatic day to day affairs of all of Chilpaea. He took a deep breath, about to identify himself, when to his surprise, his older brother spoke up.

"I am Jeremias Colcott, Seneschal of Chilpaea," said Berkley, rising to his feet with a wince, his thin dark-skinned face drawn with pain.

It looked as though a patch of his silver hair had been ripped out. He shot Jeremias a warning look, telling him to keep quiet. Jeremias' mind raced. Berkley was the Lullabyer's steward, his personal attendant and fast friend. But he did not run the country. Jeremias did. Jeremias understood then that his older brother was trying to sacrifice himself so that the younger – the more important to all of Chilpaea – could survive. His eyes welled again.

"I'll do anything you ask," said Berkley. "I only ask that you spare my little brother, Berkley, the Lullabyer's steward." He gestured to Jeremias. "He can be helpful to you. He can show you the location of the Lullabyer's treasure chambers. Please, just spare his life."

"Agreed," said Saint-Marcente nonchalantly, making a gesture.

Marshal Clauss stepped up behind Berkley, seized his hair and slit his throat with a dagger. Berkley hit the marble floor in a pool of his own blood with a thud, gazing up adoringly at his little brother. He tried to smile reassuringly just before the light faded from his eyes. The true seneschal felt cold to his core then, as though it were his blood slowly pooling on the floor. The colour drained from the room, his surroundings becoming ephemeral, surreal and dreamlike as his head swam … what was the point of carrying on?

He thought of what his brother would have said. His brother would have told him that he had sacrificed himself so that Jeremias could go on, so that he could protect and serve the country both of them loved so much. Jeremias took a deep shuddering breath. Even as a figment of his imagination, Berkley was right – as usual. Still, he knew he would never forget Marshal Clauss' cold, aloof face as the man slit his brother's throat, or the callous face of Saint-Marcente as he gave the order.

"So, Berkley," said the blonde man, rocking the baby, "where is this treasure your brother spoke of?"

Not long later, Jeremias was leading the Knight-Commander and a score of his knights through a locked door at the bottom of the palace to which only the Lullabyer, himself and his brother held a key. He escorted them down through labyrinthine passages carved into the headland beneath Maawu Palace, down to the Lullabyer's treasure chamber in a cavern deep underground. The light of torches borne by some of the knights flickered over irregular walls red as a dragon's gullet. The Lullabyer's hoard was modest, just a few million doubloons, a cache of purple-blue crystals of varying sizes and a few hundred gold and silver ingots. Jeremias knew the Lullabyer would not have cared about the gold. He would have cared about his country.

So, as the Justiquans whooped and hooted and rooted through the gold with all the enthusiasm of pigs sniffing for truffles, Jeremias whispered the words to a spell he had never thought he would utter again. It had been a long time since the seneschal had cast a cantrap of any sort, and yet the occult words imprinted themselves on his eyelids as if branded there. The purple-blue crystals swelled in his perception until they consumed his vision, pulsing and glowing brighter and brighter. Up above, he had not been able to sense them, not been able to use them. But down here, he could feel their arcane energies surging through his body in response to the words of power, making his hairs stand on end and his skin tingle. Warmth flooded his frame, bearing him high on wings of nirvana until his curly hair buzzed with latent energy.

"What are you doing?" Knight-Commander Saint-Marcente demanded suddenly, noticing the old man clinging to the wall, alight with an eldritch aurora.

"Jangala bronzaquika!" Jeremias shrieked, flinging out his hand and completing the spell.

The rugged rock floor of the treasure chamber wobbled and then abruptly gave way, crumbling like a biscuit soaked too long in tea and pitching the treasure, the Knight-Commander and his twenty knights down into darkness with an ongoing clattering boom.

3

Cave In

"Yargh!" Jamba Klach yelped as the ceiling collapsed on him.

Along with Ruffle Feathers and Lug Thorm, he had been traversing the tunnel carved into the headland beneath Maawu Palace that led from the smuggler's cove to their village hideout in the Blueschist Mountains close by, on the island's west coast.

Now, buried under rubble in utter blackness and groaning as pain split him open, he gasped in rock dust and coughed, wheezing, "Ruffle? Lug? Are you there? Are you okay?"

Letters of flame burned in the air, banishing the darkness. It took Jamba a moment to suss them, for they were facing the wrong way.

'Fine and dandy.'

Somehow, Jamba sensed the words were sarcastic. He struggled up to a sitting position and gradually eased himself out from under the rocks that had tumbled down on top of him, marvelling that he had broken no bones. His clothes were torn, and grazes and bruises painted him black, blue and red, but at least he was alive, he thought, locating Ruffle and Lug amid the swirling dust motes and debris by the light of the words 'Fine and dandy', which still hung in the air.

Then, he saw what else had fallen on top of them. Gold. And Justiquan knights. But more importantly, gold. The gold glittered in the light of the fiery words, reflecting the glitter in Jamba's own eyes as he reached out to grab a handful of doubloons and stuff them into his pocket. They fell straight back out of the hole in the bottom of the pocket, and he cursed and grabbed another handful.

"Hey!" barked one of the steel-plate-clad men, a massive blonde fellow with silvery stubble, rising to his feet unsteadily. He did not appear to notice the words scrawled in fire behind him. "Put those down. Those are property of the Justiquan army."

Jamba arched an eyebrow. "Oh? Says who?"

The blonde man drew himself up and whipped out his broadsword, pointing the three-foot steel blade at the smuggler. "I do. Knight-Commander Godfrey Saint-Marcente, at your service."

"At my service?" Jamba repeated mockingly. "Oh my, how gracious."

The Knight-Commander smiled mirthlessly. "It's a turn of phrase. But also true. You see, the service I am rendering your country is to rid it of sorcerers, witches and pagan scum. That's why we're here, you know. To help. So, *put those down!"*

He growled the last words and flicked the fingers of his spare hand. Jamba felt an eerie unseen force clamp around his midsection like an iron band, seizing both of his arms in inescapable grips, and his skin crawled as he realised he had been enchanted. He dropped the doubloons in shock.

"I thought you just said you were here to rid the land of magic!" he gasped as the unseen hands started to squeeze the life out of him.

The Knight-Commander laughed sardonically. "What can I say? Sometimes, you must fight fire with fire."

Jamba smirked as the words, 'I agree' flickered in the air for a moment behind the Knight-Commander's head.

As the words faded away, Jamba saw a flash of yellow light and the Knight-Commander suddenly face-planted the floor with a clang. Past the fallen knight, the smuggler glimpsed a small but bright golden rift that stank of rotten fruit sucking back in what looked like a furry white arm before it disappeared in a flash. Gasping in breath, Jamba beheld Ruffle Feathers buried under debris, grinning weakly. He hurried past the hanging words, 'Help me!' and unearthed the obeahman, before finding and uncovering Lug, who was dazed and battered but alive. Once the three were back on their feet, Jamba started scooping up doubloons by the handful and stuffing them in any pocket that would hold them. Lug coughed on the rock dust and glanced up. Through the hole in the ceiling, he beheld another cave, dark since all the torches had fallen. A man's head poked into view in the cave above, looking down. Lug waved. The ageing curly-haired man above thrust out a hand and waved back.

Ruffle Feathers meanwhile had eyes only for the purple-blue crystals that had fallen from the treasure chamber. He covetously snatched them up one by one, ignoring Jamba's insistences that he take only doubloons. He cared nothing for the coins. Once he had a small armful of the gems, all glittering in the fiery words' radiance, he noticed one in particular, shaped like a robed man, that seemed to call to him somehow. Picking it up and peering at it closely, he dropped it in surprise when he saw a face inside and heard a faint echo of a cry for help. Recognising the face, he picked it up again tentatively.

In the cavern above, Seneschal Jeremias Colcott watched with wide eyes as Ruffle Feathers picked up the oddly shaped crystal, a knot forming in his stomach. He could not climb down, and he did not want to hurt anyone.

"Hey, you!" he hollered in Kwi. "Old man in the red robe! Ruffle Feathers! Put that crystal down immediately!"

Ruffle looked up and saw the speaker, then tucked the crystal into his leather satchel with all the others.

"Put it down, I say!" Jeremias raged, shaking his fist. "D'you know who that is? Put that crystal back or suffer the consequences, you hear? Take any other crystal you want, but please *put that back!"*

Ruffle did not answer, only stared up at the man defiantly past the Kwi words of flame, 'Help me!' yet hanging in the air.

Jeremias scowled. "I do not want to hurt you, Ruffle."

Ruffle waved a gnarly hand, and a bubble of bright gold energy sprang up around him, Jamba and Lug, flickering and wavering, an arcane shield capable of withstanding most magical assaults.

He waved a hand again and the words, 'We both know you cannot,' bloomed in fire in mid-air.

Jeremias shook his head in vexation, but he knew the old man was right. There was nothing he could do. "You are no true obeahman, Ruffle! You're a thief and a scoundrel! Obeah is meant for healing, not summoning demons!"

Witnessing the exchange, his pockets full of doubloons, Jamba tugged on Ruffle Feathers' sleeve, muttering in Kwi, "Come on, Ruffle."

He turned to the tunnel leading inland, which had survived the cave in unlike the tunnel leading back to the cove, and cursed as over a dozen armoured Justiquan knights rose groggily to their feet to block his path with belligerent expressions and broadswords in hand.

The knights took one glance at the glowing golden aegis surrounding the smugglers, cried out in Traveller's, "Sorcerers!" and charged as one, swords pointed like lances.

Jamba thanked El Vandu that only one of them bore a shield, a steel heater shield shaped like the island of Justiqua itself with three prongs at the top. He despised fighting against shields, considering them the coward's choice. He whipped out twin wide-bladed, three-foot steel scimitars from the snakeskin sheaths at his hips, while Lug tugged a heavy iron warhammer from the leather straps on his broad back, crisscrossing his barrel chest. His boulderous shoulders bulging, the simple-minded smuggler hefted the hammer high to await the knights, a placid, faintly curious expression on his dark-skinned, egg-like face.

Simple-minded he may have been, but he swung the hammer with all the expertise of a master lumberjack felling an old oak, caving in the steel helm and skull of the first knight to come within range with a perfectly timed blow that rang like a gong. He could not bring the heavy hammer to bear fast enough to thwart the next knight's attack, though, and he thought for a moment he was about to feel cold steel in his belly. Fur sprouted across his frame, and he growled savagely. He breathed a sigh of relief as one of Jamba's twin scimitars licked out to deflect the broadsword away from his gut, while the other scimitar found its way between helmet and cuirass into the knight's gullet. Lug spat and hastily wiped his eyes with a paw as the man's blood sprayed his face.

Once he could see, he rampaged towards his remaining foes, Jamba's calls for him to stay back seeming faint and faraway behind the red haze that clouded his normally jovial tawny eyes. His wolf-like snout scrunched up in a snarl, ursine ears twitching, and he swung the hammer with unmatched ferocity in huge paws, swatting down one knight and then another in as many seconds. A sword cut open his brawny, hairy arm, and he bellowed like a lion with a thorn in its paw as his blood spilled out. His hammer took the offender in the chest, crushing his ribcage regardless of the steel breastplate etched with an inverted V in white, the symbol of the Justiquans' paradise, *Citta Pacia.*

Then, his enemies had him cornered on three sides and he backed away, flailing his hammer to keep them at bay and roaring in pain and fury as their blades shallowly flayed his flesh time and again. None dared come close enough to the monster he had become for a death blow, however, afraid of the claws, snapping jaws and wildly waving hammer that could so easily stove in a skull. Lug retreated until he was once more by Jamba's side, breathing heavily, great chest heaving.

Jamba shook his head both at the stupidity of the lagahoo and in amazement at his feat. He had singlehandedly taken down three of their opponents and wounded a fourth and fifth as he retreated. The smuggler had no further time for marvelling then, however, as the knights lunged towards him. His scimitars flicked out with practised ease to smoothly steer aside the broadswords, stealing their wielders' momentum and unbalancing them so that the ripostes would find them staggering and unprotected.

Jamba had not once been hailed as the finest swordsman in Chilpaea for no reason. Before his fall from grace, he had won several tourneys and amassed a small fortune purely on the back of his swordsmanship. That, he reflected, had been his downfall. He would never admit it aloud, but he knew he was no longer as fast or as strong as he had been in his prime. His dark hair was greying, his paunch growing, his knees achy, his eyes failing.

Despite all this, the knights were slow and clumsy in their weighty armour, their broadswords far slower than his own thinner swords. He moved among them like quicksilver, faster on his feet, his blade a blur their eyes could not follow, and blood seemed to jet from their severed throats and the major arteries in their groins and armpits as if of its own accord in the wake of the graceful looping arcs of his humming scimitars. By his side, Lug bludgeoned them down with all the tact of a blundering bear.

Despite their curious mix of strength and skill, Lug and Jamba were soon on the back foot in the face of so many foes, overwhelmed by sheer numbers. They backed away, first just one step to gain a little space, and then another, and another. Once begun, the pattern was nigh unalterable, and Jamba knew it. Many were the duels he had fought where a lucky exchange had forced a foe onto the back foot and they had never recovered. The surviving knights thronged together, providing fewer openings by constantly attacking.

To his annoyance, Jamba soon found he was no longer taking initiative, no longer initiating exchanges, only responding – and not even riposting, only parrying. He had no time for a counterattack between defensive swipes, and Lug was similarly pressed, using his iron-banded warhammer like a staff to stave off the broadswords seeking his thick neck. The repeated clang of steel on iron echoed through the caves as if a sword were being forged, and indeed Lug felt as though he were burning up in a crucible. He panted like a dog in summer, wilting. Jamba, too, was sagging like a sail without any wind.

"Ruffle!" he wheezed. "Ruffle, help us! Cast a spell! Summon your snakes! Do something, please!"

The words 'Help me!' winked out, throwing the cavern into utter darkness for a split second before the words 'I cannot without lowering my shield,' flamed into existence in their place. Smugglers and knights alike cried out in primeval terror as blackness overtook them for a heartbeat, and several men almost died in the confusion of the moment before regular combat resumed. Jamba did not know much of sorcery, but he had been around Ruffle Feathers long enough to know a little. What little he knew told him that a shining golden shield, like the one Ruffle had conjured, protected an obeahman against magical attacks, but not physical ones.

So, Jamba reasoned, Ruffle was not protecting the smugglers from the knights. He was protecting them from the seneschal. Perhaps the seneschal could wipe them all out with a word, Jamba thought uneasily, a finger of fear tracing his spine. Perhaps it was best the old man focussed all his attention on the shield after all. Still, he wished the obeahman could have been of more help against the knights. Slowly but surely, the Justiquans were battering down the two Chilpaeans, forcing them back further and further from the tunnel leading inland until they were tripping over rubble and the bodies of fallen Justiquans. It was only a matter of time, Jamba thought morbidly, before the end came.

A kerfuffle sounded above, and Jamba strained his ears to make out its source. Voices, clattering and the skirl of metal on metal echoed down faintly from above, growing louder and louder by the second. Torchlight flooded the cave overhead. Soon, Jamba could make out some of the voices. Some spoke the foreign fricative tongue of the Justiquans, but some spoke in melodious Kwi patois. One in particular was spine-tinglingly familiar.

"Magnuz! Dajuan! Colcott!" it hollered in Kwi in an authoritative bass voice loud enough to wake the dead. "Magnuz! Dajuan! Colcott! Where are you? Are you down here, Colcott? Or you, Lullabyer? It is I, General

Raoul Malone! Lullabyer? Dajuan? Colcott? Magnuz!"

Jamba's mind raced. The Chilpaean army – or part of it, at least – had somehow broken past the Justiquans in the palace and fought their way down to the treasure chamber in search of the seneschal and the Lullabyer and his son. That could be a boon if they took his side against the Justiquan knights. It could also, however, prove a fatal twist of fate if the general turned on the smugglers.

Jamba and the others walked a fine line of legality. The psychoactive drug, witch-spice, was not illegal to grow or consume in Chilpaea, nor was selling it to Chilpaeans. Selling it to Zamphish warlocks, on the other hand, was a crime punishable by life imprisonment – a fact Jamba well knew, having heard of the unpleasant fate of some of his comrades who had been caught in the past. So, he did not know whether to cry or rejoice at the sound of the general's voice. He had once considered the man a true friend when they had served in the army together in their youth. Now, he was not so sure he could count on that old bond.

"Colcott!" General Malone boomed, obviously laying eyes on the seneschal. "I'm sorry about your brother. I saw his body in the atrium. It is good to see you alive, though! Where is the Lullabyer?"

"He's dead, Malone!" Jeremias replied in a tinny tenor. "I'm sorry! We have to get out of here – but first, we have to stop those smugglers down there!"

Hearing the seneschal, Jamba cursed, "Twins be damned for this nightmare!"

The skirl of sword on sword clamoured in his ears as the general and the Chilpaeans above battled a path through the Justiquans, growing louder and louder as they drew closer and closer. Jamba fought like a cornered rat, barely able to keep up with the movement of his own looping scimitars as they performed the parrying and attack patterns that hours of training had instilled into his muscles, desperate to escape before the general found a way down to them or the Knight-Commander awoke. He was hemmed in by blades on all sides, though, and even when he occasionally did find time for a counterattack, his scimitars were always batted aside by the veteran knights. Besides these frustratingly few occasions, his blades circled in defensive patterns, unable to do aught else without leaving him exposed to a killing blow.

He was soon trapped against the wall directly beneath the treasure chamber, with the collapsed tunnel leading back to the cove on his right and the tunnel leading inland on his left. Lug stood by his side on wobbly legs, now and then clubbing at the knights with his hammer but mostly also forced into a defensive stance, wielding his hammer with both paws to knock aside the deadly broadswords ever seeking his flesh. His hirsute shoulders burned from the effort of repeatedly hefting his hammer and enduring the knights' onslaught. He wanted to do his best for his friends, Jamba and Ruffle, to protect them, but his arms were beginning to shake.

Cowering behind them and maintaining the glittering, faintly humming golden sphere around the smugglers, Ruffle Feathers cast his gaze upwards when he heard the general's voice, knowing he could be of no help to the smugglers. He had heard rumours some obeahmen could perform more than one spell at once, but he wasn't sure he believed them. It was one thing to cast a spell and write words of flame in the air at the same time. Anything more than that was beyond him. It hurt his head to try. So, instead he spent his efforts on trying in vain to see over the lip of rock above them to the skirmish so clearly being fought. The bitter scents of blood and sweat amalgamated in his nostrils to make him choke as if on toxic fumes. Now and then, bits of rock crumbled down on him, passing through his golden shield unhindered to strike him and make his eyes water. Past them, though, he could make out the dark-skinned, curly-haired head of the seneschal peeking down now and again.

Jamba could barely lift his scimitars. He started composing his last prayers to Gods and Ferrymen alike, finding a strange peace settle over him at the thought of eternal rest. A crash jarred him back to reality as a knight from above toppled onto one of those seeking his blood, crushing the man in an instant. Blessed sleep would have to wait, Jamba thought sourly. The other knights froze in shock for a split-second, and Jamba slit open the inner thigh of one so that he'd bleed to death and rammed half his other sword's length into another knight's throat, the steel blade scraping between helmet and cuirass. He ripped it back out in a spurt of gore.

The surviving knights facing him roared in outrage, but before a single one of them could swing a sword, they were – to a man – abruptly pincushioned by a buzzing barrage of arrows from above. They crumpled at Jamba and Lug's feet, armour and flesh punctured, to the smugglers' amazement. That was when Jamba realised the sounds of fighting from above had ceased. Feeling Ruffle tap his shoulder and looking up, he realised the Chilpaean soldiers must have slain all of the Justiquans in the treasure chamber when he saw Seneschal Jeremias Colcott and General Raoul Malone glaring down at him through the golden sheen of Ruffle Feathers' magical shield, backlit by torchlight.

Jeremias started to speak, but the general spoke over him in a booming, commanding bass, "Give us back the crystals, Jamba Klach. That's right. I remember you. I was sorry to hear you sold your family's estate. The Klach family was once a proud part of the court." He shook his head in disgust. "What are you doing, stealing from your own people? We are at war, Jamba, as you can see with your own eyes. Why do you not stand with us?

Help us, please, by giving back those crystals."

Jamba hesitated. Perhaps the general was right. What kind of a man stole from his own country in the midst of a war that could plunge the nation into abasement, poverty and servitude? He tasted bile in the back of his throat as he considered what he had become. The crystals *were* worth a fortune, though … He looked to Ruffle, who shook his head. Jamba clenched his jaw and opened his mouth to speak, but before he could, loud shouts resounded in the cavern above and the song of steel on steel was sung once more.

The seneschal and general glanced around to see what was happening, and Jamba, surmising correctly that more Justiquan knights had entered the treasure chamber to combat the Chilpaean army, shoved Lug towards the tunnel leading inland, grunting, "Run!"

By the time the seneschal and general turned back to the hole in the ground, the smugglers were gone, as were the words of fire that had been hanging in the air. They just caught sight of Ruffle Feathers' trailing red robe as it vanished down the tunnel, illuminated by a golden aegis.

The tunnel mouth caved in on itself a moment later, and Jeremias moaned, "No!"

4

And Cocoba Bay Wept

The horrors of the sacking of Cocoba Bay would haunt Jeremias Colcott, Seneschal of Chilpaea, until the day he died.

'Pillagers plunged in plundering paws, and Cocoba Bay wept for her lost sons and daughters, her forsaken hopes and dreams.'

Jeremias was reminded of the old poem by one of the country's foremost playwrights, written before he was born of a time when Chilpaea came into combative contact with an armada of Tzunese pirates hoping to establish a base of operations on the island at the expense of the capital's populace. Then, as now, Cocoba Bay wept. The seneschal could hear her plaintive cries on the howling wind, see her reaching out for help with arms of smog and kicking up a swell in the ocean. Carcasses stained her storm-shaded matronly stone-and-timber visage as she wept tears of blood for her lost sons and daughters once more.

Fire-lit tableaus and blood-splattered images of that night flickered across Jeremias' mind's eye every time he tried to sleep thereafter; scenes of women put to the sword and ravaged, of babes snatched from their arms only to have their brains dashed out on whichever wall was closest, of piles of dead dark-skinned men heaped half as high as the burning houses. Some of the grander structures were constructed of stone, but most of the homes were timber-built and thatched and caught like kindling so that a wildfire blazed uncontrollably through the city, infecting even parts of the docks where the Chilpaean dhows and ghanjahs sank in fiery ignominy.

The flaming city sprawled out beneath Jeremias as he escaped into the tempest, gasping for breath, from Maawu Palace with General Raoul Malone, Chilpaean soldiers all around him fighting and dying for every step he took. Even as he took it in, he witnessed the Justiquan galleys in the bay launching rocks and barrels of what he guessed to be spirits into the city, the actions strangely soundless, as if he were watching children's toys. The barrels exploded in plumes of flame with only distant booms, and tenements came crashing down beneath the boulders. Jeremias' mind reeled at the absurdity of it all, and overhead the Gods peered down through a black shroud of cloud and cackled with lightning teeth and clapped thunderous hands. The seneschal wondered if it were true that the rain was Merejulanna's tears, falling for all the sins of mankind. Somehow, he hoped so. He hoped at least one of the Gods was weeping for his country.

People scurried through the cobbled streets like ants, fleeing the Justiquan army advancing slowly from the mostly intact southern half of the docks, the armoured soldiers glinting in the firelight like silver beetles. The screams of his people clawed at Jeremias' ears, and his heart panged for every soldier that died during that mad dash as he hurtled down the hill towards the burning city with General Malone.

The city had fallen. The crusaders were already solidifying their hold on the docks and the palace, clearly preparing to plant their flag. The seneschal could not stay in the city if he wished to survive, and nor could the army, which was vastly outnumbered and already greatly depleted. The only way out was through.

The seneschal half-wished Chilpaea had a grander army then as he ran, tail between his legs, but he knew that was not the Chilpaean way. And it would be a waste of manpower, under normal circumstances. Chilpaea was an island with few enemies, and so it employed only a small standing army comprised mostly of young rotating conscripts who served only for two mandatory years before retiring and seeking a career elsewhere. As a result, Chilpaea was a country of craftsmen and artists – and, unfortunately, criminals. That, thought Jeremias, was as it should be. Warfare was not a career. Despite that, he wished he could magic up another few thousand Chilpaean soldiers right then and there as he plunged with what few hundred men the general could muster into the war-torn bedlam of the streets of Cocoba Bay.

Pale-skinned Justiquan soldiers in steel armour swarmed up every road in the dock district, blocking their every path, still pouring into the city from the quays. Defended on all sides by a throng of Chilpaean soldiers in leather armour, the seneschal and general skidded down the hill to the city through blood-slick streets and proceeded through corpse-choked avenues lined on either side by the burning husks of tall stone houses, coughing on smoke borne on the salty sea wind. The soldiers around them had to battle for every step they took, scimitars, axes, maces and hammers flailing in all directions until it seemed blood poured from the sky instead of rain.

Jeremias shed no tears when they passed his modest stone home, whose blazing thatched roof had caved in and set the timber skeleton aflame. He was almost glad then that he had no wife or children to mourn. He had lived alone. He had dedicated his life to his nation, and no woman had ever been agreeable to coming second to an island. Having witnessed the Justiquans' general deployment from their vantage on the headland, the general and his forces led the seneschal at a tangential angle to the city, knifing through its western edge as fast as possible without becoming bogged down in the centre, which was heaving with Justiquans. They sounded the alarm as they went, urging people to flee with them towards the ancient necropolis to the northeast, Jinglespur.

Pelting down one carcass-littered boulevard in the market district between two wildfires that had once been rows of terraced wooden houses, blinded by sparks and smoke and retching on the stench of burnt flesh, the small column of evacuees that the general had managed to corral ran headlong into a contingent of Justiquan soldiers coming out of a side street. The seneschal knew at once they weren't knights; they wore no tabards and were protected only by cuirasses of leather, iron or steel, rather than the full assortment of cuirass, pauldrons, gauntlets and greaves in which the knights were accoutred. Some wore battered, open-faced iron helmets; most did not. Whether they were knights or not, though, their swords drew blood as easily as did a knighted man's.

Bumping into the column, clearly also caught unaware in the midst of the pandemonium, the pale-skinned Justiquans let loose inhuman cries of rage when they laid eyes upon the natives of darker complexion and tore into them like a crocodile snapping shut its jaws on an unsuspecting flamingo. The Chilpaeans squawked just the same. The seneschal wondered what could possibly have birthed the Justiquans' sadism, but he knew the answer – the witches.

Less than a hundred and fifty years had passed since the end of the Time of Witches, barely a few generations. All peoples, Justiquans and Chilpaeans alike, remembered that time in their cultural memories only too well. The witches had supplanted the Prophet's noble ideals upon his death with their own brand of cruelty, enslaving the living and sucking in the souls of the dead to grant themselves power and immortality – or so it was said. Now, folk everywhere on Maradoum trembled at the mention of magic for fear that such sorcery would give rise to a second age of witches.

The Justiquans, in particular, who had hunted down the last of the covens and put an end to their tyranny, now scoured every continent they could reach from their little island to the northwest for traces of any remaining witches in hiding, enforcing their own supposedly peaceful doctrine on people by the sword and uprooting nations' attempts to rediscover the religions of their forefathers from before the Time of Witches, hundreds of years ago – a time from which very few records had survived, a misty and mystic dawn that none now remembered.

Jeremias had always wondered how the knights had slain the witches without magic of their own. Magic was native to human women, foreign to men. Like all men, he himself required the use of crystallized magic, or *Kun-Yao-Lin* crystals, meaning *Tears of the Gods* in Tzunese, in order to wield magic through the practices of obeah. Witches required no such crutch, being able to bend the elements with a mere thought. Now, having witnessed Knight-Commander Saint-Marcente's treatment of Jamba Klach, he suspected he knew the answer to that age-old question. The knights had slain the witches by using magic of their own, obviously empowered by *Kun-Yao-*

Lin. It was the only explanation. And it made them foes of terrible power. Not only did Justiqua wield an army of steel-clad warriors; some of them were obeahmen, too.

The seneschal tucked that thought and the despair it brought away for another day. Right now, he needed to escape. He needed to live to fight another day. For his brother. For Chilpaea. And not just him. He needed to save as many of his people as possible.

"We have to protect the civilians, general!" he shouted to General Malone, who stood beside him, tendons in his bull neck standing out as he hollered to his men to clear a path through the Justiquans and keep going with all speed.

The general reminded the seneschal of a boulder – short and round, but solid. Broad and immovable. The resemblance was only enhanced by the general's slab of a face on which grew a coating of black lichen in the shape of a fan beard. Sooty stubble like shorn black grass reigned over the general's ebon pate. He mushroomed out of tight leather armour emblazoned with the white snake, Damballah the Creator.

The general stopped in his tracks, leather boots skidding on the cobbles, to stare, bug-eyed, at the seneschal. "What?"

Jeremias took a deep breath, almost gagging on the bitter aroma of human remains. "We cannot let these people die!" he yelled, thin voice cracking and croaky. "Every soul we lose is a soul who cannot help us fight back against the Justiquans!"

"We don't need carpenters, we need soldiers!" the general snarled.

"These are *our* people," Jeremias insisted, staring the fuming general in the eye, "and they can be of more help than you know. Trust me. You do not want their blood on your hands. Not when we can save them!"

General Malone stared at him in vexation for a moment, grinding his teeth. Jeremias well understood his predicament. He did not want to risk losing soldiers to save civilians who would be of no use in a battle to take back the capital in the future, but he did not want to leave them to die either. A squadron of knights rounded the corner behind them, emerging onto their street, spotting them and pursuing them with bloodcurdling roars, and Jeremias felt his throat tighten as he realised the general would order the people to be left behind in order to get his soldiers to safety.

Instead, General Malone pulled himself together, cleared his throat and bellowed, "Scratch that, men! Spread out in front of these civilians! We have to protect them! Spread out and form a fighting retreat! Double-time! Hop to! Move it! Move it! That goes for you too, civilians! Get behind my men, *now!"*

The seneschal watched in dreadful fascination as the Chilpaean soldiers jumped to follow the general's orders, countering the Justiquans' rampage into the side of the column of innocents with a charge of their own, throwing themselves without a thought between their countrymen and the crusaders' steel spears and broadswords. There was no regulation equipment or uniform per se in the Chilpaean army; each man fought as he saw fit in whatever apparel he chose with whatever weapon he pleased. Most eschewed the shield in favour of more or heavier weapons. The Justiquans, on the other hand, wore regulation tunics and leggings, armour, helmets, and bore matching blades, polearms and shields. The Chilpaeans had trained as warriors, whereas the Justiquans had trained as an army, and it showed. In an open field, the Justiquan tactics were near invincible. In a brawl in a burning alley in the market district, however, Chilpaean passion was a powerful weapon.

The Justiquans held fast and slew their enemies without budging a foot for a short while, but as soon as their shield-line cracked when a man was battered to the ground by a Chilpaean battleaxe, their resolve crumbled. Their tactics in tatters, they fell into shambles and were quickly picked off one by one as the skirmish devolved into a medley of street fights where the natives' skill in single combat had a chance to shine. Before the Chilpaeans had a chance to slay the entire Justiquan contingent, however, the seneschal and general were ushering them on, yelling in their ears until they did as bidden.

Quickly shifting past the Justiquans, the soldiers formed a fighting retreat behind those innocents who had managed to break past the crusaders. Barely had they begun to retreat when the knights who had rounded the corner behind them bolstered the Justiquan soldiers' numbers, and suddenly the Chilpaeans were retreating far faster than they had planned, forcing the civilians to shift faster ahead of them to create space. Practically running down the street in an attempt to flee the crusaders, the Chilpaean soldiers flailed their weapons behind them as best they could at full pelt to keep their enemies at bay.

Panting and sweating in his nightclothes despite the chill night wind, thanks to the bonfires on either side of him, Jeremias struggled to maintain the pace set by the younger, fitter soldiers – as did General Malone, though he would never admit it. His knees and back aching horribly, his slippered feet cramping in agony from all the scree and burnt bits of wood he had stepped on, Jeremias forced his leaden legs to swing time and again, thinking every step might be his last. He could feel the crusaders breathing down his neck, only a thin barrier of soldiers between their blades and his exposed back.

His worst fears came alive when one of the soldiers protecting him was thrown on top of him by a blow from a shield, knocking Jeremias from his feet and crushing him under the man's insensate weight. He managed to throw out his hands to prevent his head from hitting the sooty cobbles, but he was trapped. He couldn't see what was happening behind him, but he was sure a crusader's sword would pierce his back or sever his spine at any second. Gasping in breath and moaning for help, he coughed in surprise when the weight atop him lifted. Scrambling to his feet, he beheld General Malone slinging the unconscious but clearly still breathing young soldier who had fallen over his shoulder, defended all the while by the surviving Chilpaean soldiers who had banded together when they had witnessed one of their own taken down. Jeremias admired the sentiment, but flinched at the sight of several soldiers being cut down so that the general could make his rescue. If war was purely a game of numbers, he thought morbidly, they were losing.

"Go! Go!" he shrieked, hoping to impose some momentum on their forces with his voice. "We have to get out of here!"

He could not move on without the army, though, and nor could the civilians, and so – like them – he dallied, hopping from foot to foot and shouting in terror as the soldiers were forced to stand their ground against the Justiquan onslaught for a moment or else risk a blade in the back.

Tiring of his whining, the general sheathed his own ornate scimitar and picked up a plain one from where a Chilpaean had fallen.

Pressing it into the seneschal's hands, Malone snarled, "If you want to help, *then help!*"

Jeremias gawped at him in shock. "But … but I'm old!" he protested at last, holding the sword as though he had no idea how to use it – which he did not, anymore.

He did not add that his knees were made of cotton wool, his bowels were loosening, his back hunching, his eyesight failing, his knuckles arthritic, and he had funny crimp in his neck when he awoke some mornings that plagued him all day.

Raoul nodded, uncaring. "Aye, and you'll be dead quicker than old age can take you if you don't do something about it! Take some of my men and lead the civilians towards Jinglespur. The rest of us will be right on your heels, I swear."

"No!" shouted Jeremias without thinking. "We stay together!"

The General's stern expression softened, and he said, "You were right, seneschal. Tactically speaking, it is foolish to stay for the sake of a few. But each and every Chilpaean life is worth saving. Not just the soldiers. Take our people to safety, I beg you. I'll join you as soon as I can – Gods willing."

Seeing the glimmer in his eye, Jeremias did not know what to say. He wanted to argue further, but he did not know how. He did not know how to free them from their predicament. He well understood why the Chilpaean soldiers could not turn and run without opening themselves up to attack, but he did not want to leave them behind – and not just for their sake, but for his own and his people's. Without them, he was not sure how he and the other evacuees would survive if they encountered another talon of the beastly

Justiquan army. He saw he had little choice, however, so he squared his shoulders, set his jaw and nodded.

Then, clasping the hilt of the scimitar firmly, the sensation foreign but awakening old memories, he turned to the cowering evacuees, some of whom had already gone on without him, to his shame. "General Malone will buy us some time!" he yelled as loud as he could, having to pause to cough. "We must press on without him for the time being! We must be courageous – for Chilpaea!" He had hoped for a small cheer at his words, but all he got was round-eyed stares. "Ahem, follow me, please."

A path opened up for him, and he strode through the small sea of folk until he stood in the vanguard, sweat trickling down his sides and making his armpits itch. He wiped moisture from his face and gave the crowd behind him what was intended to be a reassuring smile, but which looked rather more like a rictus unfortunately. Then, he was creeping through the night, gaining speed as his confidence and fear grew in equal measure, like a strangler fig growing around a banyan. Soon, he was rushing through the fire-lit streets with the evacuees behind him, poking his head around every corner before making the turn to check for Justiquans. Now and then, he would signal the crowd to wait and hide while a crusader squadron passed close by, and then they would resume their macabre marathon. Eventually, though, his luck ran out.

A contingent of Justiquan soldiers rounded a corner at the boundary of the temple district and the slums ahead of them, observing them and spreading out to block the way. Jeremias instantly led the evacuees down a side street sandwiched between burning stone temples built to honour the pantheon before the crusaders could reach them, and a terrifying game of hide and seek ensued, in which the Justiquans hunted down the Chilpaeans like dogs, baying for their blood. Jeremias zigzagged through tight alleys at top speed, but in the end ran straight into another arm of the Justiquan army and the game began over again with yet more soldiers on their tail. When the crusaders caught them, the carnage defied belief. The Justiquans mowed the Chilpaeans down with as little mercy as a gardener shows his weeds, plucking them up by the root and casting them out. The Justiquans did not always go for the kill immediately, more often crippling folk so they could not run, so that the soldiers could finish them off at their leisure. Jeremias' eyes watered – and not just from the choking smoke.

For the first time in decades, he fought. He swung the sword the general had given him and gasped as it ricocheted off another with an ear-splitting clang, sparks flying. He could see that, under the helmet, the Justiquan he faced was nothing but a beardless boy in leather armour. Jeremias guessed it was his first war. The young crusader fought as if at a fencing school, always with proper form, never veering from the moves he had been taught. Jeremias almost felt sorry for the boy when he punched him in the face, hooked a leg behind his to trip him and consequently plunged his scimitar into the prone boy's throat, making him cough up blood. It surprised the seneschal how many tricks he remembered from his warrior days. He cast away the guilt trying to climb him like a trellis, kicked the next soldier in the balls and then stabbed him in the belly. His slippered foot throbbed hotly from the contact.

Shocked and proud, he witnessed a few of the braver Chilpaean evacuees meeting the Justiquans head on and wresting weapons from their hands to use against them. Most, however, fled in all directions or quivered in fear behind those few men who were fighting. If it had not been for the sudden arrival of General Malone and his men, Jeremias felt certain the escape attempt would have come to an end then and there. Before the general showed up, Jeremias had no idea how he was going to extricate himself and his fellows from their predicament. Fortunately, the general had ideas.

Bulling into the blood-soaked arena of the street tucked between torched temples with his men, General Malone bellowed, "Attack the right flank! Push them back until a path opens up to the north!"

The Chilpaeans hammered the Justiquans' right flank, crushing it under the weight of their swinging scimitars and forcing the whole contingent to pinwheel as it tried to compensate and encircle the newcomers. General Malone, however, was not about to let that happen. The timing was crucial. If he waited too long, he and his forces would be trapped with no way to escape but south or east, back into the heart of the city.

As soon as the path leading north through the slums opened up a sliver, he roared, "Now! Fighting retreat to the north!"

The Chilpaeans burst into frantic action, shoving the last of the crusaders out of the way and bursting out of their confines up the street. As soon as they had cleared the avenues' mouth, they spun to face the Justiquans, holding them at bay on the west side of the street, while the evacuees finished the circling manoeuvre and pelted north, passing close by the blazing temples and tenements and crying out as sparks and spars tumbled down in their midst. Once all the evacuees present had passed by, the Chilpaean soldiers sealed the boulevard behind them and followed more slowly, methodically chipping away at the mighty war machine that was the crusader army. Walking backwards, stumbling over the corpses of their brethren, many Chilpaean soldiers never made it out of the capital. Jeremias would never forget their sacrifice, though. Thanks to them, the rest did make it.

Though they staggered on jellied legs through the edge of the slums towards the city's northern rim, though sweat poured from their dirty brows into their eyes and down bloody cheeks, when their General ordered them to charge one last time and then hightail it out of there, the soldiers complied, hurling themselves at the Justiquans in one last frenzied burst of energy before turning tail and sprinting with their last reserves away from the fire-ridden city so many of them had called mother and into the blessed solace of the night's darkness.

5

The Face in the Crystal

Jamba Klach emerged from the tunnel first, stretching and yawning, turning his cocoa face to the blissful blue sky and closing his tired eyes, relishing the warmth on his skin. Ruffle Feathers stepped out next, shading his eyes from the scorching noon sun with a gnarly hand. Lug brought up the rear in his human form once more, ambling out without a care in the world to gaze around in childlike wonder at the jungled slopes rearing leafy heads all around them, his egg-like face split by a vapid smile.

Mahoganies, mahoes, ebonies and limes stippled every rocky face, leaning into the stiff wind and watching the trio with faces hidden in old knots, their roots so large they contoured the topography. Flocks of hummingbirds, warblers and parakeets patrolled their territory, and the buzz of dragonflies and wasps never ended. Carved out by obeah by the Shadowers themselves many years ago when they had first started paying Chilpaean growers to smuggle witch-spice into Zamphia in bulk, the tunnel led straight from the west coast by Cocoba Bay to a hidden spot in the Blueschist Mountains northwest of the city.

"D'you have any water?" Jamba asked without turning, voice harsh and dry.

Halting beside him, Ruffle shook his head and waved a hand. 'No.'

Jamba nodded, expecting as much. "There's a stream by the village. We'd best press on." He saw Lug wandering off after a pretty butterfly. "Keep up, Lug!"

The seven-foot-tall muscle-bound behemoth turned to face Jamba with his hands clasped in front of him, staring at his feet as he kicked the dirt like a scolded child. "Sorry, Jamba."

Jamba gave him an unforgiving glare for a moment before tramping north along the fern-filled valley between the Blueschists where the tunnel had brought them out. Wild baui plants sprang up among the ferns here and there. The smugglers trekked through wooded ravines and up and down forested slopes all morning, exhaustion haunting their every step, the blistering sun partially kept at bay by the big fluttering leaves of the banyans and catalpas.

The village poked its thatched head out of the jungle several hours later as the great eye in the sky neared its terminus, and the trio breathed a sigh of relief as they finally stepped out of the dappled shade into the small glade nestled in a valley in the bluish mountains where the village hid from prying eyes. Witch-spice grew on tall, hairy, eight-foot stalks in husks like corn all around them as they strolled downhill towards the village, fuzzing every surrounding slope. Jamba breathed in deeply. The scent of the witch-spice, like potent turmeric, put him in mind of fond memories of drunken evenings spent in this village with his friends.

A spring in his step, his body abruptly lighter, he bounced towards the growers in sight tending the plants, hooting, "Hallo there, it's me, Jamba!"

Within minutes, the smugglers were ensconced in the village hall, sitting at a long scarred ebony table, quaffing rum, smoking baui, listening to a raucous rendition of *Hey, Kraken!* and swapping tales of their adventures with the growers and their leaders, the infamous spice smugglers, Yon Moro and Seymore Wallis. Years ago, the two intrepid warriors had begun the whole spice smuggling operation, communicating with Thetmakh, Kalif and the other Shadowers in Zamphia. They had long since retired from the high seas and now oversaw crop production.

Sat at the head of the table, Yon Moro, a Chilpaean whose dark complexion contrasted strongly with his short-shorn snow-white hair and beard, frowned pensively when he heard Jamba's tale of their exploits, pressing his lips to his clasped hands. "Hmm, an invasion is the last thing we need," he said in a rhythmic baritone in Kwi patois. "How are we to continue to trade with the Zamphish if the Justiquans are blockading the island? This does not bode well."

Seymore, a weathered seadog from Swash Isle in a simple white shirt with the sleeves rolled up and tight, dark breeches, patted his friend on the shoulder with his one good hand. The other had been wounded in a battle years ago and been amputated after it caught gangrene. An iron hook was strapped to the stump now in its place, which the old sailor used to prong a piece of venison and lift it to his moustached face.

Speaking around the mouthful in creaky old Traveller's Tongue, he said, "We'll find a way, Yon. We always do."

Yon fingered the shark tooth hanging from a thong around his neck thoughtfully; a keepsake from the creature that had taken a chunk out of his leg decades before. "I fear we may have to put a stop to deliveries for a while. The Shadowers will not be pleased."

"Better them sad than us dead," Jamba said wryly, smearing a salve made by Ruffle Feathers on his grazes. "It is safe to assume Cocoba Bay was completely overrun if the crusaders got into the palace. You should've seen the number of Justiquan ships. It's not possible the capital still stands – and if the Justiquans are attacking strategically, they will have landed ships at other ports simultaneously. The entire island could be under their control within days."

"Well, surely the army can deal with them," said Seymore off-hand, waving his hook, understanding Kwi but speaking Traveller's. "Or the

Lullabyer himself. Surely he has the magic voice for a reason."

Yon shook his head. "That's not how it works. It –"

He trailed off as words of flickering fire branded the air, stating in Kwi, 'The Lullabyer is dead. His soul is in this crystal.'

All eyes turned on Ruffle Feathers and the purple-blue gemstone in the shape of a man in robes in his hands, the size of a skull. It pulsed with eldritch power, outshining the guttering candles.

"What do you mean when you say 'his soul is in the crystal'?" Yon Moro asked softly, slack-jawed like the others.

The words of fire faded, and more took their place. 'The Lullabyer must have cast a spell in order to safeguard his soul in the event of his death. He was killed by the crusaders last night as he slept, and now his duppy, his essence, his very mind, is somehow preserved in this chunk of *Kun-Yao-Lin.* It is obeah beyond my ken.'

"How do you know he was killed last night as he slept?" Jamba asked.

The smuggler's eyes bugged as he read the words of flame that materialised in mid-air above the table then. 'Because he told me.'

"You can communicate with him?" Seymore squawked in surprise, voice reminiscent of a rusty gate.

'I can,' Ruffle replied in conflagrating letters with a wave of the hand. 'I believe that is the reason he stored his soul, so to speak – in order to pass on his knowledge.'

Yon's eyes near popped out of his skull as he realised the implications. "The Sleepers must not awaken! Without the Lullabyer's knowledge and skill, who is to pacify the Sleepers?"

'There is none.'

"Well, to whom can the Lullabyer pass on his knowledge? Can you learn the spells, Ruffle?" Yon pressed, an edge of fear in his voice as he glanced out the window at the slowly setting sun.

Ruffle Feathers shook his head. 'There is but one with the syrinx, the voice of the Gods – the Lullabyer's youngest son, Pahu Opherio. The Lullabyer asks that we bear the crystal that contains his soul to the northeast tip of the island, to the Monastery Calliope on the Hook, where we will find his son, Pahu. He asks that we do this to save all Chilpaea. He says, without our aid, the nation is doomed. And I believe him.'

"What?" squawked Seymore.

"You can't possibly go!" Jamba blustered. "Like I said, the cursed crusaders will have landed at as many ports as they can. They'll be everywhere by now, all across the island – hunting for the crystal no less, if they know of its existence! I wouldn't put it past them, the scurvy dogs! Not to mention that, if the Lullabyer truly is dead as you say, the Sleepers will awaken! They'll tear you apart if you go out at night!"

"You want to go, don't you?" Yon asked Ruffle quietly.

Raising his chin, dignified as an oak, the old obeahman bobbed his head.

Jamba raised an eyebrow, gulping rum and smacking his lips. "Even after all he did to you?"

"What did he do to him?" Seymore asked.

Jamba looked to Ruffle, who waved a hand, indicating he should tell the tale.

Jamba sighed and said, "Ruffle served the Lullabyer a long time ago. When he arrived at court, he would not tell anyone his name, only that he was there to 'ruffle feathers'. Magnuz soon recognised his wisdom and power, however, and offered him an advisory role in the palace. Ruffle accepted and lived with the Lullabyer and his family – for some years, as I understand it. Then, the Lullabyer's wife, Ladonya, fell pregnant. The pregnancy was hard for her, and she grew weaker and weaker with each passing day, wasting away before the Lullabyer's eyes.

"So, after consulting all the foremost herbalists and healers in the country in vain, Magnuz asked Ruffle Feathers if he could use obeah to save the lady Ladonya's life. Ruffle said that he would try everything in his power, and he performed a duppy dance, begging the spirits of our ancestors to help her … but the duppy would not heed his call. Ladonya died giving birth to the Lullabyer's second son, Pahu, who survived thanks to Ruffle's efforts. When his wife passed, though, Magnuz went wild with grief and, in his madness, ordered Ruffle's drink to be drugged with valerian, a sedative, and witchbane, a plant that nullifies an obeahman's powers. While Ruffle was unconscious, the Lullabyer had his soldiers cut out the obeahman's tongue with a red-hot blade, so that he could never cast a spell again." Silence drew a curtain on the hall, solemnifying the happy occasion. Jamba cleared his throat to break the tension and added, "Resourceful as he is, our clever Ruffle found a way around that, of course, and now he can cast a spell just as easily as before."

"I never knew," Yon said quietly.

Jamba nodded. "Ruffle doesn't speak of it much."

"Why would you want to help someone who did that to you?" Yon asked the obeahman.

Ruffle met his eyes and waved a hand. The words, 'For Chilpaea,' shone in the air for a moment.

"I don't understand all o' this," said Seymore slowly, puffing on a baui pipe and blowing coiling, bluish-white clouds of smoke. "So what if the Lullabyer's dead? Can't you just appoint a new one? And who are these Sleepers you were talking about?"

Yon clapped his friend on the shoulder. "You are right, old friend, you do not understand. Let me tell you a legend every Chilpaean mother tells their child. The legend goes that at the dawn of time, before the Prophet, before the Betrayer, before the witches, Chilpaea was a nation beset by thousands upon thousands of horrors indescribable who preyed on people like cattle, horrors whose name we no longer know. The populace pleaded to the Gods for help, and in response, the Gods of Dreams and Nightmares – the Twins, Panku and Pangu – granted one family the hereditary ability to sing with such power that their music could enchant the beasts, hypnotise them and put them to sleep so that they would never terrorise Chilpaea ever again. They gave the family syrinxes, like the vocal chords of birds, rather than larynxes, like the rest of us.

"This family – the Opherio family – took that power and used it to play instruments and sing and make such wonderful lullabies that the horrors retreated into their warrens dug deep beneath the island and fell asleep. The legend also says that if one of the Opherio family does not sing the Lullaby every single night, the Sleepers will awaken and consume Chilpaea in carnage and chaos. *That* is what we are afraid of, Seymore. The Sleepers must not awaken."

Seymore snorted. "Has anyone actually ever seen one of these Sleepers?"

Yon nodded sombrely. "Occasionally, one will be found in a cave or mine by those delving deep. And sometimes, the Lullabyer falls ill and cannot sing … those are dark, dark nights indeed."

Seymore shivered as a chill wriggled up his spine. Still, he protested, "But it sounds like an old fishwives' tale!"

Yon nodded, eyes distant. "Aye, but all stories have a kernel of truth."

"What d'you think, Yon?" Jamba asked.

Yon blew out his cheeks. "I think, with my leg wound, I'm going nowhere. It's you lot who'll have to make the trip if you decide to help the dead old geezer. So, it's your decision to make."

Jamba turned to Ruffle thoughtfully. "Can we speak to the Lullabyer?"

Ruffle raised his eyebrows, but nodded and placed the pulsating crystal on the table, gesturing towards it. Jamba leaned in close to stare into the shifting depths of the glowing crystal. Colours swirled into bizarre patterns like ink in water before his eyes until abruptly they settled into a configuration he recognised – the bearded face of Magnuz Opherio drawn in blue and purple blobs.

The face in the crystal frowned, and Jamba jumped as he heard the Lullabyer's mellifluous voice in his head. *"Who are you? Where is Ruffle Feathers?"*

"He – he's right here," Jamba stammered. "Can't you see him?"

The face in the crystal sniffed disdainfully. *"It's very difficult to speak through the veil, you know. It's much easier to do it in close proximity."*

"Are you in the Sunset Isles?" Jamba asked, while the others looked at him as though he had fallen off sanity's brink.

He supposed they could not hear the Lullabyer.

"No," came the reply in his head, like an echo in a cave. *"I'm stuck in this blasted crystal for now, obviously, aren't I?"*

Jamba blushed. "Oh, yes, right, sorry."

The face in the crystal rolled it eyes. *"What do you want? I'm very busy, you know."*

"Really?"

"No. I just don't want to talk to you any longer than I have to."

Jamba hesitated. "You don't remember me, do you?" The face did not reply, just peered back at him. "I won several tourneys in Cocoba Bay. I was the island's most famous swordsman not so long ago."

"Jamba Klach?" The voice sounded incredulous. *"Papa Bwa's ass, I hardly recognise you. When did you grow that ghastly beard?"*

"It's better than yours," Jamba shot back, stroking his black arrow-shaped beard.

"I hardly think so."

"No, it definitely is."

"Agree to disagree. What is it you want, Jamba Klach, once the most famous swordsman in Chilpaea and now nothing but a deadbeat smuggler who can't pay his gambling debts?"

Jamba bridled. "Ruffle has explained what you want from us. And if you want us to do it, you'd best get on my good side quick."

Jamba heard a sigh in his head. *"Oh, very well, it's a magnificent beard, truly remarkable, worthy of song and praise. Why, even the Gods would –"*

"That's not what I meant," Jamba growled. "Tell us why we should help you. What's in it for us?"

"You mean besides the obvious benefit of sedating the Sleepers and thus staying alive and saving the country?"

"Yes."

"Oh, very well, you mercenary dog. Do it and I won't have my son send my men after you to take back those crystals and doubloons you stole, sound fair?"

"You'll have to do better than that."

"Ugh, alright, alright. Gods help me that it has come to this. Begging for help from smugglers. Troubled times, indeed. Very well, criminal. Help me and not only will you and all your scummy friends have my eternal gratitude and a pardon for all your crimes, but I shall see to it that my son gives you any monetary reward you deem fit. Satisfied?"

Jamba nodded. "Now, that's more like it."

"You'll have to travel overland, I suspect. From what I saw, the Justiquans have blockaded the entire island. It's a miracle you were able to slip past their ships once. They'll sink any boat you put out."

Jamba nodded and stretched. "You're probably right."

"We should get going at once. The Sleepers may take a few days to awaken from their slumber, but once risen they will be hungry beyond belief. The sooner we reach my son so that I can teach him the Lullaby the better."

"We're exhausted, your worshipfulness," Jamba replied, yawning and gazing out the window at the sunset, which looked disturbingly like someone had slit open the horizon, leaving it to bleed out across the sky. "We need to rest – and there's no safer place than right here, surrounded by fire and friends. Have a little patience, Lullabyer. We'll leave in the morning."

"On your heads be it."

6

Jinglespur

People spoke of Jinglespur Necropolis in hushed tones, afraid the accursed duppy that haunt the place might hear them. All in Chilpaea have heard the story of Jinglespur Necropolis and the necromancer, Waddi-waddi, who conquered the ancient capital at the head of an undead army. The name of the necromancer and his zombie city caused goosebumps all across Chilpaea as mothers told the stories to their babes to frighten them into behaving. Over the years, parties were sent to investigate the old lore inscribed on the walls of the citadel at its heart, learning much about the age before the Time of Witches, though not the ultimate fate of the necromancer himself. Few returned. Now, none had entered the walled necropolis for decades. Weeds, creepers and grass had gradually overtaken the city, thrusting their roots between its paving stones, cracking and smothering them in time.

The thick, pitted fifty-foot walls of unknown black stone still stood tall and proud, however, which was why Jeremias Colcott had chosen the place as a refuge for his people after they fled Cocoba Bay.

He glared at the fortress-town-turned-necropolis silhouetted against the dusky firmament as he slogged uphill towards it alongside General Raoul Malone, a column of exhausted Chilpaeans from Cocoba Bay and the surrounding villages on his heels. The Dragon Sea cut into the south coast of the island to form a V with Jinglespur nestled in its elbow crook, high on a blowy petunia-strewn headland overlooking the surf, several leagues northeast of Cocoba Bay. The citadel's spiked spires soared high above the other towers of the city, char-black fingers clawing at the iron sky in jealousy of the Gods. The city squatted on the promontory, spider-like, ever ready to pounce with its splayed out legs of stone. The semi-circular wall trapping it against the sheer cliff-edge had five short outcroppings like spokes protruding from a wheel hub, where defenders atop the battlements could shoot arrows down on attackers in the killing fields between the spokes.

One of those outcroppings was the barbican, a tower built in front of the sole gate providing entry into the necropolis and connected to the main wall by a short stretch of stone tunnel in which was safely hidden the gate. Any invaders would be funnelled into the barbican and forced to climb to the top of the tower, only to descend it again on the far side before they could gain entry to the gate through the tunnel.

Climbing and descending the ancient black tower, Jeremias cursed when he saw that the gate had rusted off its hinges long ago and lay ignominiously half-buried and rotten in the feathery grass and ferns that had since sprouted. He made a mental note to find a metalworker and a carpenter to fix it as he strode through the threshold, trying and failing not to shiver in dread as he entered the city of the damned. The shade as he passed through the tunnel seeped into his very bones, far colder than any shade ought to be. He could see his breath puffing in the air in front of him despite the previously warm evening, and he thought he could hear a distant wailing on the sea wind.

Walking through a maze of streets past rows of surprisingly intact black stone houses with missing thatching, he felt like he was traversing a stone honeycomb. Half of the streets, making up the entire outer half-ring of the necropolis, were lined on either side not by buildings but by hundreds upon hundreds of tombstones, said to be where Waddi-waddi had interred his zombie army.

"We should not be here," whispered General Malone, darting concerned glances this way and that at the deserted black stone streets.

Jeremias set his jaw. "I know. But we have nowhere else to go. Nowhere else can offer us the same protection as this old city." He purposefully avoided calling it a necropolis.

"But the duppy of Waddi-waddi –"

"But the Justiquans!" Jeremias snapped, tired and on edge. He sagged. "I'm sorry, General. If you have a better idea, I'm all ears. If not, this is our last hope."

The General nodded reluctantly. "I fear you may be right, seneschal. It does my poor heart no good to be in a place like this, though. I'll be spooked to death before the crusaders can finish me off."

Jeremias had to deal with a hundred such complaints that evening as he tried to help organise the sleeping arrangements in the citadel for the hundreds of people who had followed him to the necropolis. Occasionally, his temper frayed and he snapped at a few folk, but for the most part he treated people with respect and patience, listening to their concerns and doing his best to make them comfortable. Eventually, they all settled into the citadel and the healers were able to tend to the wounded, leaving the wind to whistle down the empty streets of the necropolis outside. Jeremias had suggested some people could take up residence in some of the houses beyond the citadel. Nobody had liked the idea. So, everybody stayed together, cooped up in the black heart of the city. General Malone gave his soldiers no choice, commanding them to stand guard on the wall and keep watch for the crusader army despite their complaints. Everybody was on edge, constantly looking over their shoulders, their backs itching as if branded with dagger targets.

Jeremias felt it, too. Everywhere he went, he thought he could almost hear voices, on the periphery of his hearing, whispering to him, ever whispering. Their every attempt to map out the labyrinthine citadel came to a fruitless end, each and every map proving different to the one before as if the corridors were sentient, shifting around and switching places. Some mappers found multiple staircases; some found none. None found one leading down, only up.

It was not long before the incidents began.

Within hours, hallucinations preyed on the necropolis' new residents, their imaginations transporting them to grotesque tableaus, often epitomising their worst fears. One man wept as he told the seneschal of a waking dream in which he had fallen onto an ant's nest, as he had in his youth, only this time his parents had not been there to help him up. He had been unable to move, unable to do anything except scream as the insects crawled into his eyes, his ears, his nose and his mouth. One woman, repulsed by snakes, was tormented by spectacles of being squeezed to death by a boa constrictor. Another man, deathly afraid of heights, had fallen off a cliff only to lie, entirely broken but alive, under the scorching sun for hours. One woman told the seneschal she had had nightmares with her eyes open of being cut open in pregnancy, and of the heinous baby ripping its way out of her stomach with tooth and claw.

Those were the few he remembered most of a hundred such stories, the few that would stick with him, making him shudder now and then for the rest of his life. He himself had been plagued by twisted visions of roaming the palace as a duppy, unable to communicate with anyone, unable to help. Finding a metalworker and carpenter to fix the gate proved troublesome when his eyes cheated him, making him walk into walls. He saw again the faces of his brother and the Lullabyer and his son, Dajuan. The four of them had worked together for years to bring prosperity to their nation, and only now did Jeremias realise those had been the best days of his life. His heart throbbed with pain as he remembered the unique contours of their features. His brother's face, in particular, dogged his every blink, damning him with its warm, forgiving smile.

Though they dreamed, the people could not sleep. Every soul glared at the black walls with wide eyes that first night in the necropolis, sure that some fiend from the blackest gulfs imaginable would rear its horrible head to devour them all by dawn, or that Waddi-waddi would rise from the grave and storm through the gates with his ancient army of undead, or that the Sleepers would awaken. As the sun peeked nervously over the horizon to see if any such fate had befallen the Chilpaeans, however, it found them all alive, staring into nothingness with bloodshot eyes as they slipped in and out of phantasmagoric trances.

By day two, distinguishing between dream and reality was nigh impossible as hallucinations bled into each and every tiredly twitching eye. Jeremias was convinced he was drowning in Cocoba Bay alongside his brethren at one point, until he remembered to breathe. He came so close to passing out that lights danced before his eyes. By the time the moon rose, people were conversing with the walls, proclaiming them the duppy of their dead relatives or the Gods themselves. Jeremias could hardly refute their claims when a cavalcade of familiar-faced wraiths paraded through the citadel before his eyes while he was writing letters on the last of his parchment to organise reinforcements from the nearby towns of Hatbrim, Jawduck and Nirby, ephemeral, silvery and shining like starlight. He wondered then whether he ought to tell the residents of the other towns to stay put rather than invite them to the waking nightmare that was the necropolis. Their towns had no walls and few warriors, however, and so he decided that, for now, safety outweighed sanity.

His skin crawled with every step he took as he made his way then to the nook of the citadel where he knew a rookmaster to be. It took him over an hour to find the man, for the route had seemingly changed overnight. The room in which the man sat with a few others lay bare of furniture or ornament save for dusty broken remnants and thick, heavily populated cobwebs that had mostly been torn down. Thin windows set high in the walls allowed in a meagre trickle of early moonlight swamped by clouds, so many folk had been using ancient scraps of wood to start small fires. The rookmaster warmed his hands by one such fire, his wizened face gleaming in the flickering light.

"You said you managed to bring some rooks with you?" Jeremias asked the man after the initial polite preamble.

"I did," the man replied, ruffling his short grey locks as a spider abseiled down from his fringe. "I left them in their cages just outside the citadel."

"May I use some of them?" Jeremias asked. "It is of the utmost importance, I assure you."

The man raised a wrinkly hand. "Say no more, seneschal. I'll do whatever I can to help. Come, I'll show you the rooks."

"Have you quill, ink and parchment, too?"

"Of course, seneschal."

Within minutes, Jeremias had attached the requests for reinforcements to several of the birds and was scrawling a note and attaching it to the leg of one last messenger rook, the note addressed to Kofi 'Skinner' Touluz, the most feared assassin in Chilpaea. The black-feathered bird cawed disconcertingly and took off, soon blending into the void between stars.

"Thank you," Jeremias said to the rookmaster.

He was patrolling the curving wall that night out of morbid curiosity with General Malone when he heard them howling. Together with the general and the twitchy soldiers, he stared out into the darkness to the west. Nominally, the soldiers were on lookout for Justiquans. All knew what they were really on the lookout for, however.

"Sleepers," Jeremias whispered, his flesh goose-pimpling.

He could see little thanks to the clouds, but after peering into the murk for a while, he thought he saw the land itself moving, wriggling, rolling towards him like a wave. He knew after a few moments that it was but an optical illusion. The ground was not moving. It was carpeted by a thousand beasts, all moving as one.

When the first huge, shaggy black horror pounced on Jinglespur's mighty black wall and started to skitter up it towards the seneschal like a spider, Jeremias screamed, "It's the Sleepers! Run! Run for your lives! Back to the citadel!"

Hearing crunching and screeching to both left and right and guessing some soldiers had been slow on the uptake, the seneschal bounded down the stairs with more athleticism than he had known he had, propelled by terror. General Malone and the soldiers still outpaced him to the citadel, however, and the general awaited him in the doorway, beckoning. Jeremias glanced back and wished he hadn't. Hundreds of Sleepers had clambered the walls already and were pelting towards him, slavering and howling, stinking of rotting meat, barely visible in the darkness.

He focussed forward once more and forced his burning legs and arms to pump until he was safely inside the citadel and the general was slamming shut the heavy stone doors with the help of his men in the face of the horde of horrors. Sleepers crashed against the stone not a moment later, but the thick door held firm, as it had for centuries. Nobody had been able to find any hinges thus far, and it was believed the doors had been fashioned by and still operated by obeah, as did all the citadel doors.

"We should be safe in here," Jeremias panted to the frightened people by the entry. "Nothing can break down those doors. Make sure all entryways are sealed tight, even those on the roofs. Those beasts can climb. As long as all the doors are shut, we should be safe."

He prayed it was true.

Jeremias could not sleep again that night, no matter how long he tossed and turned on the cold stone floor with only his nightclothes for comfort. The howling, the babies crying and the fear kept him awake. So, like many others, he aimlessly prowled the dark halls of the citadel, eyes burning with exhaustion, lost in vivid visions. Sleepers howled at him through the thin windows, far too large to fit through, and he ignored them. Smoke from the fires wafted down the corridors like a phantom horde, obscuring his vision.

He found a door that gave onto a set of stairs leading down, and he followed the steps out of curiosity, barely thinking about what he was doing or seeing what lay before him. Down and down he went, deep beneath the citadel into the very bowels of the earth. He blinked in surprise upon finding himself in a rugged, musty cavern whose centrepiece, a purple-blue gemstone twice the size of a man, pulsed with arcane power, illuminating a lone stone sarcophagus at its foot. Jeremias' instincts screamed at him to turn and flee, but curiosity drove him on. He crept up to the sarcophagus, feeling the very air throb with the crystal's energies, and brushed away dust so that he could read the inscription etched on the stone lid in archaic Kwi patois.

His heart stopped for an instant, and he thought he had died until he sucked in a lungful of dusty air, feeling dizzy, and his heart beat again.

"It's not possible!" he breathed.

"Oh, but it is," a faint voice replied with a hint of sardonic humour. *"Welcome, seneschal, to my tomb."*

Jeremias turned to see a duppy, his heart cartwheeling in his chest and his stomach dropping away. "Waddi-waddi!"

7

Dark Smog

The blood-chilling howls of the Sleepers had haunted the smugglers' sleep the previous night, after they had left Yon Moro, Seymore and the growers' village behind. Making camp in a cave high in the Blueschists had proved to keep them safe from the warren-dwelling night time antics of the Sleepers when they rose above ground. And there was no doubt in the smugglers' minds that the horrors had risen above ground. They had spent the night in abject terror. The high, barking yowls they had heard could have come from no other throat than those of horrific monsters. The Lullaby had gone unsung, and the Sleepers once more prowled the surface.

On their second day of travel, heading northeast through the jungled peaks, they halted in their tracks when an uninterrupted swathe of white-barked, leafless trees, skeletal and gnarled into fiendish clawed shapes, stretched away before them as far as they could see to both east and west. To the west, they knew the mountains morphed into sheer razor-sharp peaks, entirely inaccessible.

'At least the boundary between the jungle and the witchwood is easy to mark,' Ruffle Feathers observed dryly, his flaming words burning in the air only long enough for the others to read.

The trio peered into the sunlit woods, wondering if the rumours of duppy roaming the trees were true.

"How do the trees grow without leaves?" quizzed Lug Thorm, staring up at the skeletal branches.

Ruffle waved a hand. 'Like conifers, they grow tiny needles instead of leaves, so fine that they resemble hairs all over the trees' frames.'

"We're not going in there, are we?" Lug asked, scratching his cheek. "I heard anybody who enters the witchwood either dies or goes crazy."

"No," murmured Jamba Klach. "Time to head east, I suppose. If all goes well, we'll be at the Belt in five days."

They gazed east as one, at the increasingly diminishing foothills and, beyond them, the plains down at sea level. None relished the idea of a night spent in the open.

"Won't the Sleepers get us if we go down there?" Lug asked anxiously, fidgeting.

Jamba took a deep breath. "Yes, Lug, they might. That's what we're afraid of. But there's nothing to be gained by worrying, as my old mother used to say. Might as well do it with a smile on your puss as a frown. So, let's go."

He started off with more eagerness than he felt, forcing himself to a good pace in order to circumvent the woods and reach the Belt, Chilpaea's cinched midsection, as soon as possible. His shins soon ached with the stress of walking downhill as he navigated one forested foothill after another, ducking mossy branches and vine nooses and trampling carelessly through the hibiscuses and passionflowers. Every step down made him sweat just a little more – and not from the effort. Every step brought him a foot closer to the plains, and the monsters from his childhood fables.

He could picture his mother as clear as day, her dark, pocked face smiling down warmly at him as she coddled him in her arms and told him the legend of the Sleepers and the Lullaby, telling him he would never have to worry because the Opherio family would always be there to protect him. In a way, he was glad his parents had passed before the Opherios. He would not have wanted her to have to live through this nightmare. Parrots, warblers and thrushes chittered overhead in the endless blue bowl dappled by the foliage of huge kapoks, mahoganies and rosewoods, and Jamba imagined the birds were tweeting him a warning, urging him to turn back and seek refuge in the mountains. He wished he could listen to the apocryphal advice, but he kept plodding down and east, his gut tightening as he went until he wasn't sure if he was constipated or diarrhetic.

The grander trees fell behind in the sprint to the plains, content to remain at rest high in the peaks, and soon smaller saplings and thicker undergrowth paved the way, ebonies, limes, coconut palms and palmettos all shouldering one another aside, vying for the syrupy sunlight; and over all of them, the lianas draped themselves like gossamer silk cloaks, sucking up all the sun's energy before it could ever reach the plants beneath.

Lost in fond memories of his mother, Jamba finished off the foothills before he knew it and stared out over the plains below with wide eyes, like a bunny that has spotted a fox. To his left, the witchwood beckoned with gaunt white fingers. Ahead and to the right, there was nothing to see for leagues save swishing feathery grass and copses of palms and cedars, but Jamba's imagination readily provided the figment of a horde of Sleepers charging across the empty space towards him, and his heart quickened. His breath came faster, and his palms felt clammy.

He cleared a suddenly dry throat and croaked, "Sooner we go, sooner we're there."

He set foot on the plains, wondering if he would soon come to regret it.

He regretted it by the afternoon, when flaming letters appeared before his eyes, telling him to 'Look behind.' He cast a glance over his shoulder, and his eyes popped out of his skull as he beheld mounted warriors thundering towards them from the south over hill and dale amid a cloud of kicked up dust, their armour gleaming in the sunlight.

"Crusaders!" Jamba spat, knowing his own countrymen did not wear steel armour, as a rule.

Ruffle bobbed his head, and Lug looked on vapidly. Jamba wondered how so many horses could possibly have survived a night of Sleeper attacks. Possible scenarios flitted through his mind for a heartbeat. Either the mounts were fresh off the boat that morning, in which case they had ridden a long way, or their stables had somehow been secure enough to resist a Sleeper attack, or there was sorcery at play.

"Run!" Jamba roared, hightailing it along the edge of the witchwood and praying they had not been seen.

His prayers went unanswered. The crusaders veered as they went, a contingent of perhaps a hundred cavalrymen clearly chasing the smugglers.

Jamba cursed, "Ah, El Vandu pisses on us yet again! They've seen us! We'll never outrun them on foot, and we have nowhere to go! The end of the witchwood is leagues away! We're trapped!" He stopped and whipped out his twin scimitars in a peal of steel, baring his teeth at his enemies as they bore down on him. "There's no choice. We make a stand here and now! Are you with me? Lug? Ruffle? Ruffle? Ruffle!"

Glancing over his shoulder, he watched in disbelief as Ruffle Feathers, followed by Lug, plunged headlong into the shadow of the witchwood, ducking skeletal branches and slipping past white boles. Jamba debated for only a split-second – death by crusaders or death by duppy? He could not give the crusaders the satisfaction. He'd rather die at the ethereal hands of the malevolent spirits of his own people. Turning his back on the crusaders, who were close enough for him to see their pale skin and hear their raucous shouts, he sprinted after his friends.

A preternatural chill hit him as he passed under the first white boughs, seeping deeper into his skin than any shade he had ever known until he shivered despite the blistering sunlight and bright blue sky. His lips soon felt numb, and he had the disquieting notion that if he stopped running, he'd never be able to move again. The shrills of the woodpeckers, peewees and pigeons and the buzzing of flies, crickets and cicadas, so omnipresent in the field not so far away, now faded away to be replaced by utter eerie silence as if not a single other living thing crept, crawled or flew in the woods. He thought he saw an infamous bloodwood tree flash past as he ran, its wood easily enchanted to cut through anything like butter, even steel. Distant wails tickled his ears, on the bleeding edge of reality and imagination, and his flesh crawled when he thought he glimpsed a shifting ethereal shape in his peripheral vision. When he jerked his head around to look straight at it, he saw nothing but mocking trees.

Then, all thoughts of duppy and bloodwoods were driven from his mind as the crusaders caught him. Hearing their hoof beats growing louder and louder, Jamba spun to meet them, his scimitar arcing out just in time to deflect a vicious chop aimed to cleave his skull apart. The ring of blade on blade echoed jarringly through the still forest, splitting its sanctity in twain, once, twice, thrice, as Jamba hastily retreated, all the while batting away the blades of the three closest crusaders who took turns to strike at him as they carefully manoeuvred their mounts around the creepy white-barked trees. Fighting on foot against a mounted opponent was difficult enough; battling several mounted foes counted as suicide, Jamba was sure. Sweat poured down his frame despite the woods' chill as he swept his scimitars back and forth, each sweep diverting another of the knights' broadswords from his flesh. A fighting man on foot had only one viable tactic against a mounted foe, Jamba knew – unseat the man. The easiest way to achieve this was killing or maiming the horse. Jamba baulked at such a measure, however, having a high regard for the majesty of the breed. It was not their fault they were ridden by genocidal maniacs, he reflected.

Finding a spare second and a yard to dash away, Jamba headed for a particularly thick tree, hearing cantering hooves close in behind him. He leaped as high as he could, placed a foot on the tree, bounced off to gain height and met the charging horseman in mid-air, catching him by surprise and bearing him bodily off his steed. The horse ran off into the woods, neighing wildly, and Jamba ripped up the winded knight's visor and rammed his scimitar into the hole in the helmet until it hit the metal nape. He had to spit out blood when he retrieved his sword in a fountain of gore. A few more crusaders managed to force their steeds through the woods to surround him then, and Jamba spun and parried like a whirlwind of steel, heart singing as he saw an unending stretch of sleep yawning open before him. He prayed to the Ferrymen to take his soul to the Sunset Isles and to avenge his death.

Ruffle Feathers, too, had an aversion for killing horses, but the lagahoo saw steaming meals on legs. Hearing his friend's roars and the staccato clanging of blade on blade, he turned to help Jamba. Sprouting fur from every pore, his face morphing into a snouted animal visage akin to that of the ghastly offspring of a bear and a wolf, Lug tore up the ground with his clawed paws as he hurtled through the woods. Snarling and spitting, he pounced high and came crashing down on one of the horsemen, smacking the man aside and opening the beast's throat with a slash of his claw. The man hit the ground hard and never had a chance to rise. Lug landed on him a heartbeat later, while lights yet danced before his eyes, and snapped his fanged maw shut on the man's head, popping it like a watermelon.

Swords slashed down at the lagahoo's back, crisscrossing it with wounds, though the soldiers found to their surprise that their steel could not easily penetrate deep into the thick hide. Expecting to see a beast dead at their feet, they stared in terror into the tawny semi-human eyes that regarded them.

Lug and Jamba leaped, claws and scimitars lashing out, and two more crusaders toppled from their mounts. Jamba retreated to gain space to fight while Lug tore open the belly of a rearing horse he had startled with a roar.

"Lug!" Jamba yelled. "Lug, come one! We have to keep moving!"

He thought for a second the bumbling meld of man and wolf had not heard him over whatever berserker rage overtook him at times like this, but then Lug loped after him on all fours and Jamba took off deeper into the woods, the supernatural cold almost forgotten. On the contrary, his lungs burned and his muscles throbbed. They could never get far, though, before they were once more at bay, forced to turn and fight or else feel the crusaders' steel in their spines.

Running and fighting, running and fighting, Jamba's shoulders soon ached from the effort of parrying heavy Justiquan broadswords. His own scimitars glanced off the knights' steel plate armour again and again, almost jarring the swords from his grasp as his grip weakened. Masterful in a duel though he liked to think himself, battling multiple opponents meant he rarely had the chance to put his counteroffensive skills to the test, ever on the back foot. He used the forest to his advantage, trying to place a tree between him and at least one of his enemies at all times, so that he could whittle down their effective numbers if only for a second or two at a time.

Through careful manoeuvring, he singled out a crusader from the pack for a moment. Leading the man away, he scrambled into a cleft in a broad white bole and then leaped down on him when he came within range. The knight tried to skewer him on his sword, but Jamba swatted it aside with one scimitar and caromed into him, knocking him off the horse. Both lay flat and winded for an instant, and then the disarmed knight began wriggling around like a beetle on its back, struggling to rise under the weight of all his armour. As he arched his back and tried to sit up again and again, he opened and closed the gap between his cuirass and helmet. Awaiting the opportune moment, Jamba slit his throat in one smooth motion before pushing himself to his feet just in time to duck one sword swipe and parry another that would have scalped him. He ran.

He could hear the horses' laboured breathing on his neck, though, and his back itched in anticipation of the sword strike that would tear it open. Then, Lug blurred past him, launching himself high into the air and walloping one man off his horse with a flung claw, before landing squarely in front of another mount and stopping it in its cantering tracks with his bare paws on its mighty shoulders, his own hairy feet sliding back on the sun-baked earth only a little. Jamba gawked in amazement, having glanced over his shoulder to be sure the lagahoo hadn't died. He needn't have worried. Lug threw the horse down on its side as if it were no more than a rocking horse carved for a babe. The creature whickered in heart-rending tones as the lagahoo sank its fangs into the beast's belly, before falling silent as the man-beast's claws savaged it and its dazed rider. Lug's maw came away bloody, dripping strips of muscle hanging from his teeth. Jamba felt his bile rise, but strangled it back down. Much as he hated the act, he was grateful for it, too.

Once more, Lug paid the price for rescuing him. The lagahoo was surrounded in a blink, broadswords rising and falling all around him and painting the white trees with his blood. Jamba's heart went out to him as he howled in pain, and the smuggler was hurtling back through the forest towards his simple-minded friend before he even knew what he was doing. His feet dug in deep, propelling him forward with pantherish alacrity so that the wind rushed through his hair. His muscles clenched up, and as a wrathful holler tore itself from his mouth, he felt powerful, alive. Springing off a fallen tree, he threw himself onto the back of one of the mounted knights, jamming his scimitar into the man's ribcage through his armpit with a roar as the knight raised his arm to rain another blow down on Lug. Wrenching the weapon back out awkwardly, he shoved the coughing corpse off the horse and stuck his own feet in the stirrups.

Digging his heels into the horse's flanks, controlling it expertly with his knees and shouting, "Hyah!" he forced the palomino steed to caracole around Lug, knocking all the other horses away for a moment. It was a risky manoeuvre and Jamba's scimitars flashed every step of the way, dissuading broadswords from beheading him time and again, but it worked. The other mounts were caught by surprise and instinctively stepped back.

Jamba reached out a hand to Lug. "Let's go!"

Lug ignored the hand but vaulted easily onto the horse behind Jamba, his heavy clawed paws settling on the smuggler's shoulders. The horse reared and whinnied as his weight came down on it, kicking two horses out of the way with its flailing front hooves, and then Jamba heeled its sides and it took off through the gap it had created at top speed, galloping and tossing its head in fear and confusion while Jamba whooped. The crusaders pursued them with curses, calling on their infernal Prophet for aid as their mounts struggled to navigate the plethora of trees without barging into one another. Atop the palomino, Jamba and Lug zigged and zagged snappily through the woods with only trees to avoid. Within seconds, they had caught the old obeahman who had led them into the forbidden forest. Glancing back in almost comical fear as he waddled, cocoa face reddened by the sun setting in a mauve corona to the west, Ruffle Feathers' features warped into a mask of confusion and then a shrugging acceptance as he beheld his friends atop a Justiquan steed. He held out a hand, and Lug hauled him easily into his lap atop the horse with one hairy arm.

Supported by Lug, Ruffle Feathers stood up on the horse's back as soon as he was seated and directed an arm towards the crusaders chasing them. Smoke billowed copiously from his fingers, only to float and swirl strangely in the dusky air before him, attached to his hand by ethereal black tendrils. The dark smog coalesced into a swarm of ephemeral nightmarish bats with bleeding red eyes, long tendrils for tails where they were linked to Ruffle's palm and horns on their heads.

"What would you have of us, master?" they gurgled as one in Traveller's Tongue in horrific phlegmy voices like drowning children.

Ruffle pointed with his spare hand at the knights on their trail, and the smoky bats bobbed their heads, turned and flapped their bizarre wings. Ruffle swiped a hand, severing the smoggy link between him and the demons he had summoned. The bats soared with unnatural speed through the woods, easily flitted around barky sentinels bathed in the sunset's pinkish radiance, and descended on the crusaders like a dark cloud, a black shroud for their doomed souls. Gibbering in panic, the foremost crusaders were torn to shreds by the bats like injured fish that venture into piranha-ridden waters.

The bats clawed and gnawed open their faces as the knights screamed, immune to fist and blade. Their tails, barbed with ghostly spikes, wrapped around Justiquan necks and tore out their throats. They did not spare the horses, either. Gore grew on the trees like springtime blossom, flecking the unearthly boughs and sullying the already tainted earth. Red suffused the sky, as if the clouds were soaking up the spilled ichor.

His nose crammed with the bitter aroma of blood, death and voided bowels, Ruffle Feathers' eyes widened as he beheld some of the crusaders circumventing his throng of demon bats, ruthless as tax collectors. He could not believe they were still coming.

8

Father of the Forest

"Hyah! Hyah!" Jamba yelled, flogging the flagging horse with the reins and kicking his heels into its sides savagely in hopes of eking every last ounce of speed from the creature.

Under the weight of three men, however, the horse was tiring fast and slowing by the second. Just as blood coagulated, so too did the red sky darken. The crusaders who had forged past Ruffle Feathers' smoky horde of demon bats were gaining on the smugglers with every passing breath, and Jamba felt helpless to prevent them. Though the bats had slain scores, dozens remained – too many for an outright fight. So, though it seemed as though he was only delaying their inevitable doom, Jamba kept the horse galloping. The leafless, white-barked, skeletal trees proved the smugglers' only salvation, temporary though it may have been. While their one horse could weave through the trees with relative ease, the crusaders' horses constantly bumped into one another thanks to their erratic courses in the increasing darkness, and they had to wait for one another time and again in order to pursue as the crow flies, or else split up and spread out, which cost them time.

Jamba could feel the woods' cold creeping up on him again now that he was no longer running. He glimpsed fleeting figures, silvery and ethereal, in his periphery amid the bone-white trees now and then, and distant lamentations reached his ears, just on the edge of make believe. He shivered as the thought crossed his mind that the woods could be a tear in the veil between life and death, and perhaps he was hearing the pleading calls of all the unborn children begging for life. He wondered if this was his destiny, after all he had been through – to die lost and forgotten in an eldritch wood, surrounded by duppy and invisible supernatural beings from the dawn of time and, worst of all, Justiquans. It would be rich, he thought wryly.

He could hear the crusaders' hoof beats closing in on him, their fricative shouts grating against his ears. He could feel Ruffle slumped against his back and knew the old obeahman would be of no further assistance. Summoning the bats had drained him, Jamba knew. Preparing to turn for a last stand against the knights, Jamba's eyes widened when the land abruptly sloped steeply down and he found himself instead hurtling headlong atop the horse down the hidden hill towards a maroon morass steaming in the dying light. He let out a yelp, sure their horse would break a leg and throw them at any second. The wind blasted his face as the horse pelted down the hill at frightening speed, lathered and labouring. Jamba blinked, sure his eyes were playing with him, but when he reopened them he saw the same thing.

Eyes in the steam, watching him.

He could scarcely even explain what he was seeing or how he knew what he was seeing, but he knew he was seeing it, knew in the depths of his heart that this was no illusion. He heard Ruffle gasp and guessed the obeahman could see them, too. Phantom figures floated above the boggy ground in the glittering steam, silvery and translucent as steam themselves. Jamba considered yanking on the horse's reins to stop it or turn, but decided against it. If the duppy wanted him dead, he'd be dead. The mount hit flat ground at a mad gallop and caromed through tall rushes the colour of dried blood under a sky the colour of rust. Tugging this way and that on the reins, Jamba helped it navigate the dry land amid the stagnant ponds, though it proved far from easy to tell where the hidden waters lay thanks to the masking effects of the red sedge. He could hear the crusaders having similar problems behind him as they too barged heedlessly into the swamp and splashed into the algae-ridden ponds with cries of rage, sending up a musty scent.

Jamba screeched like a parakeet as a pond nearby suddenly exploded upwards, and from the fetid spray came slithering with serpentine speed a thirty-foot-long Chilpaean crocodile, the largest breed of crocodile in all of Maradoum. Its hide glistened green in the sunlight, and its mammoth jaws snapped shut a hair's breadth behind the smugglers' horse's rear end, making Jamba jump. He looked back for a second and witnessed the crocodile, along with another that had appeared from the mists, converging on the shrieking Justiquans.

As Jamba and the other smugglers passed into the steam, he closed his eyes for a few seconds, letting the horse have its head and expecting to be ripped from existence at any moment by malicious spirits. Then, having not died, so far as he could tell, he cautiously opened one eye and peeked out. White swirls floated around him like vaporised cotton, and in their foggy midst, just out of eyeshot, he could hear distant wailing. It came to him more clearly now, and he realised with a start that he could understand the voices speaking to him faintly in Kwi patois.

"Turn east! We will lead you to safety! East!"

He felt but did not see ghostly hands gripping the reins alongside his own, helping him steer the horse east, and he would have broken out in a sweat if he had not already been sweating profusely. His flesh crawled at the presence of the supernatural. Behind him, he could hear splashing and screams and the grotesque snapping and tearing sounds of crusaders being shredded by crocodiles.

"What's happening?" shouted Lug. "Why are we turning?"

Jamba had no answer for the lagahoo. He could not even see their path to avoid the stagnant pools, thanks to the steam, and so he had no choice but to blindly trust the duppy who were leading him and pray they were not malevolent. He felt as if he were riding in a dreamworld, rustling through rosy rushes and sedge towards oblivion. The horse that bore them slowed to a canter and then to a trot, spent. Jamba did not lash it or dig his heels into its sides, even when it slowed to a mosey. The witchwood had them firmly in it skeletal clutches now, and it would decide their fate, rather than the speed of their horse's hooves.

Soon, the Justiquans' death cries and the sounds of crocodiles gorging themselves fell far behind, to be replaced by a goosebump-raising silence. Jamba didn't even realise he was holding his breath, afraid to make a sound, until he almost passed out from lack of air. He cautiously sucked in a breath, afraid that even such a small act could displease the duppy. He did not die a gruesome death, though, so he relaxed a jot.

He lost track of time in that unnaturally thick steam, but thought more than an hour must have passed before the steam unfolded before them, giving onto a glade surrounded on three sides by white-barked sentinels. Reddish rushes and sedge swayed in the night breeze. The sun had set, and stars winked at the smugglers from the void. In the centre of the glade, by a black algae-thick pond, grew a blue mahoe tree, the tallest Jamba had ever seen, and perfectly proportioned. Its glossy leaves gleamed in the streaming moonlight, the epitome of green, and its blue-green bole was so smooth it looked as if it had been lacquered. Its fuchsia flowers ranged in colour, running the gamut of the sunset.

"It's beautiful," Lug said softly, and Jamba heartily agreed.

In the shadow of the blue mahoe lurked a figure. Jamba directed the horse towards the tree, but as he did so he heard a strange whooshing behind him. He glanced over his shoulder just in time to see the steam that eclipsed the bog swirling, coalescing and solidifying into the form of a gigantic white snake with fangs the size of swords and great, yellow eyes with slit pupils. Upon seeing the monster, the horse threw the smugglers and galloped off into the woods, tossing its head and whinnying. Groaning on the ground, the smugglers gaped. It was impossible to tell how long the snake was, for it coiled in on itself seemingly indefinitely, its loops surrounding it like an aurora as it hung, hovering, in mid-air, not a single scale touching the earth. Jamba reckoned it was as wide as the fifty-foot mahoe.

Its forked tongue flickering in and out, the snake demanded of the smugglers in sibilant Kwi patois, "What foolishness drives the travellers here, hmm? And how dare they taint my woods with the footsteps of foreigners, unbelievers, deceivers, betrayers and scoundrels? Why? Why should I not tear the heads from the necks of such troublesome intruders into my woods, hmm? Hmm?"

Stammering, in search of an answer, Jamba was saved by a gravelly voice from behind speaking the same tongue. "Oh, knock it off, Damballah!

These are *our* people, and you know it."

Jamba whipped his head around to observe the figure emerging from the shade of the blue mahoe, and once more his jaw fell slack. The figure appeared to be a five-foot old man – but a man with the hairy legs and cloven hooves of a billy goat. From the waist up, he was indistinguishable from a wrinkly, hunched old man – save for the small horns growing from the bird's nest of hair atop his head. As he strolled closer, leaning on a witchwood cane, Jamba saw that his long unkempt beard looked to be made of algae.

"The travellers track in their filth and expect no comeuppance!" hissed the massive snake, disgruntled.

"And no uppance shall come," replied the ancient fellow with a twinkle in his evergreen eyes. "Not while Papa Bwa wanders these woods."

"Papa Bwa and Damballah!" Jamba gasped, eyes wide as his mind took flight to the fables his mother had told him as a child – stories of the father of the forest and the world serpent, two primordial Gods locked in an endless struggle, one who loathes that which he helped create and one who protects all life.

"Pay no heed to Damballah," said Papa Bwa, waving a dismissive hand towards the huffy snake, his voice deep as kapok roots. "You are safe here, my children."

"Thank you, Papa Bwa," said Lug jovially, rising, brushing himself off and extending his hand.

To Jamba's surprise, Bwa shook it with a chuckle.

"Yes," Jamba added, pushing himself up and then helping Ruffle Feathers to his feet. "Thank you, truly. How can we ever repay such a debt?"

"There is no debt." Papa Bwa waved away the words, beckoning them with a grandfatherly smile. "Come, come. I've laid out a nice picnic for us beneath the mallow."

"You will live to regret this, Bwa!" Damballah hissed as the father of the forest led the smugglers towards the tree. "Humans are a scourge upon the universe, a blight to be eradicated!"

"Shush now," Papa Bwa retorted, shooing the snake away. "Go on, be off with you if you've naught nice to say."

Jamba watched in astonishment as the snake pouted and then melted back into steam before his eyes, once more masking the woods behind him from view.

Flickers of fire in the air told him Ruffle Feathers was introducing himself to the Forest God, and he winced when he read, 'Not that I'm not awed by your presence – truly I am – but that was far from the epic clash I expected after reading the fables.'

Fortunately, Papa Bwa did not take offence, but rather guffawed loudly. "Oh, Damballah's not such a bad sort when you get to know him. Of course, on his bad days, he does seek an end to all existence. He gets a bit blue. But, luckily, I'm always here to cheer him up."

Jamba could not believe his eyes when he saw the spread laid out for them on a big periwinkle blanket under the blue mahoe, lit by the fireflies that now flitted around beneath the branches. Bread, cheese, fowl, frog, snail and strips of salted boar meat awaited the smugglers' delectation, alongside wooden pipes in the shapes of dragons and several large leather baui pouches.

Jamba murmured, "Somebody pinch me. I must be dreaming. Ow!"

He scowled at Ruffle and rubbed his arm where the old man had pinched it. Ruffle shrugged, sat down and dug in. Papa Bwa and Lug seated themselves on the blanket and reached for some of the food, and Jamba was left standing for a moment, staring around in utter disbelief. Then, he too shrugged, sat and started shoving food into his famished face, realising just how hungry he was.

"If you don't mind my asking," he said around a mouthful of sausage, "why did you save us?"

Papa Bwa tore off a hunk of bread with his teeth and chewed thoughtfully. "This is my country," he said in the end, spitting crumbs, "and you are my people. More than that, the Chilpaeans are a good people, always have been. They do not invade other countries nor torture their own earth with razing and pollutants. They look after one another, and the wildlife that surrounds them. They even found a way to pacify the Sleepers without killing them." He spread his arms and took in the glade. "They live in harmony with the Gods, and with nature."

His arms fell, and he shook his head. "These so-called crusaders are the apotheosis of mankind's darker nature, driven by greed, irrational hatred and an endless lust for power. If they have their way, all of Maradoum will be scourged of magic and their cities of stone will smother the lands, and life along with it. Why, they would even enslave the Gods if they could." He looked troubled for a moment as he said this, but then he shook off the darkness. "I know of your mission – or I can readily guess it, at least. I sensed the Lullabyer's soul as soon as it entered the witchwood. One of you carries it with you, no? And, unless I miss my guess, you are bearing it north to the Monastery Calliope to bring it to his sole heir, are you not?"

"You know of all that transpired in Cocoba Bay?" Jamba asked, surprised.

Papa Bwa's eyes twinkled as he lit a baui pipe with a snap of his fingers and puffed pungent plumes. "A God has his ways, my son. I know that the country has fallen, both south and north, but that pockets of resistance yet hold out. I know that the Lullabyer and his eldest child have been slain and the Lullaby has gone unsung. Sleepers creep from their holes even as we speak."

Jamba shot a glance up at the moon and leaped to his feet in alarm. "Gods, you're right! The-"

"Settle down, my son, settle down." Papa Bwa flapped for him to sit back down. "My, you're a jumpy one, aren't you? You're safe here in my glade, and here you may spend the night. In the morning, I'll lead you to the northern edge of the woods, and you may continue on your journey."

"Oh, thank you, Papa Bwa!" said Jamba, slumping back down on his backside with a sigh of relief.

"Be on the lookout when you leave, however. The Sleepers are an ancient, near unstoppable race, and they will hunt you remorselessly should they find you, so take care."

"Will you come with us, please?" Lug asked, face alight.

Papa Bwa shook his head, rising, patting the lagahoo's shoulder and then beginning to bandage his many wounds with linen that appeared from nowhere. "I am a minor God, with my powers greatest here in my own lands, in the forests south of the Belt. I would be of little assistance to you in the north, I'm afraid, nothing but an old bag of bones. Besides, Mama D'lo would never hear of it."

9

Prayers to the Twins

As the smugglers made their way out of the northern edge of the witchwoods, close to the Belt, Jamba Klach glanced back in time to witness Papa Bwa wave and disappear back into the mist-wreathed trees from which he had come.

"Wow," he said. "That was something. I never in all my life expected to meet Papa Bwa, father of the forest. Or to venture into the witchwood and emerge unscathed, for that matter. It's a blessed miracle we survived!"

"I liked Papa Bwa," said Lug Thorm, entranced by a bee buzzing in the meadow bursting with golden orchids shining in the morning sun beyond the woods. "He was nice."

Tramping through the meadow, Ruffle Feathers bobbed his head and waved a hand. Words materialised in mid-air, etched in flame. 'A miracle indeed. It is a miracle that we survived the night. We should be doubly grateful for that. I feel it in the air this morning. The Sleepers have arisen.'

Jamba tried to ignore the chill coursing down his spine demanding his attention. "Faugh, they've been asleep for hundreds of years. Perhaps Papa Bwa made a mistake. Perhaps they haven't woken yet."

Even as he said it, he knew in his gut it was wrong. He saw Lug clasping his hands and closing his eyes as he walked, so that he bumbled from side to side, feet getting stuck in rabbit holes now and then.

"What are you doing?" Jamba asked eventually when the lagahoo almost fell over.

Lug opened one eye to see his companions staring at him. He looked abashed. "I was just … praying to the Twins." Seeing his friends' questioning looks, he went on. "Well, it seems to me that the Twins are the ones who gave the Lullabyer his magic powers, right? Well, if that's the case, maybe if we pray to them hard enough, they'll give me the magic voice – or you, Ruffle. I thought it was worth a try. They are Gods, after all. They can do anything."

Jamba was about to castigate the man for his foolishness when it struck him that it wasn't a half bad idea, if the legends of the source of the Opherios' powers were true.

Ruffle seemed to agree, for he asked in letters of fire, 'And did it work? Did the Gods speak to you? Did they grant you the voice?'

Lug looked taken aback. "I – I don't know. I didn't speak to them, but … maybe they did without me realising it. D'you think?"

"Try it out," Jamba suggested, seeing where Ruffle was going. "Try singing a song."

"Young Janie, young Janie, came swimming to me,
Far from the bathtub, deep in the stream ..."

As Lug opened wide his mouth and started bawling out a common country tune in ear-splitting discordant tones that would make a trained singer weep, Jamba and Ruffle could keep it in no longer. As one, they broke down in a fit of giggles, clutching their sides as the laughter convulsed their whole bodies and tears streamed down their cheeks.

Lug stopped singing. "You were having me on!"

"I don't think it worked!" Jamba joked amid peals of mirth, doubled over, slapping his thigh.

Lug scowled and plodded away. "Let's just go."

The smugglers headed north through the golden meadows, Jamba singing *Young Janie* teasingly now and again. The land around the witchwood had been allowed to grow wild, no one wanting to venture near the unnerving white trees. As the smugglers approached cultivated lands, however, they had to make a choice.

"So," said Jamba, breaking a long silence, "do we stop off at Nirby or not?"

Ruffle pondered this for a moment, puffing on a wooden baui pipe carved in the shape of a dragon and blowing bluish-white plumes. 'We should avoid towns where possible. The Justiquans will target them first.'

Jamba nodded. "True, although there's not just the crusaders to consider. There's Sleepers too, if Papa Bwa was right. We'd be safer in a town, surrounded by torches. You know the legends say the Sleepers hate fire."

'Then, we will just have to light our own fire.'

Jamba rubbed a hand over his face, tugging at his beard in frustration. "But the Sleepers will see the light of a fire from leagues away! Rrg! This is impossible. We cannot make camp in town lest we're hunted down like criminals and we cannot roam the wilderness at night lest we're hunted down like animals! There are enemies at every turn!" He paused to gather his thoughts, before turning to Ruffle again. "D'you think we'll be safer if we light a fire to fend off the Sleepers or just try to hide from them in the darkness?"

Ruffle considered this, then waved a hand. 'The legends say the Sleepers can sniff you out wherever you are. They will find us. We should light a fire.'

Jamba nodded thoughtfully. "There are few places to hide in these parts anyway. The mountains are too far to the west, the coast too far to the east, so the chances of finding a cave by nightfall are slim and we just passed the last sizeable forest in this region."

"Why do the Sleepers only come out at night anyway?" asked Lug shyly.

Jamba looked at him in surprise and opened his mouth, but found he had no answer.

Ruffle scrawled letters of fire on the night. 'Many creatures are nocturnal. It is not so strange. It is likely simply how they evolved, the best time for them to feed. And, like all creatures, even the Sleepers must sleep.'

They made camp just before the sun fell in a small cedar copse they stumbled across. Jamba and Lug cleared a space for them to sleep amid the myriad fallen needles and then rooted around for wood, finding little that was dry. Ruffle started a fire with a snap of his fingers once they had stacked the sap-filled wood, and great white plumes billowed high into the purple sky like a smoke signal.

Watching them, Jamba muttered, "Every crusader for leagues will see this."

Ruffle replied in arcane words of flame, nodding to the western horizon where the sun sank in waves of peach. 'We'll be the least of their concerns soon.'

Sitting cross-legged on the ground around the small fire, they cooked some of the dried venison they had brought from the growers' village in hemp bags and devoured some of the cheese, bread and fruit they had brought along from the picnic in the witchwood. They ate in anxious silence, each darting glances around, trying not to stare into the flames, but all eventually becoming hypnotised by the crackling orange tongues. The wood popped as it burned, making them jump.

Jamba smiled sheepishly when he saw that he was not the only one who had flinched. "D'you really think the Sleepers will find us tonight?" he asked softly. "I know what Papa Bwa said, and I know the legends, but … that's all they've ever been to me. Legends. It seems impossible that the Sleepers could awaken, rise from their burrows and slaughter us all in our sleep. It just can't be."

Ruffle nodded, puffing on his pipe. 'Change is difficult to imagine, but it is coming, mark my words. They are coming. We cannot prevent change. We can, however, control how we react to it. We can flee in fear like mice from a cat, or we can stand our ground and fight and, if we die, go down in a blaze of glory fit for bards to sing of for a thousand years!'

Jamba nodded. "Right you are, Ruffle. Right you are. Are you with us, Lug?"

Lug smiled lopsidedly. "Always, my friends."

Jamba cleared his throat. "Okay, here we go then … all together now … *Young Janie, young Jani-"*

His singing was cut off by laughter as Lug leaned over to punch his arm.

"So, now that you have more of these magical crystals, does that make you more powerful?" Jamba asked Ruffle, his face becoming more serious. "I've never seen you summon so many weird bat creatures."

Ruffle pursed his lips as he manifested his response. 'Yes, in a manner of speaking. It gives me more reserves to call upon.'

Jamba nodded, pretending understanding. "So, now that the Lullabyer is trapped in a crystal, can he help us? Can we use his power, too?"

Ruffle frowned. 'He is not trapped in the crystal. He is the crystal. It is his soul given physical form. Ergo we cannot tap that crystal's power without consuming the Lullabyer's soul. And consuming souls is not something anyone should ever want to do. That way madness lies.'

"So … we can't use that particular crystal?"

'No.'

Jamba blew out his cheeks. "Okay, well, at least we have others. Can we speak to the Lullabyer? Does he have any ideas on how to put the Sleepers back to sleep? He's been doing it for decades, after all."

Ruffle shook his head and waved a hand, but reached into his satchel for the crystal carved in the Lullabyer's likeness. 'None but the Opherios can perform the Lullaby, but fine. Speak to the Lullabyer yourself.'

He placed the crystal in the loam, wriggling it back and forth to embed it. Jamba leaned in to put his face close to the crystal and saw the familiar bearded face inside composed of swirling blobs of blue and purple like ink in water. As he watched, one of the eyes floated away and then returned to its original position.

"Good evening, Magnuz," Jamba said.

"You may call me Lullabyer!" the face snapped, its voice echoing in Jamba's mind. *"Is it evening? I can hardly tell. I can barely see anything at the best of times, but stick me in a satchel all the Gods-damned day long and I can't make out a wink! It's lucky I can still sleep to pass the time ... or perhaps it's not sleep. Perhaps it's more of a self-enforced trance, a lack of awareness that allows me to rest without constant stimulation. Whatever it is, I thank the Gods for it, else I'd have gone demented by now. Can you please ask Ruffle Feathers to take me out of the bag now and again so that I don't go insane?"*

Jamba looked to the obeahman. "Magnuz asks that you take him out of the satchel more often. He's bored."

Ruffle rolled his eyes and replied in eldritch fiery words, 'He's easiest to carry in the satchel. But fine. I'll take him out more often.'

"He'll take you out more often," Jamba relayed to the Lullabyer, who sniffed, chin held high.

"Excellent. I'm used to a certain way of life, you know. Walking, eating, drinking, breathing, the one-handed dance ... I can't do any of the

things I used to do." The face sighed. *"The sooner I can pass on my knowledge to my son, the better. Then, I can finally rest in the Sunset Isles."*

"The Isles are real, then?"

"They'd better be."

Jamba stroked his beard for a second. "I wanted to ask, Magnuz, if you had any advice for us, any pearls of wisdom that might help us survive to reach the Monastery Calliope?"

"Pearls of wisdom?" the face repeated sneeringly. *"What d'you think I am – a fucking oyster of endless aphorisms? Here's some advice, smuggler. Travel as fast as you can. Hide at night. Don't die."*

"Thanks," Jamba drawled sarcastically, "that's very helpful, you miserable old bugger."

"You're very welcome."

"Can't you sing the Sleepers back to sleep?" Jamba asked.

The face in the crystal gave him a condescending look. *"I can't make noise, can I? I can't speak or sing – save in the minds of those prepared to listen. So, no, smuggler, I cannot sing the Sleepers back to sleep."*

"Seriously, you don't know anything more about the Sleepers than the rest of us?"

The face in the crystal shook its head. *"Honestly, I don't. I never much questioned my powers. They were with me from birth, and I was taught to control them as I was taught to walk and talk. They are such an intrinsic part of me that I don't even know how to explain them to an outsider, for I do not know what life is like without them. I've never even seen a live Sleeper. I saw a dead one once, and I can tell you they are huge. And horrific to gaze upon. Such fangs ..."* The face shuddered. *"I wish I'd paid more attention to the lore growing up. To be truthful, I know no more about the Sleepers than you do. They've always ... well, they've always been asleep, haven't they? I've sung the Lullaby at least once every single night of my life, except when I was ill. So, they've never risen before. Not in numbers. Not like this."*

Jamba nodded and puffed out his cheeks. "The blind leading the blind. How reassuring."

10

Djhuty the Diabolical

The smugglers sat and watched the bruised sky darken until the twinkling eyes above began to show and howls resounded across the land. Jamba shuddered as he heard the first inhuman high-pitched bark break the night. It sounded thankfully distant, but there was little doubt in the swordsman's mind what kind of creature had made such a distinctive sound. Another yowl replied to the first, and another, and another, until the horrible howling abraded their ears from every corner, some close and some far away. Hearing a howl uncomfortably nearby, the smugglers stiffened and laid hands on their weapons.

Jamba's blood froze in his veins when he heard padding in the cedar copse, just outside the firelight. He turned towards the sound and scrunched up his eyes, trying to pierce the darkness, but all he saw was trees and shadow. The smugglers' heads whipped around when they heard fallen needles rustle in the opposite direction, and again when they heard a faint growl coming from yet another cardinal point.

"They're surrounding us, circling us!" Jamba whispered tremulously as the padding and growling grew louder and more frequent. He unsheathed his scimitars with a rasp of steel. Still, he could see nothing. "Do we have enough wood to last the night?"

Ruffle swiftly tucked his pipe and the Lullabyer-shaped gemstone back in his satchel, despite its protestations, and waved a hand. 'It doesn't matter. They're afraid of fire, true, but hungry enough not to care, I suspect. Stay close to the fire, and to me, when they attack.' He hesitated for a second, and then more words winked into existence. 'I am going to attempt to summon a larger demon than usual. Such a spell is dangerous for many reasons, but the foremost is that to do so I must open a door between our world and the demon plane. While such a door is open, any demon could come through – even ones beyond my control.' He met the eyes of his companions. 'This spell could easily kill us if it goes wrong, but we are looking death in the face anyway tonight, no? So, why not spit in its eye?'

Jamba nodded. "Damn the risk. Do it, Ruffle. As you say, we might be doomed if you do, but we're definitely doomed if you do not."

Lug bobbed his head. "You are my best friends. If we die, we die together."

The love in the lagahoo's face made Jamba and Ruffle uncomfortable. Both averted their gaze and mumbled in reply. Then, Ruffle closed his eyes and began to hum a low, monotonous note while tracing arcane patterns in the air with his gnarly hands. The warm wind picked up, and the cedars whispered to one another as they swayed.

Jamba took a leather pouch from a pocket in his breeches, unknotted the drawstring and opened it, before offering it to Lug. "Witch-spice?"

Lug nodded, reached in and took a pinch of the small seeds between thumb and forefinger, then lifted them to his nose and snorted them noisily. He slapped his lips and stuck out his tongue as his pupils dilated. Jamba took a pinch from the bag, held the seeds to his right nostril and sniffed them up, wincing at the potent smell of concentrated turmeric and the feel of the witch-spice, hot as a shot of firewater, coursing down his windpipe into his lungs, where they would inevitably germinate thanks to the body's moisture and grow through the lungs like a spiderweb, invading every corner until eventually they consumed their host after enough use and burst out of its corpse to spread their seed and begin the cycle over.

Before they consumed their host, though, the little seeds imbued those who sniffed them with superhuman strength, speed and reflexes, pushing the body to its limits to wrench the most out of it. And it felt good, Jamba had to admit. It felt really good. His heart pounded, fast as a hummingbird's wings, and his eyes opened wide to suck in all the meagre light. His old aches and pains faded away, muffled by the spice's noise. Grinning like a maniac and tensing his muscles, the smuggler felt eighteen years old again, like he could take on the whole world single-handed, cross a mountain in a bound and swim a sea in one stroke. Bursting with energy, he bounced on the balls of his feet on the spot, while Lug performed some shadow-boxing.

A black hulk blurred across Jamba's vision, whipping the campfire and leaving a gash across the smuggler's left shoulder. Had he not darted to the right just in time, his throat would have been torn out. He barely had time to glimpse the huge figure as it skittered by. All he recalled was fur and fangs.

"They're coming!" he shrieked, spinning on the spot to try to cover all angles, his shoulder aflame.

Bristly umber hair sprouting all over his body and his nose lengthening into a snout, Lug scooped up and hefted his weighty iron warhammer in his paws. He was laid flat by a shaggy black assailant an instant later, though he managed a glancing blow in return that elicited a bone-chilling yowl before the creature disappeared into the darkness once more.

His eyesight augmented by the witch-spice, Jamba could make out shifting shapes in the shadows now, and he threw himself in front of Ruffle Feathers just in time when he saw a figure flit towards the unprotected obeahman. Lunging, he managed to catch the Sleeper and felt the tip of his scimitar pierce flesh. Hot red blood speckled his hand, and a thrill raced through him as he realised he had hurt one. He had drawn its blood. If it bled, it was a mere animal, no demon or ungodly horror. If it bled, he could kill it.

The black beast backhanded him with one of its many hairy, segmented legs, and Jamba staggered back under the force of the blow, his face numb. He saw the Sleeper closing in on Ruffle Feathers and flung himself after it with a holler, leaping far and fast thanks to the witch-spice, directly onto the creature's back. He crosshatched its hide with his blades in a frenzy, and then plunged one of his scimitars into its back, down to where he hoped its lungs and heart might be. The Sleeper wailed hideously and bucked like a bronco, throwing the smuggler off its back before coughing up incarnadine blood and slumping lifeless in the dirt. Jamba could not believe it. He had slain one of the semi-mythical Sleepers.

A long, thin, scaly tail wrapped around his neck while he was catching breath, squeezing until his face turned blue, lifting him off his feet and turning him to face his new enemy. Jamba baulked at the sight. Nothing familiar presented itself to the eye – no eyes, no ears, no nose – and his mind reeled as it sought a feature in the visage on which to focus. Then, the entire shaggy black face opened up wide like a flower to receive him, each weird petal lined with row upon row of sharp, hooked teeth.

Wheezing for breath, Jamba glimpsed Lug out of the corner of his eye, somehow holding two of the beasts at bay with wide swipes of his warhammer. The lagahoo could not help him. As his vision darkened around the edges, diminishing to a tunnel with a light at the end, he knew blessed sleep was but moments away.

Fate had other plans for him, however. At that moment, Ruffle Feathers' eyes snapped open, his arm shot out and violet energy sparked from his splayed fingers, igniting mid-air and tearing a hole in the curtain between realms with a ghastly whooshing, ripping sound. In heartbeats, a purple rift had formed, stinking of sulphur and hovering in mid-air, gushing mauve flames and at the same time sucking everything towards it like a vortex. The Sleeper holding him aloft dropped Jamba and scampered away into the cedars' shadow in fright, its fellows yelping and skittering after it beyond the firelight. Jamba landed on his rear end, gasping for breath and rubbing his throat and gawping at Ruffle Feathers in awe.

A tentacled horror started to squirm and wriggle through the rift, but then it whimpered as an unseen hand abruptly yanked it back out of sight. Jamba jerked his head around, and his heart beat a frenzied tattoo in his chest. The Sleepers were creeping forwards again. A whump from the rift made them slink back again a moment later, and Jamba once more ogled the magenta scar the obeahman had created.

Fingers curled around its edges as if it were solid, uncaring of the flames, and then a humanoid figure stepped through, no taller than Jamba but radiating palpable ripples of power. Limned by purple fire, it took in the tableau in the copse with eyes blazing with an unholy inferno set in an ageless, androgynously beautiful visage the colour of dusk, a dark blend of blue and black. Its upswept, spiky white locks and cloak of black feathers swayed in the warm breeze as it inhaled the night air. Beneath the cloak, it wore only a black loincloth, its form lithe and powerful. Tattoos followed the contours of its muscles, alien runes pulsing and glowing with an eldritch blue light, and in its hand it bore a staff of yellowed bone topped with a skull like that of a horned horse. It turned its fiery eyes on Ruffle Feathers, who appeared as flabbergasted as the rest of them by the apparition.

"You! Am I truly free *ghon-jamohr?"* it spoke in surprisingly soft Traveller's Tongue, slipping into a grunting guttural language at the end. "Is this *Rijak-Kohmour,* the world of day?"

Ruffle waved a hand, wide-eyed, and flaming letters flickered into existence twixt him and the figure. 'I don't know what you mean. You're not the demon I summoned.'

The demon grinned, baring needle teeth. "A mute, eh? *Johr gollac.* Well, you are human, mute, so it must be the world of day. *Shivath previk."* It stepped towards the obeahman menacingly, purring, "And no, you did not summon me. But how could I pass up such a *delicious* opportunity?"

As it raised its hands menacingly in the air, Ruffle Feathers rapidly lifted his own and fresh words of flame bloomed in the air before the demon's eyes. 'Your prey is behind you.' The old obeahman waved a hand again when he saw the demon hesitate. 'Far larger and tastier than me.'

The demon slitted its eyes at the old man, but then spun on the ball of its foot to peer into the shadows between the trees. Jamba watched a satisfied smile curl its bluish lips, giving its face a more masculine cast, and observed the pulsing of the alien runes scrawled across its body intensify.

"Prey, indeed," it crooned. "Come to me, my beauties."

It beckoned to the Sleepers, and the violet rift snapped closed at its back, vanishing in a flash of flame. As if the sound were a clarion call, the Sleepers howled as one and charged the demon and the smugglers. Its bearing regal, its chin raised defiantly, the demon directed its bone staff towards the Sleepers. Darkness pulsed from the stave, a shockwave that ate through the Sleepers like a horde of maggots on witch-spice. Great holes appeared in the mewling creatures' shaggy frames in an instant, their hair burning away with an awful stench and their flesh blackening and shrivelling around the wounds. Mutilated and warped, they died mewling, and Jamba almost felt sorry for them.

Then, the demon was among them, whacking them with the skull topping the staff and flailing the shadowy morningstar that morphed into existence in its spare hand to decimate the throng of crepuscular critters. Though it looked like a phantom weapon carved from the darkest corners of imagination where horrors lurk, the morningstar bruised flesh and crushed bone with very real force. Sleepers howled as the demon sent them flying with wallops of its ever-spinning weapons, their bodies brutalised. They had enough intelligence to pull back to the shadows then, though only after the demon had mauled over a score of their kin in mere seconds. The scene seemed surreal to Jamba, who could not believe the power contained in the demon's compact frame; it was no larger than he was, half the size of the Sleepers, and yet it packed the punch of a sasquatch. The morningstar faded from sight as if it had never been once the Sleepers retreated, and Jamba shuddered.

The smugglers stood perfectly still, afraid to move, as the demon hauled the Sleepers' carcasses closer to the fire one by one, gutted them and tossed their entrails towards their growling fellows hiding among the cedars. Then, it sat cross-legged in the dirt and began to snap the beasts' bones in its bare hands, gouging out great chunks of meat with its sharp white teeth. Blood flecked its bruise-coloured face as it chewed and swallowed. It glanced around at the smugglers and gestured for them to join it by the dwindling fire.

"You may sit," it informed them magnanimously. "I have decided to let you live on account of the good sport and fine dining *gro bakhir*. You should count yourselves lucky. Not many are the humans who can claim to have shared a meal with Djhuty the Diabolical and lived to tell the tale. What are your names, new friends?"

The smugglers sat down tentatively on the far side of the fire, as far from the demon as they could get without seeming too rude. They did not want to anger the creature by snubbing it.

When no one spoke, Jamba cleared his throat and mumbled, "I am Jamba Klach, great Djhuty … the Diabolical. This is Lug Thorm, and this is Ruffle Feathers."

The demon's fiery gaze swept over the obeahman. "You are the one who summoned me. Do not think to banish me before I finish my meal, old one. I will go when I am good and ready."

Ruffle hastily gestured, and a reply appeared, scribbled in fire. 'Stay until morning. Protect us from the Sleepers.'

Nonchalantly tossing away a gnawed bone, the demon replied, "And why would I do that? What care I if you live or die?"

'If you ever want to come back to this realm, you need me to open a door,' Ruffle pointed out in arcane letters hanging in the air, at which the demon cocked its head and nodded grudgingly. The obeahman waved a hand again. 'And, like you said, we provided you with sport and a feast. We can help each other.'

The demon slitted its eyes, but then nodded. "Very well, old one. It shall be as you say. I leave at dawn, once I've had my fill. What did you call these creatures? Sleepers?" It loudly slurped down some bone marrow and burped. "They're simply delectable."

The smugglers stacked more wood on the fire, while the demon gorged itself. Ruffle Feathers smeared a salve made from herbs he kept in his satchel on Jamba and Lug's wounds and bandaged them with strips of linen. The Sleepers prowled around the edges of the camp, growling and sniffing, but did not dare venture into the firelight again. Still, the smugglers did not get a wink of sleep that night, buzzing with the aftereffects of all the excitement, the fear and the spice. True to its word, the demon stayed until dawn.

As soon as they could see clearly by the grey light that the Sleepers had slunk off to their warrens, the demon rose to its feet in one languid motion. "It seems you're safe now, and I have had my fill." Several skeletons gnawed to the bone gave testimony. The demon casually waved a hand, and a purple rift sprang into existence with a whoosh in the same spot as the night before, flickering with magenta flames. "I am glad I did not kill you. Perhaps we'll see one another again one day."

It stepped through the rift and was gone. The ugly tear in the fabric of the world stitched itself shut in the blink of an eye with a popping sound, and only the sulphurous reek remained.

"What in Galush-Kagen's ass was that, Ruffle?" Jamba demanded once he was sure the demon was not coming back, kicking dirt over the low fire to put it out.

Ruffle shrugged and waved a hand, replying in letters of fire, 'That was not the demon I was trying to summon. Such are the dangers of demon summoning. Open a door large enough, and who knows what will come through. I have never met such a powerful entity, capable of wielding dark magic of its own. We should be thankful that it protected us – and that it did not kill us on sight.'

Scratching his beard, Jamba muttered, "That's true. At least we're still alive – and Chilpaea still has a chance." He yawned, his eyes gummy and bloodshot. "I don't know about you, but I don't think I can take a step right now. I need a few winks, know what I mean?"

Ruffle nodded, his old face haggard. 'Agreed. We'll risk a quick snooze for a few hours, all three of us. I doubt anyone wants to volunteer to keep watch.'

He looked from Jamba to Lug, who both shook their heads. Lug was already making himself comfortable, lying flat on the dirt and needles.

"What if the Sleepers come back, though?" Jamba murmured as he laid his heavy head down. "Or the crusaders? Or some forest devil? We really should post a sentry. We really should …"

11

The Witch and the Worm

The smugglers slept uninterrupted till just before noon. It was when they rose and stepped out of the cedar copse, wiping crust from their eyes, that their troubles reawakened.

A shadow swept over them, eclipsing the sun for a second, and the smugglers craned their necks to look up. Blinded by the blistering sun, they heard the sound of huge wings flapping. When their eyes adjusted, Lug yelped in alarm, Jamba gasped, and Ruffle Feathers just stared as a lindworm, smaller cousin to the dragon, descended from the sunny blue sky toward them. Native to Chilpaea, lindworms normally lived solitary lives high in the Blueschists, rarely spied by human eyes.

Jamba Klach grabbed Ruffle Feathers and tried to drag him away, shouting, "A lindworm! Run!"

Ruffle refused to budge, though, waving his arm and forming words of fire. 'We cannot outrun it. And I think I recognise the rider.'

Reluctantly reading the obeahman's advice, Jamba let go of the old man with a growl and drew his blades. "Change of plans, Lug! Hold your ground."

The lagahoo sheepishly loped back to them, having started to sprint off across the field. Jamba returned his gaze to the lindworm, seeking its rider. Though smaller than a dragon, a lindworm towered twice as high as a man, its round, bloated body wrapped in green scales as tough as jade. Birdlike in posture with two taloned legs and two membranous wings, it swung a reptilian tail as a rudder in mid-air. It glanced down at the smugglers, craning its long neck, and Jamba shuddered at the sight of its metallic golden eyes and vicious raptorial beak with smoke pluming from the nares. Twin long, ridged horns sprouted from its temples.

It screeched with enough volume to wake a hibernating bear. *"Kreekaw!"*

Wind buffeted the smugglers, and then the lindworm was landing beside them, flapping its wings as it balanced on its talons, gouging the earth, and then tucking them back to allow its rider to dismount. A dark-eyed young woman of cocoa complexion hopped agilely off its back and swaggered towards the slack-jawed smugglers, her puffy pantaloons and garishly embroidered shawl billowing in the wind. Tendrils of crow-black hair that had crept loose from the intricate knot atop her head swept mesmerisingly across her scarred features.

"Who in Bwa's beard is that?" Jamba muttered as she swept closer, brandishing his scimitars and dropping into a fighting crouch.

Lug copied him, glancing again and again between him and the woman nervously. Ruffle stood calmly as the woman approached, noting that some of the wounds on her arms and legs seemed fresh.

She stopped ten paces from them, hands on her tilted hips. "So, you're the legendary obeahman, Ruffle Feathers, are you?" she asked as if she didn't quite believe it with a mixture of awe and scorn. She spoke Kwi patois in husky rasping tones like rock scraping against steel.

Ruffle bobbed his head and waved a hand. 'And you must be the infamous witch, Mzee Malakbet. Is it Vivian or Violet? I knew your mother, you know.'

"A witch?" Lug yelped, unable to keep it in any longer. "Are you going to drain our souls?"

The woman gave him a disdainful look. "A witch I may be, but I am not a Sister of Convent. I am not an immortal. I am not one of those responsible for the Time of Witches. So, no, lack-wit, I am not going to drain your soul. Today."

Lug didn't relax his posture an ounce, still holding his warhammer before him.

'A powerful witch your mother was,' Ruffle signed, 'and a real thorn in Magnuz's side.'

The woman nodded. "I know. Mother told me of your battles often enough. She said she'd never faced a more formidable, but fair, foe. That is why I've sought you out, Ruffle Feathers. I need your help."

Ruffle's eyebrows shot up. 'What makes you think I would help you when you and your mother are devoted to the downfall of the Lullabyer and all of Chilpaea?'

The woman hesitated a moment, then sighed and admitted, "I may have had a change of heart there. I've seen what the Sleepers can do now. Nobody warned us in time, and so that first night the Sleepers awoke … we did not know they were coming. They caught us unawares as we slept. My mother saw one of the monsters looming over my bed and blasted it away without a second thought. There was another behind her, though. It took her head from her shoulders with one swing of its paw."

She clenched her jaw so tight that she trembled, fists balled, eyes glimmering. "Mother and I used to believe the Sleepers would restore order to an unbalanced nation, let evolution take its natural course by culling the weak and strengthening the strong. I see now how wrong my mother was, how wrong I was. The Sleepers are not nature's scales; they are its bane. They must be put back to sleep. Thanks to my spies in your little growers' village, I know that is your goal. You seek to bring the Lullabyer's soul to his son in the Monastery Calliope in order to train him to use the Lullaby to restore order." She ignored their dumbstruck faces. "So, why help me? Because I will not let you pass if you do not. I control the Belt, and nobody crosses without my say so."

Ruffle scowled. 'I am not saying I agree, but what is it you want from us?'

"It's my sister, Violet," said Mzee Vivian Malakbet. "She thought she could open a portal to the Sunset Isles to bring our mother back to life. Instead, she opened a door to a realm of nightmares. She's trapped in another world."

12

The Belt Repository

Jamba had wanted to ride the lindworm. He would've given his left arm for the chance. But Mzee Vivian Malakbet informed him the lindworm could not carry more than one rider and would not carry the smugglers under any circumstance. Jamba did not doubt her from the fiery-eyed glares the creature gave him or the way it kept snapping its beak threateningly at them any time they drew too close.

So, much to his disappointment, he and his friends had to hoof it north to the witch's place of stay, the Belt, an ancient fortress built into the Blueschist Mountains where they stretched across the midsection of the island at its narrowest point; a natural barrier that had once served to separate two warring factions on the island in times long gone. They had to set a brisk pace to reach it by dusk. The Blueschists' hulking outline swam into view beneath the radiant pink rays of the sinking sun, sprawling sheer and unassailable from east to west horizon, so that none could cross the island's belly without navigating the fort. The lindworm landed in front of the fortress' bluish colonnaded façade beneath a great stylized sculpture carved into the cliff wall, parts of it chipped away by time and the elements.

Jamba found his eyes drawn to the scuffed imagery of monsters with faces that opened up like flowers, their petal-like jaws lined with teeth. The sculpture depicted a man playing a damaru and singing, the power of his music compelling the monsters to flee from him. Jamba squinted. There was something else, though, something he could not quite make out. The singer was on the left, the beasts in the middle, and on the right – most of it weathered beyond recognition – Jamba thought he could make out the crumbled outlines of men in Tzunese-style armour being mauled by the monsters.

"Welcome," rasped Mzee Malakbet, "to the Belt."

"How did you take the fortress anyway?" asked Jamba suspiciously. "It must have been guarded by hundreds of men."

The witch smirked. "Yes. Hundreds of foolish, superstitious men. My sister and I resolved to take the fort immediately after our mother died, so that we would have somewhere to hole up that night, safe from the Sleepers. It took us less than a day to drive most of the soldiers out with illusions of ghosts and demons. The token force ordered to remain were brave, I'll give them that. They did not flee, despite all the horrors they hallucinated. In the end, dusk was falling, so we had to sneak in, put them to sleep and drag them out." She raised a cocoa hand. "Our touch *is* sleep."

"Blessed sleep." Jamba started forward, but Ruffle held him back.

'So, you left them to die at the hands of the Sleepers?' Ruffle demanded, jabbing an angry finger.

Mzee Malakbet shrugged. "It is possible they got to safety. Now, enough chitter-chatter. Every second we waste is another second my sister is caught in a nightmare."

She beckoned, and they followed her past the columns and up a small set of stairs to a small and unassuming iron-reinforced wooden door hidden behind a small but sturdy portcullis – the sole way to pass overland from the south of Chilpaea to the north without surmounting the hundred-foot-high Blueschists.

As they neared it, the witch waved a hand and the portcullis rose with a creak and the door swung open. "I put a magical lock on the door once we had cleared out all the soldiers," she explained, "and reinforced it to keep out the Sleepers and crusaders."

The comparatively small, sculpted and colonnaded entrance gave onto a labyrinth of caverns honeycombing the Blueschists. Vivian Malakbet led the smugglers unerringly on a zigzagging course through neatly hewn blue stone tunnels to a large smooth-walled chamber laid out with tables and chairs lit by a brushwood fire, which helped the smoke escape the tunnels. Some of the chairs had been knocked over. Cutlery was scattered on the floor, dishes lay cracked, and old bits of food were starting to fester.

"This is the mess hall. One of the soldiers put up a fight," the witch explained calmly. "Follow me."

She led them yet further into the bowels of the Blueschists until they reached a large hall, lit by another small fire and packed to the gills with shelf upon shelf of dusty old tomes.

Puffing on a dragon-shaped baui pipe and blowing bluish plumes of pungent smoke, Ruffle waved a hand with a reverential expression on his creased old face. 'The Belt Repository.'

"Yes," said Vivian. "The Belt's famous library. My mother had always talked of coming here one day to study the ancient texts. I don't think she ever truly thought she'd find anything useful, though, otherwise she would have come here long ago. My sister pored over the tomes all morning yesterday and then resolved to cast a spell she had found in one ancient spellbook in hopes of bringing our mother back from the dead." Rounding a bookshelf behind the witch, the smugglers' eyes widened at the sight of a large chunk of purple-blue crystal lying on the cold stone floor, throbbing and glowing with an eldritch light. "This *Kun-Yao-Lin* is the anchor for the portal I will create. The problem is that I cannot create the portal and defend myself at the same time, and so every time I open a door, a monster comes hurtling through before I can stop it."

She swept a rug off a bulk beyond the crystal, and the smugglers took a step back as one at the sight of the carcass of the silver-scaled horror that lurked beneath.

"It's so ugly!" Jamba breathed.

"What in the name of the Gods is that?" Lug gasped.

"This is beyond the realm of the Gods," said the witch darkly. "This is from beyond even the Nether. This is a monster from another world, I'm sure of it. This is why I need you, Ruffle, and your friends. You're my only hope to rescue my sister. Please."

Ruffle tapped a foot for a moment in thought, frowning pensively. Then, he waved a hand. 'And what would you have of us?'

"I am the only one who can create the portal, since I have studied the spell," said Vivian. "I need you to go through the portal and bring her back."

'I could study the spell and cast the portal and you could go through.'

"There's no time," urged the witch. "That could take hours. Please, we need to do this as fast as possible. It's already been a day since she vanished!"

Ruffle gestured to the scaly corpse in the corner. 'So, you want us to venture into an alien world full of monsters such as these, and you do not even know if she is still alive?'

Vivian thumped her chest over her heart, eyes blazing. "I *know* she is still alive. I feel it!" Ruffle considered this, puffing on his pipe. Eventually, the witch growled, "There *will* be a fight today, obeahman. Do this and I let you walk free. Refuse and I will torture your friends until you help me. I will stop at nothing to save my sister, you understand?"

Ruffle scowled, but Jamba knew what he would say before he even waved a hand. Murder was Ruffle Feathers' least favourite pastime, and Jamba was sure he'd rather slay mindless monsters than a beautiful countrywoman – even a witch. He suspected that was why the old obeahman had never fully triumphed over Vivian's infamous mother, Mzee Malakbet – because he was never prepared to take the final, lethal step. Even when he had fought the Justiquans, he had summoned demons to dispatch them rather than dirty his own hands.

So, when Ruffle put out his pipe and signed, 'Fine. Let's just get this over with.' Jamba was far from surprised.

He did not even object. Nor did Lug. It was the fire or the frying pan. Wordlessly, they snorted some witch-spice and readied themselves.

Vivian Malakbet took up a stance in front of the crystal, while the smugglers readied their weapons by her side. Chanting plosive occult words that made Jamba's flesh crawl and break out in goosebumps, she traced arcane patterns in the air with her hands, and in only a few seconds, runes written in flickering fuchsia fire burst into existence above the crystal, one at a time, gradually forming a circle taller than a man.

When they pulsed as one, aligned, the witch yelled, her voice strained, "Go! Go now!"

13

Otherworldly Murk

Roaring to drown out his fear, Jamba Klach leaped through the portal, praying to the Gods that his friends would follow him and that this was not all some elaborate trick. He landed staggering on uneven and alien terrain, green and squishy underfoot. It was not grass, though; the earth itself was green and spongy. Bluish liquid gathered around his feet where they indented the ground, as if he stood in a bog, and the aroma was not dissimilar. Ruffle Feathers and Lug Thorm landed by his sides, the latter snouted and furry, and Jamba sent up a thankful prayer to the Twins. At least he was not in this nightmare alone. A bluish haze hung over the world, like cerulean fog tossed this way and that by a hot, fickle breeze, and verdigrised lightning flickered in the sky, half-seen through the mist. A cawing like that of crows and a slithering, clicking noise surrounded the smugglers on all sides, and they quickly put their backs to one another.

"What is that?" Jamba hissed, cycs trying to pierce the fog.

From the otherworldly murk sprang a form so alien that Jamba baulked at the mere sight of it and the horrific squawks emanating from the round, sphincter-like maw that took up the majority of its face, complete with a few fangs that could serve as daggers. Four eyes dangled on stalks from its chin, and a hump rose from its forehead, slit with flaring nostrils. A cobra-like hood framed its bizarre visage, furry like a mane. It belched, purple tongue lolling, and blue flames sprayed from its round mouth, making the smugglers flinch. Its weird face was attached to its rounded body by a long neck. It had no arms, but waddled in a bird-like fashion on two stumpy taloned legs. Like the corpse in the library, it was armoured from head to tail in silver scales like a tiny wingless dragon. It was small only in comparison to such a legendary beast, however; it towered a few feet over Lug, the tallest of the smugglers.

Belching blue flame, it waddled nearer, abruptly picking up speed to charge at them like a scaly ostrich. The smugglers scattered out of its path, Jamba taking a swipe at it as it passed him by. His arm shook from the force of the blow, as though he had hit a metal bar, and the beast's scales were only slightly dented. His eyes widened; how could he slay such a well-armoured foe? He recalled then how his father had taught him to scale a fish; take the knife from tail to head in order to get behind the overlapping scales. He had no time to test his theory, however, as the creature's long reptilian tail lashed out to knock him from his feet. He landed flat on his back on the spongy earth, trying desperately to suck back in all the air that had whooshed out of his lungs.

The creature launched itself at Ruffle Feathers face first, but Lug intercepted it in mid-air with a swing of his warhammer, sending the horror sprawling on the ground with a squawk. Jamba was pleased to see the scales had been bent more by the blunt force of the warhammer than his scimitar; perhaps they were not invincible after all, he thought. The creature sprang up in an instant, however, and prowled towards the lagahoo, head low. As soon as it came close enough, it opened its maw wide and burped cerulean flames. Lug screeched as his fur caught and threw himself on the ground, rolling around like a railing madman to put out the fire. Fortunately, it was doused quickly, thanks to the liquid gathering in pools at their feet. The monster jumped on Lug once he was down, clawing at him with its talons and sucking in a lungful to breathe fire on him once more.

Jamba's scimitar hit the horror's long, flexible neck at an angle from behind, cleaving perfectly between the overlapping scales with a keening, grating noise and half-severing the head in one smooth motion, sending stinky white ichor flying through the air to spatter on the eerie earth. The creature cawed, stumbling about as if not yet realising it was dead, its head dragging along the ground. It accidentally stepped on its own face, tripped and hit the ground, twitching.

"Is it dead?" Lug panted.

"I sure hope so," Jamba replied between breaths, sweat running down his cocoa cheeks and into his arrow-shaped beard to make his chin itchy.

They did not have time to check. More clicking and slithering heralded more of the creatures approaching.

"Where would this Violet Malakbet have gone?" Jamba shouted over the noise as the smugglers put their backs to one another again. "Why isn't she here?"

'She must have sought shelter,' Ruffle signed, making Jamba wince. The fiery words hanging in the sky would call the monsters from every corner like a beacon.

"Aye, you're probably right," he replied as the words guttered and faded away. "Merry's tits! We'll have to go look for her, I suppose. But which way?"

Ruffle waved a hand. 'Head forwards. I think I sense her.'

Before they could take more than a collective step, another of the silver-scaled serpents lurched out of the blue fog to snap at Lug, who barely stepped out of the way in time. He swatted at the beast with his hammer, laying it flat for a moment, and Jamba tried to circle it. The serpent lunged upright in a blink, however, and belched a gout of blue flames at Jamba, who leaped back just in time to avoid all but a mild scorching. It whipped Ruffle Feathers off his feet as he was trying to cast a spell with its swinging tail, and then threw itself at Lug once more, burping fire and seeking his face with its maw. Lug backed away, knocking the thing down again and again with mighty sweeps of his warhammer, but it leaped up every time, its scales dented, eyes swinging like pendulums from its chin, licking its lips with its long, thick purple tongue. Lug walloped it back for the umpteenth time and thanked the Gods when Jamba sprang out of the mist, scimitars slashing through the back of the creature's winding neck and finally ending its life.

"Run!" Jamba yelled, taking his own advice and running back to Ruffle Feathers, helping the old obeahman to his feet and then hauling him on as fast as his old legs would carry him in the opposite direction from the ring of pulsing purple runes written in fire through which they had entered, away from safety and into the unknown of the swirling bluish mists haunted by crow calls.

Monsters sprang at them from left and right, thankfully sporadic, and the smugglers quickly developed a modus operandi of beating the beasts down with Lug's warhammer and then slitting them open with Jamba's scimitars before moving on as fast as possible, leaving the creatures' white ichor to pool on the spongy earth. They stumbled upon one pissing bluish fluid, leg cocked, and Jamba groaned as he realised what he had been stepping in all this time. At least he had not rolled around in it like Lug, he reminded himself, glancing askew at the drenched lagahoo, who was starting to smell like a piss pot. Lug battered the creature's head in with unusual vehemence, and Jamba, slicing its spine with one smooth cut, figured the lagahoo must have put two and two together as well. He grimaced when the creature's pale blood stained his hands and wiped them on his breeches. An eerie keening drifting on the wind called the smugglers further into the caracoling vapours.

A behemoth loomed out of the blue mist, and Lug yelped before realising it was only a gigantic tree. It was not *only* a tree, though, Jamba quickly saw as he drew nearer. It was a tree the size of a castle with its canopy lost in the clouds, and it was made of screaming faces. His jaw hung slack as he came close enough to make them out; myriad faces, some human, some not, all screaming, had taken the natural place of bark in this tree, as though it played host to a million tortured duppy. And most horrifying of all, a doorway in the bole beckoned.

"We're not going in there, are we?" Lug asked with a tremor in his deep voice, hands shaking on his warhammer's iron-banded wooden haft.

Jamba sighed and glanced at Ruffle. "You *did* say you thought she might have sought shelter. And this is the first … shelter … we have stumbled across, though calling it such is dubious." He rubbed a hand over his face with a groan. "Ugh, I guess we should check it out. Come on, boys. Don't look so worried, Lug. Your face'll freeze that way."

Lug straightened his features, and Jamba almost laughed. Instead, he hefted his scimitars and led the way into the tree of lost souls. The eyes of the screeching damned all watched him pass, and he tried not to make eye contact with any of them, shuffling step by step into the darkness. Ruffle Feathers gesticulated and threw up a sparkling golden bubble around them just as he had done in the tunnels beneath Maawu Palace, to protect them against magical attacks and to light their path. Jamba could only partially see through the bubble, however, as golden energy zipped and zapped across its surface. He inched forwards, thanking the Gods that the screaming faces only covered the outside of the tree. In the hollow, he placed his feet on wood as red as blood, and as he and the other smugglers plunged further and further into the heart of the tree, the keening faded to a more tolerable pitch.

The tunnel they followed wound a meandering path through the tree, only ever branching off above them, left, right and straight up, so that they always followed the same path, knowing it was likely the path any other human would have taken. It did, however, make them wonder what might have carved such a strange burrow. They heard a distant buzzing and were so sure that they were about to meet a heinous beast of some sort that when they eventually stumbled upon a sleeping silver serpent, Jamba and Lug roared as one, lifting their weapons high to bring them smashing down on the creature.

"Wait! Wait! Don't!" the creature shrieked in Kwi patois in feminine tones.

Jamba and Lug cautiously lowered their weapons, eyes wide with surprise as human arms poked out from the creature's flanks. Then, a cocoa-skinned woman stepped out, a mane of tangled obsidian hair forming a nebula around her fine-boned, scarred features, and the smugglers realised it had not been a silver serpent at all. It had been a woman hiding under the skin of a slain silver serpent.

"You must be Violet," Jamba said after a heart-pounding moment, thinking of how close he had come to scalping her.

She raised her chin haughtily, smoothing her tattered pantaloons and shawl. "That's *Mzee Violet Malakbet* to you."

Jamba almost chuckled. Instead, he shook his head. "D'you know what we've been through to find you? Never mind. Let's just get out of here. Your sister's waiting."

"Vivian sent you?" Violet asked.

"Yes."

"Oh. Excellent," Violet said briskly, brushing her hands together. "Well, then, we'd best be on our way."

14

Silver Serpents, Evil Bees and Demonic Spiders

"Why were you hiding under that hide?" Jamba asked.

"Because of the bugs," Violet told the smugglers as though they were idiots. Seeing their confusion, her own brow wrinkled and she added, "You didn't see any bugs?"

"No, but that's a good thing, right?"

"No! It's bad!" Violet shouted, clapping her hands to her face. "It means the bugs are out looking for food. It means they'll be back any second, and we can't all hide under this skin!"

Jamba raised his eyebrows questioningly. "So …?"

"So, we run!" Vivian said firmly, pelting past the perplexed smugglers, who swiftly turned and followed, huffing and puffing.

The buzzing the smugglers had heard earlier intensified until it felt like it was rattling their very bones, and then the bugs swarmed into sight. About as big as a dwarf, the droning insects flitted into the hollow on sets of translucent, dragonfly-like wings, their fuzzy thoraxes striped purple and black. Their eyes hung from their bellies on stalks, and each had a vicious stinger for a tail. They clicked their mandibles like beetles when they spotted the intruders and buzzed towards them surprisingly slowly, evidently inhibited by their bloated bodies. They looked too fat to fly, Jamba thought, though he did not discount their danger, certain that their stingers held a well of some hideous and fatal venom.

In the vanguard, Violet had only a silver dagger, but she flung herself fearlessly at the flying fiends, gutting one with a single overhead swipe so that purplish goo rained down on her long, raven hair. Spitting out the blood and the words to a spell – words that made Jamba's ears itch and his nape tingle – Violet slew another swathe of the bugs with a wave of legendary green witch-fire. The bugs dropped, incinerated, out of the air, but the flames had no effect on the blood-red bark.

The smugglers sprinted after the witch through the path she had opened up, whacking back the bugs closing in on them from all sides even as they ran. Carving open the creatures like watermelons, the smugglers were soon as saturated in purple gooey gore as Violet. Worst of all, it stank like cat sick, making them gag so much they could barely breathe. Jamba's arms ached from waving his swords above his head, and Lug's tongue was lolling out of his mouth like an overheated dog's. Just when it seemed they must be overwhelmed by sheer numbers, surrounded by stingers on all sides, their flagging arms failing to keep up with the insects' onslaught, Ruffle Feathers finally managed to establish the concentration required to cast a summoning spell.

Dropping his eldritch bubble and reaching into nightmare gulfs, he opened a door once more and beckoned through some old friends. The light of the bubble winked out. A greenish rift ripped open the veil between worlds this time, bathing the hollow in a ghoulish glow and eking vapours that smelled like the flatulence of a diarrhetic skunk and making the smugglers retch all over again. The sight that followed was not much more appetising. Grotesque creatures the size of dogs skittered out of the rift on eight legs like arachnids, their bodies protected by spiky salmon armour, like crabs. Once a couple of dozen had passed through, the rift snapped shut with a *pop,* plunging the smugglers into darkness with only a faint pinprick of bluish light ahead to indicate the way out.

The demons' mandibles waggled enthusiastically at the sight of their buzzing meals, and they screeched like eagles. They did not ask their master who their target was; they were too simple-minded for that. Ruffle had to keep a constant tether on them to keep them focussed on his enemies and not on himself or his friends, and the effort was draining. There was little that could stand against the demonic spiders, however, for they ate through anything and everything they came across save metal. The insects' advantage of flight was nullified in the confines of the hollow, where the spiders could jump up and catch the bugs in their mandibles with ease, squeezing the life out of them and greedily guzzling their lavender blood.

Hightailing it past and vaulting the demonic spiders where necessary, the smugglers made for the pinprick of light with all haste, Violet Malakbet leading the way. Jamba was almost more afraid of the spiders than the giant purple bees. He hated spiders. None of them attacked him or any of the others, though, for which he was grateful. With the demons distracting and dispatching the bugs, the smugglers burst out of the hollow and into the fey bluish light of the mist once more, gasping for breath, barely able to hear themselves think over the omnipresent buzzing and the screams of the faces in the tree.

"Back to the portal!" Jamba hollered, tugging on the others' sleeves, unsure if they could hear him.

He stared to shuffle through the fog and was glad when he felt Ruffle Feathers latch onto his shirt. He glanced back to see they were all close, keeping hold of one another lest they become lost in the vapours. Much to his relief, the screaking spiders flanked them as they went, still pouncing up into the air to try to snag any bug that drew too near, though it was more difficult for them now that the insects had room to fly about in the open air. Still, they made a remarkable deterrent, Jamba thought. Some of the alien bees targeted the spiders instead of the humans, but most of their attacks bounced harmlessly off the spiders' shells. Here and there, however, Jamba caught a bee landing a lucky blow, its stinger slipping between the cracks in the armour. Those demons unlucky enough to be jabbed swelled up to five times their normal size in heartbeats and then exploded, spewing hot green goo all over the smugglers.

Jamba was just beginning to think they were making good progress when he heard a sound that chilled him to the bone – the clicking and slithering of approaching silver serpents. It rang out from all corners, ubiquitous in the mist and closing in fast. Jamba tried to quicken his pace to escape the noose he sensed being drawn about them and bumped headlong into one of the horrors he was trying to avoid. He lashed out with his scimitars at the beast in surprise, but his blades ricocheted off the silver scales. The serpent had him pinned to the spongy earth in an instant, the few knife-like fangs in its sphincter-like maw kept at bay from his face only by his scimitars at its neck. Its scales grated against his blades as it stretched its long neck to reach him, and he knew it was only a matter of heartbeats before he was alien fodder.

Lug hit the scaly serpent so hard it flew at least a yard through the air before crumpling in a heap. Jamba took the lagahoo's proffered hand and hauled himself to his feet, wondering if blessed sleep would ever come. His bones ached with weariness. He saw then that the silver serpents had them surrounded on all sides and were depleting the demonic spiders' numbers with alarming rapidity, crushing them under talon, snatching them up in their jaws and belching blue flames into their scurrying ranks. The spiders put up a valiant defence, and when several of them were able to swarm over one of the scaly horrors at once, the monster was chewed to death with frightening speed. One on one, however, they were no match for the aliens. They could not eat through the tough scales and had to scrabble them out of the way with their pincers before they could take a bite. It would not be long, Jamba knew, before the spiders were eradicated and the serpents and bees were at the smugglers' throats. Casting around, he caught sight of a flicker of magenta in the distance and recognised it as the circle of runes.

"Run for the portal!" he hollered hoarsely, springing into action.

Lopping off the eyes of one of the scaly horrors with a well-placed slash, Jamba darted around the squawking blinded creature and forced his leaden legs to propel him across the soft earth in a mad dash for safety. He escaped the beasts' encapsulating ring, but others were closing in fast, appearing out of the bluish fog like figments of a lunatic to claw at him with talons, burp tongues of blue flame in his direction and try to gobble him up whole. Despite this, he stopped long enough to turn and see if the others had followed, swiping at the monsters to keep them at bay. As he watched, Lug hammered a path through the silver serpents to reach Jamba and – as the others followed him through the gap – Violet brought up the rear, immolating bugs and serpents by the dozen with a never-ending stream of spooky green flames spewing from her hands.

"That's it!" Jamba crowed triumphantly, dodging a bite and spinning to continue his hurtle towards the portal.

A silver serpent's swinging tail took him in the midriff, sending him soaring several yards through the air into the horror-ridden mists. Flat on his back, he watched in agonised breathlessness as Lug and the others overtook him, powering on towards the portal, clearly not having witnessed his stoke of misfortune. As he stared, the last of the spiders was overwhelmed by the ever-increasing horde of rampant scaly monsters, burnt, trampled and then chewed to death. The beasts' eyes pendulumed back and forth as they settled on the lone smuggler then, and Jamba felt a stab of fear lance through him. The oversized insects buzzed towards him in a dark cloud. There were too many for him to fight, and one by one the aliens were gradually blocking off all avenues towards the portal, towards his friends.

Scarcely able to breathe, he thrust himself up with a wobble, scooped up his scimitars and took off, slaloming between the silver serpents and lashing out with his blades only when necessary to distract, block or knock aside one of his many enemies. Jumping between two of the horrors, their jaws snapping shut where he had just been, he landed in the path of a third, ducked and spun under its lunging neck and ploughed on, losing little momentum. A bug dove down, trying to prong him with its stinger, and he pirouetted around it. Past all the shifting forms in his way, he saw that his friends had arrived at the portal and appeared to be battling a bed of silver snakes. Scaled figures loomed out of the vapours left and right, and burps of blue fire soon started to burst in front of him like fireworks, narrowly missing him and singeing his skin. He did not cry out or slow, though. Pumping his arms and legs, he ran like his life depended on it, for it very much did.

He heard Lug's plaintive cries even over the monsters' pervasive squawks. "Jamba! Jamba! Quick, Jamba, run!"

A swathe of serpents blocked his path, and Jamba gritted his teeth and threw himself forwards, skidding feet first through the legs of one of the belching monsters, feeling its jaws snap inches from his head and blue fire whoosh past his face. He worried his beard might be alight, but he did not stop to check. As soon as he had slid under the beast, he was up again and running. A few bugs made beelines for him, and he zigzagged out of their path. He vaulted a swinging tail and kept going, staggering past bursts of blue flame and gnashing teeth. A serpent lunged for his legs, and he cleared the beast in one great hurdle, smacking its tail out of the way with a scimitar as he went. His path was clear. He was going to make it back to his friends, make it back through the portal to his own world, to safety. Then, a scaly horror leaped out of the smog and tackled him to the ground, once again knocking the wind out of him.

Jamba looked up with desperate eyes just in time to see Violet Malakbet jumping through the portal. A pang of fear made his whole body jolt as if struck by lightning – they were leaving without him! He sprang up again, coughing and wheezing, and pelted forward as fast as he could – at about the same pace as a prize-winning snail. The monster that had tackled him was on him in a flash, its fetid breath in his face, its long purple tongue licking his cheek as its jaws sought his skull. Holding it back with his scimitars, Jamba's strength was about to give out when another of the beasts headbutted the first, knocking it aside and then straddling Jamba itself to claim the meal for its own. The first beast did not much like that, so it retaliated and the two started scrapping over the right to eat the smuggler, while Jamba looked on in horror, unable to move thanks to fear and crippling pain.

When one of the horrors started to slink away, mewling, it appeared the contest was over. The first beast had won. It mattered little to Jamba. By now, he knew his friends must be long gone. They had all probably jumped through the portal and closed it behind themselves, he thought, sealing him in this nightmarish realm forever. He hoped so, anyway. Blessed sleep could not be far away now. He prayed to the Ferrymen, as he so often had – they knew where he wanted to go by now.

He closed his eyes as the serpent's slobbering maw descended towards him – then snapped them open again when he felt a strange heat and heard the beast grunt and topple, lifeless, to the ground. Jamba sat up and stared in shock at the smoking watermelon-sized hole in the beast's scaly side. It looked like something had punched clean through the monster.

A demon looking like a five-foot long snake doused in oil and lit swam in the air before his eyes, hissing in Traveller's, "The master wishes you to join him!"

Jamba glanced left towards the second beast that had sought his blood, and his mouth hung open at the sight of a second blazing snake slithering down the scaly horror's gullet only to reappear from its gut in a spray of whitish gore and seek a bug to slay in the green-lightning-wreathed firmament.

"Move, mortal!" the floating snake hissed, the flames wreathing its body crackling.

"Aye, aye!" Jamba replied, pushing himself up once more despite all the protests from his aching frame and limping towards the portal.

Violet had evidently returned, for she stood now alongside Ruffle Feathers and Lug by the portal, incinerating silver serpents wherever she laid eyes on them. A few silver-scaled horrors came frothing out of the fog to intercept Jamba, but this time he did not have to dodge or lift a finger. Ruffle Feathers' burning demonic snakes flitted across his vision time and again, coring demons like maggots in apples. By the time Jamba came abreast of the beasts, they were dropping at his feet, dead. He glanced over his shoulder and wished he had not done so. A veritable horde of scaly horrors and evil bees was swarming towards him out of the mists – too many for even the demonic snakes, he thought. He forced himself to a quicker pace, but still only just reached the portal a step ahead of the fast-moving monsters.

"Go!" he roared at his friends as he drew near. "Jump!"

Violet did not need to be told twice. She was gone as soon as he said go. Ruffle Feathers waved for Lug to follow the witch, but the lagahoo stoutly shook his head, making Jamba's heart swell with affection even as he scowled at the burly man's stupidity. So, rolling his eyes, Ruffle leaped through the portal after the witch, vanishing in a blink into the rippling air between the blazing purple runes. Lug waited until the last possible second, until Jamba had hared past him and hopped through the portal. Only then, whacking back the frontrunner of the horrific horde, did the lagahoo make his exit from the other world.

Arguably, Jamba thought, he left it too late. Two of the monsters managed to spring through the portal at his back before Mzee Vivian Malakbet could seal it shut with a sound like the popping of a pig's bladder. In the ensuing darkness, the two silver serpents wreaked carnage in the library in the Belt fortress, squawking and smashing into bookcases and burning books with their ghastly breath. The demonic snakes were nowhere to be seen. Jamba and Violet scrambled to their feet, having fallen to their knees thanks to the disorientation of the jump between worlds. Ruffle Feathers and Lug were still on all fours, spewing up their guts.

It was a miracle the beasts did not kill them in all the kerfuffle, Jamba thought. Though his head gonged and he felt like he had swallowed a nest of hornets, he launched himself at one of the horrors, scimitars cleaving down. His blades glanced off the tough silver scales, and the monster spun and whacked him back with its long whipping tail, before pouncing on the prone smuggler. Jamba rolled aside just in time to avoid the gouging talons, hearing them scrape on the stone floor where he had been as he wriggled to his feet and sprang at the monster again. This time, he managed to loop one blade behind the beast so that it slid under the scales and into the flesh. The horror swivelled as he did so, though, cawing like a crow, and Jamba could tell he had not struck deep, though creamy ichor welled from the wound.

He waited until the last moment as the creature bulled towards him, before sidestepping and bringing his scimitar swinging down on the back of its neck in what he thought was a winning cut. The beast writhed aside somehow, so that its scales once more protected it from the worst of the blow, and then its jaws were gnashing in the smuggler's face. Jamba retreated step by step, trying in vain to bat the beast's head away with his scimitars.

His back hit a wall, and he tried to sidestep once more as the monster leaped again, but it anticipated the move and caught him with a raking bite to his already wounded shoulder, a couple of its fangs gashing open his skin again and making him hiss in pain. He was about to retaliate with what he suspected might be the last sword stroke of his lifetime when abruptly the beast burst into greenish flames, rapidly shrivelling and melting in the inferno until all that remained was ash. Beyond the beast's remains, by the spell's dying light, Jamba witnessed Vivian Malakbet with her hand outstretched. Behind her, Violet Malakbet stood panting over the carcass of the second silver serpent in a pool of its white blood.

"Thanks," Jamba gasped, before collapsing on his face and letting blessed sleep take him, if only for a time …

15

A Camel in a Horse Race

Jeremias Colcott walked in the land of the dead.

The sky was a shroud, crimson-edged at the horizon. Something like rain deluged the place, so that everything was wet, and yet not so – as if in a dream, where knowledge replaces reality. Jinglespur Necropolis had blurred into a phantom of its former self, faintly outlined and ethereal as the thousand duppy that roamed its blue-hued streets. Jeremias had the feeling he could walk through the walls if he wished, for he was little more solid himself than his transcendental environs. He was just one more ghost in a world of ghosts.

"Why are they here?" he asked his mentor, the infamous deceased necromancer, Waddi-waddi.

Strolling beside him without a care in the world, Waddi-waddi glanced at him askew, raising his bushy eyebrows. His face was strong, with a hooked nose and lantern jaw. His head forewent hair, but his chin relished it. A long beard braided with small bones and bird skulls clinked with every movement, hanging down to his barrel chest. His ears were pierced with sharp bone slivers, and charmed bracelets and anklets adorned his wrists and ankles, the charms formed from the skeletons of the demons he had slain in life. Jeremias had expected the necromancer to be a scrawny, ascetic type and had been surprised to meet the stout powerhouse in person. Though shorter than the seneschal, the ebon-skinned necromancer was banded with thick cords of muscle from bull neck to meaty calf. He wore only sandals and a black robe with the sleeves rolled up to let his brawny forearms breathe.

"The duppy?" he asked in a voice like the tolling of a funerary gong. "They are lost souls, trapped by their own unfulfilled wishes, unable to let go of the material world and move on to the world of spirit. Some seek revenge, others await lost loves, and some cannot even remember their own names they have dwelled so long in the darkness."

"You mean move on to the Sunset Isles?" Jeremias asked.

Waddi-waddi shrugged. "If that is their destiny. There are many afterlives to which souls flock after death."

"Why did you not flock after them?"

Waddi-waddi grinned at him. "I am no bird of a feather. I am a lone wolf, prowling the sunless underworld, awaiting my chance to see the light again! One day, I shall find a way to be reborn and walk in the green fields of my homeland once more."

Jeremias rolled his eyes, unwilling to provoke another ramble about resurrection. "Yes, well, until that day, perhaps you could teach me your secrets, like you promised, so that there will be a homeland for you to return to."

"Of course," agreed Waddi-waddi equably, the zealous light fading from his piercing fuchsia eyes. "But first we must finish attuning your spirit to this realm. The longer we remain here, the more at home you will feel and the more you will be able to accomplish. The world seems ephemeral to you now, as if you can barely touch it, no? Soon, you will swim through the world of the dead like a fish in the sea. But it requires patience, my friend. One step at a time. Have you been performing your exercises?"

"Yes." Jeremias had indeed been trying his best to stick to the rigorous exercise regime laid out for him by the necromancer and could already feel and see the benefits in his swelling frame.

Waddi-waddi nodded, pleased. "Good. That is good. Strength in mind is nothing without strength in body. Keep it up. One day, you will be able to do more than mere dream-walking. One day, you will be able to bring the dead back as zombies to serve your whim, to conjure demons that call you master, to cast fire and lightning from your fingertips." He levitated up into the air above the ghostly throng in the street without a visible flicker of effort. "One day, you will be able to fly."

Jeremias felt a hand on his shoulder and heard his name being called, as if from faraway. He blinked rapidly and opened his eyes with a splitting headache to see that he was no longer roaming the dream-streets, but once more sat cross-legend in the ancient crypt beneath Jinglespur's citadel, where lurked the giant crystal that housed the soul of Waddi-waddi and the sarcophagus that bore his remains.

He looked up into the concerned doe-brown eyes and open, honest face of Dreyfuss Alamoigne, the only soul to whom he had shown the location of the crypt. As one of General Malone's most trusted soldiers, Dreyfuss had grown into Jeremias' good graces during their tenure at Jinglespur, and the seneschal knew he needed a man he could trust with this secret. So, since somebody needed to be able to relay messages to him while he was ensconced in the crypt, Jeremias had chosen Dreyfuss for the duty.

His leather armour creaked as he shook the seneschal's shoulder. "Seneschal? Seneschal? Hello? General Malone says you're needed on the wall at once."

Strangely saddened to be confined to flesh once more, Jeremias rose to his feet with a sigh and said, "Lead on, Dreyfuss. Thank you."

The tall soldier bobbed his stubbly head and led the seneschal up into the citadel, past a cavalcade of hallucinating folk chasing duppy and out into the indecisive weather. The sun shone in the east, but from the west flew a bank of grey clouds tossing drizzle at the land. Jeremias thought he glimpsed a rainbow in the distance.

By the time he reached General Malone's side, rain, the great equaliser, warm and wet, pitter-pattered on the heads of the Chilpaeans inside Jinglespur Necropolis, just as it did on the heads of the Justiquans outside the walls. The sky was a blank slate awaiting the momentous events of the day, just as was Jeremias. From the rampart atop Jinglespur's curving wall, he stared through the drizzly morning mist at the enemy army, slowly amassing in their thousands on the field beyond the wall just outside of arrow range, in a haze of his own.

In his mind's eye, he kept replaying the events of the last few days, seeing again and again the duppy of Waddi-waddi manifesting from the giant chunk of *Kun-Yao-Lin* buried beneath the necropolis. The notorious necromancer consumed his thoughts, and he wished only for whatever farce was occurring to be over so that he could return to his studies.

"How many?" he asked General Malone.

"Thousands," responded the general tersely. "Infantry and cavalry. A few knights. Not many yet from the look of it. But still only a fraction of their force. These will be the frontrunners, the scouts. The heavies will come later. Still, they have us outnumbered already, even with all the reinforcements from Hatbrim, Jawduck, the Belt and the surrounding villages."

"What d'you think happened at the Belt? D'you believe the tale of duppy and demons?"

"I have no idea."

"D'you think they'll parley?" Jeremias asked, nodding to the crusaders.

His question was answered when a knight in steel plate armour on a spotless steed the colour of milk rode out from the Justiquan army bearing a white flag, surrounded by a handful of infantrymen in studded leather.

"We'll go together," grunted the general, turning away.

"Wait," said Jeremias, holding up a hand. "There's no need for both of us to die. Look around, general. These people are on the brink of collapse. And we are besieged. We need a general now. We need *you* now, more than ever. You understand tactics. You understand strategy and discipline. You can keep these people alive. I cannot. I am but a glorified clerk when it comes right down to it. And the time for paperwork is over. I am but a camel in a horse race now, general – useless."

Not long later, Jinglespur's newly forged iron-reinforced gates were opening noiselessly on oiled hinges to emit the seneschal and a few Chilpaean soldiers. Passing under the walls' shadow and traipsing up and down the barbican tower to emerge into the rainy daylight of the field north of the fortress made Jeremias' skin crawl. He took a deep breath, savouring the scent of wild petunia and the sweet smell of soaked grass, but still his heart pounded as he heard the gates bang shut behind him. The knight stopped halfway between the army and the gates, within the Chilpaeans' arrow range. Jeremias walked forward slowly to meet him, knees knocking, grateful that Dreyfuss Alamoigne and a few other soldiers were with him. General Malone watched, impotent and infuriated, from the wall.

"Greetings from Knight-Commander Godfrey Saint-Marcente," said the middle-aged knight in Traveller's Tongue in a sibilant hiss, his bone-white hair gleaming, his pale skin reddened by the blistering Chilpaean sun. He carried his steel helm under his left arm. Jeremias wished he had worn it to mask his ophidian face. "My name is Marshal Clauss. I speak on behalf of the Justiquan army. Whom do I address?"

"You do not remember me, then?" Jeremias asked scornfully, voice shaking as he remembered the night he had met the man, the night of the Lullabyer's demise.

He had never known he could hate a man so much. He longed to gouge out the man's eyes, to rip out his windpipe with his teeth and spit down the hole. He wanted to wipe the man's bloodline from the face of Maradoum. He trembled with the urge. He wished he could tear the man limb from limb using the power of the *Kun-Yao-Lin* crystal secreted beneath the citadel, the gemstone housing Waddi-waddi's duppy, but he could not sense its energies at such a distance. Indeed, even in the citadel he could not sense it – only in the cavern beneath. He could not sense any other crystals anywhere in the necropolis either, though he had tried. He thought sourly that Ruffle Feathers would surely be able to sense it from a league away. Jeremias had never been much of an obeahman, he reflected. He had known few spells in his youth, had forgotten most of them now, and of those few only a small fragment had ever been battle cantraps.

"No," replied the marshal, raising white eyebrows a notch.

"My name is Jeremias Colcott. You killed my brother."

The marshal tapped a finger on his chin for a moment and then nodded. "Ah yes, Colcott … The seneschal, no? You're the seneschal's brother, I remember now. So good to see you again. My, haven't you done well for yourself." He smiled, his eyes gleaming mockingly.

"Speak your piece, vermin, and begone!" Jeremias snarled, sick of the sight of the man.

Clauss' smile evaporated. "Very well, Colcott. As I'm sure you know by now, we have taken Cocoba Bay by right of conquest. We are not here for wholesale slaughter, however. We wish only to cure the world of the disease of magic. So, here are our terms. Open the gates and surrender to us. Any magic-users among you will be executed. The rest are free to leave."

"Even if I did believe you, even if we were harbouring magicians by the score, I'd still never surrender to you!" Jeremias growled, wrath coiling in his belly like a riled serpent, tightening like a noose. "I don't believe a word you say, though, and I will protect my people from you until the day I die. You will never set foot inside Jinglespur!"

Marshal Clauss sighed. "I understand. You are emotional. Is there anyone else more rational with whom I can speak?"

"I speak for all of Chilpaea when I tell you to go jump off a cliff, scum!"

Marshal Clauss gritted his teeth and said quietly, "I will not forget this insult, Colcott. Mark my words. You will live to regret this."

A chill coursed up Jeremias' spine at that, but he joined the other soldiers in jeering and swearing at the Justiquans as they retreated back behind their lines.

"Was that wise, seneschal?" asked Dreyfuss.

"No," replied Jeremias, "but it was fun!"

The Justiquan infantry stomped forward as one, shaking the earth with their tread, and Jeremias and the others dashed back to the safety of the walls. So it begins, thought the seneschal as the thrum of arrows caught his ear.

16

Devil's Bog

The smugglers left the Belt the following morning after a night spent deep in the safety of the fortress, where they could not even hear the Sleepers howling and clawing at the portcullises and walls all night long. Exhausted, they had slept deeply. Now, as dawn ladled light over the land, they stepped out of the north side of the Belt, bidding farewell to the witches, Vivian and Violet Malakbet.

"It's a shame they did not wish to join us," said Lug Thorm, ambling through the jacaranda-laden meadow beyond the Blueschists and admiring the buzzing bees and flitting dragonflies.

Though he trampled the turquoise flowers underfoot, they sprang right back up in his wake.

'Their mother implanted deep suspicions in them of the Lullabyer,' Ruffle Feathers told the lagahoo in words of fire hanging in the air. 'Did you see the engraving on the façade, of the Sleepers attacking the Tzunese men? Those witches take it literally. They believe the Lullabyer has the power to use the Sleepers on his enemies, not just put them to sleep. They believe such power is too great for one man – or even one family.' He shook his head. 'At least, Vivian has come to understand that we need the Lullabyer – not as a weapon but as a shield against the Sleepers.'

Lug frowned. "If she understands that, then why did she not join us?"

'Because,' Ruffle replied, stuffing his dragon-shaped pipe with the herb, baui, 'she does not expect us to survive.'

"*I* do not expect us to survive," muttered Jamba Klach, fidgeting at the bandages on his shoulder beneath his dirty shirt. "Where are we to shelter tonight when the Sleepers come if we are avoiding the towns?"

Ruffle pointed, puffing on a pipe that had seen no flames and blowing thick clouds of aromatic smoke. Jamba never knew how he lit his pipes. It was the way of obeahmen, he supposed.

Ruffle waved a hand, coughing. 'We go east through Devil's Bog. Perhaps the Sleepers will not dare to tread there. Perhaps we will be safe.'

Jamba's jaw hung slack. "Safe?" he squawked in a strangled voice. "Do you even hear yourself? Safe in Devil's Bog? It's a miracle we survived the witchwood, and now you want us to risk our souls in Devil's Bog?"

Ruffle nodded, dreadlocks bobbing. 'There are too many towns to the west. The Bog is the only way.'

Jamba sighed and ran a calloused hand through his salt-and-pepper hair. He walked stiffly, itching at his bandages. "I knew you were going to say that," he groaned.

The forested swampland of Devil's Bog on the east coast of the hourglass-shaped island yawned open before them that afternoon, steamy and mysterious. Jamba did not feel the unnatural cold of the witchwood seep into him when he first stepped into the shadow of the cypresses, maples and willows this time; rather, he felt warm and cosy and abruptly very sleepy, as if he could lie down quite happily amid the hibiscuses and never rise again. The swampier parts of the swamp were easy to decipher thanks to the greedy mangrove trees sucking at every waterline, so prolific that they formed a carpet in places, with hoary intertwined roots that looked like a bed of half-submerged brown snakes. Reeds swayed in the algae-thick water, alongside lily pads and lotuses, their blooms decadently beautiful in the austere green and brown uniformity of the forest.

The further in they travelled, the more flowers they saw, as if the splendour of the place were secluded from the world by a buffer of blandness. Magnificent tabebuias aflame with flowers soon towered over them, alongside pouis, bauhinias and guangos, all hung with beards of moss and bursting with colour. An orchestra of chirping woodpeckers, warblers and peewees and droning flies and mosquitos greeted them and stayed with them from the outset.

Jamba thought he caught movement in his periphery and stalked on, on edge, his hands on his sword hilts at his hips, certain they were being watched. He could sense eyes in the trees. After a couple of hours, he finally spotted a lithe figure flitting between the boles in the distance, her dark breasts and buttocks exposed to the dappled sunlight. He spotted another not long later, then another, and another, until he was sure they were positively surrounded by naked beauties hiding among the trees.

"We are not alone," he whispered to Ruffle.

The obeahman nodded and waved a hand. 'I know. But they have done us no harm yet. Let's just keep moving and try to put the Bog behind us.'

Jamba nodded, though he knew his hackles would be up if he had any. The forest soothed him, though, the birds' tweeting and the bees' buzzing forming a natural lullaby. The sunlight was soft as cotton on his skin, the flowers sweet as honey. He blinked, wondering when and why he had sat down among the hibiscuses. His eyes were so heavy, his limbs leaden. Was it finally time for blessed sleep? he wondered as his eyes closed and he slumped to the ground. The last thing he saw was the naked beauties closing in on him.

Then, Lug was shaking him awake, shouting, "Jamba! Jamba! Help, Jamba!"

The smuggler forced his gummy eyes open. He had never felt so tired in his life. Sleep was in his very bones.

"What is it, Lug?" he groaned, blinking. "I'm so tired. I need a rest."

"No!" shouted Lug. "It's the soucouya! They've enchanted you and Ruffle to make you sleep! I managed to keep them away from you, but they've stolen the Lullabyer's crystal! We have to get it back!"

Jamba's eyes snapped open as the last effects of the spell wore off. Dusk was falling fast. He was surprised he was still alive if the legendary soucouya had indeed seduced him with supernatural sleep. It was said any man who fell under their spell never lived to tell the tale – although Jamba had often wondered who had first told the tale if that were true. He helped Lug shake Ruffle Feathers awake. The obeahman was harder to wake than a rock, but eventually they prised his eyelids open and slapped him into consciousness.

Gazing at them with bleary eyes, the old man mumbled, "What? What?"

"The soucouya stole the Lullabyer's crystal," Jamba reiterated. "We have to retrieve it before sunset and get to safety, or Chilpaea is doomed."

"Just five more minutes," Ruffle moaned.

"No," said Jamba firmly, "now!"

He hoisted the wizened obeahman to his feet. "Which way did they go, Lug?"

They were soon dashing through the forest after Lug, Jamba half-dragging Ruffle Feathers. The soucouya moved like spirits, leaving no trail that Jamba could see, but Lug claimed he could smell them and moved unerringly in one direction. Jamba snorted some witch-spice to restore his concentration, as did Lug, then Jamba stuffed some of the stinky little seeds up Ruffle Feathers' nostril too, and the old obeahman's eyes snapped wide open.

As the sun teetered on the brink of the world, reaching out its last red rays, the smugglers arrived at a gargantuan old silk cotton tree in the heart of the forest. In the crook of its splitting trunks, some fifty feet up, was nestled a huge treehouse built of a hundred different types of wood with a roof thatched with palm fronds. A red-skinned, horned figure with a long tail tipped with a barbed arrow swaggered out onto the balcony and leaned on the balustrade. His scarlet eyes sparkled in the light of sunset, his angular face cruelly handsome, and he wore only a boar-skin loincloth.

"The forest devil!" Lug gasped. "Bazil!"

Jamba gulped. All children knew the tale of Bazil, the forest devil, the lord of Devil's Bog, evil-doer, child-snatcher, a black God as old as time itself. Jamba had never expected to meet him, though. It was said he raised the children he snatched as his own, only ever taking beautiful young girls to transform into his slaves.

The devil grinned down at the smugglers, revealing a mouthful of canines. From behind the enormous tree's bole peeked out a number of pretty dark-skinned faces, whom Jamba recognised as the beauties he had seen before.

"Welcome, strangers," sneered the devil in an unctuous voice. "Not many are there who find my home and escape with their eyes – and you shall not be among their number!"

Flaring into a rage, Bazil flung out his hands and creepers and vines responded to his will, enwrapping the struggling smugglers' limbs in seconds and lifting them off their feet so that they dangled in the air like fish in the fist. The smugglers could not break free; the vines were thick as boas. At least, Jamba thought, he would find blessed sleep with the pleasant scent of passionflower in his nostrils. He groaned as the vines started to retract, slowly quartering him like a man with his limbs tied to four horses. He could feel his bones on the verge of popping out of their sockets, and he screamed in agony.

Suddenly, the vines hung slack as a magenta rift split open the veil between worlds with a whoosh and gushed flames into the forest, a purple scar hanging in mid-air. Jamba watched, open-mouthed, as a tentacled entity from nightmare gulfs jetted out of the crackling rift to land on the forest devil, smothering his face with its smooth black body and grabbing him in a deathly hug with its long, sucker-lined tentacles. Its beak snapped in anticipation as it glared at him with seven magenta eyes. Bazil's screams came out muffled, and he staggered back and forth on the balcony, trying to rip the thing off his face.

Eventually, the creepers and vines ensnaring the smugglers fell away completely, dropping them to the floor as the forest devil switched his attention to a new enchantment. He laid hands on the clingy cephalopod, and it burned. It did not seem to mind, though, having sprung from a fiery world stinking of sulphur. So, the smugglers watched as the forest devil waved his hands and once more creepers and vines responded to his will, circling the tentacled demon's limbs and slowly prising them free. Finally, the demon was pulled from his face with a squelch, still attached momentarily by strands of some sort of goo or saliva that swiftly broke as the distance between them increased, snapping back one way or the other.

Jamba shuddered, and Bazil sucked in a great breath, leaning on the balustrade for balance now. Bazil glared at the smugglers as he panted and made a gesture. The vines tore the demon apart, and purplish gore rained down on the smugglers' heads. The rift snapped shut.

Ruffle Feathers waved a hand while the forest devil yet gasped for breath like a landed fish, and words formed of bright orange flame burned into existence in mid-air between the smugglers and the devil. 'Give us back what you have stolen.'

"I wouldn't piss on you if you were on fire!" Bazil retorted hoarsely, rubbing his throat.

Ruffle frowned. 'Give us back what you have stolen, or I will summon a more powerful demon to deal with you.'

Bazil blanched. "It will avail you nothing, you know. The Lullaby will not be sung in time. Chilpaea is doomed."

'Just give it back to us. You must hate the crusaders as much as we do. Give it back to us and we will rid the land of them once and for all.'

Bazil cocked his head. "Now, why do I almost believe you?"

He held out a hand, and the familiar crystal in the shape of the Lullabyer appeared on his palm. He tossed it down to them, and Jamba caught it deftly, quickly checking it for scuffs and tucking it in his bag, while the face in the crystal raged at him for his carelessness.

Ruffle Feathers bowed. 'Thank you, Bazil. We will leave now. We are sorry to have disturbed you.'

"Go," said Bazil. "You are too late anyway."

17

Island's Children

The smugglers could not escape Devil's Bog before sundown, so they spent a fitful but warm night in the forested morass, sleeping in shifts and watching out for soucouya, Sleepers and the forest devil. Magnuz Opherio sulked when they tried to address him, barbing that he was lucky they hadn't dropped him off a cliff or into a river by now, so they soon gave up.

To their surprise, dawn found them unmolested and they were able to walk free of the Bog the following morning after the scorching sun melted the fog and evaporated the dew. Hills confronted them, and they spent the majority of the day hiking up and down grassy crests and valleys, the sun a hot hammer on their brows, their calves burning. Sticking to the hills, they skirted the nearby villages lining the Mardy Grae River to the north, seeing black plumes of smoke spiralling into the sky at times in the distance.

"Why didn't the Sleepers find us last night?" Jamba Klach asked as they traipsed up yet another hill.

Ruffle Feathers shrugged, putting away his pipe, and signed, 'Perhaps because Bazil and his soucouya patrol the Bog, keeping out intruders. Perhaps we simply got lucky.'

Lug Thorm shivered at the thought of the Sleepers. "I'm just glad we're still alive."

"Speaking of which," said Jamba, "what are we going to do when night falls? Just set up camp in the hills and hope for the best?"

'We keep moving,' Ruffle responded in words of flame. 'If we keep moving in the darkness with no campfire, perhaps we will be fortunate enough to escape the Sleepers' attentions while they focus on the towns.'

Jamba blanched. "That's cold-blooded, but I guess there's some logic there. And what about sleep?"

'We'll sleep in the morning. Or when we're dead.'

Near dropping from tiredness, the smugglers ploughed on even after the world purpled and darkened and the distant howls commenced. Jamba wondered if he'd be able to react in time if a Sleeper attacked and doubted it. He felt heavy and sluggish, his mind numb. All he could do was focus on the next step, and the next, and the next, seemingly into oblivion.

"Spice, Lug?" he asked, voice thick.

"Aye," agreed the lagahoo, taking a pinch from Jamba's pouch and sniffing it.

Jamba noticed the change in him right away. He stood straighter, eyes rounder, positively jigging with energy. Jamba snorted some himself, wincing at the heat in his nostril and chest and the potent scent of turmeric. He felt the witch-spice spread through his lungs and buzz through his body like a jolt of lightning, boiling his blood for the night to come. His eyes snapped open wide, and he walked with a new spring in his step. Nobody spoke after that, afraid to bring the Sleepers down on them.

The beasts found them anyway. The smugglers heard the howling growing closer for hours before they stumbled upon a lone limping Sleeper in the darkness of the cloudy night, one of its hairy rear legs hanging by a thread. It howled at the sight of them, and the smugglers hurried to dispatch it before it could bring its brethren down on them, knowing it was already too late. By the time Jamba and Lug had bludgeoned and stabbed the creature to death, they could hear its kin bearing down on them.

"Do something, Ruffle!" Jamba cried, brandishing his scimitars and spinning on the spot, peering into the shadows.

Ruffle Feathers traced arcane patterns with his arms, and the air thrummed and crackled with energy, making Jamba's hairs stand on end and his teeth itch. The obeahman waggled the fingers of one hand, and from them oozed thick plumes of black smoke that swiftly coalesced into a ghostly horde of nightmarish bats with eyes bleeding red and horns atop their heads, all connected to Ruffle by their long smoky tails.

"What would you have of us, master?" they gurgled as one in the voices of the drowned.

Ruffle pointed with his spare hand at the Sleepers jumping out of the night to torment his friends. The bats bobbed their heads, turned and started to fly away, speeding up exponentially once Ruffle severed their link to him with a swipe of his hand. Like speeding arrows, they soared through the air to swarm the Sleepers, smothering them like a wriggling skin and gnawing them to the bone in seconds.

Still, Sleepers sprang around them and through them, despite the mutilation they incurred doing so. Jamba and Lug blanched as Sleepers tore towards them with faces ripped open, legs missing and great bloody holes in their flanks. Lug stove in their heads with his warhammer, while Jamba took out their legs with swipes of his scimitars and then speared their brains, thankful that the beasts were slower than usual due to their injuries. The bats flitted this way and that as a devouring cloud, but more and more Sleepers came skittering out of the darkness all around them.

"Run!" yelled Jamba, bounding northwest towards the plains and knocking a Sleeper out of the way with a slash of his scimitar that severed one of its flexible petal-like jaws in a spray of gore. "I have an idea!"

Letters of fire flashed before his eyes as he ran. 'Wait! We should veer east! I've told you what lies in this direction!'

"I know!" Jamba shouted. "Where d'you think I got the idea?"

Dodging lunging Sleepers and batting them away with warhammer and scimitar if they came too close, the smugglers made it to the bottom of the hill, hearing the yowls of the bat-beleaguered beasts behind them. The plains stretched away before them, but Jamba, in the vanguard, turned back on himself and plunged into the fire opal mine that cut into the hill, knowing it had lain deserted for years – ever since it was learned what had happened there.

Stories told that, after the Age of Witches when the lore of the time before was lost, mining crews had found the mine empty of folk and tools, but full of fire opals. Not long after the mining had begun, however, the workers had been visited by murderous duppy who told the miners they had once been obeahmen in the time before the witches, using magic to mine the fire opals, but that the great necromancer, Waddi-waddi, had found and destroyed them for defying him. Now, their duppy haunted the mine, scaring away all workforces eventually by killing them or driving them insane.

Jamba had dual hopes for the mine – either that the Sleepers would not dare enter on account of the duppy or that the funnelling effect of the narrow passage would help reduce the creatures' advantage of numbers. As the Sleepers came scurrying into the mine behind the smugglers, Jamba cursed, writing off the first notion. He would have to rely on the tactical advantage of the terrain then, he supposed, and the obeahman's wiles.

He turned to Ruffle Feathers, a desperate look on his face. "Please, tell me you have a trick up your sleeve."

Ruffle Feathers regarded him in exasperation, panting and sweating, doubled over. 'I have already summoned a throng of killer bats. What more do you want from me?'

"Merry's tits!" Jamba cursed.

Letters of fire assuaged his fears. 'Give me a little time, and I'll come up with something.'

"Thanks, Ruffle! Stand your ground, Lug. We need to give Ruffle a little time to save our skins, understand? Not a single Sleeper gets through!"

His hands trembled, and his temples pounded as the Sleepers bore down on them in a black wave, scurrying halfway up the walls and leapfrogging one another like crickets. Their howling barks echoed down the tunnel, reverberating until it was all Jamba could hear. Their fetid scent, like dead wet dog, was all he could smell, and he wanted to scream, to flee. Instead, he tightened his grip on his scimitars and brandished them before him, weaving a well-known attack pattern in the air again and again to calm his nerves. Beside him, Lug stood still, blinking and licking his lips, fur sprouting all over his frame and his nose extending into a lupine snout. Jamba wondered where the demonic bats had gone.

Then, the wave crashed down on the smugglers, and Jamba was

battling for his life against multiple Sleepers, chopping at any swinging paw he saw in a frenzy of bloodshed, frantically attempting to hold his ground. Lug fell back before the onslaught, and Jamba only lasted a couple of seconds longer before the weight of the press began to tell, forcing him back, step by grudging step. Attack patterns went out the window as he did whatever he had to do to stay alive, parrying and blocking and dodging, only occasionally finding enough breathing space for a retaliatory blow and even then failing more often than not to puncture the hulking beasts' thick hides and reach a vital organ. Sleeper claws started to sneak through his guard, carving him apart bit by bit.

"Ruffle!" he screamed as he was forced back another step. "Time's up! Whatever you're doing, do it now or we have to retreat further into the mine!"

Ruffle Feathers extended a hand, and a crackling doorway to another world burst open in mid-air beside the smugglers, brimming with violet fire. Nothing happened. Nothing stepped through.

Jamba saw words of flame flicker to life above the head of the Sleeper he was currently clobbering. 'Shout Djhuty the Diabolical!'

Though the words stuck in his craw, Jamba shouted in a strangled voice, "Djhuty! Djhuty the Diabolical! We need your help! Dhjuty! Please, oh great Djhuty the Diabolical, grant us your aid!"

He had thought his words theatrical overkill, a mocking testimony to Ruffle's foolishness, but to his surprise the androgynously handsome head of Djhuty the Diabolical did indeed poke through the fiery-edged rift just then, an inquisitive expression on its blue-black face, its upswept ivory hair swaying in the warm wind.

"You called?" inquired the demon in urbane tones in Traveller's Tongue.

"Yes!" Jamba yelled, before remembering to show a little more respect to the demon who might rip out his tongue on a whim. "Please, Djhuty, we've called you for a feast! See all these Sleepers? They are yours to gorge upon! Help yourself!"

Djhuty hummed thoughtfully, still only halfway through the rift. "Hmm, *kafi khohum,* I don't know. I'm pretty full, and there are a *lot* of them. More than I can handle, maybe. Definitely more than I can eat. What do I gain by helping you? *Medhja ruuk."*

"Gain?" Jamba shrieked. "You'd gain my eternal gratitude for a start! Just please, help us! We'll die if you don't!"

The demon shrugged. "That's really not my concern, *sivul calim.*" It was about to duck back through the rift and out of sight when it stopped and looked back, its face alight with curiosity. "I say, what is that? I daresay I'll stick around to find out."

It stepped through the rift, and it sewed itself shut behind the demon and disappeared with a popping sound. Then, Djhuty waded into the wave of Sleepers until it was hip-deep in blood and broken bones, shattering the beasts with its skull-topped staff and the ghostly morningstar it manifested in its spare hand. The Sleepers clawed at the demon's black feather cloak, but Jamba did not witness a single feather fall off and wondered what demonic bird they had come from. The tattoos contouring the muscles banding the demon's supple body pulsed as it fought, bathing the nocturnal monsters in an eerie cerulean glow.

Jamba wondered what the demon had been speaking of, but did not ask, grateful for the dark entity's help, whatever the reason. Knocking aside Sleeper legs and mandibles with penduluming sweeps of his scimitars, the smuggler heard a faint hum welling up from below him and at the same time felt the earth beneath his boots begin to vibrate, gently at first but shaking more and more violently with every passing second while the humming ramped up to a crescendo. Expecting another earthquake, Jamba thought his heart was going to burst in his chest from stress. There was no way to escape the mine. The wave had become a black flood. The smugglers would be buried alive alongside all the Sleepers. Jamba's heart slowed a little at that thought – buried. Blessed sleep, at last. He would welcome the Ferrymen with open arms.

The mine did not come tumbling down on top of him as expected, however. Instead, a spectral form flitted through him from behind, making him jump back from the coldness of its touch, and floated on towards the Sleepers baying for his blood. Jamba thought the foremost Sleeper would leap straight through the translucent, silvery man in robes, but it did not. The spectral robed man cut through its open mouth, teeth and all, deep into its body with a simple chopping motion of his hand, almost splitting it from nape to grapes. Jamba gawked.

More and more duppy, all robed men and women, floated past him, beyond the need for such mortal concerns as walking, and proceeded to lay into the Sleepers with a flabbergasting array of sorceries, conjuring fireballs and tridents of lightning, ice spears and earthen swords, the weapons just as ephemeral as their wielders but dealing real damage to the beasts, who yowled as they were burned, frozen, electrocuted and cudgelled to death by the dozen.

Jamba stood with both his jaw and swords hanging slack, watching the brutal but eerie battle unfold. "What is happening?" he croaked, his throat drier than Sharikhafar Desert.

'It is the duppy of the obeahmen slain a thousand or more years ago by the necromancer, Waddi-waddi,' answered Ruffle Feathers in letters of flame. 'They have come to our rescue!'

"Why would they do that?" Lug asked.

'I don't know. Just be grateful that they did. Be patient and we may get the chance to ask them.'

"I don't understand," said Lug, brow furrowed. "Shouldn't we be afraid of duppy? Aren't they evil spirits?"

'It's not quite that simple,' Ruffle replied, 'but in broad terms, yes. While these spirits live only for vengeance, however, it is not vengeance against *us* that they seek. So, there is no reason we should not be allies.'

Djhuty shook its head in awe. "Your little island really does love you, you know that? *Fayn shajh!* Just look at this! You are her children, and she will do anything to protect you. You have to admire it, in a way."

Ruffle smiled at the demon. 'Chilpaea is our mother, and we would do anything for her.'

18

The Invisible Farmhouse

Bandaged and drugged, the smugglers slept in the mine at daybreak for a few hours. Djhuty the Diabolical returned to his own infernal world when it became clear he would not get what he wanted – a chance to speak with the spirits who had saved them, who all ignored the demon as if he didn't exist despite his prying questions. It did not matter, Jamba Klach thought thankfully. The duppy protected them during the deadly midnight hours, until the horizon gave birth to the sun and dawn finally banished the horde of Sleepers to their deep-dug warrens.

The smugglers tried speaking to the spirits too, before passing out on their blankets on the hard rock floor. The duppy did not ignore them, but nor did they reply save to bestow the saddest of smiles. When Jamba awoke shortly before noon, wiping crust from his eyes, however, he spotted Ruffle Feathers communicating with one of the duppy in sign language, their fingers forming fast and intricate patterns that only they understood. Like the others, the duppy was robed and hooded, his silvery face gnarly with a bulbous nose, jutting chin and butting brow. His eyes fixed on Jamba for just a moment, and the smuggler thought he saw a flash of colour in them if only for a split second – a purple blink – and then it was gone. The duppy bowed to Ruffle Feathers, who bowed in return, and then the spirit simply faded from sight, like fog in the morning light.

"What did he say?" Jamba asked through a half-stifled yawn as he stood and stretched, his back cracking like an old bough and his wounds protesting.

Ruffle turned and waved a hand, and words of fire blazed into view. 'He told me his story. He was the overseer of the mine in ages past. He learned sign language because he was deafened by the sorcerous explosions that the obeahmen used to excavate the fire opals in his time. By all accounts, the miners here were once mighty magic-users in the time before the witches."

"But that was thousands of years ago!" Lug Thorm blurted, amazed. "Have the duppy really been here all that time?"

Ruffle nodded. 'They are trapped by their own fury, until they find vengeance against the one who slew them – and since Waddi-waddi himself has been dead for thousands of years, the chances that they'll get their wish are looking slim.'

"Did you tell them that?" Jamba asked.

Ruffle frowned. 'Don't be foolish. Of course I did not.'

Jamba sighed. "Poor souls." He turned to gaze down into the depths of the mine, where the dirt tunnel, propped up by wooden beams, extended away into darkness. "Thank you for saving us, my friends," he said, placing a hand on his heart and bowing. "You will not be forgotten." He turned back to the others. "Let's go. We're wasting daylight."

The smugglers hastened out of the mine, breathing easier once the midday sunlight bathed their skin in a golden glow. Only then did they realise how unnaturally cold the mine had been. Jamba shivered at the recollection, praying he would never see another duppy in his life. He did not want to see people either, though.

"We're going to have to travel through civilized areas soon," he said reluctantly. "I know of no way to skirt Billygoat Bridge if we're heading northeast – or Shearer village for that matter. Or Jemel on the other side. There's no crossing for leagues to the west, and east lies the city of Dos Rios on the coast, where the Justiquans have doubtless landed in their thousands, just like they did in Cocoba Bay." He rubbed a hand over his face, tugging at his arrow beard and leaving a smudge of dirt on his cheek. Nobody said anything. It complemented the smudge on his other cheek quite well. "We'll just have to pray the cursed crusaders haven't made it this far inland."

Leaving the hills behind and venturing out onto the plains, where they felt vulnerable as the rabbits they occasionally saw in the long yellow grass, the smugglers instinctively hunched and crept across the grassland to the farmlands beyond. There, they stuck to the thorny hedgerows between fields, stalking in the shadows past burned out husks of farmhouses towards Shearer village in the distance. Half the crops had been trampled by booted feet and Sleeper claws already. The smugglers feared they already knew what they would find when the village came into sight.

Black thrushes tweeted in the big blue sky, casting flitting shadows on the travellers. Shaggy billy goats stopped cropping the grass to baa at them as they passed, the older creatures' horns long, ridged and magnificent, arching over their napes. Lug smiled and waved to the animals, before trying to shush them when their bleating intensified. Hiding in the shadow of a prickly green hedge, the smugglers squinted at the village. Even from a distance, they could make out the wall of stakes surrounding the previously unwalled town and the two men in glittering steel plate armour barring the entryway.

"Ferrymen's bunghole!" Jamba swore, sweating in the afternoon heat. "I don't remember that palisade being there before. That means the crusaders have taken Shearer already."

Ruffle nodded by his side, his words of fire forming smaller than usual for stealth. 'I think you're right. Still, as you said, we must find a way through. It would add days to our journey to trek west all the way to Braeburn Crossing. And we cannot risk Dos Rios. We must cross the Rio Boae here and now.'

"I know," murmured Jamba, "but how? We could try to sneak around the edge of the village, maybe create a distraction? I don't know if we'd be able to reach the bridge from outside that wall, though. Probably not …"

"Or we could just leg it through the middle," said Lug, shrugging.

Jamba opened his mouth to retort sharply, but paused for a moment's consideration. "Our furry friend may have a point. The crusaders may not even be on the lookout for us yet this far north. We may be able to simply pass through unnoticed."

Ruffle snorted. 'Fat chance. You think the Justiquans haven't been communicating by pigeon and rook? Let me assure you that they have. Not to mention whatever magical means of communication they have. It's safer to assume they're looking for us already. I think I know of a way we can make it through in disguise. But first we need to sneak into one of the farmhouses closer to the village. I have a friend there who may be able to help us – if he yet lives.'

Jamba glanced at the old obeahman with a hint of a mocking smile. "I didn't know you had friends."

Ruffle grinned. 'I'm the life of the party, me.' Then, his expression hardened. 'Follow me.'

Like all the others, the farmhouse they sought was in ruins, charred beams and rubble scattered amid a field. Ruffle Feathers strode straight past the wreckage undeterred and knocked on the air with a *thump thump thump.* Jamba and Lug had to pick their jaws up off the floor when a door opened in the middle of the field, materialising from nowhere as it did so. Through the door, they could see what appeared to be the kitchen of a farmhouse, with a chopping board complete with venison laid out on a countertop in the foreground and shelves stacked with herbs, spices, fruit and vegetables behind. Jamba surreptitiously peeked around the back of the door, but saw only the field in which they were stood. Flabbergasted, he scratched his head and ogled the ageing man in the doorway. Clad in a bloodstained apron over a blue tunic, the bull-necked stranger grinned, threw wide his brawny nut-brown arms and engulfed Ruffle Feathers in a bear hug, smothering the little obeahman's face in his bushy golden beard.

"Ruffle Feathers!" he boomed. "So good to see you, my old chum, it's been so long! Look at you! You've gotten so old! How long's it been? Ten years? Something like that. Let me look at you. My, you're a sight for sore eyes! I feared those Gods-damned crusaders had gotten you too, like so many others. Did you here about Vandeveld? Or Crithon? Or Tito? All dead, I'm sorry to say. These crusaders are nothing but blood-crazed war dogs, every one of them, I swear it! Nothing but dogs!"

Gasping for breath once the stranger released him, Ruffle glanced nervously towards the village and scribbled words of fire in the air with a wave of his hand. 'Joto Esponzo, it is good to see you too, my friend! May we come in? We're in something of a pickle.'

"Of course, of course!" Joto replied in his deep, jovial voice, stepping aside and waving for the smugglers to enter. "Do come in!"

Jamba gulped, unsure whether he wanted to set foot inside a house that – by all outward appearances – did not exist.

He grabbed Ruffle's robe before the obeahman could take a step and hissed, "What is this? Where are you taking us? Is this doorway some magical portal?"

Ruffle gave him a patronising look. 'I'm not taking you anywhere except in there.' He gestured to the door. 'It's just a farmhouse, Jamba. It's invisible. That's all. It's how Joto escaped the Justiquans' notice – and the Sleepers' too, I imagine.'

"He's an obeahman, too?"

Ruffle nodded and beckoned for Jamba to follow him inside. 'Yes, and one of my oldest friends.'

"Well, you never mentioned him," Jamba muttered as he trod nervously through the threshold, glancing at the frame the entire time and observing with wonder the grassy field just outside the door and the kitchen nook just inside. "Why can't you turn things invisible? It'd be a handy trick for hiding from the Sleepers at night."

Ruffle fixed him with a withering look. 'All obeahman have different talents.'

Sensing the old man's irritability, Jamba dropped the subject. Once inside, he could see the field through the open windows, feel the breeze on his skin. When the door latched quietly behind him, he felt queasy.

Taking off his bloodstained apron and laying it on the counter, the big man, Joto, ushered the smugglers through the kitchen to his living room, where comfortable leather armchairs awaited them on thick maroon rugs by an empty hearth.

Joto picked up a decanter from a round mahogany table, unstoppered it and sniffed it with an appreciative hum. "Mmm, the finest firewater in all of Chilpaea, guaranteed. Who wants a cup?"

He poured a measure of amber liquid for each of them into several clay cups.

"How are your goats still alive?" asked Lug.

"I'm not sure!" Joto laughed. "They're wily! Not all of them have survived, but they do seem to hide well at night."

Jamba coughed and wheezed upon his first sip of the firewater, his gullet afire.

Then, eyes watering, he managed to croak, "That's good stuff!"

Joto quaffed it like water and smacked his lips. "So, what brings you to my neck of the woods at such an ill hour, my friend?"

Ruffle lit his pipe with his unseen arts and waved a hand. Letters of flame materialised in mid-air. 'We are on a quest to save Chilpaea, my old friend, and we need your help.'

He puffed contentedly and nodded to Jamba, who proceeded to explain all about the Lullabyer trapped in the crystal and their mission to deliver the crystal to the Lullabyer's son in the Monastery Calliope to save Chilpaea from the Sleepers. Taking the Lullabyer-shaped chunk of *Kun-Yao-Lin* from his satchel, Ruffle showed it to his friend. Both gaped when the gemstone shone brighter and brighter, eventually emitting a blinding flash of light that made them all avert their gaze for a moment.

The smugglers' eyes popped out of their skulls to witness the Lullabyer standing before them then, albeit in a strange and spectral form. As tall as he had been in life, the Lullabyer's entire frame appeared to be composed of the same stuff as the crystal itself, though appearing softer, less brittle, swirling with blues and purples all over, translucent as a duppy and glittering as if star-ridden. Even his regal robes and long, once-silver locks tied up in a topknot were washed mauve and cerulean. His face was just as it had been in life, hard, so angular it was almost jagged, softened only a little by a tightly trimmed beard.

Joto blew out his cheeks, eyes wide, and ran a thick-fingered hand over the short-shorn blonde fuzz on his scalp. "Wow. It is hard to dispute your tale, tall as it is, with the proof standing here before me."

"How did you do that?" Jamba squawked in amazement.

The Lullabyer smiled smugly, his lips moving but his voice sounding inside their heads rather than in their ears. *"The longer I spend trapped in that cursed crystal, the more I test my boundaries and discover what I am capable of. It is difficult to explain, but I believe I am using my soul's energy to ... project a manifestation of myself. I have not lost all my wiles just yet, smuggler."*

"He can hear us then?" Joto asked, surprised.

"I can hear you," replied Magnuz Opherio.

Joto jumped, then rose from his armchair and bowed. "Greetings, Lullabyer. I don't believe we ever had the pleasure of meeting in life. My name is Joto Esponzo, and I am at your disposal."

"A pleasure, Joto." Magnuz nodded to him. *"Thank you for taking us in during our hour of need."*

"You're welcome. Anything for Chilpaea," said Joto, before turning back to Jamba and Ruffle. "So, what is it you need from me?"

'We need a way to pass through Shearer village undetected by the cursed crusaders,' Ruffle answered. 'We need disguises and – I am sorry to ask – a few billy goats. We could use your help on our quest too, my friend.'

The smugglers all glanced at the staircase in the corner when they heard a baby's cries coming from upstairs.

Joto smiled and shook his head. "The rest I am happy to provide, but I cannot join you, my friends. I wish I could, truly. But I cannot. My wife and child need me here, especially with so many Justiquans around."

"You have a new-born?" Magnuz asked.

"We do. Her name is Grace."

"Congratulations! I understand, of course."

"Thank you."

19

Rio Boae

Bidding farewell to Joto Esponzo, the smugglers stepped out of the farmhouse and back into the field. By the time they turned around, the door had closed and the house, by all appearances, had vanished. Jamba Klach was too afraid to reach out a hand to test if it was still there, so he cleared his throat and set off across the field with shoulders squared, beelining for the entrance to Shearer village with Ruffle Feathers and Lug Thorm struggling to keep up with his brisk pace, tugging along a billy goat apiece. Lug's little billy goat was so afraid of him that he had to practically drag it along while it dug its hooves into the ground and refused to move. The Lullabyer's duppy terrified the beasts even more when he manifested in the middle of the field, and the smugglers shooed him away as if he were a goose at a picnic.

"But I get so bored in the satchel!" Magnuz Opherio stamped a foot like a tantruming child, before folding his arms and pouting. *"Fine, I'll go."*

He disappeared in a flash of light that the smugglers prayed had not been spotted by any of the soldiers by the village. Jamba was breathing hard by the time they were drawing near the guarded entrance, thanks to stress rather than labour. Sweat glistened in his arrow beard in the sweltering sunlight.

He glanced back to see Ruffle and Lug falling behind again. "Hurry up!" he hissed.

"We're trying!" Lug grunted, his huge shoulders bunching as he heaved his goat another few feet. "But these goats are stubborn as mules!"

Jamba surveyed their disguises. Like him, Ruffle and Lug now wore sheepskin coats slung over their shoulders to hide their weapons, plain tunics and woolly leggings – the classic garb of the billy goat farmer. The pièce de résistance was the wide-brimmed straw hats all three wore to hide their faces. Their usual gear was stowed in a large leather sack slung over Lug's huge shoulder, which they hoped would pass as grain for the goats. The smugglers could see a few dark-skinned folk herding sheep through the village, so they knew not every farmer had been slain and prayed they could blend in once past the wall.

Jamba slowed down so that the trio could time their entry into the village with another hangdog sheep farmer. Mimicking the man's stooped shuffle, trying to look as small and inoffensive as possible as he drew near the guards by the entrance, Jamba forced himself to breathe normally. His swords, normally belted at his waist, felt strange strapped to his back, out of place. The wool itched. He shuffled forward behind the other sheep farmer and his sheep, keeping his face down so that the hat would hide his features, not daring to look up to see where he was going.

He almost walked straight into one of the guards, who grabbed his sore shoulder not an inch from the hilt of one of his scimitars and said gruffly, "Oi, you don't look familiar. Who are you? What's your business here?"

Jamba forced himself to resist the urge to hiss in pain or look up. He merely bobbed his head and adopted a yokel accent as he said in Traveller's, "Oh, don't mind us, good sir knight, we're merely a bunch of billy goat farmers, come to sell our billy goats across the river. These here are me brothers, Hurb and Murb."

"And what's your name?" the guard asked suspiciously.

"Oh, I'm Able," Jamba replied, not wanting to rhyme yet again, sweating profusely. "Pleased to meet ya."

"Well, Able, there's no record of your transaction on our lists," the guard said condescendingly, making Jamba fear they would turn him away. "I suppose you haven't been here since the change in rules, though, eh? So, we'll let you off this time. In future, though, all entrants into and transactions taking place in Shearer and Jemel must be reported ahead of time to Major Rubens, understood?"

Jamba bobbed his head again. "Understood, sir, understood. Thankee, sir, thankee."

He was walking past the guard with a sigh of relief when the Justiquan reached out and grabbed his sheepskin coat, tugging it clear of one scimitar handle. Jamba hastily put it back, but the damage was done.

"Hold on!" the guard snapped. "Why have you got a sword like that? Let me see your face!"

Jamba glanced up despite himself and locked eyes with a pale-skinned blonde moustached man who had taken off his helmet in the extreme heat and now carried it tucked under his arm.

The guard blanched at the sight and bellowed, "It's them! It's the smugglers!"

He reached out to seize Jamba, but the smuggler headbutted him in the face before he could say another word and the man fell back with blood spraying from his broken nose. Jamba had no idea how Lug wrenched his warhammer off his back so fast, but regardless the other guard at the gate was smashed off his feet a moment later, his helmet dented and his skull likely popped.

"Run!" Jamba yelled, taking off at a sprint down the dirt street cutting straight through the village.

Lug had already released his billy goat, and now Ruffle let his go too, both tearing after Jamba. The billy goats hopped away, bleating, back into the fields. The smugglers could see the bridge ahead of them past the surviving wattle and daub shacks, some of which had clearly been burned down like the farmhouses. Like the entrance, though, the bridge was guarded – by a whole squadron of knights in full armour this time. A bugle sounded, and more Justiquan soldiers in leather armour started to pour out of the buildings to the left and right of the bridge.

"Ruffle, look out!" Jamba cried.

Ruffle Feathers was already waving his arms as he ran, however, as if sculpting the gusts into eldritch patterns. The air thrummed, and the wind howled. Jamba's skin crawled as if a thousand creepy-crawlies were skittering all over it, and he knew the old obeahman was practising his arcane arts. He felt the supernatural heat singeing his skin as two eight-foot long snakes, blazing as if doused in lit oil from head to tail, flew past him in an orange blur, weaving through the air effortlessly towards the crusaders, who – to the smuggler's amazement – held their ground, heater shields raised. The demonic serpents melted their shields in an instant, incinerating some of the knights from existence altogether. They gobbled up knights by the handful, swallowing them after a single snap of their jaws. They only needed to pass near to a foe to melt his armour, fusing it with his skin in an incredibly painful process that left half-dead men mutilated and screaming on the ground. The stench was ineffable, metallic and acrid and bitter.

The smugglers ran past the horrifically blackened bodies of the dead and dying, gagging on the reeking black smoke. The snakes cleared a way for them as they went, barring any of the soldiers from reaching them with their long serpentine frames, and within seconds of entering the village, the smugglers had set foot on Billygoat Bridge. True to its name, the bridge was clogged with farmers trying to shepherd their sheep and billy goats across. Once they spotted the demonic snakes, however, all the farmers cleared the way, either running to the opposite shore or leaping off the bridge in terror. The livestock were not so smart, however, and mostly milled about, bleating in fear. Jamba winced as he watched one farmer jump into the fast-moving murky water only to be immediately entangled in the constricting loops of a twelve-foot Chilpaean boa and dragged under. A sheep suffered a similar fate a split second later. The Rio Boae could be a dangerous place.

Stuck on the bridge, trying to dodge past the remaining sheep and billy goats still blocking the way, the smugglers' hearts sank when they spotted knights and Justiquan soldiers on the far side of the bridge awaiting them with weapons bared. Jamba glanced back, and his gaze hooked on a fat man in armour – Major Rubens, he presumed. Unlike the rest of the knights' steel plate armour, consisting of a cuirass, pauldrons, greaves and gauntlets, this man wore specially crafted laminar armour made of steel bands fitted together broadways to account for his ample gut. Even his helmet was unique, wider than the rest and topped with a spike. He was chanting alien words; words that chilled Jamba to the bone and made his ears itch as though bugs were crawling into – or out of – them.

"A magician!" Jamba whispered, feeling terror well up in his gullet like bile.

The bridge shook, and the wobbling smugglers watched in horror as the rushing brown river decided it had had enough of horizontal life and stood up. Water rushed up, contrary to its nature, to form the vague adumbrate of a twenty-foot-tall bulky humanoid figure sans the neck, and then it froze in place, sheening over with frost that glittered incongruously in the late afternoon sunlight. The rest of the river continued on its course, but part of it remained in place, frozen solid and yet far from immobile. As the eerie magic-formed creature stomped towards the bridge, shaking the ground with its footsteps, sunk to its ankles in the fast-flowing river, Jamba saw words of fire flash before his eyes.

'It's a Gods-damned golem! Kill the Justiquan magician!'

20

A Warm Wind

Jamba wasn't sure if the words were directed at him or the giant demonic snakes coiling in mid-air, snatching up soldiers and lashing knights into the river with their fiery tails. He hoped the latter. Though the otherworldly serpents had devastated the Justiquan ranks, enough soldiers yet stood between him and the fat man in armour to deter him from making an approach. He watched with hopeful eyes as the demonic snakes spun and speared towards the rotund magician, but before they could reach him the giant golem stretched out its long arms and wrapped thick icy fingers around each of the snakes' tails, yanking them to an abrupt halt, their knife-sized fangs gnashing mere yards away from the armoured magician.

The serpents twisted and launched themselves at the golem, biting and burning. Chips of ice sloughed off the golem where the serpents wounded it, and water trickled into the river where it began to melt under the eldritch heat of their bodies. It was not finished yet, however. The smugglers and soldiers watched in awe as the golem made whip-like motions and slammed the snakes' heads down on the rocky shore, shaking the earth. He brought them crashing down again and again, until the demonic snakes' bodies started to freeze from the tail end, the fire there diminishing and then dying to leave behind bare black scales that were soon rimed with frost.

Finally, the golem released one of them and grabbed the other by both ends, head and tail, squeezing the life and fire out of it. Its flames died out on its head and tail, only persisting in the middle of its long body, guttering like a spent candle. Just before they could completely sputter out, however, its twin shook off the beating it had taken and reared up with a hiss, its fires burning bright once more. Speeding through the air with a sound like steam hissing from a kettle, the serpent punched a hole straight through the golem's melting middle. The golem made no noise, for it had no mouth, but it waved its arms like it might be in pain, flailing and then dropping the snake still in its grip. The freed snake's fires swarmed back over its entire frame in a heartbeat, crackling, popping and whooshing with venom.

Together, the demonic snakes laid into the golem from all angles, gouging holes in its icy body left, right and centre. Even when it managed to seize hold of one or both of them again, the other was always at hand to bite the snatching hand and free its fellow. Within seconds, the golem had been chipped down to half its size, its long arms gnawed down to stumps, and its legs melted up to the knees. Pocked with holes, it collapsed and disintegrated into the river with a great splash.

Ruffle waved his hands, urging the serpents to unleash their demonic fury on the magician who had forged the golem. To his dismay, however, the snakes shook their heads, their fires weak. One of them chewed through the veil between realms, biting open a jagged, fiery-edged rift through which both rapidly disappeared. As soon as their tails flicked out of sight, the rift snapped shut with a *pop* and the smugglers were alone on the bridge with the livestock, trapped between a rock and a hard place. The only blessing that Jamba could see was that the fat man in armour was leaning on his knees, huffing and puffing, evidently exhausted by his sorcerous feats. Jamba glanced at Ruffle Feathers and cursed inwardly. The old obeahman looked ashen and grey.

"Can you summon anything else to help us?" Jamba demanded.

Ruffle shook his head, eyelids heavy.

"Don't just stand there!" the fat man in armour managed to yell in a warbling voice. "Kill the smugglers! Kill them all!"

"Get behind me," Jamba ordered Ruffle, standing with a wide stance in the middle of the bridge. "Lug, protect Ruffle from the soldiers on the other side, got it?"

"Got it!" Lug grunted, hairy as a bear with a wolfish snout.

Most of the knights in Shearer had been melted inside their armour by the demonic snakes, so Jamba faced predominantly soldiers in studded leather cuirasses and vambraces, while Lug had the misfortune to face Jemel village on the far side of the river, where more of the knights had survived the snakes' onslaught. Parrying a high swipe and retorting with a slash at the torso, Jamba discovered to his frustration that the cuirasses were toughened enough to resist a tangential attack. He plunged his other scimitar straight through the leather, skewering the man's heart before ripping out his blade in a spray of hot blood, satisfied that the armour could not withstand a puncture.

After that, he slashed at the soldier's arms whenever a blow to the neck did not come easy, forcing his enemies to flinch or drop their weapons entirely and thus expose their jugulars. Fast on his feet, he flitted back and forth with perfectly balanced footwork, stabbing and slashing, pirouetting around clumsy blows and riposting in a wink. Bodies piled up on the bridge, making it harder for the soldiers behind to reach him. As they started to trip over one another, he used it to his advantage, hacking them down the second they lost their balance.

For most, a parry and retort was sufficient, such was his speed. Some, however, bogged him down in swordplay for longer than he liked, and for these he pulled out his bag of tricks, blinding them with the sun's reflection on his blade, manoeuvring to put their own comrades in their way or striking at an unexpected spot to fell them as fast as possible. One man resisted all of Jamba's tricks until the smuggler booted him in the balls, poleaxing him. Jamba had once believed in courtly honour and etiquette on the battlefield.

Now, he saw no reason not to kick a man in the plums if it meant surviving the night.

Despite all his strength and speed and the years spent honing his skills with the blade, however, sheer numbers soon began to tell and Jamba became more and more overwhelmed, less and less able to retaliate and forced more and more into defensive positions. He cursed as he was forced back a step to dodge a vicious swipe aimed at his neck and fought in a frenzy to regain the step lest one of the soldiers slip past his guard to wound Ruffle Feathers, but he could not find the time to regain the space he had lost. His scimitars blurred, trying to keep up with all the blades coming for him. He realised he was slowing down with a pang of terror when soldiers' swords started to sneak past his defence in the scarlet glow of sunset, spilling blood from his arm and thigh. Shallow wounds, they nevertheless jarred his confidence and concentration.

"Lug, we have to get out of here!" he roared.

Behind him, Lug was also tiring. Initially beating down knights and soldiers alike with his great warhammer like a bear protecting its cubs, bending armour and pulverising the flesh beneath, he had now begun to flag to the point that he barely had the strength to lift the hammer. It was knocked from his grasp by one knight, and he tore off the man's helmet and ripped out his windpipe with his teeth, guzzling his blood for a moment. That made him feel better – until one of the soldiers cut open his ear. Had he not dodged, he'd have lost his head. He fixed the offender with a glare and raked the man's face open with a claw, making him totter back, screaming, into his fellows, knocking one off the bridge to be lost in the murky water. Lug scooped up his hammer in the lull, but it felt unusually heavy in his paws.

A warm wind blew by, warmer than was natural and scented of baui, hibiscus and jacaranda. It felt soft as silk on the lagahoo's fur, and somehow soothed his soul, reminding him that everything would be alright, that everything happened for a reason. Jamba felt it too, and inhaled deeply without fully understanding why, relishing the breeze. The billy goats' ears pricked up as they felt it, and as one they turned their golden eyes on the crusaders thronging on either end of the bridge. Jamba gawped as the billy goats abruptly pelted past him en masse and rammed the Justiquans he faced, knocking them back or butting them off the bridge entirely. He glanced over his shoulder to see that the beasts were likewise aiding Lug.

The Justiquans recovered from their surprise quickly, however, and the pained bleating of dying goats soon rang out over the waters. As if disturbed by the sound, the river roiled like a thousand maelstroms had taken root. Given a second of space by the billy goats, Jamba ogled the churning water in awe, seeing scales swirling in the murk. He realised with a start that the waters were seething with Chilpaean boas. They slithered up out of the river by the score and wrapped themselves sinuously around the Justiquans one by one, binding them in a lethal embrace. Jamba blanched at the sight of the crusaders' faces turning purple and their eyeballs popping from their sockets as they were squeezed to death.

The river reared up once more then with a great roar like a waterfall, cascading upwards into the unmistakeable shape of a woman as tall as a tree, the foam forming her hair. A voluminous feminine voice reverberated in the air, seeming to come from everywhere and nowhere.

"You dare to impugn my waters, filthy Justiquan?" the voice shrilled in Kwi patois. "This is *my* country! This is *my* river! And I will see you dead before you sully it again!"

The water comprising the woman arced up out of the river to sluice down on the fat Justiquan magician, Major Rubens, laying him out cold. Jamba thought he might have drowned and was disappointed to see his big gut moving as he sucked in a breath. The few soldiers not washed away by the flood, slain by snakes or butted off the bridge by goats brandished their swords nervously at the smugglers.

"What in the name of the Twins is happening?" Jamba turned just in time to see Ruffle Feathers beckon him before jumping nonchalantly feet first into the rushing brown river to disappear from sight. "Merry's tits! Come on, Lug! We're out of here!"

Jamba took a deep breath and vaulted into the river, followed a second later by Lug. The powerful current whisked them downriver in a heartbeat, and the smugglers were lost in a world of whooshing water and bubbles.

21

Building Blocks

Jeremias Colcott could fly.

He had no wings. He did not flap his arms. He simply soared through the iron sky in the land of the dead by the power of his will, high above the ground and far from the red rim of the horizon, looking down on the throng of duppy milling aimlessly in the streets. From his vantage point, he could even see beyond Jinglespur's curved wall. Something like rain pitter-pattered down on him, ethereal as he was himself. There was no sign of the Justiquans' stockade here in the dreamworld. Horrors and fantasies, dreams and nightmares prowled the wastes and bountiful lands beyond the necropolis. Just as Jinglespur appeared as a phantom of itself, blurring and oscillating, so too did the world outside forever shift scene, so that at one moment Jeremias beheld a joyous parade, the next a cavalcade of corpses.

"Is there something wrong with my eyes?" he asked Waddi-waddi, who flew by his side. "I cannot piece together a clear image of what lays beyond the wall."

"That is because nothing lays beyond," replied Waddi-waddi in gulf-deep tones. "There is no wall. There is only a projection of the city, cast by the minds of those within its walls, all filling in gaps for each other to form a cohesive image. A semblance of reality reassures the dreamer. Beyond the walls are the wilder dreams, the darkest nightmares. Venture beyond the wall and you will certainly be lost in the madness."

Jeremias gulped. "You have been there?"

"I have. There is little else for me to do save wander the dreamworld while I wait for a way to return to the land of the living. I was lost for a long time before I found my way back home, and I had to slay a horde of nightmares to return. Imagine, if you can, every bad dream taking shape out there, and you will have some idea of what I faced."

"Dreams become real here?"

"Of course. This is the dreamworld, after all. Dreamers hold the power here – although they do not know it. Have you ever had a dream where you half-knew you were awake and you felt as if you could dictate the dream? Most people have. That is how we dreamwalk. That is how we control our nightmares."

Jeremias hummed. "Hmm, I have had dreams like that, now that you mention it. Why is it that we so seldom remember dreams?"

"Dreams are representations of our truest fears, our deepest desires – the building blocks of the soul. Most people are not ready to come to terms

with the truth about themselves, and so they choose not to remember their dreams where their wishes were fulfilled or their terrors came to life. It is a way of staying sane."

"But you don't worry about such things?"

"Ha!" Waddi-waddi barked with laughter. "No, I have long since left such concerns behind. I know who I am. I am a coward who fears to be powerless, and thus I crave power."

Jeremias blinked in surprise at this frank admission. "You call yourself a coward with no shame?"

Waddi-waddi shrugged. "Everybody is afraid of something. What are you afraid of, Jeremias?"

"Of failing in my duty," the seneschal replied without thinking.

Waddi-waddi nodded. "A noble goal. And what is your deepest desire?"

"To matter," Jeremias replied, surprising himself. "I want to matter, to lead an important life."

Waddi-waddi nodded. "A common goal. And one, it could be said, that you have already achieved by attaining one of the highest possible ranks in your country short of the title of Lullabyer itself."

"I don't feel as if I've achieved it."

Waddi-waddi chuckled. "We never do. It is what gives us passion, my boy. A blessing and a curse, eh?"

Jeremias nodded. "Indeed. So, are you going to actually teach me anything today?"

"We are *learning," Waddi-waddi assured him. "Simply by being in this state, in this realm of being, your body and mind are becoming more attuned to the dreamworld. The more attuned you are, the more you will be able to achieve here."*

As they soared across the necropolis yet again, Jeremias could not help but track the phantasmagoria occurring beyond the wall. Every insanity he could dream of was enacting itself out there. Sentient plants were eating folk, surrounded by giant spiders. Chasms of fire and darkness yawned everywhere he looked, splitting the land before his eyes only to re-seal. The sea sprang out of its bed to drown whole houses. Demons of all shapes and sizes flitted through the air and rustled through the undergrowth. Jeremias' head hurt as he tried to keep up with the train of fantastical images running through his head.

"How do you slay a nightmare?"

"By turning it into a dream."

"What is that?" Jeremias asked, pointing past the wall, where a dark speck in the red-edged sky was growing larger by the second.

Waddi-waddi stared for a few seconds, before grunting, "We are not the only dreamwalkers this night, it seems. One of the Justiquans has mastered the art. You must flee or he'll kill you! Quick, back to your body!"

Startled, Jeremias spun in the air and sped towards the spectral citadel, towards his body. He stopped to look back when he saw Waddi-waddi was not following and witnessed the speck resolve into the shape of a man in a suit of steel plate armour sans the helmet, with hair as white as ivory and a face flat as a snake's. In his hand was a shining white broadsword, straight as an arrow.

"Marshal Clauss?" Jeremias breathed in shock, recognising the Justiquan commander from the parley a few days earlier.

A heartbeat later, Clauss was over the wall and above the necropolis, crashing into Waddi-waddi with all the force of a preying falcon and bearing him back. Jeremias thought for a moment that the infamous necromancer had been slain, before he saw that Waddi-waddi wielded his own weapon – one Jeremias was sure he had not borne a few moments ago. Nevertheless, the necromancer now twirled a twinkling staff of gleaming white energy in his hands, batting the sword away time and again as it sought out his spirit form.

"Get out of my way, whoever you are!" Jeremias heard Marshal Clauss shouting. "I have no qualms with you, stranger. My quarrel is with your rotten-mouthed friend!"

Jeremias smirked at that.

"Then, your quarrel is *with me, Marshal Clauss," replied Waddi-waddi, lashing out viciously with the stave of light and making the Justiquan retreat or else have his head clobbered, "for, you see, Jeremias Colcott is my friend and pupil. I am Waddi-waddi, the most powerful obeahman this island has ever known! Remember my name, quim, for one day it will spell your doom!"*

"You are merely a spirit," Clauss spat, though his eyes had gone wide at the name. "You do not possess the energy to defeat me in this form!"

"Flee, Jeremias!" Waddi-waddi cried, before hurling himself at the marshal, his staff blurring to thwack the man on the head.

"Ow!" Clauss whined.

He launched his own assault then, faster than even Waddi-waddi could match, Jeremias saw as he glanced over his shoulder on the way to the citadel, and eventually the marshal's sword snuck through to pierce the duppy's chest. Not a drop of blood spilled.

"Now, get out of my way!" Clauss snarled in the necromancer's face.

Waddi-waddi grinned. "You cannot kill what is already dead, fool!"

Clauss threw him aside in disgust and glided after Jeremias, gaining by the second. Panicking, Jeremias urged himself to greater and greater speed, surprising himself time and again. He did not stop to open the citadel doors but flew straight through them, the cold of the stone making him flinch.

Once inside, he saw that Marshal Clauss had caught him and now swam in the air alongside him, smiling wickedly, sword in hand.

Letting out a yelp, Jeremias shot up just in time to dodge a swipe that would have cut him in half, flying as fast as he could along the ceiling, through a door and up a set of stairs towards where he hoped his body would be. It seemed like the citadel changed its layout every day, though, and he was hopelessly lost in only a few minutes, flying around in circles with the Justiquan hacking at his heels. After what seemed an interminable age, he finally flew back downstairs and found his body there. Clauss hovered between him and his body. He charged the crusader and slid under the arcing broadsword, missing it with his nose by a margin no wider than a bee, and slumped into his body.

He awakened in cold sweat with a gasp.

The throng of the demented within the citadel walls increased day by day. Jeremias had come to dread his tours of the odious corridors, wondering what he would see each morn. Would it be a man smearing his own faeces on his face, or a woman singing to a butterfly, or a child trying to bash its brains out on a wall? He never knew. But it was always something. That day, he saw a young boy eating bugs, a young girl dancing around a diseased corpse and a man just sitting and staring at a black wall with a look of terror written on his face, completely oblivious to the world and all attempts to help him. The people stuck inside the necropolis were slowly but surely losing their minds, Jeremias was sure of it. The only thing he was not sure of was how far along in the process he was himself. Had he become mired in the swamps of insanity already, or was he one of the few to yet toe the rare dry ground? He was not sure.

By the time he emerged from the citadel, the sun had almost reached its zenith and blazed down on the necropolis, casting short shadows. The heat redoubled the stench of death and decay hanging in the muggy air. He guessed he must have inadvertently been up late with Waddi-waddi. It was hard to keep track of time in the dreamworld. Seconds that felt like hours might be only minutes. Muffling a yawn, the seneschal watched in horror as Justiquan soldiers swarmed up onto the sunlit rampart from the ladders leaning against Jinglespur's spoked semi-circular wall, slaying the Chilpaean warriors standing guard.

"A breach!" he screamed, pointing. "Look out!"

Further along the wall, knocking down both ladders and attacking crusaders, General Raoul Malone heard the seneschal's cry and followed his finger.

Spotting the peril, he barked, "Dreyfuss, Shambak! With me!"

Pelting along the wall with surprising speed for his age, the general barrelled into the Justiquans on the wall alongside the two soldiers he had called to accompany him. Leaning to dodge a stabbing sword as he went, Malone lopped off the offender's sword arm at the elbow just above the vambrace with a precise slash, making the man holler in agony and stumble back as blood spurted from the wound. Malone shoulder-barged the man to the ground, knowing he would soon bleed out, and pushed on, parrying two blows from two foes in quick succession before punching one back. Crossing blades again with the second, he overpowered the crusader in a show of strength, shoving him straight over the crenellated battlements and off the wall. The man's shriek as he fell was abruptly cut off.

Turning back to the soldier he had punched, Malone found the Justiquan harrying him with blow after skilful blow and was forced to give ground for a second. Then, he planted his feet, blocked an overhead chop and kicked the man's ankle. Though the Justiquan wore a pair of steel greaves to cover his calves, he still crumpled beneath the kick. He tried to block the general's scimitar when it came for him, but could not manoeuvre his sword into a useful position on the ground. Malone's sword clove open his skull in a shower of bone shards and brains. Before his body hit the ground, the general was already disembowelling his next victim, slipping his blade into the man's side past his armour straps.

Observing from a street inside the necropolis, Jeremias felt sick at the sight of all the blood being spilled and at the same time wished he were yet hale enough to wield a blade again without being more hindrance than help. He knew he could not, though. He had tried taking up a sword the first day of the siege, but had scarcely been able to swing it and knew he had achieved nothing but getting in the way of younger, fitter men. For three days, the Justiquans had been whittling down the Chilpaean forces with sheer numbers, and Jeremias was starting to lose hope. The only solace came at night, when the Sleepers emerged to besiege the Justiquans' log-walled stockade while the Chilpaeans hid inside the black citadel, which proved impregnable to the beasts.

So, he watched, shifting from foot to foot and fidgeting, as General Malone barged men off the wall left and right. When one landed at the foot of the wall inside the necropolis, stirring and groaning, Jeremias hastened over, grabbed the man's fallen sword and jammed it in his throat in the chink between his armour and helmet. Hot blood washed over the dark leggings and pale tunic so graciously provided to him by one of the folks from Jawduck. He dropped the heavy sword on the cobbles with a clatter and spat out bile. He had never liked killing.

Casting his gaze up to the wall once more, he saw that General Malone was in trouble. Enough Justiquans had managed to top the wall now to protect those still climbing the ladders, so that more and more were gaining the rampart by the second. If the breach was not closed quickly, it could spell the

Chilpaeans' end, the seneschal knew. Malone knew it, too. He was hurling himself against the crusaders tirelessly like a breaker against a cliff wall, sparks from the skirling steel flying through the air as his scimitar clanged against breastplates and broadswords.

Dreyfuss yet fought by his side, jabbing his iron-headed spear at the crusaders' weak points. Shambak had already fallen, Jeremias saw with panging heart. Young and lithe, Dreyfuss was fast enough to catch the crusaders out by tripping them with his spear, before vaulting on them and pronging them while they were prone. As he did so, though, one of the Justiquans broke ranks and charged him, screaming angrily – presumably because of the death of his comrade, thought Jeremias, watching with a dry mouth. The Justiquan aimed his broadsword to take the Chilpaean's head clean off. Just before it made contact, though, Dreyfuss flowed out of its way, swaying and spinning his spear and walloping the man with the haft, sending him staggering towards the battlements. Leaping high, Dreyfuss booted him over the edge before he could regain his balance and then whirled his spear towards the remaining Justiquans as he landed to prevent another rush, catching one man on the helmet with a gonging noise and decking him. Dreyfuss stamped on his sword arm, jabbed at the other crusaders to keep them back, and then impaled the man beneath his boot.

Despite their skills, against so many foes Jeremias was sure it was only a matter of time before the two of them were overwhelmed. Feeling dread well in his heart, he picked up the sword again, just in case, feeling nauseated. Malone and Dreyfuss were pushed back by sheer numbers, the general taking a slash to the shoulder and the solider limping from a cut to the leg. Punched in the face, the general went down. Roaring like a wildcat, Dreyfuss stood over him, penduluming his spear back and forth across the width of the rampart while the crusaders tried to snap its wooden haft with their swords, closing in on the lone Chilpaean soldier like a pack of wolves.

Jeremias' heart cramped in his chest at the sight, and he yelled, "Get up, Malone! Get up!"

The seneschal was so focussed on the general that he did not notice a band of Chilpaean warriors approaching from the opposite direction along the wall, having sealed a breach of their own. As the Chilpaeans slammed into the Justiquans with all the force of fury, cutting them down left and right until none remained on the rampart and then kicking down their ladders, Jeremias breathed a sigh of relief, recognising them as the reinforcements from the nearby town of Hatbrim. General Malone rose woozily to his feet, helped by Dreyfuss, and nodded his thanks to the Hatbrim warriors, clasping hands with their ample-framed mayor, Bo Yaak. As ladders clattered against the wall once more, Bo Yaak hollered heartily and helped the general throw them back, his braided beard billowing in the warm sea breeze.

Jeremias swept the wall with his gaze, coming to rest on Wam Guir, captain of the troops from the Belt, who had apparently been ousted by duppy, and Zov Lorr, captain of Jawduck's minor military force. He was glad they had come. Without them, he doubted they would have had enough soldiers to hold the wall. Even now, it was a close call, hundreds pitted against thousands. Wam Guir led his men with charisma, swearing like a sailor, with so many colourful phrases flying from his tongue that his men could not help but chuckle even in the midst of battle. Zov Lorr was a more taciturn type, the better fighter, who led by example.

Wam Guir festooned himself with garish garments and had allowed his hair and beard to grow long and wild. Zov Lorr wore tight, gauzy pale vestments better suited to the hot climate, his face and head shaven. Both, in their own way, were masters of their craft, though, thought Jeremias. Wam Guir could evoke greatness from his men with his words alone, encouraging them to walk through fire on his behalf, while Zov Lorr's cold shoulder had his soldiers fighting their hardest just to earn a single rare word of praise.

For some reason Jeremias could not explain, the two got on like a house on fire and fought side by side almost every day, their troops beside them. Jeremias watched Wam Guir save Zov Lorr from a sword in the gut, hammering his huge two-handed axe with butterfly blades into the would-be disemboweller's thigh, eliciting a shrill of pain. He yanked out the axe with a roar and a geyser of gore and buried it in the Justiquan's neck even as he toppled over. Trying to recapture his stuck weapon, however, he was a sitting duck when the next leather-clad crusader topped a ladder and hopped over the battlements to stand before him. Fortunately, Zov Lorr was at hand to parry the blow that would have taken his life and riposte, his exceptionally curved sword – a shamshir – taking his opponent in the face rather than the throat as the man tried to duck. Jeremias winced at the mangled mess the man's face had become and was glad to be free of the sight when Zov Lorr shoved him off the wall.

The Chilpaeans fought for hours every day, not having the numbers to switch out as often as did the Justiquans, and were bone-weary by each dusk. As the sun sank in ignominious flame that evening and the crusaders pulled back to ensconce themselves in their stockade, Jeremias took the stone steps up to the rampart to join General Malone, Bo Yaak, Wam Guir, Zov Lorr and Dreyfuss Alamoigne in staring after their seemingly numberless foes across the meadow of petunias.

"Another day survived," he said as he joined them, knees aching from the climb. "Well done, men. Tremendous work. Truly. Congratulations all around."

"Thank you, seneschal," replied Bo Yaak, ponderous as a bear. "You honour us with your words."

Malone clapped the seneschal on the shoulder and smiled tiredly. "Another day survived."

"It hardly feels like the time for congratulations," said Zov Lorr in his deep, sombre voice. "I lost good men today, just as I did yesterday."

Wam Guir threw an arm around his friend's shoulder. "He's not trying to make light of our losses, Zov, buddy. He's just seeking the silver lining – and I mean, what else is there to do? Every cloud has a silver lining, so they say, and we've got nothing but clouds right now. It's a Gods-damned thunderstorm out there, in fact!"

Zov Lorr glanced up at the clear sky, confused. Wam Guir rolled his eyes.

Jeremias fixed his gaze on the stockade, wondering whether he would see Marshal Clauss in the dreamworld again. When the Sleepers' howls split the night, the Chilpaeans retreated to the haunted safety of the citadel.

22

Ambush at Bessaroca

Borne by the undertow, the smugglers washed up on a coral shore, coughing and spluttering. Jamba Klach realised it was not an ordinary shore as soon as he blinked his eyes clear of water. He could see fish swimming past the windows for one thing, the blue light from their bioluminescent barbels illuminating the palatial bud-shaped coral cavern in which he found himself. He rose and spun around, fly-catching, taking in the curving aquamarine, salmon and fuchsia walls, the high ungulate ceiling, the brimming bookshelves, the cabinets, the table and chairs, the small bed in the corner, the sizzling cauldron set above a fire on a tripod in the middle of the room spewing bluish smoke, and the workbench laid with pouches, herbs, cups, spices, gizzards, mortar and pestle and yellowed parchments. He felt like he was standing inside a tulip.

He stepped out of the water onto the blue and mauve floor, crossed to the window and gazed at the perch and killifish flitting past. Trying to figure out how he was not drowning while on the riverbed surrounded by fish made his head hurt, so he stopped trying and turned to the mysterious woman stirring the cauldron. Her ebon-skinned face was creased with laughter lines, crows' feet, the marks of weather and all the signs of a life well lived. Her long hair was grey and lustrous, tied back in a loose ponytail, and she wore what looked like nothing more than an oversized pillowcase that shielded her from prying eyes from neck to thigh. Her breasts were sagging, her bottom the size of a boulder, and yet she somehow epitomised the word 'handsome' in Jamba's mind. He could think of no other word for her. He could sense the power pulsing from her like ripples in a pond.

He bowed to her. "Mama D'lo? Is that you?"

"So some call me," she replied in a voice husky yet mellifluous, maternal as a hug. "I have had many names over the centuries. Mama D'lo is one of my favourites, though."

"Then, that is how I shall address you," Jamba said, placing a hand on his chest and bowing again. "Thank you, Mama D'lo, from the bottom of my heart for saving our lives. I cannot thank you enough. How can I ever repay you?"

"Yes, thank you!" Lug said, his face and frame free of fur once more, and Ruffle Feathers added his gratitude in letters of flame.

"There is no need for repayment, my child," the woman replied, wafting away the offer with a wrinkly hand. "I am always happy to help my children in the struggle against the cursed outsiders. I only wish I could do more, but these wily Justiquans are surprisingly powerful in the mystic arts."

"Too powerful for a Goddess?" Lug asked without thinking, amazed, and Jamba struck him lightly on the chest in reprimand.

The woman frowned. "A minor Goddess. And I did not say *too* powerful. Not alone, anyway." She held up a finger. "A finger is a finger." She clenched her hand. "But a fist is a fist. See?"

"Yes, of course," Jamba replied, clueless. "So … this is your home?"

"When I need it to be," Mama D'lo replied. "I take many forms, and not all of them require such accommodation."

"Are we at the bottom of the Rio Boae?"

"We are. At the deepest spot in the whole river."

"We are grateful for all you have done," Jamba said, "but is there any way you can help us reach the Monastery Calliope with all haste? We must get the Lullabyer's duppy to his son to teach him the Lullaby. Chilpaea cannot repel the invaders and the Sleepers at the same time."

Mama D'lo hummed thoughtfully. "There is a tributary stretching north. I can take you to its furthest reaches. That is as close to the monastery as I can easily bring you, though, I am afraid. My power resides in the rivers and streams, not on the land." She fixed Jamba with a knowing look. "You're lucky your lagahoo friend here prays to the right people, you know, smuggler. You, on the other hand, can't stop talking about Merejulanna's milk-makers! Despicable."

Jamba blushed and Lug grinned.

"We would be most appreciative if you could take us as far north as you can," Jamba said, feeling his ears burn and trying to ignore Lug elbowing him in the ribs.

Mama D'lo nodded. "You can spend the night here. You'll be safe from the Sleepers in my little hideaway. In the morning, I'll take you to the furthest reaches of the tributary."

"Thank you again."

"That smells delicious," said Lug. "What are you cooking up in there?"

"Supper," replied the mother of rivers with a maternal smile.

The smugglers guzzled down Mama D'lo's delectable fish broth and a barnacled gourd of rum. She bandaged their wounds and they slept deeply and peacefully that night on the hard multicoloured floor of the coral cavern, their dreams for once sweet and free from troubles. They awoke the next morning to the mouth-watering scent of bammy, callaloo, hard dough bread, plantains, ackeee and saltfish. How Mama D'lo had found the ingredients they did not know. Nor did they ask. They wolfed it all down without complaint and moaned with pleasure when the Goddess handed them each a coral cup of piping hot cocoa tea.

Once they were stuffed, Mama D'lo instructed them to submerge themselves in the water once more. No sooner had they done so than they were whisked away by a supernatural current and borne with mind-bending quickness to the far reaches of the Rio Boae's northernmost tributary. Coughing and spluttering, their heads awhirl, the trio washed up on a rocky shore in a jungled gully, inundated by the buzz of wasps and mosquitos and the warbles of cuckoos and parrots overhead in the cloudy morning sky. Mama D'lo was already awaiting them, standing on a mossy boulder nearby.

"This is the end of the Blue Eye tributary," she informed them. "This is as far as I go. North, you'll find the Hook and the monastery. Best of luck, my children. And remember, Chilpaea is counting on you."

With that, she dove into the warm, crystal-clear water of the tributary and was gone in a splash.

"Thank you!" Jamba called after her once he had regained his breath, echoed by Lug.

Discarding their disguises in favour of their usual clothes – which they were thrilled to see that Mama D'lo had somehow cleaned – the sodden smugglers set off uphill through the jungle, passing by palms, ebonies and limes, the floor carpeted here and there by mimosas and fogfruit. Lug whistled a cheerful tune. Ruffle Feathers lit his pipe and produced the shining Lullabyer-shaped crystal from his satchel. Magnuz materialised mid-step beside them, ethereal and composed of glimmering blue and purple light.

"Ah, it feels good to stretch the old legs once again," he said, smiling, stretching out his arms to bask in the dappled sunlight and taking overlong strides. *"Even if I don't have any legs. So, what've I missed since the farmhouse?"*

Jamba filled him in, and the Lullabyer spat a blue-purple glob of phlegm that disappeared the instant it touched the ground.

"Cursed Justiquans!" Magnuz snarled, clenching his fists. *"I'll see them suffer for what they've done!"* He took a deep breath, relaxing his hands, then said, *"D'you know the difference between a Justiquan and a dung beetle?"*

"No," said Jamba. "What's the difference?"

"There isn't one. Both are armoured scum peddling shit."

Sweating under the baleful noon sun, they topped a rise and gazed down on the Hook, the curving promontory extending out west from the northeast corner of the mainland, the far end of which was lost in the distance. The west side of the sloping Hook reared high, cliffs jutting out of the surf, while the east hung low, at sea level in places. Where the promontory began, a fishing village comprised of a cluster of simple timber huts had sprung up on a beach on the east coast. A row of small boats was pulled up on the fine white sand, nets drying nearby in the sun. The Hook was so narrow that there was no way of passing by the village without being seen, save hanging off the western cliff edge like a limpet. So, the smugglers started downhill for the ruin of the village, Bessaroca, necks itching as if they had targets on them as they stepped out of the shade of the jungle and into the open once more. Magnuz reluctantly returned to the depths of the crystal lest he be spotted and give rise to unanswerable questions. As they came closer, they saw that most of the boats had been splintered. From the detritus of the torn down huts and the poorly cleaned bloodstains on the walls of those still standing, the smugglers could tell the Sleepers had ravaged the village. Jamba was surprised it was still standing at all.

"I don't see any Justiquan activity," Jamba said as they entered the village, their approach noted by the few dark-skinned residents but not causing any ruckus. "I guess this place is just too small for them to care about."

Ruffle Feathers waved a hand, conjuring words of flame. 'Unlike Oldport further north. I fear we'll meet far greater resistance there."

Jamba nodded with a sour expression. "At least we should be able to stock up on supplies here. I wouldn't mind some salted fish."

Nodding amicably to the fishermen they passed, the smugglers traipsed through the half-wrecked sandy village to its centre, where the largest structure was hung with a sign proclaiming it the 'Bessaroca Bazaar'. Bazaar was a grand name for what proved essentially to be a log-built tavern coupled with a supply store, Jamba thought, stepping into the shade and running his eyes over the rods, tackle, nets, bait and the bar, behind which a rough-shod woman almost as burly as Lug was cleaning a cup with a dirty rag, her silver hair tied back in a tight bun that drew her ebon-skinned face taut where it was starting to wrinkle. She wore a rum-stained apron and nodded to them as they strolled over to the bar. In gravelly tones, she agreed to get them what they needed. The smugglers paid the woman with doubloons stolen from the treasury beneath Maawu Palace, and she disappeared into a back room stocked with boxes and barrels, returning several minutes later with several full waterskins and a sack full of dried fruit, salted meat and fish, cheese and hardtack.

Stepping back out the door, Jamba remembered to add hard dough bread to the list and doubled back – just in time to witness an ebon-skinned figure in dark breeches and a loose charcoal shirt springing out of the wild ackee and doctorbush framing the Bazaar, twin steel swords poised to come chopping down. Jamba squawked as he was almost split open from tongue to balls and stumbled back out of the way of the blades, toppling down the few flaking white wooden steps leading up to the doorway and bowling over both Lug and Ruffle Feathers.

Trampling his friends in a mad scramble to regain his feet, Jamba yanked his scimitars out of their snakeskin sheaths – at his waist once more, where they ought to be – and surveyed his foe for a split second, a shiver seeking solace in his spine. The straight swords the man bore glittered ominously in the blistering sunlight, looking thinner and lighter than any longswords Jamba had ever seen. The man's stubbly face, like his frame, was wolf-lean, with something of the vulture in his hooked nose and deep, dark eyes. His long raven hair was tied back in a ponytail at his nape so tight that it drew his visage taut as a drum skin, giving him a skull-like mien. Jamba doubted he could frown if he tried.

The would-be killer rushed Jamba wordlessly, evidently hoping to put an end to the conflict before the smugglers could rally. Jamba leaped off his wailing friends to meet the man head on, scimitars whistling through the air to come crashing down on the man's blades in a symphony of ringing steel. The man parried perfectly, shifting into a counterattack with all the grace of flowing water, and Jamba found himself admiring the man's form and footwork even as he feared for his life. He was facing no untrained warrior, he knew. This man was a true swordsman, a master of the craft like Jamba himself. Jamba baited the man, letting him think his counterattack would find the smuggler off-balance, before pirouetting around and under the swipes seeking his throat and lashing out to his right at his enemy as he passed. His swords hit nothing to his surprise, and once more he marvelled at the vulture-faced man's speed, watching as he leaped away with all the grace of a deer. Jamba threw himself at the man in an all-out attack, panic bubbling up inside him as he wondered if he had finally met his match.

Rarely did he meet a foe who could wield dual swords as skilfully as could he. Bearing two blades in battle was a hindrance more than a help to the uninitiated, but to the well-trained ambidextrous warrior it doubled the potential killing output, opening up a whole new world of moves and strategies. The two men ranged through the most well-known of the dual-wield attack patterns to get the measure of one another, their blades chiming time and again as they met as if in a choreographed dance. At first, cutting high and stabbing low, they then inverted the patterns, cutting low and stabbing high, and then – finally, when both had survived the appetiser of swordplay – they introduced the variants to the patterns that both had invented over their years of practice and experience. Their true skills shone through as each was forced to improvise and adapt to unexpected techniques thrown at them by the other.

Jamba fought dirty. He tried every trick he had up his sleeve to throw his enemy off-balance, tripping, punching, elbowing, kicking, kneeing, even spitting. His opponent did not so much as scowl when the spittle flecked his cheek, however. His face was an empty canvas devoid of emotion, while Jamba's rictus would have made a dead man envious. Sweating buckets,

Jamba forced his tiring body into the most flamboyant of the attack patterns he had ever devised, leaping and twirling with fatal speed, his swords flashing in circles in the sun, scything the air as his attacker sprang back to reassess. Jamba finally came to a halt, breathing hard, and the assassin darted in with his own schemes and sly styles.

Jamba's patterns were colourful pictures of intricate passion. His foe's were a blank canvas with only enough direction to craft an image. The man had stripped the mechanisms of fighting down to their bare bones, removing all that was fluff. What remained was a wolf-lean killing machine. Not a single step was taken or move made that did not help him try to kill Jamba. His every breath was taken to the purpose and, stripped of all the flourishes, his swordplay was fast – scarily fast, thought Jamba, watching the man's swords flicker in his periphery again and again and only just catching them in time to prevent them from plunging deep into his flesh. The would-be assassin's wiry muscles bunched to propel him with the force of a tossed spear at the smuggler over and over, and Jamba watched in horror as the wide open path to victory transformed into a crumbling precipice.

Finally, tiredness won out. Jamba ducked a vicious swipe aimed to take his head from his shoulders, but slipped in the sand as he tried to reposition and was flat on his back before he knew what had happened. His enemy loomed over him, silhouetted against the endless blue sky, swords raised for the killing blow, and Jamba felt peace settle over him like a shroud. It looked as though sleep had found him at long last. It was about time, he thought.

Fire flashed before Jamba's blinking eyes, and his foe was forced to back away or else be incinerated by the letters of flame that swam into existence, crackling and whooshing, hovering in the air above the fallen smuggler, proclaiming, 'Kill my friend and I will tear you apart limb from limb.'

Jamba's attacker's mouth hung open at the sight of the words for a moment. He recovered quickly, though, and peered past them to where Ruffle Feathers and Lug had regained their feet.

"This is your doing, then?" he asked Ruffle in a high-pitched, twangy voice, indicating the words with a jab of his sword.

Ruffle nodded, brows drawn together in a thunderous expression. He waved his hand, and the words of flame faded away only to be replaced by more.

'I can summon a demon with a thought that will flay the skin from your still living body purely for pleasure, so stay back unless you wish to experience the most horrific demise a demonic mind can envisage.'

The man with two swords smirked. "You are Jamba Klach, Ruffle Feathers and Lug Thorm, are you not?"

"No, the fellows you're looking for just left," said Jamba, panting on the ground and pointing. "If you hurry south, you might be able to catch them."

Ruffle Feathers waved a hand, and Jamba felt sick as he watched words burn into existence in mid-air. 'We are. Who are you?'

"I am Kofi Touluz, called 'Skinner' by some. Seneschal Jeremias Colcott has authorised me to confiscate the Lullabyer crystal from you and return it to him at Jinglespur by any means necessary. Hand it over and there need be no more … unpleasantness."

"Kofi Touluz?" Lug repeated slowly, tapping a broad finger on his lantern jaw. "The Skinner? The assassin?"

"*You* work for Colcott?" Jamba asked, propping himself up on his elbows, voice laden with scepticism.

Kofi Touluz cocked his head. "I work for whoever pays me. Now, be good chaps and hand over the crystal."

Ruffle waved a hand. 'We are on a quest at the Lullabyer's behest to bring his spirit to his son at the Monastery Calliope to save all of Chilpaea from the threat of the Sleepers. We cannot give up the crystal now. You may tell Jeremias that the crystal will be returned when the time is right.'

"I am no messenger boy!" Touluz snarled, brandishing his blades. "I will not return empty-handed. Give me the crystal."

Ruffle Feathers' satchel glowed with an unearthly light, brighter and brighter, until a blinding flash made all present shield their eyes for a moment. When they uncovered them, a man formed of pulsing cobalt and lavender light stood before them, glittering like the sky at night, ethereal as smoke. His face was sharp as the rocks off the coast, softened by a clipped beard and surmounted by a severe topknot.

"Lullabyer!" gasped Kofi Touluz, swords hanging slack.

"Do you serve Colcott or do you serve me?" Magnuz Opherio demanded of the assassin, drawing himself up. *"Chilpaea is in peril, Kofi Touluz, and I need your help to save it."*

It was then that Jamba finally took notice of the villagers rushing past them, some giving the Lullabyer a perplexed look, some unmindful, all dashing into the Bazaar.

One woman carrying a baby halted and said, "Get inside, you fools! The Sleepers will be here soon!"

The Lullabyer glanced up at the purpling sky, before returning his cool gaze to the assassin. *"What will it be, Touluz?"*

Kofi bowed sarcastically. "Long live the Lullabyer."

23

Izulu

The last few minutes of blood-dipped sunlight that day found the smugglers sniffing spice and barricading themselves in the Bessaroca Bazaar along with the rest of the villagers. Having endured a week of Sleeper attacks, the villagers, led by the meaty woman in the rum-stained apron who owned the Bazaar, had cobbled together a simple survival strategy – hide in the biggest, sturdiest building, surrounded by torches.

"Are these folk all that remain?" Jamba Klach whispered to the woman, Brenda Bree, affectionately known as Big Brenda.

Big Brenda nodded, her silver bun bobbing. "Some fled for Dos Rios or Oldport when the attacks began. But yes, this is all the folks who have survived the past week – those that chose to stay."

His heart heavy, Jamba counted perhaps thirty people in a village that had once housed a couple of hundred. "And the Sleepers have never managed to break in here?"

Big Brenda shook her head, honing a machete on a whetstone with long rasping strokes. "Not yet they haven't. And if'n they do, we'll make 'em pay." She waved her blade. "These walls are thick, built to last."

Jamba ran his eyes over the boards nailed over the windows and the makeshift barricade by the door, comprised of stacked, turned over tables and chairs. The doors had long since been torn clear. Unlike most of the thatched huts, the Bazaar's roof was shingled. A few children huddled behind the bar with the women. The light from the circle of torches outside flickered through the cracks in the boards over the haggard, fearful faces of the men stood by the windows and door, one or two with rusty swords, the rest bearing daggers, hatchets and clubs.

"Jamba, you're with me by the door," said Kofi Touluz. "Ruffle, stand behind us. Lug, cover that window on the left."

"Whoah whoah whoah," said Jamba, waving his hands. "I give the orders here. Just who d'you think you are?"

Kofi shrugged, expressionless. "I was just trying to be helpful. But fine. Where would you have us, oh great master?"

Jamba considered this, fuming. It made sense for him and Kofi, being the most skilful warriors, to stand by the doorway where the fighting would be thickest. Equally, it made sense for Ruffle Feathers to hang back. The only part of Kofi's plan that Jamba could change was Lug's placement, so he cleared his throat and said, "Kofi, you and me by the door, with Ruffle behind us to provide support. Lug, cover that window on the *right*, please."

Lug Thorm nodded amicably. "Will do, boss."

Kofi rolled his eyes. The glow around the edge of the boarded-up windows was fading fast.

"Can you summon a demon, Ruffle?" Jamba asked quietly. "Djhuty perhaps?"

Ruffle put away his pipe, nodded and waved a hand. 'I will try. Look after these people, will you? They're good folk.'

His words of fire still made a few villagers flinch, but most had gotten used to it now. It was far from top of their priorities. Ruffle promptly sat on the floor, cross-legged, and closed his eyes to attune his mind to the task. Jamba nodded to himself; he knew what the old man meant. The obeahman knew, as did he, that without them, without the completion of their quest, these people could not hold out indefinitely. They would soon be dead.

Overhearing him, one of the villagers, a thickset man with a bushy beard and a hatchet, leaned over to ask, "A demon? What in the name of Kagen's ass do you mean, summon a demon?"

Hearing the man's less than subtle voice, the ebon-skinned villagers rounded on the smugglers with shocked visages and Jamba raised his empty hands to placate them.

"My friend, Ruffle Feathers, is an obeahman," he explained, loud enough for all to hear. "He is capable of summoning – *and controlling* – entities from other worlds, conjuring them forth to do his bidding. You will all be perfectly safe from any creature he summons, I assure you, and with his help perhaps we can all make it through the night unscathed, eh? We are Chilpaeans, the strongest of folk. We do not yield to crusaders. We do not yield to Sleepers. We stick together. And we fight. Right?" A few murmurs of agreement met his words, though still some troubled glances were thrown Ruffle's way. "So, stick with me, good people, and we'll survive the night, I promise."

"Hear hear!" one man cried, and then the rest were cheering mutedly.

Jamba smiled sheepishly at the applause. Kofi rolled his eyes again.

"I miss the Lullaby," said Lug as he watched the sun sink beneath the horizon.

Jamba nodded. "Don't we all."

The first gut-churning yowls of the Sleepers cracked the quiet of the night not long later, making the children whimper.

Hearing skittering on the sand outside, Jamba yelled nervously over his shoulder, "Ruffle, now would be a good time to do something!"

He got no reply, save the shifting of shadows in the gloaming. From the scurrying sounds, the growling and the pained hissing, he knew the Sleepers were ringing the hut, trying to extinguish the circle of tall, frond-wrapped torches planted in the sand. Their capricious light illuminated shaggy hides now and then, segmented legs and scaly tails. A storm descended on the village in a fury, booming and bellowing, crackling with lightning and seething with rain. The torches spluttered out one by one beneath the tempest's roar, and darkness abounded, its total dominion prevented solely by the few candles in the Bazaar flickering in the howling gale coming in through the doorway.

The children screamed, and Ruffle Feathers' satchel, tossed into the corner behind the bar, shone like a violet star was trapped within. A light flashed, seen only by the blinking children, and the Lullabyer materialised before them, ethereal as smoke, twinkling like the night sky, and formed entirely of blue and purple light. The children did not scream, only gawped.

The Lullabyer smiled down at them, kneeling by their side. *"This storm is awfully loud, isn't it? Hello. My name is Magnuz. I was once the Lullabyer, you know, ruler of the entire island."*

The children were not convinced until their mothers swayed them. Magnuz would forever wonder why the mothers had been so accepting of his appearance. He supposed nothing could surprise them anymore, and in their state of shock they were willing to accept anything that improved their lot even a little. Some appeared to recognise him, too.

He asked gently, *"Would you like to hear a story to pass the time until morning, children? I'm sure I know more than a few."*

"Yes!" gasped one of the children, a boy with an unruly mop evidently desperate for distraction. "Please, tell us a story!"

"Very well," said Magnuz in the long-honoured lilting tones of the storyteller. *"Once upon a time, a band of smugglers set out to steal the Lullabyer's carefully collected treasure. What they didn't know, however ..."*

"Get ready!" Jamba shouted as the skittering drew nearer and nearer.

A slobbering horror, all black fur and rows of sharp teeth, threw itself onto the barricade by the door, growling and slobbering and trying to claw its way inside. Jamba sprang forward to skewer it, only to find his way blocked by Kofi, who coolly slid one of his swords into the beast's neck, behind its flower-like face, making it yelp and retreat into the night, its blood staining the barricade.

"Stay out of my way!" Jamba growled, and Kofi gave him a quizzical look.

Jamba knew he was being petty, but he did not care. The sight of the assassin who had so nearly killed him irked him like an itch he could not scratch. Big Brenda took the next one, burying her machete deep into one of the petals that served as the monster's jaws, sending its blood spraying through the air. The crippled creature hurriedly backed out of harm's way, but its companions were not long in taking its place. As the storm intensified, the doorway became clogged with huge, shaggy Sleepers, all pawing and gnawing at the tables and chairs in their way, trying to scamper over them to get to the juicy meat inside.

Jamba finally saw a chance to wet his blade and shuffled forward to hack at one of the horrors, hoping to cleave open its skull. It slipped on the chair it was stuck on, and he gave it only a glancing blow, almost kneecapping Big Brenda by his side as his sword ricocheted away. He gave her an apologetic look.

"Their bones are strong as steel. You should try finding a weak spot to attack," Kofi advised, stabbing a Sleeper in the collar and making Jamba grind his teeth in vexation.

Spitefully, Jamba brought his sword down on the creature's head again, jarring his arm as though he had struck an ironwood tree. Gritting his teeth and telling himself it was his own idea, he slashed open one of the beast's petal-jaws, making it growl in pain and flinch to one side, before stabbing it deep in the neck. As the monster lurched back out onto the beach, it almost ripped his sword from his grasp and Jamba was pulled onto the barricade as he tried to hold on.

A Sleeper pounced before he could recover his balance, and he saw blessed sleep inside its rows of fangs. Kofi Touluz smacked it back with both blades, using brute force to save Jamba's life. Regaining his footing, Jamba nodded his thanks to the assassin, though the nod stuck in his craw, burning like bile. Kofi ignored him, continuing to calmly slit open Sleeper after Sleeper with his blurring blades. On his other side, Big Brenda whacked any Sleeper that came too close with her machete, using sheer brawn to bully them back.

Jamba tried to help, but his mind was hazy with the after-effects of too much witch-spice. His arms felt numb as bricks after his duel with Kofi, and he struggled to focus even when his life was on the line. He forced himself to stay standing though all he wanted to do was take a nap, forced himself to hack and stab at his enemy again and again though he could barely see them through sleep-crusted eyes. He was slow in reacting to one Sleeper leaping onto the barricade, and the monster was able to yank one of the villagers, a man with a dagger, out into the night. Jamba winced as he heard the man's screams followed by the sounds of bones snapping and guts being guzzled in the darkness, just out of sight.

He was not the last to fall.

As another man was stolen from the Bazaar, Jamba croaked hoarsely, "Ruffle, we need your help! Please!"

Behind him, Ruffle Feathers painted invisible arcane charms in the air with his gnarly fingertips and the women and children behind the bar gasped as a fiery-edged rift ripped open the curtain between worlds in the middle of the Bazaar, gushing purple flames and sulphuric smoke. The women screamed and hid the children's eyes when a monstrous pit-black bird the size of an ape came cawing through the rift, flexing talons, snapping its silver beak, swishing its barbed, scorpion-like tail back and forth and fixing the obeahman with a blood-red glare. It flapped wide feathery wings to hover, at the end of which large crimson claws clenched and unclenched. The rift sewed itself shut behind the demon with a *pop.*

"What would you have of me, master? *Kakaw!*" the bird squawked in metallic Traveller's.

'Where is Djhuty?' Ruffle asked in blazing letters hanging in mid-air.

"He sends me in his stead," the demon bird replied. "I am Izulu. *Kakaw!* Djhuty told me fine feasts await in this world."

Ruffle frowned, but waved a hand. 'Your feast awaits you outside, Izulu. Kill the black, furry monsters on the beach, but leave my friends be!'

Izulu bobbed its raven-plumed head, beat its wings once and soared out of the Bazaar above the intruding Sleepers' heads, disappearing in a blink into the night as if it was kin. Frowning and wondering if he had been ripped off, Ruffle Feathers gasped when lightning smote a Sleeper down on the beach outside in a bright flash. The lightning had not been golden, however. It had been the colour of blood, the colour of Izulu's eyes.

Ruffle grinned as he beheld the demon bird swoop down over the Sleeper horde outside, illuminating and scorching the beasts with bolts of crimson lightning spat from its long beak. As it passed over the throng again and again, the obeahman saw more and more Sleeper corpses piling up on the sand. A shaft of moonlight broke free of the storm during a lull, and the old man witnessed the bird perched atop a heap of shaggy corpses, tearing at them with its beak and throwing back its head to swallow their flesh before more Sleepers chased it away and it took to the air with a disgruntled screak once more. The lone demon could not cull the entire herd, however, and no matter how many it killed, it could not dissuade the brainless monsters from seeking to tear their way into the Bazaar like bears trying to reach honey.

The smugglers and villagers were granted little reprieve. By the door, Jamba, Kofi and Big Brenda fought fiercely to protect their own, cleaving down beast after beast on the barricade until the carcasses were piled high, hearts panging every time one of the men was snatched out of the door. The boards over the windows were soon smashed in as the horrors tried to force their way in through apertures too small for them, and Lug and the villagers had their hands full slaughtering Sleepers to prevent them from widening the windows to the point that they could slink inside.

By morning, Jamba was convinced a lack of sleep was taking its toll on him. He had felt clumsy and ill-coordinated all night, having to be saved from certain death time and again by both Kofi and Big Brenda. Eyes leaden, he thanked them both by the tangerine light of the morning rays, while Izulu plucked out dead Sleepers' eyeballs nearby. In the faint dawn light, the dead Sleepers seemed surreal, as if such a strange meld of creatures could not exist. Eyeing their creepy insectoid legs, reptilian tails and hairy, flower-like jaws, Jamba shuddered.

"Come with us to Oldport," he said to Big Brenda as the two stood on the beach outside the bazaar, making one last-ditch effort to convince the woman. "You'll be safer there."

Big Brenda shook her head and spat on the sand. "It's full of Justiquans, so they say. Ain't no safer there than we are here. No, I think we'll stay, thank you. This is our home, and we'll fight for it to the last man. Or woman."

Privately, Jamba thought that would likely be in but a few days' time, but aloud he said, "Very well. Good luck, Brenda. El Vandu bless you."

Ruffle Feathers conjured a fiery rift for Izulu to return to whatever demonic plane he called home.

Before it left, the demon bird cawed, *"Kakaw!* My thanks for the feast, human. I will not suck out your brains through your eyeballs this night. Perhaps Djhuty was right. Perhaps you *are* worth keeping alive. *Kakaw!* So long, human! Until we meet again."

Ruffle bowed with a wry smile, and the demon swooped through the rift before it closed.

Then, along with Kofi Touluz, the smugglers put Bessaroca behind them as the rising sun gilded the ocean and the remaining villagers – little more than a score of them – started dragging the corpses of the Sleepers down the beach to be washed away by the tide, leaving long red smears in the sand. The air was fresh once they escaped the bitter aroma of death and decay, as if cleansed by the storm. The seagulls' caws were interspersed here and there by the harsher cries of the turkey vultures feasting on the rotting flesh of the slain Sleepers.

The smugglers spied a Justiquan patrol down the road ahead of them towards noon – a mounted officer in steel plate and a score of infantry in leather – but did not change course. There was nowhere to hide anyway. The dirt trail they trod ran down the middle of the Hook with nothing on either side for leagues but scrubland interrupted only by a few stunted, leaning trees up on the western clifftops.

Ruffle Feathers summoned a swarm of demons that coalesced from smog spewed from his fingertips, and the killer bats rolled over the crusaders like a black wave, shredding anything and anyone in their path, gnawing through cloth, leather, flesh, bone, even steel armour as if it were soft as rotten fruit. The officer's scream was cut off abruptly as the demons coated him like a second skin, and the infantry shrieked in horror and scattered at the sight of his fleshless skeleton a few seconds later. They did not get far. Those that fled north, east or west were eventually found by the demon bats. Those few that ran south, hoping to cut through the smugglers and find their way to freedom, were mown down like wheat by Jamba, Kofi and Lug. The smugglers encountered no more resistance on the road after that.

24

Jungle of Dreams

"I have been having the strangest dreams of late," said Jeremias Colcott as he dug at the earth inside Jinglespur Necropolis with his bare hands, the dirt gritty under his fingertips.

"Oh?" said Waddi-waddi, raising an eyebrow.

"Dreams of memories not my own, of places I have never visited, people I have never met, emotions I have never felt."

"It is an effect of the dreamworld," said the necromancer quickly. "So many dreams impinge upon your own, because you invite them by attuning yourself more and more to the land of the dead."

Jeremias nodded unsurely. "I guess that makes sense."

"How go your exercises?"

"Very well, thank you. They help me meditate. My mind is a blank slate as I go through the motions."

"Good ... good. Keep it up. It will help more than you know."

Jeremias unearthed a human skull and held it up to the faint scarlet light rimming the horizon so that phantom rain speckled it faintly. "I found one."

"Excellent," said Waddi-waddi, clapping his hands. "And do you sense its energies? There is power in bones, a small modicum of the spirit left behind in the physical remains."

Jeremias studied the skull and shook his head. "I don't sense anything. It's just a skull."

Waddi-waddi shook his head disappointedly. "Nothing is as it seems in the dreamworld, Jeremias. Remember that. Very well, I suppose you are not yet ready. I had hoped you would be a faster student, but it appears we will have to accelerate the process."

"What do you mean?" asked Jeremias, gently placing the skull down where he had dug it up and standing to face his mentor with furrowed brow.

"I mean we have no time left for me to teach you. The Justiquan marshal will kill you here in the dreamworld if you do not learn to protect yourself. There are those who thrive under pressure. I suspect you are one such person, Jeremias, so I am going to apply some pressure. Don't beat yourself up – I'm much the same myself."

The necromancer grinned, snatched the seneschal's hand and flew, quick as a blink, out beyond Jinglespur's curving wall, only stopping once they were out of sight of the necropolis entirely, lost in a jungle of dreams.

"It's time to sink or swim," said Waddi-waddi, releasing the

seneschal's hand and smling wickedly. "Find your own way home, seneschal, or you are no longer worth my time."

With that, he turned and disappeared into the horizon in a heartbeat. Jeremias gave frantic chase, but before he could get far, he slammed face first into a monster as tall as the sky, a demonic bear with horns and spikes and fangs and long claws. It roared with ear-shattering volume and swatted Jeremias out of the sky with a hefty paw. The seneschal didn't even have time to scream. He only grunted as he hit the earth hard and lay there, wheezing.

At first, he was sure he was going to die. He could not fight a bear as big as that. It was impossible. He hated Waddi-waddi in that moment.

He could not give up, though. His people needed him. So, he pushed himself to his feet and watched the bear slowly advance on him, thinking. This was the dreamworld. Here, the dreamer controlled the dreams. And that was all this bear was – a figment of the sleeping mind, a terror conjured to life.

"How do you slay a nightmare?" he had once asked the necromancer.

Waddi-waddi had replied, "By turning it into a dream."

He was the dreamer, and this was the dreamworld, Jeremias told himself. He had the power here. He wondered how Waddi-waddi had summoned the staff of light to fight Marshal Clauss and decided it must have been a spirit weapon, conjured straight out of the psyche. If Waddi-waddi could do it, then so could he.

Ignoring the bear's stomping footsteps as it drew nearer and concentrating hard on the recalled sensation of a sword hilt in his hand, Jeremias breathed slowly and deeply, letting the sensation of the sword in his hand consume his mind until he was absolutely certain that he did, in fact, hold a sword in his hand. He opened his eyes to behold a scimitar clasped in his fist, glowing an ethereal white.

He grinned. "You're in for it now, bear!"

Flying back up into the air by the power of his will, Jeremias circled the bear's great head like a vulture, darting in now and then to slash at an ear with his blazing white sword before rapidly retreating to dodge the swiping paw that inevitably came for him. This continued for some time until Jeremias noticed that, though he was opening glowng white wounds in the bear's head, they were healing as quickly as they formed. He was doing no lasting damage.

Frowning, Jeremias was about to launch a more concerted assault when another thought struck him. The sword was a dream – he had summoned it himself. The bear, too, was a dream, summoned by a frightened sleeping mind – probably one of those within the walls of the necropolis. Jeremias took a deep breath and told himself the bear was nothing but a figment of his imagination. Seeing the bear's paw coming for him once more, he squeezed shut his eyes, imagining a cuddly little teddy bear in the monster's place. A few seconds later, having not been struck, he cracked open an eye to peer out and gasped at the sight of a sentient teddy bear on the ground, waving at him and smiling amicably.

Jeremias descended to pick it up and stroke it with a wry smile. "There, you're not so scary, are you?"

The bear shook its little head. Patting it and setting it down, Jeremias flew back up into the air and continued on his way through the land of the dead with a proverbial spring in his step and a whistle on his lips. He wasn't sure he was going the right way, but figured one way was as good as another in the dreamword. He would end up where he wanted to be, because he was the dreamer. The journey proved far from easy, however, and he encountered a medley of night terrors along the way. Sometimes, though he had been flying over the shifting shadows of nightmares, he would suddenly find himself not flying at all, but snared in the web of some poor tortured soul's bad dream. One second, he would be flying contentedly; the next, he would be stuck, buried in the ground or trapped in a tree hollow with a whole swarm of bugs crawling over him, trying to creep into his mouth, eyes, ears and nose. Once, he even found himself falling for no reason, fear of being dashed on the ground like a dropped snail welling in his heart. Normally, he had no fear of heights, though, and guessed he was afflicted by the dream itself, or the dreamer.

He dug his way out of the ground when buried with the help of a shovel he manifested from nowhere and cut his way free of the creep-crawly-ridden tree hollow with a shining white sword. When falling, he found he no longer remembered how to fly, but it did not matter. He transformed the hard flat ground awaiting him into a cushion on which he landed gently.

Other nightmares, more external in nature, plagued him, too. A pack of lions came loping towards him along the clouds as if they provided solid footing. Raptorial birds attacked him from on high, and maggots squirmed out of an apple when he stopped to pick one from a tree. When he dropped the apple and tried to flee, a boa constrictor sprang out of the branches to wrap its thick body around him and begin to squeeze him to death. A murder of duppy even cornered him against the ground, filling the slate-grey sky. Jeremias petted the lions as kittens when they approached him and fed the preying birds crumbs that he summoned from nowhere as he had done the ducks on the shore of the Agua Alta many times. Feeling his ribs creak and crack in his chest upon being entangled by the boa, Jeremias had hastily assured himself it was but a too-tight coat and, sure enough, upon squeezing shut his eyes and reopening them, he found himself wearing a coat made from snakeskin. When the duppy cornered him, it was but the work of a moment to imagine them as sentient storm clouds and then stroll through their deluge unharmed.

The scenery changed with every passing heartbeat, tableaus flickering in and out of existence, ever in flow. Hills transformed into plains and then reared up into mountains, only to sink into gulfs and then sink even deeper until they formed lakes of lava in the centre of the world. Rivers gushed into streams, and oceans shrank into lakes, and bountiful forests thrived a heartbeat from barren deserts. Once, he even saw Jinglespur ahead, but somehow knew instanty it was not the true necropolis. This one was a caricature of the place, leering at him with scorning eyes and towers for teeth. Painting it in calico, he had sauntered, grinning, through a pantomime, playing up to the troubadours and actors who materialised from thin air.

All manner of creatures, real and apocryphal, scurried through the necropolis, forest, hills, mountains, gulfs and dunes. Jeremias stumbled across numerous monsters for which he had no name. Upon morphing one such beast with two heads, six eyes, four horns and eighteen legs into a bunny rabbit, which hopped away, fluffy tail bouncing, the seneschal turned to see that he stood in Maawu Palace before the Lullabyer – and he was naked. For a moment, a wave of embarrassment washed him under, but then he smiled wryly and reclothed himself with a thought, the apparition of a stern Magnuz Opherio fading as fast as it had formed, as did Maawu Palace behind him, drifting away like smoke on the wind.

Joy and imagination his twin swords, the seneschal battled his way through a horde of nightmares and finally saw Jinglespur silhouetted against the blood-red horizon, recognising it this time as the true necropolis by instinct. Surging towards it both on foot and in the air, depending on where the fantasies dictated he be, he broke free of the jungle of dreams and soared over Jinglespur's spoked wall with a sigh of relief.

As he did so, a figure flitted down from the sky and almost took off his head with a blazing white sword. Yelping in alarm, Jeremias veered aside and cried out when the sword raked his arm. Flying as fast as he could, he made for the citadel and his body. The assailant gave chase. Glancing over his shoulder as he went, Jeremias recognised the man as Marshal Clauss and cursed inwardly, fearing he would die at the crusader's hands thanks to Waddi-waddi's foolishness. Fear stuck in his craw, and the marshal overtook him, blocking the way to the citadel so that Jeremias had to come to a halt. Snarling in anger at his imminent demise, the seneschal conjured his own scimitar of bright white light from a fantasy and awaited the Justiquan's onslaught.

Marshal Clauss bore down on him with the inevitability of the passing ages, and Jeremias could not escape. He felt slow and old. No matter where he turned to flee, Clauss stood in his way. Crossing swords with the marshal, the seneschal felt the weight of despair dragging him down. He could not keep up with the crusader's swordplay, and Clauss' sword snuck past his guard again and again to nip his shoulder, his legs and his side. In an emotional nadir, he realised the marshal was toying with him, as a cat does a mouse.

Clauss battled him back away from the citadel, sneering, "I was wondering where you had gone, Colcott. It's time for you to pay for those insults you cast my way!"

So saying, he laid open Jeremias' chest and pulled back his blade for the final thrust. Gasping in agony, the seneschal blinked in surprise when his would-be killer was abruptly borne away from him by a blur. His eyes widened when he saw that the blur was Waddi-waddi, and the ancient necromancer was once more pitted against the marshal in a dream duel.

Ephemeral sparks burst from their scraping swords, and Waddi-waddi screamed, "Flee, Jeremias! Back to your body at once!"

The seneschal needed no further prompting. He turned away and sped back into the citadel, ghosting through the walls like a duppy until he found his body and dipped his soul back inside.

Waking with a start, sweaty and shivering with Waddi-waddi's death cry lingering in his ears, Jeremias tried to rise and grunted as agony lanced through his body from the wounds Clauss had instilled. Lifting his tunic, he studied his chest. No wound showed there, but the pain remained. Jeremias lay back and tried to think positively. He was not truly hurt, he told himself. It was only the remnants of his dream percolating in his mind ...wasn't it? Marshal Clauss had haunted his dreamwalks night after night of late, waiting for him out in the murk of the spirit world. Most every night, Waddi-waddi saved the seneschal at the cost of his own life, and always the nexy day the necromancer was ready to teach again – for as long as they had before the crusader found them.

By the time the pain from his phantom wounds had faded, the sun had sailed past its peak. Jeremias shambled past the crazed caracoling crowds and out of the citadel into a dim drizzle to witness fewer warriors than ever before manning the necropolis wall, to a man engaged with the Justiquans essaying a coup. Jeremias saw a few bodies at the base of the wall and wandered over to where a few civilians had volunteered to clear away the corpses, trying to ignore the ignominious trails of blood left behind the bodies as they were carried away on makeshift stretchers. The laments of the wounded under the ministration of the few healers they had rang in the seneschal's ears, making him wince in pity. Everything was wet – just as it was in his dreams. The line between dreams and reality blurred in his mind, and he wondered if he could still fly.

The seneschal's gloomy spirits lifted a little at the sight of General Malone and Dreyfuss Alamoigne at the heart of the defence, the former hollering orders and the second protecting him as he did so, his spear striking with snakelike speed. Further along the wall, Zov Lorr and his troops from the town of Jawduck swam in perilous straits where a boulder had smashed the battlements and left a deep and jagged groove in the top of the wall. The crusaders had completed construction on siege weapons inside their stockade the day before and rolled them out in plain view under scorching sunlight to point them at Jinglespur. No warning had been given. The catapults and ballistae had simply started to fire, sending boulders slamming into the pit-black wall while huge bolts tore men off the rampart. The wall had shuddered and crumbled under the impact, and Jeremias had once seen two men pronged by the same bolt. He worried the ancient necropolis could not hold out for long against such powerful weapons.

Justiquans were swarming up ladders onto the parapet where a boulder had struck, and Zov Lorr and his men were struggling to fight their way down to the ladders to prevent the breach from growing any larger, unable to find decent footing on the uneven part of the rampart, where stones slid out easily from underfoot, sending both Justiquans and Chilpaeans plummeting to their deaths. Jeremias watched with his heart in his mouth, wondering if this was the end for their last stand as Zov himself leaped into the breach, shamshir swinging faster than the seneschal's eye could follow and laying steel-plate-clad knights low left and right in the blink of an eye. Blood jetted from severed jugulars, and slit visages spied through helmets.

One of the knights managed to catch the Jawduck captain's sword on his own then, however, and punched Zov Lorr hard in the face with a gauntleted fist, almost knocking him off the wall as stones crumbled underfoot. Fortunately, the shifting stone worked in Zov's favour, giving him a second to retreat while the knight wobbled. The captain looked dazed, Jeremias thought – as well he might after such a blow. Zov's men tried to pick up the slack left by their captain, but the breach had formed and, like a cancerous growth, was growing larger and larger by the minute as more and more Justiquans climbed the ladders and gained the broken section of rampart.

Fortunately, Jeremias was not the only one who had witnessed Zov Lorr's plight. Wam Guir hurtled past his friend, roaring at the top of his lungs, and flung himself on the crusaders with a wild war cry, invoking Galush-Kagen, the God of Blood. His double-headed axe hummed out in wide, sweeping arcs to occasionally lop off heads or arms but more often simply whacking Justiquans off their precarious footing to fall to the ground far below with loud clangs. Zov's men, heartened by the display of bravery, rushed to the captain's aid. They jumped down on the Justiquans, uncaring of the swords pointed up at them, batting the blades out of the way and bearing the crusaders down so that they could be pinioned or stamped to death. Wam Guir fought in the thick of it, yelling inarticulately as he bashed in helmets and dented cuirasses with his blunting blade.

Jeremias watched the tide turn with a dawning sense of relief. Zov

Lorr leaped back into the fray then, his shamshir whining as it slaughtered. Together, Wam Guir and Zov Lorr skirmished their way to the ladders, clearing the sundered parapet of foes and pushing the ladders back off the wall so that those still climbing fell to their deaths, or at least ended up with a bruise or two. Jeremias managed a small smile as he watched Wam Guir heft his axe high in the air and holler in victory, rain pitter-pattering his wild mane.

The seneschal's smile vanished as his gaze flicked still further down the wall just in time to behold a ballista bolt impale a defender in a spray of blood, casting him off the wall to land mere yards away from Jeremias and skid to a halt. Up on the rampart, the mayor of Hatbrim, Bo Yaak, bellowed in fury at the loss of one of his men and charged headlong into a breach rapidly forming on the wall to vent his wrath. His glaive scythed through the Justiquans trying to form up with surprising speed for a polearm, thwacking and hacking, stabbing and shoving. His men vied to stay by his side as he pushed into the midst of the enemy, swords swinging frantically. They could not keep up with their bear of a leader, however.

Soon, Bo Yaak fought alone, an island in a sea of knights. Still, he did not succumb, but used his glaive to maximum effect, slitting throats and thighs with the long, curved blade and smacking back foes with the haft. The crusaders sought in vain to pierce the whirling weapon's defence, and Jeremias watched in awe as the mayor wrought carnage among them, ploughing straight through them all the way to the battlements, where he threw down the last of them with the help of his soldiers and cast away the ladders leaning on the wall. He threw up his arms and grinned, and then a boulder careened into him, killing him instantly.

Jeremias covered his mouth with his hands in shock, shaking. One second, the mayor had been there, alive as alive can be. The next, he was gone along with a swathe of his men, the section of rampart where they had been standing brutalised and broken. Jeremias turned to behold the boulder as it rolled to a stop in the middle of Jinglespur alongside so many others. He saw a smear of blood on it and hastily looked away lest he vomit. He puked anyway. If the siege weapons' barrage kept up much longer, he knew the Chilpaeans holed up in the necropolis would be done for.

25

Demon Spawn

Oldport, a sprawling town on the Hook sloping down to the sea, had once been the hub of northern Chilpaean trade, harbouring a hundred ships a day from the Sultanate, Swash Isle, Zamphia and Al Kutz. No longer. As the town of Dos Rios to the south grew, it absorbed all of Oldport's business, being more centrally located, until Oldport became a ghost town, harbouring but a few fishermen. No longer.

Now, seen by the smugglers ensconced among the rocks on the Hook's western bluff, the whitewashed town was abuzz with activity. Jamba Klach watched in disbelief as his countrymen, chained wrist and ankle, were prodded onto huge Justiquan ships at spearpoint by the crusaders in their scores. He followed the line of dark-skinned prisoners with his eyes from the docks far below on the east coast all the way through the town to Urugulu Prison up on the west coast, carved into the cliffs. The groups of prisoners were escorted every step of the way by armed and armoured knights, while the populace thronged the streets in protest, howling their fury and pelting the crusaders with rocks, rotten fruit and even dung as their loved ones were taken away.

Jamba eyed the overcast sky uneasily; they did not have long before the sun set. "If we're going down there, we'd better do it sooner rather than later. Perhaps we can slip through the town while the Justiquans are distracted by the riot."

Words of fire blocked him as he started to move. 'We have to help our imprisoned countrymen!'

Jamba turned back to face Ruffle Feathers. "But what about our quest? We *are* helping them by putting a stop to the Sleepers!"

Ruffle crossed his arms, jaw set, and Jamba sighed. "You're right, of course, my friend. We should help our countrymen. Come on. Let's get down there before dark. It's got to be safer in the city than out here after sundown – crusaders or no crusaders."

"Is this how you always do things?" asked Kofi Touluz, following as Jamba started sneaking through the rocks. "Just charge in pell-mell with no plan of any sort whatsoever?"

"I have a plan," said Jamba without turning. "We're going to take that prison. Looks like the safest place to spend the night. Want some spice, Lug?"

The lagahoo nodded his assent, grabbed a pinch from the leather pouch when Jamba offered it and sniffed it noisily.

Following suit, Jamba let out a soft, "Wooh!" as a jolt like lightning shook his entire body and his eyes came into razor-sharp focus.

He felt as if he could lift boulders and outrun wolves. His fingertips tingled with energy.

"May I have some?" Kofi asked politely.

Jamba narrowed his eyes at the assassin, then grudgingly offered him the pouch.

All roads into Oldport were fortified with earthworks and barricades and watched over by squadrons of Justiquan soldiers. So, spectated by gulls, the smugglers snuck into the city along an old goat trail high on the bluff that passed through a grove of dogwood, fiddlewood and wild ackee on the edge of town. Oldport was too large for the crusaders to cover every angle of approach, too vast for a palisade. So, the smugglers made it into the slums easily. Giving the heavily fortified prison a wide berth, they made for the town centre, where the riot was crescendoing.

Chilpaeans had flocked in their hundreds to the town square, built around a limestone fountain depicting the Twins, to try to cut off the crusaders ferrying their folk through the town to the docks. Joining the back of the baying mob and then sidling through with a shove here and an elbow there, the smugglers soon arrived at the front of the crowd, where the knights were pushing people back with polearms to create a path.

About to leap on an armoured crusader and stab him to death, Jamba stood statue-still when a stranger in the crowd did the honours for him, a dreadlocked woman with a dagger in her fist and a war cry on her lips. The knight's hot blood jetted over Jamba's face before the man fell, and the smuggler licked his lips without thinking, tasting the man's tangy, metallic blood. Then, other figures were popping out of the roaring crowd all around him to lay waste to the Justiquans – dark-skinned men and women in simple tunics and breeches. Disgruntled residents, Jamba presumed, admiring their spirit.

The dreadlocked Chilpaean woman wielding a knife shouted to the prisoners in Kwi patois, "Hang on! We'll get those chains off you as soon as possible!"

She could not get near the prisoners, though. None of the townsfolk could. Unarmoured and wielding knives, daggers and clubs, they outnumbered the knights but were no match for them in one on one combat. The knights closed ranks around the prisoners, disciplined and calm, and used their heater shields to rebuff their screeching assailants before slicing them open with broadswords and staining the town square red. Jamba found his gaze drawn to the blood-flecked faces of the Twins depicted in the fountain and wondered if it was an omen.

Seeing the dreadlocked woman and her fellows being pushed back, or outright slaughtered here and there, Jamba finally recovered from his stupefaction and leaped to their aid. His scimitars flashed in the dwindling sunlight, slipping between a knight's cuirass and helmet and sending his head flying through the air in a spray of gore. Then, the knights took notice of him, shouting and pointing, and he gulped. The crusaders' halberds – a vicious meld of spear and axe – swept out, not to propel the populace away anymore but aimed to kill, and carved bloody swathes through the brave Chilpaeans who had broken out of the crowd, scything down multiple foes at once. Screams echoed around the square. Jamba watched in horror as one halberd gutted two warriors in a single swipe, and then the halberds were coming for him.

Frightened, he darted out of the way of the first few swipes of the long polearms, dancing this way and that, his scimitar clattering against the thick hafts. Then, however, he relaxed a little, having gotten the measure of the weapons and the men wielding them. The halberds were heavy and slow, and it proved ultimately facile to slip past one when it was overextended. In close quarters, the halberd-men had no resort save daggers, which took too long to draw, and so Jamba opened up their throats before they could react. When faced with multiple foes at once, however, the smuggler could no longer easily weave past their halberds, for every time he tried to pass one, another was there to prod him back.

The crusaders forced him back, step by step, into the throng and then laid about them with reckless abandon, chopping down innocent Chilpaeans like so much firewood while Jamba looked on in horror. The crowd split, but rather than flee, they encircled the Justiquans like a crab's pincers and pinched. Jamba saw their minds snap in the crazed look in their eyes, heard it in their animalistic howls. His mouth hung open at the sight of bare-fisted men beating down men in armour with bloody knuckles, of women stabbing knights in the gaps in their helmets with kitchen knives, of children grabbing crusaders' legs so that they could not move. His foes were stabbed in the back one by one, and blessed sleep was averted once more.

Glancing left, he was glad to witness a furry Lug putting dents in the knights' armour with his mighty warhammer. Glancing right, he could take or leave the sight of Kofi Touluz slashing his way through his armoured foes with all the slow-going ease of a pioneer hacking down vines in the jungle. He knew Ruffle Feathers was behind him somewhere; the old obeahman always was.

The evening became a hazy blur of blood and death for Jamba after that. Swept up in the righteous furore of the riot, the smugglers blazed a trail of carnage through the town, freeing group after group of slaves on their way uphill to Urugulu Prison and leaving piles of armoured bodies strewn in the cobbled streets in their wake. It soon became clear why the populace had failed to take the prison before their arrival, however. Roaring and spitting with rage, the people of Oldport all pressed up against a ten-foot barred metal fence topped with spikes, unable to squeeze through or surmount it while the Justiquans rained down arrows and crossbow bolts on them from the roof and windows of the fortress-like prison cut into the cliff face. Jamba could see no gate to allow entry anywhere. Wolves' faces, depicted in intricate detail in wrought iron all along the fence, snarled at him, glittering in the crimson light of sunset. He eyed the sky with a feeling like someone was treading on his grave. The sun was hidden behind the prison now, silhouetting the grand old building against a red-gold backdrop. They did not have long.

Bodies started to heap up at the front of the crowd by the fence, but still the people of Oldport flocked to the prison, undeterred by the buzzing bolts and arrows. Half of them pinged harmlessly off the fence. Eventually, the projectiles ceased and the prison's iron-reinforced doors banged open to emit a squadron of knights, in their midst an iron-haired rake of a man with a pointy chin beard, immaculately attired in a long black coat over a creamy doublet and tight black trousers with a linen ruff at the neck.

"I say, what's all this to-do?" he shouted in Traveller's in tones as polished as his boots. The smugglers had snuck close enough to the front of the crowd to hear him over the mob's baying for blood. "It simply won't do! You ought to know your places by now, savages. Fret not, however, for I am an educator, forever at hand to teach you."

He lifted a hand and made a strange stabbing motion with all his fingers. As he did so, the wolves' faces wrought all along the fence came alive, growling and gnashing their iron fangs, mutilating the Chilpaeans pressed up against the metal. The rest of the crowd backed away, screaming, as their loved ones were mauled by deadly decorations.

"I, Major Thedes, command you all to return to your homes at once!" shouted the iron-haired Justiquan, tucking his hands behind his back. "Disperse, I say! Disperse!"

"A pox on you!" the dreadlocked woman spat at him, epitomising the crowd's response.

Jamba pushed his way through to her, while the mob unleashed sonic fury on the prison from a safe distance. "Ahoy there," he shouted to get her attention. "You were very brave back there in the town square."

She looked him up and down, then nodded grudgingly. "You, too."

"I'm Jamba Klach." The smuggler sheathed a sword and extended a hand, which the woman shook briefly. "I'm not from around here, but I'd like to help you free your people."

She gave him a hard, penetrating look, and he felt strangely naked. "Is that so, Jamba Klach?" she asked sceptically, raising an eyebrow. "Well, my name is Ithina Roe, and I'll believe your words when I see you in action."

Jamba dipped his head. "As you say, lotus flower."

"Don't call me that!" Ithina snapped.

Jamba grinned as he backed away into the crowd to find his friends. "As you say … Ithina."

"Where have you been?" asked Lug when Jamba found them.

"Never mind that." Jamba dismissed the question with a flick of the wrist. "We need to find a way past that cursed magic fence. Any ideas, Ruffle?"

The obeahman waved a hand, and his words of fire flickered in the air above the crowd's heads, hardly noticed amid the pandemonium. 'Burning through it or breaking it down are the obvious solutions.'

"Good! Summon those snakes of yours then, and let's break into prison!"

'That's the problem,' Ruffle replied. 'The snakes will not come. Either they are ignoring me, or they are still too glutted or too wounded from our battle at Billygoat Bridge. They are not answering my call.'

"Bwa's beard!" Jamba yelled in frustration, tugging at his own facial hair. "What else can you summon?"

Ruffle shook his head. 'The bats cannot break down the fence. The spiders cannot eat through iron. Izulu cannot tear it down, and Djhuty is unreliable at best. I have not made contact with many other fiery demons capable of burning through this, unfortunately.'

"Well, what *have* you made contact with?" Jamba demanded, pointing at the western horizon, where the sun was almost out of sight behind the prison. "We are almost out of time!" A troubled look crossed over Ruffle's face like a storm cloud, and Jamba leaped on it. "That! Whatever you just thought of, put aside your doubts and *do it!* Do it *now!"*

Ruffle grimaced and waved a hand. 'You do not understand the danger! The only other demons I know of capable of torching a path to the prison are the offspring of one of the most terrible demons I have ever encountered, Shazarad, a being we do not want to enter our realm at any cost! If I summon its children, it is possible it will draw the demon's attention. You think Sleepers and Justiquans are bad, but this demon will not destroy just Chilpaea – it will consume the whole world in fire and blood. It could wipe out our island in a day! It is not to be underestimated.'

Trying his best to ignore the shiver wriggling up his spine like an icy centipede, Jamba barked, "Just do it, Ruffle, or we're dead men!"

Ruffle set his jaw and nodded, and Jamba breathed a sigh of relief. The obeahman closed his eyes, and Jamba knew he was concentrating. A few minutes later, he whirled his arms around seemingly at random, but the smuggler felt his hairs stand on end as his skin broke out in goosebumps and knew something was happening. The air crackled with energy. The fabric of space and time warped, then bent and ripped with a sound like a scrap of parchment being torn in two magnified tenfold. A crimson rift spitting fire and choking fumes rent the world open between the crowd and the fence, and Chilpaeans and Jutsiquans alike backed away in awe and terror as giggling grated on their ears. Jamba did not know how to explain it, but he instinctively sensed what everyone else did – this giggling was no playful vocalisation of good-natured mirth. This giggling was the sound a madman makes as he sadistically flays the flesh off his victims. This giggling was the apotheosis of evil.

Demon Children burst out of the rift – Jamba did not know what else to call them, given Ruffle's description. Ordinary children they were not, however. Only half a dozen made it through the rift before Ruffle waved a peremptory hand and it snapped shut, winking out of existence in a cloud of fire and red smoke. Flickering with flame from head to toe with skin the colour of blood, eyes like bottomless pits and crowns of sharp little horns all over their scalps, Shazarad's Children were nightmares given form.

Waddling on chubby little legs, only three feet tall, the Children spread out in all directions like a dire ripple, even towards the horrified crowd, before Ruffle Feathers waved an arm and commanded them, 'Leave the townsfolk! Kill the pale-skinned Justiquans on the other side of the fence!'

The Children halted in their tracks, some doubled back, and then all of them were streaming towards the fence as one, tottering like toddlers and giggling like the crazed. They waddled straight through the fence like it did not exist, and indeed it melted like heated butter in their wake, shrivelling up and glowing red-hot where it had been melted in an instant. The iron-wrought wolves snapped at the demons, but the Children paid them no mind and the wolves melted just as fast as the rest of the fence.

The Children toddled towards the crusaders ringing Major Thedes, who promptly called for reinforcements, his cultured voice strained. A bugle sounded. Knights and soldiers poured out of the prison, and the archers on the roof and in the windows rained down a storm of arrows and bolts on the demons. The shafts burst into flames once they got within a few feet of the fiery little beings, the metal heads liquefying in mid-air to drizzle down as molten metal, burning a few unfortunate screaming soldiers like lava.

The Children toddled on. Mastering their fear, the crusaders sprang to the attack, jabbing and chopping at the demons. Their swords sagged, red-hot, before they could strike, and those in steel plate foolish enough to venture too close were fused horrifically with their melting armour. Jamba watched the Justiquans' eyebrows sizzle off their faces as they darted in to attack. The Children made no move to defend themselves or retreat, rather waddling towards their enemies as fast as their tubby little legs would carry them with outstretched arms. Jamba winced at the sight of the Children taking crusaders in their embrace, hugging one or both legs tight until the Justiquans had become living torches, their howls raking the ears, the scent of their burning flesh putrid in the nostrils. Soldiers burned up until only ashen statues of them remained, which crumbled and wafted away in the breeze as soon as the Children released them to seek their next target. The townsfolk stood and watched, slack-jawed, not one taking a step to follow the demons through the fence torn asunder.

Panicking, Major Thedes made clawing motions with his hands, and the fence came alive once more – what was left of it. Uprooting itself from the ground, the length of the fence reared up serpent-wise and came crashing down on the demons. It burned away before it made contact. The giggling Children were only a few yards away from Major Thedes and the retreating Justiquans now. The major pawed the air again, uprooting more of the fence, heaving it high in the air and bringing it slamming down once more. Ruffle Feathers' eyes widened as he sensed a shift in the fence's energies and witnessed a fine rime form over the iron, twinkling in the last red rays of the day.

Enhanced by an eldritch frost, the fence endured the infernal flames long enough this time to lay the Children flat with a bang that shook the earth. Ruffle felt fear clamp icy fingers around his heart as he watched the demons' flames gutter and heard the whoosh of the wind in the absence of their insane chuckles. One brave knight sprang forward in that moment and brought his broadsword stabbing down on one of the prone Children. Ruffle Feathers took a step forward involuntarily at the sight, but he was too far away to intervene.

The broadsword impaled the demon through its bloated little belly, and it eviscerated the man who had slain it with a scream visible as a shockwave that shook the sky before it too died. Blood and bits of bone sprayed high in the air where the knight had been only to come raining down on the rest of the Children as they rose unsteadily to their feet, clutching their heads, their fires reawakening and burning back brighter than ever before, incinerating the fence that had laid them low. Fixing angry, abyssal eyes on the crusaders, the Children toddled towards them with outstretched arms.

The Justiquans retreated into the prison, Major Thedes commanding the door to be shut as soon as he was inside, leaving a few men trapped without. Those unfortunate enough not to make it inside railed at the major, pounding on the door before they were wholly consumed by the Children's conflagration. In the end, it made no difference whether they made it through the door or not. The Children waddled through the door as if it were a cobweb, torching it with their mere presence, and disappeared into the depths of the prison.

"Quick!" shouted Jamba, coming to his senses as the demons disappeared from sight. "Ruffle, lead everyone into the prison before the sun sets! Lug, Kofi, come with me!"

"Where are we going?" asked the lagahoo.
"To rescue our countrymen from those cursed ships down there."

26

Boom Tower

Finding Ithina Roe among the crowd, Jamba Klach grabbed her arm and told her his plan. With a bob of her head and a wave of her hand, she agreed and gestured for five of her fellow townsfolk to accompany them. Jamba was glad to see the men held daggers or stolen Justiquan swords. Together, the group hurtled east downhill through the deserted city streets, racing the waning sun through the shadowy city until they arrived at the boom tower on the shore of the arm of land north of the harbour. Its head yet basked in sunlight, while its base was cloaked in shadow. Watching the sunlit half shrink, Jamba was reminded of how little time they had.

"How did the Justiquans make it past the boom in the first place?" Jamba asked Ithina between breaths as they approached the lone rounded whitewashed tower, whose stucco was peeling in places.

"I heard they sent a group of rowboats to sneak past the chain at night," Ithina replied, eyes glinting angrily. "Their soldiers overwhelmed the token force in the tower in minutes and lowered the chain so that their galleys could sail in unhindered. By morning, they were already docked. That scoundrel, Major Thedes, and his men slew our mayor and massacred the rest of the armed forces in a single day – those who did not escape. Then, the abductions began. None of the ships have yet sailed away, though, so if we can find a way aboard, we can rescue everyone who has been enslaved."

Jamba nodded resolutely. "That's the plan."

Justiquan knights buzzed around the tower like bees around a hive, armoured in steel plate. Jamba cursed at the sight of them, peeking aroud the corner of a house, but there was no time for subtlety. He turned to the others.

"Well, looks like we've got a fight ahead of us. I'd normally tell you all to be careful and take your time picking them apart, but sunset's almost upon us. So, haste is the name of the game today, understood? Get in there, kill those wretches and save our kinfolk. On me!"

He sprang out from behind the house and rushed the Justiquans across a stretch of open ground. Arrows from the tower's slitted windows pinged off the paving by his legs as he ran, one cutting open his cheek. Zigging and zagging, he charged on, a wild war cry bubbling up out of him involuntarily as the thrill of the fight overtook him. He did not look back, but he could feel Lug's panting breath on his neck and hear the pounding footsteps of the others. He heard a cry of pain from behind and prayed it had not been Lug or Ithina, but he did not stop.

Once he was close to the knights hastily forming a shield wall between him and the boom tower, the archers dared not loose their shafts at him for fear that they would wound their own, and so all that he had to contend with was the score of knights blocking his path. He wished then that Ithina had brought more men. Eight against a score – plus however many lurked inside the tower – was poor odds, he knew.

Still, he did not stop. Lashing out at the blades peeking over the top of the shields to keep them out of his way, he kicked viciously at two of the knights' legs in quick succession, downing both of them. A split-second later, as the other knight' blades sought his flesh, Lug was barrelling through the gap in the shield wall Jamba had created, a whirlwind of fur and fangs in their midst. His blood flew as swords sliced him open, but his hide was tough and they did not pierce deep. In return, he clawed open their faces with a bestial roar and sank his wolfish fangs into their throats to tear out their windpipes in great bloody sprays. A heartbeat after he was through the gap, Kofi was too, blurring past Jamba to parry the swords aimed at the smuggler and riposting with the venom of a scorned woman, his sword swishing through thighs and necks.

"Thanks!" Jamba gasped, deciding that perhaps the assassin was not so bad after all.

Then, he was flailing his scimitars once more, surprised and pleased to find Ithina by his side, unharmed but for a few scratches trickling blood, bloody dagger in hand. She flew, screaming, at the closest knight like a banshee, clawing at him with her steel talon to make him raise his shield, before ducking his swiping sword and severing his hamstring where his greave did not protect him as she spun around him. Blood spurted, and the man groaned as his leg gave out beneath him. Ithina was at hand behind him to cup his chin, lift his head and slit his throat.

Caught up observing her peerless ferocity, Jamba almost fell prey to a pair of broadswords and had to leap back to avoid disembowellement. Colouring with shame and hoping Ithina had not witnessed it, he sprang back into the fray, swirling both stabbing broadswords around with his own scimitars as if in a malestorm until both knights were forced to drop their blades by their own twisted wrists. Jamba glanced over his shoulder to see if Ithina had beheld this remarkable feat – she had – but was punched in the face for his absence of mind by one of his disarmed foes.

The gauntleted fist rocked him back a step, but he recovered quickly enough to chop off the fingers of the first man to reach for his dropped sword, making him rear up and holler in agony. Jamba put a scimitar through his mouth to put an end to all the caterwauling, wincing at the arterial spray as he ripped his blade out again. The second knight had hesitated too long to attack, stunned by the sight of his comrade's gruesome demise. By the time he did try to jump on Jamba, the smuggler was ready and smote him down with both swords ringing on his breastplate. Once the Justiquan was flat on his back, he protected his face with his gauntlets, so Jamba stabbed him in the groin and left him to bleed out, moving on to his next opponent.

The next man in his eyesight hefted his broadword, but yelled over his shoulder, “Close the door!”

The door stood blessedly ajar. Jamba parried his blade and then booted down the man who had shouted, before vaulting his upturned body, which was disarmed and wriggling like a beetle, in order to sprint with all he had towards the well-scarred but intact thick wooden door. He knew that if it was closed and locked, it would be nigh impossible to open again from the outside and their misson would be scuppered. He wished Ruffe Feathers were with them then, knowing too the old man could’ve easily burned down the door with the help of the Children. As it turned out, the obeahman and his fiends were not needed. The crusaders inside were slow off the mark, and though two of the knights in the conflict turned and raced Jamba for the gate, they could not keep up with him in ther steel plate armour, for he wore only breeches and a dirty shirt. As soon as the door started to close, pushed from the inside, Jamba shoulder-barged it wide open again and fell upon those inside like a fox in a henhouse.

The two knights behind him could have stabbed him in the back then if not for Lug, who had hurtled after his friend as soon as Jamba started moving and mauled the two before they even reached the door. The smugglers were inside. In a few seconds that felt like an eternity, the remaining crusaders outside were slain, along with two of Ithina’s friends. With no time to mourn, the remaining four Chilpaeans prowled into the tower. They gutted it like a cleansing fire, showing the Justiquans no mercy, and soon had the run of the place. Stepping over a score more bloody bodies of armoured knights and soldiers in leather armour, Jamba approached the windlass that operated the boom almost reverently.

“Lug,” he said softly, “would you be so kind? Put those big muscles of yours to use.”

Lug bobbed his head, his fur fading back into his skin. “It would be my honour … what are we doing exactly?”

Jamba grinned as the lagahoo began to crank the windlass. “We’re raising the boom, my friend, to block off the bay and prevent those damned crusaders from escaping on their infernal ships with our noble brethren!”

“And what’s a boom?”

“It’s a chain strung across the mouth of the harbour that can be raised to prevent access, or lowered to allow it. The chain will scupper the hull of any deep-keeled ship that tries to pass over it.”

“But they weren’t trying to sail away,” Lug pointed out, brow furrowed.

Jamba nodded. "But they will as soon as they find out what's happened to their friends in the town."

Lug made an understanding, "Ah," noise.

"The ships!" one of the Chilpaean men keeping watch shouted from outside the tower just then to reinforce the smuggler's point. "They're embarking!"

Jamba grinned at Ithina. "Let's go tell them how it is."

Even by the dimming vermillion light of sunset, it was impossible for the Justiqans aboard the galleys departing the docks to miss or neglect the sight of Jamba, Ithina and the other Chilpaeans all hollering at them from the north shore, waving crusader helmets in the air. The ships stopped in their tracks, knowing what it meant to see Chilpaeans in control of the boom tower, and rapidly sent a rowing boat over to investigate.

Jamba shouted to the knight and the soldiers in the longboat in Traveller's, "We have raised the boom! Tell your captains to turn back to shore immediately. Return to us the slaves you have taken, and we will lower the boom and allow you to escape with your lives. You must know by now that Major Thedes and all his men are dead." Jamba prayed that were true.

"What's to stop us from slaying you and retaking the tower?" demanded the knight in the rowboat in the same tongue, a sunburned fellow with freckles.

Jamba gestured to the sun half-hidden by the horizon. "Time, for one thing. Numbers, for another. We far outnumber your token crews now that the major and all his men have been killed. Perhaps you didn't hear how they died? They were slain – to a man – by fiery demons … demons we would have no trouble turning on you next!"

The knight, Freckles, blanched. "I must admit we had heard rumours of such a thing. Very well, if you will spare our lives and allow our departure, we will return your slaves … I mean your people."

"Turn back to the docks," Jamba commanded. "I'll meet you there."

Only once he was sure the galleys had turned and were indeed sailing back to the docks did he and Lug and Ithina leave her friends at the tower to hightail it to the quays. They arrived just as the Justiquans moored, the last rays of the red sun peeking past the cloudbank to glint on the rippling waves. The knight to whom they had spoken embarked from the ship, strolling down the gangplank and onto shore to stand before a sweaty Jamba, a furry Lug and a large crowd of Chilpaeans who had run down to the docks to see what was happening when the ships had set sail. Jamba tried to remonstrate with the townsfolk, telling them to ensconce themselves in the prison at once to hide from the Sleepers, but they ignored him, intent on seeing their loved ones again.

The knight waved a hand at the men still on board, and they began to shove the now unchained Chilpaeans onto the gangplank to follow the knight to shore. Jamba noticed the Chilpaeans coming off the ships were all skeletal, some with patches of hair falling out, and ground his teeth.

"Your countrymen are returned to you," said Freckles. "Will you keep your word and grant us safe passage?"

Jamba longed to sink his sword into the man's eye, but the sun had almost set. "Aye, we'll keep our word – if you keep yours. You're not leaving until we've checked every ship for hidden slaves. You're not leaving here with a single one of our people."

The knight bobbed his head. "Very well. Make it quick, though. We have no desire to be here after dusk."

Jamba and Ithina personally checked the corners of every ship as fast as they could and discovered to their surprise that the Justiquans were as good as their word, on this occasion. The holds had been emptied, the slaves all returned. Satisfied, they bade Freckles a sour farewell, signalled the men still posted at the boom tower to lower the harbour chain and watched the Justiquan galleys sail out of the bay and away to the north by the final radiance of a sun just barely clinging on.

As the sun set and shadows swept through the town and the Sleepers' howls echoed through the streets, the Chilpaeans raced for the prison, among them the freed slaves who were reunited with their friends and families in brief emotional scenes of hugging and weeping.

Jamba noted the irony. He had never been so desperate to get to prison in his entire life as he was that night.

27

Imprisoned

The Children hollowed the prison like termites in a table leg. Major Thedes and his men were never seen again. The Chilpaeans turned out the cells, freeing scores of their imprisoned countrymen.

"Why were you so afraid of summoning those demons?" Jamba Klach asked Ruffle Feathers once the Children had been sent home and the smugglers, along with half the populace of Oldport, were holed up in Urugulu Prison for the night with what remained of the fence – now a lifeless lump of metal once more – barricading the burned out entryway. "I mean, they *were* terrifying, but all demons give me the heebie-jeebies, so why them in particular?"

'A magician summoned their sire once by accident in Al Kutz in my youth,' answered Ruffle in words of fire, chewing on salted pork, 'and it destroyed an entire city, all of Messipea, before myself and a group of obeahmen were able to throw it back into its own realm by the skin of our teeth. I lost many friends that day to that cursed demon, and I swore I would never again let it see the light of our sun. Summoning its Children was a risk. We could have inadvertently drawn its eye to us.'

Jamba's flesh crawled, and he itched his bandages uncomfortably, sniffing more spice despite Ruffle's disapproving look. "Well, let's just pray it doesn't find us then. We're alive still, at least – thanks to you. I don't know how we'd have made it this far without you."

He had spoken the words off-hand, hoping to cheer Ruffle up, but he found that he meant them.

Ruffle gave him a cheeky grin and a wink. 'You wouldn't have made it this far without me. You'd be dead in a ditch in the witchwood.'

Jamba returned the grin, tearing off a chunk of hard dough bread with his teeth. "You're probably right."

"Don't say that!" Lug Thorm objected miserably, barely visible in the darkness as he took the proffered spice pouch, lit only by meagre cloud-riddled starlight streaming in through the murder holes and the clogged entryway.

"What?" asked Jamba.

"Don't talk about being dead in a ditch," replied Lug, snorting a few seeds. "You'll jinx yourself!"

Jamba rolled his eyes. "It's okay, Lug. I'm not really dead in a ditch. We're all fine."

They all jumped as a huge Sleeper banged particularly loudly on the fence blockading the entryway on the far side of the bare stone room. Then, it started to scrabble at the edge of the fence with the claws on the end of its segmented legs, trying to tear it out of the way. It yowled in vexation at the demonic spiders holding the fence in place with vice-like pincers and tried again, some of its fellows catching on and joining in.

"Looks like they've figured it out," observed Jamba as the spiders struggled to hold on. "Well, at least we found a moment to chuck some food down our gullets." He tucked his loaf back into his bag, then rose, drew one scimitar and crossed the room to lift an iron torch out of its sconce. "They'll be through any second now."

Lug was beside him in a blink, furry as a bear, his snout long and full of sharp fangs. In his paws, he bore his warhammer. Kofi Touluz took his place on Jamba's left, likewise armed with sword and torch. Last to rise was Ruffle Feathers, propping himself up on creaky knees and rubbing his achy back.

Jamba glanced from face to face, the cockles of his heart warmed by the notion that his friends would stand by his side even in the face of a horde of bloodthirsty Sleepers. "No rest for the wicked, eh?"

"We've got your back," Ithina said behind him, bloody knife in hand.

Jamba nodded to her. "Thank you. We'll take the first shift."

The Sleepers ripped aside the fence, snatched up a few of the arachnids and gorged on them. As they savaged the skittering horrors, however, the rest of the demonic spiders swarmed the Sleepers in the vanguard, snipping with pincers and gouging with mandibles. Gnawing a few down to the bone, the demons were eventually overcome by sheer size and numbers and trampled under the Sleeper stampede.

The Sleepers stormed through the barbican, funnelled by the narrow tunnel, the sole entrance to the prison, its walls charred by the passage of the Children. At the end of the tunnel, the smugglers awaited them behind another stretch of fence wedged against the lintel by more of Ruffle Feathers' demonic spiders. The Sleepers bounded through the tunnel with frightening speed, growling and slavering, skittering up the walls and along the ceiling. They smashed into the length of fence with enough force to judder it and jolt the spiders back a step.

The demonic creatures knew their task, however, and bent to it with a will, screeching as they rammed the fence tight against the entrance once more. Piling up on top of one another in their frenzy to taste flesh, the Sleepers were like fish in a barrel when the smugglers started jabbing blades and torches between the bars, stabbing and burning. The acrid aroma of burned hair and flesh filled the room, and Jamba gagged, but did not stop thrusting even when his torch caught in a Sleeper's tangled mane and set its face ablaze and it snapped at him with fiery fangs. His scimitar took it in the maw, and it fell back with a screech.

The smugglers fought for as long as they could. Eventually, limp with fatigue, they started to make mistakes. Most of the Sleepers' paws were too wide to fit through the fence's tight bars, but occasionally a smaller specimen managed to snake a limb through the gap. One such diminutive beast caught Lug unawares, raking open his arm as he bashed in the skull of another of the monsters. The lagahoo hissed in pain and swatted at the offending paw with his hammer, but it shifted out of the way and scratched him again as his hammer fell. Blood saturating his fur, Lug growled and tottered backwards. A burly, bearded Chilpaean caught him before he could fall, lowered him gently to the ground and took his place, jabbing a torch and a scavenged Justiquan broadsword at the horrors jammed against the length of fence.

Kofi slipped in a blood slick and banged his head on the bars. Ruefully rubbing his aching cranium and accepting that he was lucky not to have died, he retreated and let another do battle in his stead for a while. Jamba fought on the longest, until he was dropping with exhaustion and he mistimed a blow, getting his scimitar stuck in a Sleeper's ribs as it twisted away. Determined not to lose the weapon, he instinctively propped a foot against one of the bars for greater leverage and heaved. The weapon came loose in a spurt of blood, but so too did a section of his boot as a Sleeper took a bite out of the foot on the bar.

Yelping and hopping back from the fence, Jamba gestured for another to take his place and passed on the torch. Hastily sitting down by Lug, Kofi and Ruffle, he took off his ruined boot and sock and lifted his foot towards the torchlight. A bloody bite mark showed where the pinkie toe on his right foot had been.

"Those bastards ate my toe!"

Regardless, the smugglers only had a few hours' reprieve. The townsmen took turns battling the Sleepers with stolen swords and torches, but before the sun rose, all were as exhausted as the smugglers and the dreadlocked woman asked Jamba and Kofi to take another turn. Knowing he'd do almost anything for the woman, Jamba agreed wearily. Kofi sighed but pushed himself to his feet. Lug nodded amiably and hefted his warhammer. Ruffle Feathers had never taken a break, nor could he for the duration of the night, for his demonic spiders were the bolts holding the fence in place. All knew that if the Sleepers won past the fence, they'd be able to spread out and surround the townsfolk inside and, by dint of sheer numbers, would doubtless be the only living beings in the prison by dawn.

So, the smugglers fought on, jabbing torches into slavering flower-like faces, skewering beasts when they were pressed up against the fence and hacking off or brutalizing any furry limb that made it past the bars. The corpses piled up until the Sleepers were climbing over heaps of their fallen fellows to reach their intended prey, as single-minded as a crab trying to crack open a clam to get at the gooey goodness inside. The weight of the carcasses leaning against the length of fence started to tell. The creepy arachnids were beginning to skid back with every impact on the fence, unable to take the combined weight of the creatures on the other side. Sleepers pawed at the stone doorframe, some managing to hook their claws around the edge of the fence to try to rip it out of the way entirely.

Seeing the danger, Jamba shouted, "Cut off their fingers!"

Taking his own advice, he swiped at the appendages shoving past the fence, his scimitar skirling against the wall as he hacked off claw after claw. A skinny Sleeper limb snuck between the bars to disembowel him while he was distracted, but fortunately Kofi Touluz was at hand to lop off the claw before it could do any damage. Seeing the assassin save his life from the corner of his eye, Jamba nodded to the man, and Kofi nodded back. Then, both were thrusting their torches and swords at the horrors trapping them in the prison once more, adapting to one another's movements so that they did not hinder but helped.

Despite their newfound synchronicity, one powerful Sleeper threw itself at the fence with such force that it staggered the demonic spiders for a second and squeezed its bulky body through the gap it had created between fence and threshold and skittered up onto the ceiling in a heartbeat. Kofi lunged, impaling the Sleeper that tried to follow it, whose bulk blocked those behind it, giving the spiders enough time to slam the fence back into place. The Sleepers howled in fury as the entryway was sealed once more, but one of them was already inside.

The fighters who had been taking a rest now sprang to their feet, weapons in hand, shifting towards the rear of the room to protect the doorway leading deeper into the prison, where the women and children were hiding. Ashen and sweating with the effort of controlling so many spider demons, Ruffle Feathers could do nothing but pray the townsfolk defended him. They had all congregated at the back of the room, though, leaving him sitting cross-legged, alone and unprotected.

Seeing this, the Sleeper on the ceiling yowled in anticipation of an easy meal and pounced, flinging itself down toward the obeahman. Realising the peril the old man faced, the dreadlocked woman, Ithina, ran back across the room and launched herself high in the air, booting the Sleeper with both feet away from the demon summoner and catapulting it into one wall. She hit the ground hard, but two of her friends had followed her lead and now leaped on the Sleeper as it scrambled to its feet, whacking at it passionately but unskilfully with Justiquan broadswords.

The Sleeper gained its feet, tore the face off one man, curled its tail around another and flung him into the wall with bone-crunching force, and then it was upon Ithina while she was yet winded. It bore her back down to the ground with its weight, and she gagged at the smell of its fetid breath and filthy fur. She managed to get her dagger between them, though, and the creature's own momentum drove the blade deep into its breast. It sagged down on her limply before it could take a bite, and Ithina wheezed for help. The townsfolk cried out in apoplexy, thinking she had been slain, and pronged the beast with sword after sword before they heard her cries and realised she yet lived. They carefully dragged her out from under the beast, eyeing it nervously the entire time. It did not move.

Drenched in blood, Ithina gave herself a disgusted once over, before turning to the townsfolk. "Thanks."

28

Discord

Against all odds, the smugglers and the townsfolk of Oldport held the Sleepers at bay until the first rays of dawn. They cheered tiredly as they watched the beasts slink away, back to their warrens dug deep underground. Ruffle Feathers finally allowed the demonic spiders to return to their home realm through a ghoulish green portal that stank of rotten eggs, his face grey and his fingers atremble.

Their wounds bandaged, the smugglers slept a few hours in the safety of Urugulu Prison, before forcing their weary bodies to rise once more. Puffing on his dragon-shaped baui pipe, Ruffle Feathers grimaced as he once more beheld the corpse of the demon Child slain the night before, left untouched out in front of the prison. Its bloated body had turned purple and putrid overnight. It reeked of putrefaction. The smugglers set forth out of the town's north gate towards the end of the Hook and the Monastery Calliope under a grey sky and a warm drizzle. Gulls squawked overhead, seeking shelter.

Treading a dirt trail between verges of lush green grass as the land rose until cliffs fell away to the ocean on both sides, Lug elbowed Jamba in the ribs. "Did you kiss Ithina goodbye?"

"It's none of your business," Jamba replied, one corner of his mouth turning up as he affectionately shoved the lagahoo.

"Mwah mwah mwah!" Lug chased him, making kissing noises.

Jamba ran away, limping and laughing. "Get away from me, you filthy beast!"

Lug halted in his tracks, a hurt look crossing his face. Lagahoo had been hunted near to extinction in ages past for being 'filthy beasts' deemed unfit for the same privileges as mankind. Chilpaean society had become more tolerant over time, as it became understood that the lagahoo were sentient creatures, not innately harmful monsters, but still they were regarded with distrust in many corners of the country.

Jamba sighed. "I'm sorry, Lug. You know I didn't mean it. I may not say it often, but … you and Ruffle are my best friends."

Lug brightened. "You mean it?"

Jamba slung an arm around the lagahoo's broad shoulders. "Of course. We're going to save the country, and then we're going to retire rich men!"

Lug grinned. "I like the sound of that."

Magnuz Opherio materialised beside them in twinkling, shifting hues of blue and purple, ghostly as steam. *"That's all well and good, but first we have to find my son."*

'Tell us about him,' suggested Ruffle Feathers in arcane blazing letters.

"His name is Pahu. He is small in stature, but strong in intellect. He once found a bird with a broken wing and begged me to let him nurse it back to health. That is, perhaps, all you need to know about him."

'What happened to the bird?'

"I squashed it underfoot," said Magnuz.

Ruffle ruminated on this awhile, then asked, 'Why did you send your youngest son to the monastery, while the older learned the ways of statesmanship and war? I apologise for the probing question, Lullabyer, but I have always wanted to know and it may prove relevant.'

Magnuz nodded. *"The boy was soft. He had no place on the battlefield, nor in court. So, I decided to ship him out of the way, give him a profession at which he could excel. At the time, I believed Pahu would not be needed for the Lullaby. I had believed, before the invasion, that Dajuan would be my heir, and so he was the one to whom I taught the ways of obeah, battle and statesmanship. I only wish now I would have taught them both, but I had no way of knowing what would happen."*

The Monastery Calliope reared up before them as daylight dimmed, a grandiose storeyed structure crafted of brownish bricks with a slate roof, perched on the edge of the promontory some hundred feet above the waterline like a gull about to take flight. Though grand in size, the only decoration on its façade consisted of pale blue lichen and pitted, weathered walls. The Hook veered west at its far end, so that the monastery was silhouetted against the dying sun and the bruised, cloud-mottled sky as the smugglers slogged uphill towards it. They did not see the two brown-robed and cowled figures emerge from the building until they stood in its shadow.

"Who goes there?" demanded one of the two monks in a nasally voice, his dark-skinned, shaven face pudgy and round, reminding Jamba of a peach.

Since the Lullabyer had retreated to the depths of his crystal a couple of hours ago, the monk saw only the three smugglers and the assassin, all armed to the teeth – save the old man.

Jamba held up empty hands, soaked to the bone. "We're here to see Pahu Opherio. My name is Jamba Klach. This is Ruffle Feathers, and this is Lug Thorm."

"And why do you wish to visit the Lullabyer's son?" the nasally man asked snootily.

Jamba opened his mouth to reply, but before he could, he was blinded by a flash of bright light. Blinking, he observed through squinty eyes that Magnuz Opherio once more stood alongside him, crafted of blue and purple light, translucent and shining like the stars.

The Lullabyer frowned at the gawping monks, his mellifluous voice ringing in their heads. *"Because his father has much to teach him! Now, get out of the way, monk!"*

The monk cringed and bowed hastily, muttering, "Of course, of course, Lullabyer, apologies, apologies, most revered. Right this way. Erm, my name is Prior Pacho Senza. This is the Abbott, Kobo Mosh." He gestured to his grey-bearded, friendly-faced companion. "Welcome to the Monastery Calliope, Lullabyer, and may I say we are most honoured to have you, most honoured!"

Most of this was spoken to Magnuz's back as he swept past the flabbergasted prior and abbott and wafted through the thick, scarred wooden door to the monastery as if it didn't exist. The monks almost tripped over themselves in their hurry to pursue, and the smugglers followed along behind them, forgotten. Prior Pacho Senza accidentally ran into the Lullabyer in his haste once inside, their bodies overlapping for a brief moment before the prior pulled back, horrified, and kowtowed, muttering apologies.

Magnuz did not appear to notice. He was staring around, open-mouthed, at the good-natured frolicking transpiring in the room. Everywhere, he looked, dreadlocked monks lounged on fabric couches beneath pieces of questionable artwork, drinking wine and rum and smoking baui, reading, drawing and painting or else strumming lutes and beating drums, all singing and conversing with obnoxious volume. Silence slowly settled over the room, like snow high in the Blueschists, at the sight of the ephemeral Lullabyer highlighted by the meagre light streaming in through the door and the high, thin windows.

"What in the Gods' name is all this?" Magnuz snapped, heard by every soul in the large, painting-festooned room. *"I thought you were spiritual men, not debauched damsels!"*

A rotund fellow put his hands on his hips defiantly. "We are monks devoted to the Goddess of Music, Calliope. What better way to worship her than to pass our days in the warm glow of smoke and song?"

"Smoke and song indeed," the Lullabyer sneered. *"I see you have become weak left up here all alone! Look at you, you fat frog! Of what use are you besides smoke and song?"*

One young monk stepped forwards, putting down his damaru drum, barely old enough for whiskers, but with a single thick, dark dreadlock hanging down to his lower back. "Father?" he asked in a soft, melodious tenor. "Is that you?"

"Pahu," Magnuz said peremptorily, *"pack your things. We're leaving at the crack of dawn."*

Pahu appeared not to hear him. "What happened to you, father? Are you a duppy?"

"Yes, after a fashion," Magnuz admitted. *"I was slain by Justiquan crusaders in Cocoba Bay, and my soul was caught in a* Kun-Yao-Lin *crystal."* He gestured to the smugglers. *"These men carried the crystal across Chilpaea at great peril to bring me to you. Dajuan is dead. The Sleepers have awakened, son, and I must teach you the Lullaby or Chilpaea is doomed. You are to be the new Lullabyer, Pahu."*

Pahu gaped. "Wait, you're dead?"

"Yes, I'm dead!" snapped Magnuz. *"Are these toxic fumes addling your mind? Did you not hear a word I said? I am dead. Your brother is dead. The steward is dead. Half of bloody Cocoba Bay is dead! Half the country, even! And, against my better judgement, you are the new Lullabyer!"*

Pahu shut his mouth and narrowed his eyes. "And just where is it you want me to go? Why can't I learn the Lullaby right here?"

"It is not only the Sleepers from whom you must save the country, my son," Magnuz bit off the words. *"It is also the Justiquans. You must avenge my death – and your mother's and brother's! You must retake Cocoba Bay and cast the cursed crusaders out of Chilpaea once and for all!"*

"And just how in the blazes am I supposed to do that?"

"The army cannot have been completely destroyed – I hope. They must be holed up somewhere. We will find them, and you will lead them – to victory!"

"I'm not going anywhere with you. This is my home. Ever since you exiled me here."

Magnuz crossed his arms. *"The Justiquans are holding your baby sister, Patma, hostage. Would you let her die? And besides, it was no exile. I sent you here to learn monasticism to properly honour the Gods who gave us our gifts."* He glanced around. *"Clearly, I made a mistake. There was nothing for you to learn here but bad habits."*

"And what would you have preferred I learn, father?"

"Strength, self-discipline, courtly etiquette, history, law, warrior skills ... anything but song and smoke!"

"And yet being Lullabyer revolves around a song, no?"

Magnuz frowned. *"There is more to being Lullabyer than singing a song."*

"Is there?"

"Yes!"

"Whatever you say, father. The point is I'm not going with you. I am sorry to hear about my mother and brother … and about Patma … but if, as you say, the capital has fallen to these crusaders, there is nothing I can do to retake it, is there? I have no army, no magic, no Lullaby. It seems to me we might as well let the Sleepers kill all the crusaders. We've been safe enough here in the monastery so far. We'll survive."

The Lullabyer looked like he was about to snarl a reply when the abbott stepped between father and son and laid a hand on Pahu's shoulder. "A word, Pahu?"

The abbott led Pahu away to an alcove in which was set a statue of an ugly troll bearing a lute. "First of all, Pahu, know this. I do not ask you to go. You are my most remarkable student, gifted and kind and wise. Losing you would grieve all of us here at the monastery greatly. What I do ask of you is that you not let spite cloud your judgement. I know your hate for your father, and – having seen him now and heard him – I can well understand the emotion. As I have taught you, though, there is no place for it. Hatred leads to evildoing, my son, and that is our souls' bane.

"We have seen the Sleepers. Some of our brothers have even died at their hands. We know the Lullabyer speaks the truth. Without you, Chilpaea *is* doomed. And so is your sister. You are the only living Opherio, the only living soul with a syrinx capable of singing the Lullaby and sending the Sleepers back to sleep. You are the only one capable of doing this. Some would say it is why you were born. Do not let your hatred for one man doom a whole country, Pahu, or I fear you will regret it all your days."

"But I don't know *how!"* Pahu protested in a small voice, teary-eyed. "I wouldn't know the first thing about saving the country or being the Lullabyer!"

Abbott Mosh smiled and wiped a tear from the young man's cheek. "As you said, it's only singing a song. You are my finest student, Pahu. There is nothing you cannot do if you set your mind to it. I ask only that you sleep on it. You can decide in the morning – if we survive the night."

Pahu Opherio told his father he'd decide in the morning. He and the other monks then proceeded to drink rum, smoke baui and sing cheerful shanties until the sun set behind a storm, despite the Lullabyer's caustic remarks. Ruffle joined in jovially, puffing until he was red in the face and coughing like a chimney, and Lug downed cup after cup of rum until he was swaying on his feet. Jamba sat in one corner, sipping at his cup of rum and wondering how the monks planned to survive the night if they were all in a drunken stupor.

The answer was not long in coming.

As the sun was dropping off the edge of the world amid a raging tempest, the monks changed their tune. The joyful melodies sank with the sun to be replaced by an eerie, jarring otherworldly descant that nevertheless still drowned out the thunder and rain. Jamba could not pinpoint exactly what made his skin crawl, being no musician. The drums beat off-kilter, the lutes twanged off-tune, the trumpets blared off-pitch, and the pipes shrilled erratically with no discernible rhythm. Knowing they could play their instruments well – for he had heard them do so only a moment ago – Jamba could not at first discern the reason for this cat's choir.

Not until more than an hour after night had fallen did he figure it out. Suddenly, it hit him like an arrow from the dark.

"Hang on a second," he said to no one in particular. "The sun's gone down and the Sleepers haven't attacked yet! What's going on?"

Pahu looked to the abbott, who nodded, freeing him from the dirge. The Lullabyer's son strolled over to sit by Jamba on one of the couches.

"It's the music," he said loud enough to be heard over the grating tune. "We knew the Lullaby sent the Sleepers so sleep, so we decided to experiment with other types of music. None of the other monks have syrinxes," he touched his throat self-consciously, "but their music is powerful nonetheless. After a bit of trial and error, we discovered that discordant music keeps the beasts at bay. It seems they dislike the off-beat rhythms as much as we do – if not more."

For the first time since they had been taken to Mama D'lo's underwater cavern, the smugglers slept through the night, jarred awake only briefly now and then by a disharmonious toot.

29

The First Note

Pahu met the smugglers in the common room dressed for travel the following morning, a pack slung over his shoulders, his brown woollen robe cinched at the waist by a sash, sandals on his feet, damaru wrapped in canvas in hand.

Magnuz Opherio manifested in glittering blue and purple light, and Pahu said, "I'll go with you. The abbott was right. Chilpaea should not suffer just because I resent my father."

Magnuz shook his head. *"Ungrateful snotty little brat, aren't you? Come on, then. Pick up your feet. We've a long way to go."*

He turned on his heel and wafted out the door. Pahu gritted his teeth, regretting his decision already.

'Thank you for agreeing to come with us, young man,' Ruffle Feathers wrote in words of flame hanging in mid-air. 'Ignore your father. From what I have seen, I think you will make a wonderful Lullabyer.'

"He's right," added Abbott Mosh. "You will do great things, Pahu, I know it. Now, go with our blessings and may Calliope be your muse."

Pahu turned to leave, but stopped when a nasally voice said, "Hold on! Where d'you think you're going?"

Pahu spun to see Prior Pacho Senza, also carrying a pack. "To learn the Lullaby, find the army and save Chilpaea."

"Not without me you're not!"

Pahu turned a pleading expression on Abbott Mosh.

The abbott chuckled. "I ordered the prior to accompany you, to keep you company and keep you safe and to continue your training."

"Are you sure *I* won't be continuing *his* training?" Pahu asked with a smug smile.

The abbott winked at his student. "Just take him along for the ride. Who knows? He may prove useful."

"I heard that," said the prior testily.

"Off you go, off you go!" the abbott shooed them both. "Off and save the country! May the Gods watch over your every step! Bye! Buh-bye!"

Shepherded out of the monastery, Pahu and Pacho blinked at one another when the grinning abbott slammed the door in their faces.

"Well," said Pacho, clearing his throat awkwardly, "I suppose that's it. We'd better be on our way. Don't want to be stuck out here come nightfall."

He glanced at the rainy morning sky and gulped.

"Indeed not," agreed Pahu, laying a hand on the door for a moment and murmuring. "Goodbye, abbott."

"Keep up!" Jamba shouted to them from down the road, and the two monks lifted their hems and hurried after the smugglers, their sandalled feet soon saturated by all the puddles.

The smugglers led the monks downhill along the path running the length of the Hook back towards Oldport, the tall wet grass glistening bright green on either side of them and swaying with heavy feathery heads like drunkards – or like monks at the end of the night, thought Pahu, wishing he could play his drum but not wishing to let the downpour warp the wood. He could still sing, though. His voice rang out over the Hook, strong and true, pure as the rain and powerful as the distant thunder, crackling like lightning now and again as he strained it.

Jamba Klach had never thought to hear a tempest in a voice, but he heard it now. Lilting as a storyteller's, vibrant as a showman's, coaxing as a horse-whisperer, Pahu's melodies had a direct line to the heartstrings and he tugged on them remorselessly, painting vivid pictures with his songs until the smugglers felt like they were strolling through a descant, surrounded on all sides by heart-warming choruses and verses. He sung epics of battles, sailors' shanties, hymns to the Gods and commonly known feel-good tunes, his cadence rising and falling to the occasion to perfectly match each and every melody he chose, soughing through the grass in tones to outmatch the wind. The storm gradually let up as he sang, diminishing into the distance with sullen booms, until fluffy white clouds scudded through blue skies overhead and the sun began to dry the travellers' rain-drenched garments.

"So, what's it like out there?" Pahu asked the smugglers, leaving Pacho behind to catch up with them. "You travelled all the way from Cocoba Bay, right? Did you encounter many crusaders?"

Lug looked away shyly, and Ruffle smiled amiably at the young man, puffing on his baui pipe.

Jamba nodded, still limping a little. "Oh yes, you could say that. We were chased into the witchwood by a pack of them as soon as we hit open ground. Then, we ran into them again at Billygoat Bridge. We had to jump in the Rio Boae just to get away! And, obviously, we had to make our way through Oldport, where the blasted Justiquans had set up camp in their hundreds in Urugulu Prison."

"What happened?" asked Pahu, wide-eyed.

Jamba glanced at him askew as they walked. "We killed them. This is our country, Pahu, not the Justiquans'. We can't just let them take whatever they want. We went through a lot to get here. A lot. Lug almost lost an ear. I lost a toe. But we did it all to find you, to bring you and your father together so that we can save the country we love."

Pahu nodded. "Well, thank you for everything you've done. I only hope I can meet your expectations."

Materialising in pulsing tones of translucent, glittering blue and purple, Magnuz Opherio said, *"You had better, or Chilpaea as we know it will be lost forever."*

Pahu gritted his teeth and directed his words towards Jamba. "Where are we going?"

"To Dos Rios," answered the Lullabyer, hands clasped behind his back, looking straight forward as if he could already see their destination. *"General Cuevo was stationed there with two thousand troops. We did not pass the city on our way here, so we have no way of knowing its condition or what happened to them. We're going to find out. Hopefully, they had more luck with throwing out the invaders than we did at Cocoba Bay."*

"You really think we'll find the city unoccupied?" Pahu asked sceptically, finally turning to his father. "Even Oldport was taken. The Justiquans will have known the strategic importance of Dos Rios."

Magnuz glanced at his son. *"That they will. We shall see."*

Pahu walked in silence for a while, before he said, "When will you teach me the Lullaby? Surely the way will be easier if there are no Sleepers to plague as at night. I'm not sure Pacho and I can keep the beasts at bay alone."

"You can't?" Jamba squawked in surprise.

Pahu shook his head. "I doubt it. It took all of us at the monastery combined to create music powerful enough to rebuff the Sleepers."

The Lullabyer sniffed disdainfully. *"You are more powerful than you know, Pahu. You require no more voice than your own. What you do need is practice."*

He made a sound then, a sound both familiar and alien to the smugglers, a sound they had heard almost every night of their lives before the last two weeks, and yet one they could never fully understand, being unable to reproduce it. The Lullabyer sang an eerie trilling note that sounded like two overlapping voices singing at once in differing but complementary pitches. Reverberating with an eldritch timbre, it hung in the air, almost palpable in its power.

"Practise that note," said the Lullabyer, *"and when you have mastered it, we will speak more of your education."*

Pahu, Pacho and the smugglers gaped at him. Even Kofi Touluz raised an eyebrow.

Knowing he could not yet replicate the note, Pahu bobbed his head and, staring at the ground, muttered, "Yes, father," before falling back to walk by Pacho's side.

Jamba thought about talking to the Lullabyer about the way he spoke to Pahu, instinctively disliking the old man's tone – as he knew Pahu must. It reminded him too much of his own father. He decided, on reflection, to say nothing, however, not wanting to interfere in a family that was not his own. What right had he? he asked himself.

Pahu tried to replicate the note a hundred times that day, driving the smugglers mad, but he could not echo his father. His voice came out garbled and disjointed, jarring the ears that heard it and making them wince. Magnuz made no comment, neither judgement nor advice, only repeated the note whenever his son asked.

By the time Oldport swam into sight on the southern horizon late in the afternoon, Pahu was ignoring his father's remonstrations and smoking baui with Ruffle Feathers, sick of the note, vowing never to sing it again. The sight of a harbour clear of Justiquan ships lifted the smugglers' hearts, and they found a new spring in their step as they moseyed into town.

Before vanishing to allay suspicions among the townsfolk, Magnuz Opherio ordered his son, *"Pahu, listen to me. You must go into town – into the middle of the town – and seize the people's attention. You must make them listen to you. If we are to succeed in our quest, we need every helping hand we can get. So, you will ask them if they know the location of General Warfa or any of the surviving soldiers and you will ask them if any of them wish to conscript. Understood?"*

Pahu nodded miserably, obviously not relishing the idea, and it struck Jamba that Pahu had been secluded in the monastery for years, living a cloistered lifestyle. He likely wasn't used to speaking to large crowds. The smugglers found Ithina Roe in the town square, overseeing the burning of bodies on pyres – Chilpaeans first, Jamba noticed.

After greetings had been exchanged, the dreadlocked woman said, "I hate to have to burn our countrymen, but there's simply too many to bury before rot sets in. We have to cleanse the city – once and for all."

Jamba nodded. "I'm sure the Gods will understand. We're on our way to cleanse Chilpaea, in fact – by fire, if necessary – with the new Lullabyer by our side."

"The new Lullabyer?" Ithina asked sceptically, gauging Pahu. *"He* is going to save the country? How old is he? Fourteen?"

"Sixteen, I think."

"The fate of our country rests on the shoulders of a sixteen-year-old?" She blew out her cheeks. "Good luck."

"You won't join us, then?"

Ithina regarded him in surprise, then she took a deep breath. "You know I want to save Chilpaea from the crusaders, you know I do. But I can only do so much. And my part to play is here, saving and rebuilding my own home. My people need me. I cannot leave. I'm sorry."

Jamba looked her in the eye and nodded. "I understand. You said before that some of the Chilpaeans posted here managed to escape. Do you know where they went?"

"The Justiquans drove them out of the city," replied Ithina without hesitation, "and those who survived retreated to Pog's End on the north coast under General Warfa's leadership. They survived a couple of days – some of us here in the city helped smuggle supplies to them – but then one morning, the gates were found hanging off their hinges and the soldiers were all gone. Blood and bones is all that was left."

"The Sleepers got them?"

"I fear so. Why do you follow this young boy, Jamba? Why cross the country to bring his father to him?"

Jamba shrugged. "For doubloons, of course. And a pardon."

Ithina Roe shook her head.

Just then, as rain started to pock the cobbles once more, Pahu climbed up on top of the rim of the stone fountain depicting the Twins, waved his arms and shouted, "Can I have your attention, please? Can I have your attention?"

Unlike when he had been singing, however, his voice came out now weak and weedy, thin as a reed and croaky as a frog. Nobody paid him any mind.

Jamba climbed up beside the young monk and hollered, "Oi, listen up! This here's the new Lullabyer, I'll have you know! He's here to help us! You'd do well to give him your ear for a few seconds. Where's the hurt?"

The folks nearby grieving and clearing bodies from the streets to dump onto pyres started to gather around the fountain. Jamba patted the monk on the shoulder.

Pahu took a deep breath. "I am on a quest to save Chilpaea, and I – I know you're busy and sorry to bother you – but I would like to ask for your help. You see, I can't do it all alone."

"How are *you* going to save the country?" one man sneered.

"Well, my friends and I are going to find the army – if it still exists, if they're not all dead, that is," replied Pahu. "And – and we're going to take back Cocoba Bay. And Dos Rios. And … the whole country."

"What about the Sleepers?" yelled a woman.

"Oh yes, I'm going to learn the Lullaby, so that I can put them back to sleep," said Pahu.

"You don't even know the Lullaby?" a man called in disbelief.

"Well, no, not yet."

Silence distended a few seconds into an awkward millennium.

"So," Jamba shouted eventually as people started to drift away, returning to the task of disposing of bodies, "who is with us? Who will help us take back Chilpaea?"

Nobody replied, and the small crowd dispersed as the rain thickened.

Jamba clapped Pahu on the shoulder again. "Well, we tried, lad. Guess it's just us."

"I forgot to ask if anyone knows where any of General Warfa's soldiers are," said Pahu, hanging his head.

"I asked Ithina," said Jamba. "They're all gone. Half killed by the crusaders, the rest by Sleepers in Pog's End."

"All of them?" asked Pahu, round-eyed.

"I'm afraid so."

"Then … what do we do? I'm just a monk. I've known nothing but the monastery these past eight years. I don't know how to do … any of this."

"I don't know what I'm doing either," said Jamba, shrugging and wiping rain from his eyes. "There's nothing to do but carry on. We go to Dos Rios and we see what remains of civilisation there."

Pahu nodded. "And if it's just the same as here? How are we to win if everyone is dead or refuses to join us?"

"What kind of talk is that?" asked Jamba lightly, punching the monk on the arm. "Of course we'll win. We're Chilpaeans! We'll spend the night here and be on our way in the morning."

"I thought you did a wonderful job, Lullabyer," grovelled Pacho, his robe saturated, "just wonderful!"

30

An Abysmal Performance

"We had metalworkers dismantle the fence and forge it into gates for the prison to keep us all safe from the Sleepers at night," Ithina Roe explained as she led the smugglers out of the gale and downpour, past the thick iron gates back into Urugulu Prison. "We slew most of the Justiquan soldiers posted outside the city. The rest fled south."

Barred gates had been bolted in place at the front of the entry tunnel to the prison and at its rear. The front gates had already been ripped off the walls and reinstalled, Jamba surmised from the scars in the rock. He marvelled then at the supernatural strength of the demonic spiders Ruffle Feathers had summoned the last time they had been ensconced in the prison, which had done what solid stone could not in holding back the beasts. The night was dark thanks to the deluge, so the murder holes were windows to a hissing abyss.

Together with the townsfolk, the smugglers hid in the prison that night and, sure as the summer monsoon, the Sleepers came for them. It took the monsters hours to rip aside the front gate again, but eventually they did. Then, they were all mashed up against the inner gate, crammed on top of one another like sardines in a net, dripping and smelling like dead wet dog. The gate creaked under their combined weight as those behind continued to try to surge forwards, half-crushing those at the front. The warriors among the townsfolk in the chamber immediately inside the prison gripped their weapons tight with grim expressions, knowing they might not live to see the morn.

They took the first shift that night in lieu of the smugglers, stabbing at the Sleepers with daggers and stolen Justiquan broadswords and jabbing torches at them through the bars until a pool of blood eked into the room, carrying with it the stench of carrion. Bodies piled up against the gate, and the metalwork began to give, its fresh bolts slowly crumbling loose.

"So, how did the four of you get swept up in all this?" Pahu asked while chewing on freshly caught and cooked red snappers provided by the people of Oldport.

Around a mouthful of fish, Jamba said, "We're witch-spice smugglers. We just happened to be passing through a secret tunnel under Maawu Palace on our way back from Zamphia when the ceiling collapsed and your father's treasure fell on our heads. So, we snagged the crystals – and some doubloons – fought off the Justiquans and scarpered."

"Smugglers?" Pahu burst out, shocked. Then, he laughed, the sound rich and full of life. "I bet that warmed my father's heart to no end – being rescued by smugglers, of all people!"

Jamba smirked. "That it did."

Magnuz Opherio manifested in a flash of bright light. *"Obviously, it was not ideal,"* he said testily, his stern melodious voice ringing in their heads, *"but half my city lay dead. My options were limited."*

"Hang on," said Jamba, raising a hand, brow furrowed, "can you hear us all the time, even when you're in the satchel? Even when … we're asleep?"

"Yes, I can hear you," replied Magnuz, *"and yes, I have heard you ... stroking the monkey ... when you thought everyone was asleep."*

He pinched his cheek and flapped it to make a gross squelching sound. Lug and Ruffle Feathers regarded Jamba in disgust. Jamba shrugged.

"Perhaps now would be a good time to test the strength of your music," Jamba suggested to Pahu, clearing his throat and switching his gaze to the howling monsters by the squeaky gate so that he did not have to make eye contact with his friends. "Spice, monk?"

Pahu shook his head, confused, and took up his damaru with jittery fingers. "No, thank you. Pacho, will you join me in a tune?"

"Of course, Lullabyer, of course."

"I'm not the Lullabyer yet, Pacho, but thank you."

Pacho strummed his lute, and incongruously sweet notes filled the dark, dank prison.

"What should we sing?" Pahu asked.

Lug piped up then, to everyone's surprise. "Sing *Young Janie* … please. My mother used to sing it to me … before she passed away, killed by human hunters."

"No," barked Magnuz. *"Sing something more appropriate."*

Pahu blinked, then smiled and tipped his head. "Very well. *Young Janie* it is."

Magnuz tutted and rolled his eyes. The warriors were enraptured when the monks started to play, spellbound when they began to sing. The beat of the drums tuned in to the beat of the pulse, and the lute strummed the heartstrings. Their voices harmonised seamlessly, transporting every man and woman to a realm far from the one they saw with their eyes, lifting them up and bearing them high on a cloud of delight. Lug teared up, dabbing at his eyes with the hem of his filthy tunic.

"Young Janie, young Janie, came swimming to me,
Far from the bathtub, deep in the stream ..."

The Sleepers paused when the monks' first notes broke the night air, and the warriors held their breath, wondering if the nightmare was at an end. Then, the monsters snarled and growled and slavered and beat at the bars keeping them out with just as much venom as ever, clearly still trying to get inside and feast on the flesh of those within. The warriors let out their breaths in disappointed sighs.

"Well, that was abysmal," Magnuz Opherio observed. *"Try it again."*

The monks tested different tunes for hours, but nothing could abate the flood of horrors in the tunnel. They tried to make discordant music as the monks had done at the monastery, but their fingers moved tentatively, producing only lacklustre arryhthmic sounds that had no visible effect on the beasts. Eventually, the gate gave way, slowly sliding out of its sockets in the wall with a loud grating noise.

"Ready your weapons!" Jamba hollered, brandishing scimitar and torch, Lug and Kofi Touluz by his sides.

Seeing fur sprout all over Lug's muscular frame and his face morph into a wolfish snouted mask, the monks gasped.

"Is he a lagahoo?" Pahu asked.

"He must be," replied Pacho, sniffing. "Wild beasts."

Pahu tutted. "Nonsense, Pacho. It's been established they're as civilised as we are. Do we not eat meat?"

Ruffle Feathers was ready. As soon as the gate was ripped aside, he commanded the crimson-eyed demon bats he had summoned to swarm across the entrance and devour anything that tried to pass through. The monks watched open-mouthed as the smoky bats formed a flitting screen across the mouth of the tunnel in place of the gate, gnawing on the Sleepers even as the beasts passed through their ethereal bodies. Not all the Sleepers were completely halted by the screen of demons, but they were slowed, confounded and half-chewed to death by the time they burst through, yowling in agony and laying about them in mindless rage. Jamba was still not sure if they had eyes, but he suspected that if they did, they had likely been ravaged by the bats. The beasts seemed to leap around the prison in a blind fury, careening into walls and biting one another as often as they did any of the warriors inside.

As the townsfolk backed away, the smugglers stepped to the forefront, placing themselves directly in front of the tunnel to take the brunt of the Sleepers' assault. The huge black beasts were so fast and frenetic, though, that landing a death blow proved far from simple. Jamba resorted more and more often to thrusting the torch into their shaggy visages as it offered a sure method of holding them at bay. The problem with that, however, was that it drove the beasts up onto the walls and the roof in their frantic efforts to escape the flames, and they scuttled deeper into the room overhead on their many segmented legs, screeching and blazing like an entomophobe's nightmares come to life, only to drop down on the warriors behind the smugglers, biting and clawing and lashing out with their scaly tails.

Ithina and her fellow townspeople tried their best to put the beasts down, but the monsters soon cleared a swathe through the warriors, slaying a slew. Jabbing his scimitar and torch into the faces of those Sleepers still accosting them from the tunnel, Jamba glanced over his shoulder to witness the townsfolk's predicament. There was nothing he could do, he knew. He was the lynchpin of the defence, stood in the centre between Lug and Kofi. If he turned away for even a moment, they would all be overrun in a matter of heartbeats. So, he fixed his gaze forward once more and stabbed and thrust and lunged and prayed to the Twins and whoever else might be listening that Ithina and the others could handle the Sleepers at his back. If not, this would be his last night on Maradoum before blessed sleep claimed him and the Ferrymen bore him upriver to the Sunset Isles.

Fortunately, he never felt any teeth in his back and the next time he found a spare half-second to glance over his shoulder while at the same time torching a Sleeper, he saw Ithina and her fellows panting beside several Sleeper and human corpses sprawled on the ground.

Jamba shouted, "Don't let them slip past overhead!"

Though it was more troublesome, he made a conscious effort to step up the pace of his fighting to account for the beasts scuttling past him. He still lit them up with the torch when they burst through the screen of bats, but now he went the extra league to make sure he finished the job if at all possible, stretching as far as he could to reach the leaping Sleepers as they tried to flee to the walls and ceiling. Blood pattered down on him like rain as mortally wounded Sleepers sailed over his head, their intestines spilling from their slit open bellies. His arms and shoulders soon burned like they had been beaten with sticks, and he was eventually forced to concede that he needed a break, long after Lug and Kofi had already retreated for a drink and let others take their places at the vanguard. Breathing hard, Jamba joined them and accepted a waterskin with a nod, taking a long draught and smacking his lips.

He was granted only the briefest of reprieves, only enough time to catch his breath. A fire-wreathed Sleeper skittered up onto the ceiling over the heads of the warriors in the front line and dropped down on those behind with a yowl, mauling and burning two men to death in as many heartbeats and then scuttling towards Ithina and her companions, who readied weapons with horror etched on their visages. Witnessing this, Jamba sprang back into the fray, a part of him terrified, a part of him exalting at the opportunity to pit his skills against a fearsome foe. He could admit, if only to himself in the back of his mind, that he revelled in the chance to impress Ithina.

As the beast bore down on her, Jamba hit it from the side, one scimitar missing the monster's strange snout where it pulled up abruptly and the other skating off its ribs instead of puncturing its lungs as the smuggler had hoped. Jamba could not believe his poor luck. He was all elbows and knees around the dreadlocked woman, he thought ruefully as the Sleeper smacked him down with its snakelike tail and pounced on him bodily, its claws gouging into his flesh and making him grunt. He held the Sleeper back with his sword at its throat, but could find little leverage to slit its throat, though the blade gouged lightly into its neck and its blood drizzled down on his face like an ill omen. He jammed his second sword into the beast's side over and over, feeling its hot juices spray over his arm. The beast roared in his face vehemently, then abruptly coughed blood in Jamba's eyes as Ithina stabbed her dagger deep into its flank. More of the townsfolk joined the dreadlocked woman in jabbing steel and iron into the monster until it slumped down dead on top of Jamba.

Crushed, Jamba wheezed, "Get this stinking thing off me!"

A few burly men hauled the Sleeper off Jamba while Ithina and the other warriors protected them from the next Sleeper to creep across the ceiling and drop down in their midst. Jamba chafed at being protected like an infant, but could not lift the Sleeper off himself. The men who had helped him gasped at the sight of Jamba's more and more tattered, blood-soaked shirt and breeches and the plethora of wounds they scarcely hid, but the smuggler ignored them and hastened to Ithina's side, determined to prove himself.

He was about to skewer a Sleeper on his scimitar as it leapt at him when Kofi carved it out of the air with his twin straight swords, grinning maddeningly. "Oi, bugger off and find your own Sleepers to kill, you glory hound!" Jamba yelled, almost pronging the assassin by mistake when he tried to jerk his thumb over his shoulder with a forgotten sword in hand.

He hastily apologised when Kofi's face darkened, and the assassin turned away from him to smite down the next Sleeper wordlessly, artfully dodging the whipping claws and tail and darting teeth to carve dual red tracks down the Sleeper's side with his blades before gutting it when it reared up high in response.

Jamba bristled. "Gods-damned assassin always showing off …"

When a hulking Sleeper launched itself with a bellow like the tolling of a funerary gong at Ithina, Jamba gallantly stepped in to intervene, only for Ithina to shriek when his scimitar almost lopped off her arm as she made to jab at the monster. She pulled back hastily, but so too did Jamba, afraid to hurt her, and so neither of them attacked the beast. The Sleeper landed heavily on the dreadlocked woman, bearing her to the ground, and Jamba hacked at it thoughtlessly, flailing with wild abandon as fear twisted his heart in his chest that he might have caused the death of one so beautiful. A shred of rationality returned, and he booted the beast off her to find her scratched and bruised but alive. As the townsfolk tore the Sleeper that had hurt her to shreds, Jamba helped her to her feet with a wry smile.

"Sorry," he said.

She rolled her eyes. "Let's just concentrate on killing these things."

Jamba focussed on the fight then, allowing all other thoughts –

including those of Ithina – to drift away like smoke on the wind. His entire being battle-devoted, his vision tunnelled down to whatever opponent or opponents he faced in that instant, for no other time, place or creature existed in his consciousness. As he found his focus, Ithina found that she did admire his swordplay, his speed, strength and skill. He saved her life a half dozen times and hardly seemed to notice, not glancing at her once, his gaze always hungrily seeking out the next victim for his blades. It was not his skill with the blade that she truly admired, though.

When the townsfolk in the front line tired, Jamba smoothly took their place, taking the brunt of the Sleeper assault on his shoulders, albeit with Lug, Kofi and a few other warriors by his side. He stood front and centre, scimitars awhirl, unflinching in the face of the throng of hundreds of monsters torn straight from fable, each capable of tearing him limb from limb if they got hold of him. Watching him, Ithina recalled their conversation by the fountain in the middle of town.

Once more, she shook her head, murmuring. “You do this not for doubloons, smuggler. You do this for love of your country. And *that* I can admire.”

31

The Broken Drum

Dawn found the smugglers and those townsfolk who had survived the night dropping with weariness, having endured countless waves of Sleeper assaults. The demon bats, visibly fattened, faded away under the morning light. Ruffle Feathers, Lug Thorm, Kofi Touluz, Pahu Opherio and Pacho Senza slept for a few hours by the prison entrance once the Sleepers grudgingly returned to their warrens, while Jamba Klach snuck off to another room with Ithina Roe. Blinking tiredly but smiling stupidly, the smuggler returned to kick his companions awake before noon.

"We're wasting daylight," he said, yawning. "We need to be at Bessaroca by nightfall, or else find somewhere else to take shelter. And there is nowhere else."

So, the smugglers and their companions shuffled out into the grey morning light and began the slog south along the breezy east coast towards the village where they had first encountered Kofi Touluz. Once again, a warm deluge prevented the monks from playing their instruments as they journeyed down the dirt trail through the grassland. Pahu spent much of the time trying to replicate the sound his father had made the day before and felt he was coming close. Seagulls swooped in close to see who was making such a racket now and then. Lug waved to them cheerily.

They did not stop for lunch – much to the monks' disappointment – and so Pahu approached Ruffle Feathers while the old obeahman was gnawing gummily but gamely on some salted beef in the afternoon. "Hello there," he said with a shy wave. "You're Ruffle Feathers, aren't you? I've heard great things about you, you know. People say you're the wisest, most powerful obeahman in all the land."

Ruffle nodded, tilting his head to chew at the tough beef with his few remaining molars.

"You don't say much, do you?"

Ruffle waved a hand, still munching, and letters of flame marched along beside them in mid-air, hissing in the rain. 'Only when there is something to say. Talking this way tires me, you see.'

Pahu nodded, amazed. "I see. Do you mind if I ask how you became a smuggler and what brought you here?"

Ruffle froze and scowled and waved his hand. 'Ask your father.'

He took the Lullabyer crystal out of his satchel, holding it out so that rain spattered it. It pulsed and glowed with an eldritch blue-purple light, and then a blinding flash heralded the appearance of Magnuz Opherio in ethereal form, his entire body seemingly carved from light itself. The spectral Lullabyer glared at Ruffle Feathers as soon as he materialised. Pahu looked on nonplussed.

Magnuz's deep voice rung in their heads. *"I knew this day would come. I know what you want, Ruffle. You want an apology after all these years! And you know what?"* He took a deep breath as if he was about to launch into a tirade, but then he sagged, hanging his head. *"You probably deserve one. Somehow, it's hard to stay angry when you're dead."* He cleared his throat and stood straight, looking Ruffle Feathers in the eye. *"I'm sorry for what I did to you, Ruffle, truly. I ... I lost my head in my grief over Ladonya's passing, and I made some ... regrettable decisions. Why did you give me false hope, though, obeahman? I've longed to ask you all these years ... why did you lie to me?"*

Ruffle Feathers shook his head, lips pursed. 'I did not lie. I promised I would do all in my power to save her, and I believed it was within my power at that time. I had heard tell of the duppy dance, but never performed it successfully myself. I thought I could. To this day, I do not know why Ladonya died. Perhaps I simply needed more power. The duppy dance is no easy piece of obeah, and the duppy are fickle at best.'

Magnuz clenched his fists. *"I remember now. That's what you said back then, too. I was just so angry ... at myself, at the Gods, at Ladonya ... at you. And I took it all out on you. You did not deserve that."*

Ruffle stuck out what remained of his tongue, a scarred, mutilated stump, and the Lullabyer flinched.

The obeahman waved a terse hand, forming words of fire. 'You should be sorry. You have no idea of the pain I suffered, the pain I still suffer.'

Magnuz was silent a long moment. Then, he said, *"Why did you agree to help me, Ruffle, when you hate me so?"*

Ruffle glanced at Pahu. 'For the same reason your son left the monastery – Chilpaea does not deserve to fall because of your idiocy and my spite. We must rise above such pettiness for the sake of our country, for the sake of all.'

"What happened between you two?" asked Pahu softly.

Ruffle put his hands on his hips and regarded Magnuz expectantly.

The Lullabyer sighed. *"Ruffle Feathers used to be one of my most trusted advisors. He promised me he could heal your mother, Ladonya, when no one else could. Pregnancy was ... difficult for her. I took Ruffle at his word and invited him to Ladonya's bedside. He performed his silly arcane rituals, but ... nothing happened. She did not get better. She passed away giving birth to you. Ruffle did, however, manage to save you, Pahu, when everyone else told me you were doomed along with Ladonya."* He turned to Ruffle. *"And for that, I am grateful."* He spun back to Pahu. *"For what I viewed as his failure to save Ladonya, I had Ruffle Feathers' drink drugged one night with valerian and witchbane and ... and I had his tongue cut out, so that he could never tell a lie, or cast a spell, again."*

Pahu gaped at his father. "You never told me that. That's atrocious!"

Magnuz nodded. *"I am not proud of my actions. My temper was ... out of control."*

"I can't believe you agreed to help him after that," Pahu said to the obeahman.

Ruffle nodded and cracked a wry smile. 'It was not an easy decision. Thank you for the apology, Magnuz. It means a lot.'

"Does that mean I'm forgiven?"

'Let's just focus on saving Chilpaea,' Ruffle replied as Pacho caught up with them.

"What'd I miss?" asked the older monk, glancing from face to face as Ruffle Feathers walked away, following Jamba and Lug down the beach.

Magnuz disappeared in a twinkling, and Pahu explained to Pacho what had happened.

"I think they're all mad as wild dogs," commented Pacho flippantly, smoking a crudely carved baui pipe.

"I just can't believe my father could so such a thing," said Pahu. "It's scary what he's capable of ... what I might be capable of."

Pacho fixed him with a serious look. "You are not your father, Pahu."

Far from reassured, Pahu took up practice of the eldritch note once again, taking off his sandals and walking in the lapping surf, closing his eyes and listening to its soft swish and roar. The smugglers made good time along the beach and were soon sipping water from chipped cups in Big Brenda's Bessaroca Bazaar while the rain gushed down outside.

Jamba smacked his lips once he had downed his cup. "Ah, thanks, mighty fine of you." He set the cup down and indicated the gaping hole in the shingled roof overhead, where one of the thick rafters had been snapped in half. Buckets had been laid out on the soaked floor beneath it to catch the rainwater pouring in. "Been having some troubles, have you?"

Big Brenda nodded and spat on the ground, then swept some more water out of the bazaar onto the beach with a broom. "Aye, some of those stinky bastards snuck in here last night, as you can see. We barely held 'em off. I don't have the materials to patch her up, nor time to fetch 'em."

"You should come with us," chimed in Pahu, seeing his chance to make up for his blunder in Oldport's town square. "We could use your help to save the country, and – like you say – it is too risky to stay here."

"You should come with us," Jamba agreed, "but we will need to stay the night here, if that's alright, Brenda? I think this is the safest spot twixt Oldport and Dos Rios, even with the hole in the roof. That big machete you carry always makes me feel better." He winked at her, and she grinned.

"Where are you going?" she asked.

Pahu had rehearsed his answer in his head this time. "We're going to find the remnants of the army, I am going to finish learning the Lullaby, and we are going to retake Cocoba Bay and save Chilpaea from both the crusaders and the Sleepers. The first step on the path to victory is to stop at Dos Rios to see if General Cuevo and his soldiers will join us."

Big Brenda nodded slowly. "It'll be tough, but I think I can convince the villagers to follow you. Helping us survive the night would be a big mark in your favour. One thing's for sure – we can't stay here."

When the sun fell and the sky turned black and the bone-chilling howls began, the few surviving villagers in the Bessaroca Bazaar quailed. Not so the smugglers. Jamba and Kofi inhaled some witch-spice and honed their blades on whetstones, telling crude jokes, while Lug pulled faces with the children, trying to reassure them. Pahu and Pacho readied their instruments, and Ruffle Feathers sat down cross-legged on the floor and closed his eyes to concentrate, observed by the silent ephemeral Lullabyer.

The Sleepers rolled over the countryside in a skittering wave of shaggy black fur and segmented legs, shaking the very earth with their tread such were their numbers that night. The villagers trembled, the fetid scent of the beasts filling their nostrils. The Sleepers prowled around the torch-lit bazaar in their hundreds, determined to wipe out this smear of humanity once and for all. The braver among them darted in close time and again to swipe at the torches, gradually knocking them over one by one until all had been doused in the sand.

Then, they swarmed over the bazaar like ants, clawing at the boards nailed over the windows, where a furry Lug awaited them with hammer held ready should they get through. They threw themselves at the barricade of turned over tables and chairs blocking the doorway, only to be met by Jamba and Kofi's cold steel. Worst of all, they sprang up onto the roof and leaped down into the bazaar through the hole in the ceiling.

The windows yet intact, Lug barrelled into the first of the horrors to drop down, bearing it bodily away from the children, tossing it to the ground and then bringing his warhammer singing down on its skull in an explosion of brains and skull shards. More dropped down through the hole or else skittered inside, crawling along the ceiling and along the log-built walls, however, and Lug flicked his gaze this way and that, trying to pick a target. He settled on the closest and moved to wallop it. The Sleeper slyly shifted out of the way, scuttling under the horizontal blow and leaping on Lug from behind when he overbalanced and staggered, rending him open with its claws and trying to catch his skull in its peculiar jaws. Shrieking, Lug capered about, desperately trying to avoid the deadly rows of fangs.

While he was distracted, another of the monsters jumped down from the rafters onto the bar with a bang and snapped at the few surviving children hiding behind the bar, missing by mere inches as they flinched. Pahu, having been playing his drum softly to entertain the children, rose to his feet, pulled like a puppet by sympathy towards the whimpering younglings. The Sleeper heard him coming and spun to meet him – just in time to take the monk's drum to the jaw, knocking it heels over head off the bar. It landed on its back, wriggling like an upturned beetle trying to find its footing. Screaming in rage and fear, Pahu loomed over the fallen Sleeper and brought his damaru down again and again on its skull, careful to avoid its tooth-lined petal-like jaws. Blood sprayed the monk, the walls and the bar, and the Sleeper yowled in pain, but it did not die. It writhed and lashed out, clawing open the young monk's arm. Pahu cried out in pain and dropped the ruined remnants of his drum.

Ruffle Feathers' eyes snapped open, and he threw out a hand. Where he pointed, a rift snapped open in the middle of the bazaar, purple as eggplant, smellier than rotten eggs, roaring with eldritch flames. An androgynously handsome, indigo-skinned figure stepped through the rift a moment later, naked but for cloak and loincloth, his upswept shock of white hair instantly recognisable. In his hand, he bore a staff topped by a skull like that of a horned horse, in fact the skull of a rival demon. The pulsing blue tattoos inscribed across his body shifted with the play of his muscles, and his black feather cloak billowed in the hot wind billowing through the rift at his back.

He took in the tableau with eyes dancing with unholy flames and nodded to Ruffle Feathers, speaking Traveller's Tongue in an urbane accent. "We meet again, *ghon-jamohr*. I have come for another feast, *dezhvak golur*. I am pleased to see you do not disappoint."

With that, he pointed his bone staff at the creatures swarming Lug. From the skull at its tip flew tendrils of darkness, tentacles blacker than the deepest abyss, which wrapped themselves around several Sleepers, including the upturned beast Pahu had been battling, binding them tight and yanking them back into the tip of the staff. Watching closely, Ruffle could not say exactly what happened, but it looked as though the creatures were somehow shrunk down in the blink of an eye and sucked into the skull's maw.

The demon waved a long-fingered hand, his tattoos swirling and pulsing, and a horde of tiny crimson bugs were hauled through the rift at his back as if by a whirlwind, borne up on unfelt and unseen arcane winds to the roof, where they clung together to form a seal across the gaping hole in a matter of seconds, shutting out storm and Sleepers alike. The rift disappeared in a flash. Not all of the beasts in the bazaar had been slain, however. With tentacles still shooting from his staff to seize, shrink and devour Sleepers, Djhuty the Diabolical waded into the melee, thwacking monsters to death with his stave and the shadowy morningstar that appeared in his off-hand between blinks.

The bazaar was clear in heartbeats, though the smugglers and villagers could still hear the creatures pounding on the shingles and log walls. The only remaining entryway was the door, where Jamba and Kofi and a few resident warriors remorselessly hacked down beast after beast trying to clamber inside, their blades blurring and buzzing like bees, stinging and stabbing at weak spots. Djhuty took over from them, sending tentacles out to snag the Sleepers as they tried to slink inside, and the smugglers fell back with weary sighs, cracking achy backs and flexing sore fingers.

"Thank you, Djhuty," said Jamba.

The demon gave him a disdainful look. "I do this not for you, *sivul calim.*"

"Well, thanks anyway," Jamba muttered as he sloped off to sit by Pahu and Pacho and catch his breath for a moment.

Magnuz Opherio was standing over the sitting monks, mid-tirade. *"I spent days pouring my energies into that damaru, carefully crafting it with my own hands and mixing the wood with my own blood, sweat and tears – and you smashed it in just a few seconds, you lousy clod! Do you know the difference between a weapon and an instrument, Pahu? An instrument is used for playing music, you bumbling buffoon, not bashing Sleepers' brains out! That is what weapons are for! That damaru was one of a kind! We needed it to subdue the Sleepers! Now, what are we going to use? Don't tell me you'll use another drum, because you will not. A special damaru crafted by a fully versed Lullabyer is the only tool that will put the Sleepers back to sleep. You have doomed us all, Pahu, you infernal fool – and for what? To save one child's life?"*

Pahu glared up at his father. "Yes! And there must be another damaru we can procure from somewhere – or else I can craft one."

"There are non-!" The Lullabyer paused and stroked his blue-and-purple beard thoughtfully. *"You may be in luck, you pest. There may be one. But only one!"*

"Then, we will find it," Pahu assured him.

The Lullabyer scoffed and turned away. *"Not likely. More likely we'll all be dead by tomorrow evening. But we must now try, I suppose."*

With that obscure warning, he evaporated back into the obeahman's satchel.

"What just happened?" Pahu asked Jamba, sweat streaming down his cocoa-skinned face as Pacho bandaged his arm.

"Your father just chewed you out, boy."

"Please, don't call me boy. I meant, what did Ruffle Feathers just do?"

"Ruffle Feathers summoned a nasty demon called Djhuty the

Diabolical," grunted Jamba, "who dines on the Sleepers as if they're wild pigs. We're lucky he came. We'd have all found blessed sleep if not."

Pahu watched Djhuty eviscerating beasts by the doorway with staff and morningstar for a moment, wrinkling his nose at the overpowering aroma of death, before saying, "Lug told me Ruffle summons demons after we saw the bats in Urugulu Prison, but it's hard to understand … Why would someone risk such a thing?"

"People will risk much for power," replied Jamba. "Besides, it's in his bones. He couldn't *not* be an obeahman if he tried. He sees the world differently than you or I do, boy – ahem, young man. Trying to understand the ways of obeah, for us, is akin to a dog learning to tell a lie."

"You're saying we don't even know how to talk, much less use that skill to subvert the truth."

Jamba tapped his nose.

32

The Hidden Grotto

Djhuty the Diabolical and his bugs defended Bessaroca Bazaar all night, never seeming to tire, only refilling his energy now and then with a quick snack of Sleeper meat and brains. This the villagers carefully hid from the children – although the sounds the demon made as he sucked out the beasts' bone marrow would likely haunt the poor youths until the day they died, Jamba suspected. When dawn burnished the land and the Sleepers finally slunk back to their deep-dug warrens, the smugglers and villagers licked their wounds and lay down to sleep and Djhuty began his meal in earnest outside on the rainy beach.

By the time the smugglers awoke again a few hours later, the demon and his bugs were gone and several Sleeper skeletons lay picked clean on the bloody sand. The storm had abated, and the air would have smelled fresh – if not for the carrion. The sun blazed down, encouraging putrefaction, alighting on the black-and-white plumage of the flock of vultures pecking at the dead meat. Big Brenda had talked the rest of those who lived at Bessaroca into following Pahu and the smugglers – if only as far as Dos Rios – and so Jamba Klach, Ruffle Feathers and Lug Thorm, who had begun the long journey alone, now set out with a village at their back.

Plunging uphill into the thick jungle south of the Hook, Jamba wondered how they'd ever go anywhere sneakily again as babies cried and men and women chatted loudly at his back, swapping jokes and stories or else complaining about the omnipresent bugs buzzing in their faces. Not to mention the monks. Pacho played his lute incessantly now that the rain had abated, accompanied by Pahu's rich, melodious tenor in song after song. Magnuz Opherio manifested shortly after noon, glowing in the dappled sunshine.

Pahu took a deep breath and approached his father. "Hello, father," he said stiffly. "Last night, you said there was one last drum we could use to put the Sleepers to sleep. Where do we find it?"

"We wouldn't need it if you hadn't smashed the first one," Magnuz growled, drawing himself up and smoothing his apocryphal robes. *"And it's a damaru – no mere drum."* He sighed. *"As luck would have it, before I died I heard tell of a magical grotto where the first Lullabyer, Sabr Kaesar, was said to have hidden his damaru upon his death. Legends say he foresaw a time when it would be needed. I researched the ancient stories from before the Time of Witches meticulously and, just before my untimely demise, I came to the conclusion that the grotto must be located somewhere close to our*

current location, on the east coast, north of Dos Rios. With the Gods' grace, we'll be able to find it before we reach the city tomorrow."

"But … it must be well-hidden if no one else has found it, no?" Pahu asked, privately wondering if such a place even existed.

Magnuz nodded. *"Yes. The legends say only the voice of a Lullabyer, an Opherio, can open the door."*

"What door?"

"That is what we are going to discover. I have only cryptic clues to go by. One text referred to it as north of what is now Dos Rios on the coast. Well, it translated from Old Kwi as 'off the coast', but that makes no sense. Another claimed it was by Hogshead Rock. Another stated the Lullabyer's voice was required to 'lift the smashers', whatever that means."

Pahu felt excitement well in his chest, but said nothing. An inkling of an idea had come to him upon hearing his father's words. The smugglers stuck to the east coast as they journeyed south, occasionally forced to venture deeper into the rainforest when the beach transformed into a bed of jagged black rocks here and there, but otherwise swishing swiftly through the sand with the gleaming ocean on their left and the chittering jungle on their right. They passed the remnants of a village that afternoon; all that remained was driftwood. Pahu observed Lug's face fall at the sight of a crib smashed to splinters.

"So, Lug, how did you become a smuggler, if you don't mind my asking?" the monk asked the lagahoo, nibbling on a watermelon he had picked in the jungle.

Chewing hard dough bread and spraying crumbs, Lug said, "I lived peacefully with my people in the woods as a child, until the humans came. They killed my people, my family, and burned the woods. I became a sailor and wandered the seas for many years, lost, seeking a new home. That's how I found Jamba and Ruffle. I tired of guarding merchant ships and pirating, and so I signed on to smuggle witch-spice for a group of growers in the Blueschists. Jamba and Ruffle Feathers were my crewmen. I knew then, as I know now, that I had found my new family."

He smiled, and Pahu smiled back at the sheer joy in the lagahoo's eyes and his guttural voice.

"Everybody deserves a family who loves them," said the young monk.

Late in the day, they followed the coastline inland and arrived at Hogshead Rock, observing the huge promontory shaped vaguely like the head of a wild hog silhouetted against the plum sunset. Fortunately, it was low tide, so a thin strip of beach, normally flooded, remained at the foot of the jungled headland.

The smugglers stopped to gawk up at the Rock, and Pahu walked past them onto the unwelcoming, pebbly beach, buffeted by the wind and sprayed by the surf. "Wait here," he told them as he went.

The smugglers watched him go. No one followed, not even Pacho or Magnuz. Standing alone a hundred feet away down the beach, Pahu shouted to them, his voice borne easily on the wind so that they all heard it as if he stood by their side.

"I don't think the last part of your translation was correct, father. I don't think the text said 'lift the smashers'. I think it said 'lift the breakers' – the waves! Which means the first part of your translation was correct, after all. The door we seek *is* off the coast!"

He cleared his throat and began to sing, quietly at first but growing louder and louder by the second until his tenor drowned out the very ocean, ringing across the waves with such passion and control that many of the villagers teared up to hear one of their favourite tunes sung so beautifully. For Pahu sang no ceremonial palace song, no hymn or dirge. He sang a tune as old as time and well-known as the sky. He sang *Young Janie.* Lug and many of the villagers from Bessaroca joined in almost immediately upon recognising the melody, and Pacho hastily strummed his lute to accompany the Lullabyer's son. Jamba joined in before he even realised it. It did not matter. None could hear the lute or even their own voices over Pahu's crescendoing cadences, which seemed to swell like the ocean at high tide.

As if blown by the power of the young monk's voice, the surf stopped lapping the shore and reversed, its waves rolling backwards away from Hogshead Rock and out into the ocean. The waterline bowed, retreating until a basin was revealed in the bay. The smugglers gawped, slack-jawed, at the stone staircase revealed, leading down to a barnacle-ridden door set in the seabed.

Pahu gestured for them to enter, still singing. Everyone else had stopped singing and started staring, eyes bugging. Jamba looked around and took a deep breath. It looked as though everyone else was too afraid to move, so it would have to be him, he supposed. As he put out a foot to take a step, however, Ruffle Feathers and Lug Thorm bounded past him, giggling and pushing one another like children, scooping up wet sand and hurling it at one another as they raced towards the sunken door. Jamba smiled wryly and followed them at a run, allowing exhilaration to replace his fear and whooping in delight as he felt the salty sea breeze on his skin. He grinned at Kofi Touluz as the assassin drew level with him, hopping over rocks and coral, skidding on seaweed and skirting the confused clams and mussels. Pacho hurried after them, holding his hems and cursing under his breath, with Magnuz Opherio walking alongside. Nobody else moved.

"We'll be back!" Jamba called to Big Brenda, seeing her and the villagers still standing on the pebbly beach.

Still singing, Pahu slowly walked down into the basin in the bay where the sea had once held what it thought was undisputed tenure, and approached the ancient door. The smugglers tried to pry it open, but it did not budge an inch despite its age. Nor had its wood rotted away, Jamba noted with goosebumps. As Pahu drew near, however, the door simply swung inwards with a creak of its own accord, as if propelled by the monk's voice. Once all were inside, Pahu's singing trailed away and the door slammed shut behind them.

"Do you think it's safe to stop?" he asked in the soft whisper demanded by the reverential air in the dark, dank, downward sloping subterranean passage in which they found themselves.

In answer, they heard the ocean roar back over the top of them, but only one or two drops of water made it past the door. A trickle of light eked in around the doorframe, only lighting the way for a few feet.

'I think we're safe,' replied Ruffle Feathers in words of fire, 'but you may need to sing again to let us out.'

Pahu nodded and stared down the length of the rugged, mossy tunnel that lay before them, extending down into darkness outside the flickering light of the obeahman's fire. "Kaesar's grotto," he whispered.

"Yes," agreed Magnuz quietly, stepping up to stand beside him. "We found it. Come. We must find his damaru."

The smugglers and monks padded as quietly as they could along the rocky passage, having to duck here and there or sidle sideways. Ruffle Feathers wrote the word 'light' in letters of crackling fire, and the word wafted ahead of them to banish the darkness. In the lead, Pahu flinched when the word's radiance washed over an eight-foot figure blocking the way. Vaguely man-shaped, the figure was made entirely of whitish stone, like the bedrock. It had no eyes or ears or nose or fingers, only a blocky head atop a boulder of a body help up by two trunk-like legs.

It spread two club-like arms wide, and its slab of a face split open to rumble in the tones of a rockslide, "Who dares seek entry to the tomb of Kaesar the Great?"

Pahu backed away rapidly, noticing that the fiery word 'light' had become the words, 'It is a stone golem, a creature of magic, presumably created as a guardian for the drum.'

"I'll deal with this," Lug growled, tugging his warhammer from the strap on his back and stalking forward purposefully.

He dealt the huge statue a tremendous blow to the chest that would have shattered a boulder, Jamba was sure, and yet the golem did not even flinch. It lashed out with surprising speed, sending the lagahoo flying back with a surprised yelp to land on his back, winded and wheezing.

"Maybe I can slip past it," said Jamba, trying to dart past the golem and receiving a hefty whack for his troubles that left him seeing stars. Flat on his back, he rolled over and crawled away from the moving statue, grunting, "Gods grant me blessed sleep."

The golem did not advance on them, only stood its ground, and so Pahu took a deep breath and started to sing the first song that sprang to mind, his voice a little wobbly with fear at first but fast finding its footing. Back on his feet and feeling only a little woozy, Jamba started to hear the old sea shanty, *Hey, Kraken!* sung in such a place.

"I'm sorry," rumbled the golem, "you do not sing the song I seek."

Frowning, Pahu attempted a number of other tunes, with just as little success. The golem would not budge.

"You must sing the Lullaby to pass,' Magnuz said at last, solidifying what all were thinking. *'And I have not yet had the time to teach it to you. Nor can I in anything short of weeks. Even with our syrinxes, it takes a lot of training to teach the voice to harness the notes required. We cannot pass by song. We must find another way."*

Ruffle Feathers waved a hand. 'I have an idea. Get behind me.'

He stood still with his eyes screwed up in concentration for a minute, and then he drew invisible arcane sigils in the air with his fingertips and thrust out his arms. Two snakes slithered out of his splayed palms, both ten feet long and wreathed in flame from head to tail.

Curling in on themselves in mid-air, they hissed in sibilant Traveller's in unison, forked tongues flickering in and out, "What would you have of us, master?"

Ruffle pointed down the tunnel, and the snakes bobbed their heads.

"As you wish," they hissed, turning and meandering through the air like eels in the sea.

Side by side, with barely enough room to move, the snakes scorched the mossy tunnel walls as they sped towards the golem. Seeming to sense danger, the golem raised its arms to stop them, but the demonic serpents punched it from its feet in the blink of an eye. A heartbeat later, the golem was charred black, melted and crumbling. Pahu and the smugglers stepped over it carefully in the snakes' wake, but it did not move. Cauterising the walls, the serpents hurtled down the tunnel together, burning a path through a small army of golems until finally they reached a large cavern, where they coiled in on themselves sulkily to wait for their master, their appetites far from sated by the stony aperitifs.

The smugglers and monks found them there, hovering above a seemingly bottomless abyss. In the centre of the cavern, atop a spire-like stone pedestal extending down into darkness, sat a damaru, beautifully crafted and etched with playful patterns. Though he knew it must be ancient, Pahu thought the damaru looked somehow free of the warping which ought to have plagued it. It looked good as new – so good that it glowed. The only way to reach the damaru, however, was to cross a sliver of a stone path some twenty feet long, completely unsupported underneath, from the tunnel mouth to the pedestal.

"I'll go if you want," Jamba offered quietly.

Pahu shook his head, squared his shoulders and said, "No. I must do this. It is my responsibility."

The edges of the narrow path crumbled as soon as Pahu set foot on it, and Jamba caught his breath, watching the young man venture out over the pit. He peered down into the blackness, but could see no bottom. Pahu took another step, and another, and another. He was almost halfway across, with no rail or handhold in sight to help him balance, when the path creaked, crumbled and jolted, pitching the monk from his feet. The smugglers cried out as he slipped off the ledge and then let out sighs of relief when he managed to grab hold of the path before he plummeted to his death.

He pulled himself back up onto the path and sat there, shaking and hugging his knees. "I c-can't do it!" he said eventually, teeth chattering. "I'll fall if I take one more step!"

"You listen to me, you little piece of –"

"You can do this, Pahu!" Jamba yelled swiftly, cutting off a scowling Magnuz. "Just a few more steps. Just picture yourself somewhere happy – like back at the monastery! Imagine you're just taking a few steps towards the monastery. And when you get there, everything will be okay. This is about more than me and you, remember? You have to be brave for the others, for the people of Chilpaea. We need you to be brave, Pahu. We believe in you."

Pahu wiped his eyes, gritted his teeth and rose slowly to his feet. Then, he walked quickly to the pedestal, carefully picked up the damaru and walked back. Jamba watched him with his heart in his mouth the entire time, imagining leaping into the pit to somehow try to save the monk if he fell. But he did not. Jamba breathed a huge sigh of relief when he made it back to the tunnel, as did all the others. Jamba thought he even saw the Lullabyer exhale heartily out of the corner of his eye.

Pahu held up the damaru, breathing hard. "Got it. Let's go."

They turned to leave, but the demonic snakes descended on them, hissing in Traveller's, "Wait! You promised us food, obeahman! Where is our repast? You know the deal. Either you supply us with blood, or we drink yours!"

Ruffle nodded calmly and waved a hand, scribbling words in the same tongue in glyphs of flame in the air. 'The sun will soon set. Your meal awaits you outside. Follow us back to the surface.'

"Very well," said the serpents in sibilant tones, "but if you are lying to us, we will suck the brains from your skull and the marrow from your bones, old man!"

Now that the golems had been pulverised, the journey back through the tunnel to the barnacled door was quick and easy. Pahu sang *Young Janie* once more to reopen the way, and the smugglers and monks waited until they heard the roar of the ocean above fade to a muffled background noise. Then, the door swung open of its own accord and they sauntered out into the dregs of sunlight. They waved for the others to join them, assuring them it was safe, and Big Brenda and the villagers from Bessaroca hesitantly made their way down the sloping sand to the door and squeezed inside.

"We'll spend the night here, safe from the Sleepers," Jamba told them cheerily, while Ruffle Feathers explained to the demonic snakes in words of fire that if they but waited outside the door, above the ocean, until the sun set, Sleepers would rise up from the earth and they could dine on as many as they pleased.

The serpents bobbed their huge heads, satisfied. "Very well, master, but if these beasts do not come, as you say they will, rest assured that we will find and devour you, no matter where you hide – be it beneath the waves or inside a mountain. We *will* find you."

33

Dos Rios

The demonic snakes did not come barging down the ancient underwater door and eat Ruffle Feathers that night, so Jamba assumed they filled their bellies with Sleepers outside, as the obeahman had promised. Though the circumstances were peculiar and all were afraid that the door might give at any moment and they'd all be drowned, the smugglers and villagers had one of the best nights of sleep they'd all had in weeks in Kaesar's Grotto, entirely unmolested by the abominable Sleepers.

Awakening at an unknown time the next morning, Pahu sang the door open, rolled back the waves like a carpet, and a mass egress ensued. The snakes had gone, though the charred cheeks of Hosghead Rock attested to their antics the night before. Hiking south along the jungled east coast, Jamba Klach was soon sweating out of his eyes under the muggy summer sun. He almost fell into the stagnant water when they ran into a marsh, saved from face-planting only by Lug's swift reflexes. Glancing up at the twittering warblers and hummingbirds looping through the swamp's rising steam, he shook his head, cursing himself inwardly for his daydreaming.

Circumventing the swamp, the smugglers and villagers ventured inland, where the rainforest fell away to be replaced by tilled fields. Trekking uphill, Jamba felt cold despite the sun at the sight of the untended crops and burned out farmhouses. The ruins reminded him of the farmhouses near Billygoat Bridge, which had all been torched by the crusaders. He shuddered as they passed close by one house and saw the scratch marks on one charred wall, and somehow he knew that this time, whatever had happened was far worse. Skeletons were scattered in the field, left where they lay so that they had become half-buried and snared in grass and blue snake weed.

"Give that caterwauling a rest, would you?" he snapped at Pahu that afternoon, sick of the constant grating sound of the young monk trying to perfect the note his father had taught him. He regretted his words immediately. "I'm sorry, Pahu. It's just … I just hate seeing Chilpaea this way, ravaged, helpless … You're definitely getting better. Don't let this crotchety old fool keep you from your practice."

Pahu smiled understandingly and let loose another warbling note that came close to the mark. Clouds swept in to mask the sun.

"Ahoy there!" a voice startled them as they traipsed along a thorny hedgerow at the edge of a field, close to the blackened husk of a farmhouse whose roof had caved in.

Caught daydreaming again, Jamba whipped out his scimitars at the sight of a lone dark-skinned man approaching from the wrecked farmhouse, bedecked in a ragged green cloak and a Chilpaean soldier's leather cuirass over a tunic, breeches and boots. The haft of a battleaxe poked up over his shoulder. Lug gawped and Ruffle continued to puff on his pipe.

"Who goes there?" Jamba shouted.

"That's what I was going to ask you!" the fellow said, chuckling, and Jamba noticed that he was swaying as he walked and carrying a gourd in one hand. His clothes were dirty, his blue-black mane and beard unkempt, eyes glazed and broad face slack. "Would you, by any chance, be the smugglers I've been told to look out for? Jabba, Rough Feathers and Bug?"

Jamba cocked his head. "Who told you to look out for us?"

"Why, Mama D'lo, of course," said the man as if it was obvious, stopping ten paces away and swigging from his gourd. Jamba could smell the rum. "She told me to be on the lookout for a band of smugglers passing through this way. She has a message for you."

"What message?"

"What was it? Ah, yes. She told me to tell you to jump in the Mardy Grae and she'll whisk you upriver to the source in the hills southwest of here to speed your journey."

Jamba blinked in surprise. "Oh. What a nice gal. And who might you be, noble messenger?"

The man chuckled sadly. "Noble? No, not me. Name's Wagnar Long. I'm a deserter. I abandoned General Warfa and my comrades at Pog's End and … and I just ran away. I've been hiding out in that half-ruined farmhouse ever since I found it. There's nowhere else since Dos Rios was sacked and burned to the ground. I'm glad Mama D'lo gave me a purpose again – she told me I would be helping the new Lullabyer to save Chilapea, I hope that's true – but now … I don't know that I have anything left to live for … except rum. I cannot look myself in the mirror, I cannot take back what I have done. I have nothing and no one, and soon I will be dead at the hands of the Sleepers."

"You *have* performed a great service to Chilpaea today," Jamba told the man, sheathing his swords. "We all make mistakes. We all deserve second chances. Would you like to meet the new Lullabyer?"

Wagnar raised an eyebrow. "Truly? I would like that, thank you."

Jamba nodded and beckoned Pahu to join them. "This," said the smuggler, clapping a hand on the monk's shoulder, "is Pahu Opherio, future Lullabyer of Chilpaea. Pahu, this man, this soldier, Wagnar Long, has just delivered a message vital to our efforts to retake the country. Tell him what you told me, Wagnar."

Jamba could see the soldier standing a little straighter as he delivered the message again, the embers of his pride flickering to life. By the time he finished speaking, he was standing stiffly at attention.

"Thank you for your service," Pahu told the man, and Jamba's heart could have burst with pride when the monk added, "We could always use a strong sword arm like yours to help us cast out the crusaders."

"But I-" Wagnar began, sagging.

Jamba cut him off. "It does not matter what we have done in the past, Wagnar. I am a smuggler. But I am here, doing my best to save the country, because it is what must be done. Will you join us? Will you do what must be done?"

Wagnar stood straight again, chin up, and barked, "Yes! I'll do anything you need of me, Lullabyer!"

Jamba nodded. "Good. Now, fetch your things. Welcome to the crew."

Pahu smiled.

The land tilted up towards Dos Rios and then cratered when it reached the city, as if bowing down to its human overlords. The clouds darkened. Standing on the crest, looking down on the second biggest city in Chilpaea as rain pitter-pattered down, the smugglers were lost for words. They had not believed Wagnar's words until now.

"I told you," the deserter said quietly.

Jamba had heard of a meteor strike in Quing Tzu once. He could not imagine even a meteor could have caused more damage than had been done to Dos Rios. Two rivers converged on the port city, flowing separately into the sea. Both ran red with blood, where they ran at all. Detritus dams had formed in places from the wreckage of the hundreds of houses. Not a single flower, not a blade of grass grew anywhere in sight. The earth lay scorched and bare. Carrion birds circled over a maelstrom of ash blown by the salty sea wind. The city had been annihilated. The smugglers could not see a single building left intact, and the harbour lay bare of ships.

"What could have done such a thing?" Pahu whispered, dread welling up within.

"I talked to a survivor," Wagnar said, "tried to nurse her back to health. She said she was here when the city was destroyed. She said … she said the Sleepers were roaming the streets in their thousands at night, that they were culling the Justiquans towards extinction. She said that almost all the crusaders were dead when … when their commander, Major Kaos, lost his mind and set the entire city ablaze with dark magic in an attempt to wipe out the Sleepers. She said she could hear him laughing as he burned … She didn't make it. Her wounds were too grave."

"And what about the people?" Pahu gasped.

Wagnar shook his head. "There was no evacuation. Those not killed by the Sleepers were put to the torch."

Pahu paled. Dos Rios had been a bustling hub of commerce, home to thousands. Now, it was a ghost town, home to naught but duppy and memories.

Watching the sun start to sink out of sight amid waves of crimson clouds, Jamba said, "We'll never reach the Mardy Grae by sundown. We need to find shelter *now!* Any ideas, Wagnar?"

Wagnar rubbed his thick tuft of beard for a moment. "It's far from a sure thing, but I'd say your best bet is the mayor's house. It was built like a small palace, and it's bound to have a cellar." He shrugged. "Perhaps the cellar survived."

Jamba nodded and looked around. "Unless there are any better ideas … no? Very well, lead us to the mayor's house then, please, Wagnar, with all haste."

"It's just on the other side of the Rio Boae. Follow me."

As soon as the smugglers set foot in the blackened boulevards, they could hear it. Just on the edge of their hearing, in their periphery, duppy wafted this way and that, wailing their endless lament. Choking on ash kicked up by the warm breeze, the travellers tiptoed past husks of houses and piles of rubble and timber that might once have been shops and schools, feeling like trespassers. Every now and then, a crow's harsh call echoed through the city, making them jumpy. Witnessing a carrion bird ripping a strip of flesh from a charred corpse, Jamba blanched and hurried on. Thanks to the devastation and the slope, the travellers could see all the way to the ocean to the east, their vision only obscured here and there by semi-shattered walls. Jamba squinted, making out a lone figure in the distance.

"Who's that?"

Still following Wagnar through the torched avenues, the smugglers watched the figure draw closer, altering course to intercept them. Eventually, it came close enough to be seen clearly, even through the billowing ash clouds.

"Bwa's beard!" Jamba exclaimed. "The poor guy's been burned to the bone! How is he still alive?"

The man who approached had no clothes, no skin, only raw red flesh exposed to the dwindling sun. He moaned with every step – as well he might, thought Jamba, trying not to imagine the agony the man must be facing.

"Who are you?" Jamba called to him as the convoy came to a halt.

"I had a name once," the man groaned. "It matters little now. For now I am become death, the destroyer of worlds."

Wagnar's eyes went wide, and he yelled in a strained voice, "It's Major Kaos! Run!"

"Hold still, pagans, for your time has come!" the major shrieked, throwing out his arms.

From his burnt palms flew fireballs the size of dogs with bestial roars, most crashing into piles of rubble where the smugglers darted out of the way, but a few careening into some of the fleeing villagers and incinerating them on the spot, leaving behind nothing but ash. Crying out as flying rock shards cut his cheek, Jamba darted around one ruined wall and ducked behind a second, beckoning for the others to join him. Fireballs scorched the air by the dozen, exploding on impact and sending deadly slivers of stone slicing through the villagers. Jamba watched several of them nearby cry out and collapse with a clenched jaw.

As soon as Ruffle Feathers crouched by his side, he hissed, "You have to do something, Ruffle! We cannot fight magic!"

Ruffle bobbed his head and closed his eyes to concentrate with deafening bangs sounding all around him. One of the ruined walls behind which they hid disintegrated under the force of a fireball, however, sending masonry soaring up into the air to rain down on their heads. Cursing and ducking, the smugglers hobbled away, the villagers trailing after them, hiding behind ruin after ruin while Major Kaos blasted the wreckage apart even further with every passing second. Ruffle Feathers tried to find a moment to concentrate enough to cast a spell again and again, but it was nigh impossible when he could not stand still for longer than a second or two before he was forced to move again or else be blown to smithereens. Finally, gasping for breath and crouching behind half a wall, he waved a hand and formed eldritch words of flickering flame in mid-air. Jamba scarcely had time to read them before they had to flee for their lives once more.

'This is hopeless! I need a distraction!'

Jamba gritted his teeth and nodded as rocks hailed down on them. "Be quick, then! I don't want to be the live bait for long! Lug, stay with the villagers and try to hide them as best you can."

With that, he dashed out into the open, running back the way they had come and hollering at the top of his lungs. He did not have to pretend to be frightened. He was scared witless. The wind rushing over his face, he coaxed his legs to speeds they had not known since he was a young man, flying down the street and vaulting the piles of rubble in his path at full speed. Within seconds, he was gasping for breath, streaming with sweat, he had a cramp in his side, and his leg muscles burned. Still, he did not stop, spitting out the coppery taste of blood in his mouth and pushing on. He knew if he stopped, he was a dead man. He could hear the booms and bangs of the fireballs as they chased him down the street, feel their heat as they exploded at his back.

Eventually, one caught up with him, hitting the stone under his heels and sending him soaring through the air to land in a sore heap on the cobbles with a groan. The next fireball flew past his face, incinerating the air where he would have been standing if he had kept running. He took little solace in the knowledge, knowing that the next ball of unearthly flame would be directed at his face.

He scrunched up his eyes, muttering, “Oh, well. Blessed sleep at last.’

He reopened one eye cautiously a few seconds later when he did not burn to a crisp, and his mouth fell open at what he saw. A demonic cephalopod – much like the one that had almost smothered the forest devil, Bazil, only larger – had its tar-black tentacles wrapped tightly around Major Kaos’ body. Jamba reckoned it must have been six foot tall in body and thought it might be able to reach twenty if it splayed its tentacles. Roaring flames engulfed the Justiquan’s entire body, spouting from his pores, but the demon did not seem to notice. The fire flickered over its abyssal body and winked out. Its hide was so black that it seemed to suck at the meagre light, draining its environs. It squeezed tighter and tighter, its tentacles coiling until Jamba heard the grisly sound of snapping bones and ear-piercing shrills of pain.

He looked around for the rift that had spawned the nightmare, but saw nothing. He looked up. The rift hung, gushing violet fire, in the air above the major’s head. Ruffle Feathers had dropped the tentacled demon down on him, Jamba then understood, a wave of relief washing over him. He glanced back down and flinched at the sight of the demon slowly shoving the major’s body into its huge beak and down its gullet without chewing, its seven blazing magenta eyes now in sight.

“Thanks,” he said, returning to Ruffle, swallowing bile, “I think. That thing is monstrous!”

Ruffle nodded, smiled and waved a hand. ‘Yes, I was finally able to go dreamwalking in the demon plane again last night, and I made a new friend.’ He frowned and spat. ‘The cursed crusaders fly the night sky above Chilpaea just as they tread her shores. The sooner we throw them out, the better.’

Jamba was not sure what this meant, but it gave him chills, so he did not ask. He was sure he would not understand the answer anyway. He had asked about dreamwalking once and been subjected to an utterly incomprehensible lecture about the power of the spirit and astral projection.

He only said, “Let’s get to this cellar before dark.”

34

Phantom Revenge

Picking themselves up and dusting themselves off, the smugglers and remaining villagers left those who had fallen behind, wishing they had time to bury them but well aware of the half-sunken sun. Thanks to the crater in which it sat, dusk came early to Dos Rios. Wagnar Long led them south through the burned out city, weaving past rows of dilapidated houses once full of families, now empty but for ghosts. Everywhere they went, the demonic cephalopod slithered along behind them, its tentacles squirming to propel it. They made it to the Rio Boae without encountering a single other soul. The wind whistled mournfully through the streets.

As they crossed the large, arched bridge spanning the river's mouth, Jamba Klach wasn't sure if he was hearing the swish of the water beneath or the sound of a thousand scuffing duppy footsteps. He debated sniffing some witch-spice, but his lungs were burning so he opted against it.

A fog rolled in off the sea, casting the city in an ephemeral twilight just before true dusk descended. Jamba could not even see the other side of the bridge as he crossed it. It felt as if he were crossing into another world, a world cold and grey. He shivered and banished the thought, forcing his feet to keep moving. Nothing awaited them on the far side but more fog, fire-gutted tenements and the wail of the wind. Jamba told himself it was the wind, anyway. He jumped when he felt an ice-cold hand on his cheek and spun to look behind him with crazed eyes, meeting the demon's violet gaze for a moment.

Ruffle Feathers nodded as he came abreast and patted him on the arm. 'Even you, whose senses are stunted, can feel the presence of the spirits around us, can you not?' Jamba nodded. 'The souls of those who died here are not at rest. They roam the city, seeking vengeance against those who slew them. I suspect they saw what we did to Major Kaos. Perhaps it appeased them, for now they follow us like lost puppies.'

Jamba shuddered. "You see them?"

Ruffle nodded, eyes distant. 'I do. There are hundreds of them. Thousands. A sea of lost souls.' He shook his head, eyes glistening. 'This must never be allowed to happen again, Jamba.'

"It won't. We won't let it."

Just then, the sun slipped over the high western horizon and shadow consumed the city.

They all looked up in alarm, and Jamba said urgently, "Wagnar, where is this cursed mayor's house?"

"This way!"

The deserter loped off through the detritus-littered, fire-marred streets, zigzagging with a surety that reassured Jamba. The smuggler's blood iced over in his veins when he heard the howls, though. As always, they seemed faraway at first, as if echoing up from the warrens dug under the island, but rapidly growing closer.

"The Sleepers have awoken!" Jamba yelled, fear squeezing his heart until he thought it might burst at the thought of being caught out in the open again.

"We're here!" Wagnar yelled, skidding to a halt beside the ruins of a grandiose building.

Jamba could tell it must have been huge from the foundations and the sheer volume of tumbled down rubble. "It could take us days to find the cellar under all this!" he cried in frustration.

Wagnar shook his head. "There will be a trap door behind the house. Most of the bigger houses have them."

He led them around the wreckage, hopping over beams and bricks, to the rubble-strewn garden, barely recognisable as such. Not a single bud sprouted from the scorched earth. Wagnar started digging through the debris without a word, and Jamba joined him with a groan, keeping one eye on the ever-darkening sky as if the sun might pop back up over the horizon at any moment. He heard scuffling sounds close by, which sent shivers racing up and down his spine, and he prayed it was only the duppy rather than the Sleepers, even while terror of the duppy snatched at him with rimy claws.

Thankfully, it proved Wagnar had been correct and they did quickly uncover a large, wooden trap door, which Lug smashed open with a single hefty wallop of his warhammer. The boom of the lock smashing and the wood giving way reverberated through the city, though, so the smugglers and villagers quickly darted down the stone stairs inside and pulled the ruined door to behind them in the hopes that it might mask their presence at least a little. At the bottom of the stairs, though, Jamba knuckled his eyes in despair at the sight of the solid iron-reinforced wooden door built into the wall before them. He tried the handle. It did not budge.

He rapped on the door hard with his knuckles, yelling, "Is anybody in there?"

He heard faint whispering in Kwi from inside. "What should we do?"

"Don't tell them we're here! Just keep quiet! Shh!"

"I can hear you!" Jamba shouted, trying to speak loud enough to be heard by those inside but not by the Sleepers outside – a delicate balance. "I know you're in there! Please, let us in or we'll perish out here!"

"I'm sorry about that, truly," said a deep sophisticated voice inside, sounding almost apologetic, "but it is not my responsibility to look after you."

The howls drew in on them from all angles like a tightening noose, and Jamba knew the Sleepers were upon them even before the villagers sent up a cry of dismay and fear. He turned to see glimpses of the shaggy beasts past the broken trap door as they tried to claw their way inside. Even as he watched, they ripped aside enough planks to squeeze their skittering bodies through, only to be met on the stairs by Ruffle Feather's tentacled entity from gulfs beyond nightmare. The demon wrapped its tendrils around several of the monsters at once, blocking the entire staircase and crushing the life out of them even as they bit and clawed at it, spilling fetid purple ichor. Between the demon and the door quivered the smugglers and the villagers, trapped between a hammer and an anvil.

"Come now, we're fellow Chilpaeans!" Jamba yelled at the door, seeing that the Sleepers were contained for the time being. "Just listen to my voice! Have you ever heard a Justiquan speak such perfect Kwi? Let us in if you cherish your countrymen, I beg you!"

"Go away!"

Tiring, Jamba said, "Listen here, whoever you are, I am very very tired. I have had a long day. I am out here with the future Lullabyer trying to save this godforsaken country so that you and people like you can enjoy it free from the Sleepers *and* the crusaders, so let us in, damn your eyes!"

"I'll never open this door!" shouted the man inside.

Jamba was about to reply when he heard a kerfuffle within and felt the ground quake beneath his feet.

Then, he heard screams coming from behind the door. "It's the Sleepers! They're inside! Open the door! Open th-argh!"

The shouts were cut off by a garbled scream, and the smuggler heard the sound of a key being frantically jammed in the lock. A moment later, the door swung open with a whine and a dark-skinned portly fellow in dirty but expensive purple attire popped out like a cork, only to lay eyes on the tentacled demon awaiting without and turn back. He hesitated for a moment then, unsure whether to face the Sleepers or the demon. Jamba pushed past him, unsheathing his scimitars and striding through the door, Kofi Touluz and Lug Thorm hot on his heels.

Jamba gaped at the gory tableau within for a heartbeat. Three Sleepers were feasting on the corpses of two men within, while more of the beasts' heads were poking out of the huge hole in the floor where the flagstones had been torn asunder. The Sleepers had burrowed up into the room from below, Jamba guessed, astonished. Seeing their leather armour and their dropped swords, he assumed the two men must have been the portly man's bodyguards. He snuck up behind one of the munching beasts and rammed one sword through its neck, the other through its belly a split second later. Still, the screeching Sleeper did not die immediately, rather writhing and batting at the smuggler, scratching him with its claws and breathing its last fetid breath in his face as Kofi jabbed one of his own swords into the monster's back. Spotting them, another of the Sleepers yowled.

Wrenching his swords from the Sleeper's corpse, Jamba brandished them before him. "Come then, my pretties, 'tis a fine night to die!"

Kofi gave him a concerned look, making Jamba laugh uproariously as he took his first swipe at a lunging Sleeper, almost severing one of its legs as it tried to claw at him and then stabbing his second blade into the creature's breast, only to feel it jar against bone. He ducked under the monster's petal-like gnashing jaws and pirouetted to one side, cleaving open the beast's belly with a scimitar en route and making it yip in agony as its guts slipped out. It tried to chase the smuggler, tripped on its own intestines and face-planted the floor with a thud. Jamba manoeuvred behind the corpse, so that the next Sleeper to attack him had to hurdle its fallen comrade to do so. As it leaped, he rolled aside, barely dodging the flailing claws, and came up beside Lug, who was busy bashing in the brains of another monster.

"Switch!" shouted Jamba, and the two smugglers swapped places, Lug whacking back the Sleeper chasing Jamba and Jamba spearing Lug's battered opponent through the ribs.

Both Sleepers fell as one. Kofi whirred past them, slashing at the segmented legs of another Sleeper as it tried to skitter out of the hole in the floor.

"Everyone, get inside now!" Jamba roared, voice hoarse.

Despite the monsters unearthing themselves from the flagstones, Ruffle Feathers and the villagers, accompanied by the sheepish portly fellow in expensive gear, hurried through the heavy door. Ruffle held the door open and beckoned the demonic cephalopod once all the villagers were through. The demon tossed aside the Sleepers it was squashing to death and squirmed through the door as fast as it could, shaggy beasts breathing down its neck every squelching step of the way. As soon as it made it through, Ruffle slammed the door shut in the faces of the cavalcade of hungry monsters and turned the key. The Sleepers outside threw themselves against the iron-reinforced barrier, and it shook, but held. Ruffle could hear the beasts mewling in vexation and clawing at the wood.

Inside the room, the ravenous cephalopod had needed to invitation to join the fracas. It threw itself in headfirst, saving the smugglers from the maws of multiple beasts as it enwrapped them in its long, thick tentacles and squeezed. Seeing more meals scurry up out of the hole in the floor, the demon laid its beak and body across the entryway, unfurling tentacles down into the tunnel to scoop up its prey and deliver them to its maw. Trying to count its tentacles made Jamba dizzy. He watched in awed dread as the demon simultaneously slaughtered the handful of Sleepers still in the cellar and at the same time blocked off those still seeking entry. He drew in a deep breath, using the lull to more fully take in his surroundings. Besides the blood and bodies, little of interest presented itself in the bare brick cellar, save for barrel upon barrel of what Jamba could only assume must be hooch of some variety.

"My throat's dry as a nun's crack," Jamba said to no one in particular, sheathing his scimitars and sidling towards the nearest barrel. "Think I'll just wet my whistle."

Almost nobody noticed, being intent on watching the gruesome battle between beast and demon. One man, however, did. The portly fellow, garbed in a plum silk cloak, a shirt patterned with flowers and pantaloons with gold-threaded hems, pushed his way out of the crowd and shoved his stubbly face as close to Jamba's as he could reach. Almost a foot taller than the man, Jamba gazed down on his grey frizzy hair in bafflement.

"You will *not* help yourself!" raged the man in a nasally falsetto, spots of colour in his chubby cheeks. "D'you know what that is? That's a cask of Dun Valley Rum almost aged to perfection! It would fetch a fortune, so keep your grubby mitts off it, you rapscallion!"

"And who's going to stop me?" asked Jamba nonchalantly. "You?"

"Do you know who I am?" demanded the man, drawing himself up. "I am Falam Burr, Mayor of Dos Rios, I'll have you know, and as such, you will address me by my title, if you please."

"You're the coward who wouldn't open the door to save his own countrymen," Jamba corrected him. "And I *am* taking your rum. It'll go to waste otherwise."

Jamba grabbed a pewter cup from the top of one of the barrels and moved to pour himself a drink. Mayor Burr seized his arm, but Jamba shrugged him off and pushed him away easily, before kicking out the spigot.

Dark rum started to gush out of the barrel, and Jamba filled himself a cup, hoisted it to the outraged mayor and said, "There's rum to be had here, folks! Help yourselves! Courtesy of our fine mayor."

"What are you doing?" asked Kofi quietly. "This is no time for nonsense."

Jamba shrugged and drained the cup. "The demon has the Sleepers in hand. No need to fret."

Despite the proximity of the monsters in the underground tunnel, whom they could hear snarling and baying for blood, the smugglers and villagers were eventually pulled down to sitting positions by exhaustion, propped against barrels or the walls. The smugglers drank rum and ate some of the rations they had brought from Oldport, while the villagers partook sparingly in their own foods borne thither from Bessaroca.

After eating a little, Pahu took out his new drum and, stroking it with reverent fingers, started to play. Jamba suspected he was doodling, making it up as he went along, for it was like no song the smuggler had ever heard, and yet its rhythms seemed somehow as old as time, fitting together unexpectedly like pieces from different puzzles. Jamba watched his hands at work, stroking, tapping, slapping and rubbing with the heel of his hand, the monk played the drum in a hundred different ways all at once, dextrous as any master craftsman.

Pacho joined in with the invented melody after a while, and it was clear where Pahu had obtained his skills. The older monk played the lute with immaculate talent, and yet somehow he could never quite match Pahu's energy levels, always falling short. Jamba did not think it had anything to do with the monk's age either. He was no musician, but he could tell instinctively that Pahu had the gift – the gift that makes a true musician what they are. Music swam in the young monk's veins. He devoted everything to it, his time, his mind and his body, and it showed in his music. Jamba could hear the passion ringing in every drumbeat. It electrified him, making his hairs stand on end as if he were witness to greatness.

Silvery spirits slowly materialised in the cellar before the smuggler's eyes, men, women and children, all ethereal as smoke. Some of them struck at the demon and the Sleepers with spectral swords, but their blades passed through the monsters as if they did not exist. Most, however, had their eyes fixed on Pahu, clearly enthralled by his spontaneous tune. A row of ghostly children sat at the monk's feet alongside those yet living and breathing, all staring up at him with adoring eyes, and he smiled back at them, gentle as dew. Jamba wondered if he was imagining it or if the ghostly children, indeed all the spirits, were glowing brighter and brighter with each passing second.

"Why can we see them now?" Jamba asked Ruffle Feathers quietly, noticing that Magnuz appeared as gobsmacked as the rest of them by the turn of events.

The obeahman's eyes were wide, his mouth agape. He waved a hand. 'I do not know, truth be told. The duppy in the fire opal mine were obeahmen with knowledge of how to control their energies to manifest change in the physical world, but these men and women … they have no such knowledge, no such control. That is why they did not appear sooner. The only explanation is that they are somehow drawing energy from Pahu's song.'

Magnuz Opherio winked into existence by their side in a flash of light. *"Opherio music is a powerful tool – a weapon in the wrong hands."*

An inhuman scream brought all eyes swivelling back to the hole in the floor. The demonic cephalopod reared up away from the aperture, purple blood pouring from a score of wounds, missing several tentacles. Its remaining limbs squirming, it propelled itself rapidly away from the entryway, keening, uncaring of the duppy it passed through. Several Sleepers bounced up out of the hole in a blink, roaring and gnashing rows of teeth.

They chased the demon down before it could flee further than a few steps and latched on to it, locking their eerie jaws around its body and tentacles and ripping chunks of flesh from its frame.

"Looks like it bit off more than it could chew," Jamba muttered as he rose to his feet and whipped out his scimitars all in one smooth motion. "Weapons ready!"

Kofi and Lug were by his sides in a blink, several of the villagers joining them a second later holding hatchets and scooping up the corpses' swords. They watched for a moment, holding their breath in hopes that the demon might yet prevail, but then several more of its tentacles were ripped off and it was swarmed. The beasts scrabbled at the cephalopod's unreflective hide with their claws and teeth until they finally tore through and started to shred its bright mauve insides as it gave voice to an ear-splitting death note.

Jamba pounced while the Sleepers were still distracted guzzling the demon's blood, slashing his swords across the spines of two of the monsters in quick succession. One went limp, trying to drag itself along the floor with just two of its legs, but the other rounded on the smuggler with a yowl and sprang at him. Jamba hopped aside and cut deep into one of the segmented legs as he did so, further crippling the creature. It hobbled towards him, and he edged around it as it snapped at him, giving Lug the chance to crush the horror's skull with his hammer.

By his side, Kofi's blades blurred, crisscrossing a Sleeper with wounds until it finally lost patience and lunged, at which point the assassin smoothly dodged and raked the beast's side with his swords, eliciting a mewl. Jamba sank his swords into the monster's other side and Kofi stabbed it in the neck, and finally it gave in, its jaws slowly closing like a flower going over. The smugglers and assassin were given no respite, though, for Sleepers continued to bubble up out of the hole in the floor like ants from a nest. Jamba saw several of the brave villagers go down and wished he could have protected them, but he was hard-pressed to defend himself.

He noticed something then, rising above the ruckus of the melee on sonic wings – a song. Pahu and Pacho were still playing, he realised, growing louder and louder, and the duppy all around them seemed to be reacting. No longer were they all facing the monk, enamoured by his music. Now, as one, they turned their unseeing eyes on the Sleepers and advanced, some of the men with spectral weapons in hand, the women and children barehanded. Before Jamba fully understood what was happening, the duppy threw themselves fearlessly on the Sleepers, bearing them back in a phantom wave, pummelling them with fists and slashing at them with swords and axes. Unlike their earlier attempts, though, the duppy were now somehow capable of touching the Sleepers, of hurting them, even killing them, Jamba saw with awe. The monks' music drowned out the Sleepers' screams.

35

Dirge

Though they could harm the Sleepers, the duppy in the mayor's cellar in Dos Rios could not themselves be harmed. The Sleepers' jaws and claws passed through them like smoke. The monks played all night. The duppy slew all night, until finally the smugglers and villagers knew that morning had come by the cessation of scratching on the thick wooden door. They threw wide the door and thus banished the Sleepers inside with shafts of sunlight. By the rays of the virgin sun, Pahu and Pacho inspected their blistered and bleeding fingers, wincing but proud.

"How did you do that?" Magnuz Opherio asked his son quietly.

"I don't know," replied Pahu guilelessly. "I just played. I just … felt it. I felt the duppy's sorrow and their rage, and I … I don't know … I tapped into it, somehow." He regarded all the duppy yet thronging the cellar, even more incongruous in daylight. "Thank you all for your aid last night. Thanks to you, Chilpaea may yet have a future. I … I do not know if I possess the power to grant you this, but it is my greatest wish that you – all of you, my countrymen, my kinsfolk – that you find peace. Your vengeance is accomplished. We will take it from here. Rest your weary heads in the Sunset Isles now, my friends, for you have earned it. Go with my blessing."

Smiling, the duppy winked out of sight one by one with a flash and a faint *pop*, and somehow Jamba knew that they had not merely faded from sight. The icy feeling that had consumed him ever since he had entered the city wafted away on the warm morning wind, and he knew the duppy had obeyed their new Lullabyer. They had finally been laid to rest. The cynical smuggler wiped a tear from his eye and sniffed, more grateful than words could express.

Wagnar gave it a go. "Oh, thank you, Pahu, thank you so much, you kind, sweet man! Thank you! Ah, to think my ole ma and pa might have been among those spirits you saved! I grew up here as a child, you see. To think you might have laid my family's souls to rest …. Ah, 'tis a blissful thing, young man, a blissful thing. I thank you from the bottom of my heart, and if there's ever anything I can do for you – *anything* – I will always be by your side, just waiting for you to ask!"

Pahu smiled and clapped the bigger man on the shoulder. "Thank you, Wagnar."

Catching a few winks, the smugglers and surviving villagers left the cellar behind shortly before noon, the mayor electing to come with them rather than be left alone.

They wandered south through the city's skeleton and soon laid eyes on the mouth of the Mardy Grae River glimmering red-gold in the morning light, its slow unhurried waters reflecting the waves of colour crossing the sky. As they reached its bank – once strewn with ferns and flowers and fruiting mango trees, Jamba recalled, now bare but for dirt – Mama D'lo rose out of the river to greet them, her flowing form comprised entirely of a shapely waterspout, the foam her hair. She stood no taller than Jamba this time. Though the morning was muggy, the smuggler shuddered as he recalled her previous incarnation at Billygoat Bridge.

"It is good to behold you once more, my children," said the River Goddess in a soft, seemingly omnipresent tone that reverberated down from the sky as much as it gurgled up from the water. "What took you so long? Never mind that. Just jump in. I'll take you to the river's source in the hills to the south." She swayed from side to side, taking in all the flabbergasted villagers. "Are you all coming?"

That same afternoon, the smugglers and villagers washed up on the shore of the Mardy Grae by its source, leagues to the south, saving them a full day's travel. Spluttering and coughing and dizzied, they thanked Mama D'lo and bade her farewell.

"I don't know why you're saying goodbye," she said, stepping out of the river. The water sloughed off her like a snakeskin, cascading to the ground to reveal her as she had been in the underwater coral cavern – as an ebon-skinned, grey-haired matronly old woman with laughter lines marking her wizened features. Strangely, she was dry as jerky. She wore a loose creamy gown, embroidered with wavy blue lines. She clapped her frail hands, and her turquoise eyes sparkled. "I'm coming with you!"

Stupefied, the smugglers stuttered their agreement. Pahu's power only continued to grow as they traipsed south up and down grassy verges towards the Belt. The evening after they left Dos Rios, they hunted for somewhere safe to spend the night, finding nothing in the end but an empty village in a valley in which stood a colonnaded stone temple dedicated to the Twins, the Gods of Dreams and Nightmares who had, according to legend, gifted syrinxes and the ability to sing the Lullaby to the Opherio family at the dawn of time to quell the Sleeper menace.

Magnuz spent all day with his son, finally teaching him to master the first note of the Lullaby and moving on to the second, and the third.

Jamba smiled with pride at the sight. "He is learning quickly," he said to Prior Pacho Senza.

Pacho bobbed his head, puffing on his pipe. "He was quite the gifted student at the monastery, picking up tunes as fast as we could lay them down. I daresay he remembers more of them by heart than me at this point. I was never the fastest learner. I think Abbott Mosh appointed me as prior more for my organisational skills than my musical talent." He gave Jamba a sad smile that made his chubby cheeks quaver.

"Have you always been a monk?"

The prior nodded, his gaze faraway as he blew plumes of smoke. "I've never known any home but the monastery. I was told by the previous abbott that I was left on the monks' doorstep in a wicker basket when I was but a mewling babe. They raised me. It is, you may believe, passing strange for me to be traipsing across the island, witnessing horrors and wonders I only ever dreamed of. Half the time, I don't know whether to laugh or cry."

Jamba smiled ruefully. "Isn't that the truth." He slung an arm around the monk's shoulders. "You know, you're not so bad, Pacho. Share some of your baui with me tonight?"

Pacho smiled. "Oh, very well, smuggler."

When they bivouacked down in the temple, a warm breeze whispering past the pillars and through the empty doorway, Jamba said to Mama D'lo, "Thank you again for coming with us, Mama D'lo. Your presence makes us all feel better, but I wanted to ask – can you help us fend off the Sleepers?"

"No, my child," replied Mama D'lo with an apologetic smile. "Only when we were by the river could my powers protect us."

So, Pahu and Pacho took up practice of their instruments in much the same way they had done in the monastery, using drum and lute to create screeching, guttural discordant music that grated against the ears rather than flowing smoothly, both praying the tone-deaf melodies would keep the Sleepers away as they had at the monastery. Pacho worried they would not have enough power between only the two of them, but Pahu simply played. Once again, the young monk seemed almost to shine with passion as he tapped his damaru confidently. Jamba could practically feel the eldritch energies emanating from him. The Sleepers did not bother them that night to the monks' surprise, held at bay by the awful racket.

"I told you," said Magnuz Opherio smugly, crossing his arms. *"You are more powerful than you know, Pahu."*

The following sunset alighted on the smugglers and villagers on the edge of Devil's Bog, so rather than risk the devil's wrath again, they made camp that cloudy night on the outskirts of the steaming swamp in a small forest of cedars and mahoes, choosing to pass through during daylight hours. Pahu and Pacho set up a rhythmless, unmelodious tune to banish the Sleepers and were competing with one another to go to greater and greater lengths in their efforts to achieve discord. The smugglers plugged their ears as the drum hooted and growled and the lute twanged and barked like a mad dog.

Pacho was grinning from ear to ear when a poison dart took him in the neck. Jamba knew it was poisoned from the way the monk's veins and face turned blue within seconds and the way he swelled up like a puffer fish when he died. Pahu leaned over to check on his friend and, in so doing, dodged a second dart aimed for his throat. The music skirled to a stop, and Sleepers could be heard howling close by. Drowning out that bone-chilling sound, however, was another – the crow-like cackling of a decrepit hag high in the treetops, nude as the day she was born.

Her wrinkly old face and saggy ebon-skinned frame glowed clearly visible in the firelight for a heartbeat before she dashed away to the south, swinging through the trees from branch to branch like a monkey and screeching in Kwi in scraping singsong tones, "That'll teach you to mess with the forest devil! The Sleepers will come for you! And if they don't get you, the Justiquans will!"

"Ragh!" Pahu let loose an animalistic roar of rage and pain, and Jamba felt it almost sweep him off his feet. "Who was that?"

Ruffle Feathers waved a hand. 'Tan my hide if that wasn't Ol' Higue! She is the forest devil's beloved, a sorcerous hag as old as Chilpaea itself, some say.'

"Legends abound about her," Jamba growled, scimitars in hand. "She's believed to have slain hundreds of men, women and children in the Bog over the years. She's a monster!"

Before he knew it, the drum was in the monk's hands again, its skin dancing under the young man's insistent tapping fingers and palm. Music flowed from it like a babbling brook, dark malevolent music, tortured and manic. Jamba feared the Sleepers would overwhelm them then, with only one monk to hold them at bay, but to his surprise they did not. In fact, he thought he saw them beyond the firelight, hundreds of them, all bounding south with bloodcurdling roars, straight past the smugglers and into the morass where the wrinkly old woman had fled. Soon, he lost sight of them.

For hours, Pahu played off-kilter feverish music, his face set and grim, his dead friend by his side. Nobody spoke. Eventually, the Sleepers returned. Jamba could see them slinking about in the shadows between the trees beyond the fire's glow. He could smell their fetid breath. One of them padded forward slowly to the edge of the firelight, making all the warriors grab their weapons and the women and children scream and scurry back in fear. Before anyone else could do anything, though, Pahu stood before the beast, nose to nose with it. The Sleeper bowed its head and opened its jaws, gently placing something on the ground at the monk's sandalled feet. Jamba gasped. It was the wrinkly old woman, Ol' Higue – or rather, her corpse. She looked as if she had been mauled by bears. Still tapping the drum, Pahu nodded to the Sleeper and it retreated back into the shadows once more.

The young monk then turned to face his father, the smugglers, the assassin, the deserter and the villagers. "The Sleepers will not bother us again tonight so long as I play. Rest, if you can."

36

Gone Brother Gone

Jamba Klach was growing concerned. And he knew Magnuz Opherio was, too.

They had watched Pahu germinate from an innocent young monk to a warrior when he had faced his first Sleeper. They had then seen him grow into his gifts. And last night, they had seen him blossom into something they had never seen before – a force powerful enough to not only subdue and restrain the Sleepers, but to control them and set them against his foes like bloodhounds. Though the Sleepers did not raid their camp once, few slept well that night. All eyes watched Pahu as he played his grating tune.

By the rosy rays of the morning sun, the smugglers buried Prior Pacho Senza in a shallow grave under a tall mahoe. Stone-faced, Pahu played the traditional funerary song, asking the Ferrymen to usher the monk's soul to the Sunset Isles, accompanied by a villager skilled enough to use Pacho's lute.

When the last notes of the song and the monk's tuneful tenor drifted away on the wind, Pahu mumbled, "Thank you for everything, Pacho. You were my family. The family I chose." He wiped away a tear, voice breaking. "I pray you rest easy in the Sunset Isles."

Tiptoeing and ever on the lookout for the devil and any trouble he might be brewing, they ventured into the steamy morass. Once more, Jamba felt the muggy heat of the place seep into him, purging his sweat, but there was nothing supernatural about the feeling this time. The sun blazed down, hot as rage.

"Pacho was a good man," Jamba said awkwardly without preamble, patting Pahu on the shoulder.

Pahu nodded, puffing heavily on Pacho's baui pipe. He would not talk to anyone that day as they walked, would only reply if addressed in a monosyllabic monotone. He did not even play his drum. He walked through the forested swamp with his head down, not noticing the grand old willows dipping their hoary fingers in the algae-ridden stagnant pools that abounded, or the white-brown reeds and lily pad blooms whispering in the wind, or the moss-draped, flowering tabebuias, pouis and bauhinias. His ears twitched now and then, though, as he absorbed the mosquitos' buzzing and the warblers' and peewees' chittering songs, searching for life's meaning in the disharmony. Lost in melancholy musings, he almost walked into a pond and had to be steered out of the way by Jamba just before a thirty-foot Chilpaean crocodile burst out of the brackish water and snapped its jaws shut just short of them. The smugglers and villagers ran away screaming.

Though his back itched as if a target hung there, Jamba Klach was surprised to spot no sign of either the soucouyants or the forest devil by sundown. He thought the swamp seemed brighter, less oppressive than before, the birdsong louder and heartier, the trees sighing in relief. As the blazing eye in the sky shrank to a fiery blip on the horizon, his heart felt unexpectedly light. He was sorry to have lost Pacho and all the villagers that had died on their long journey, but it gladdened his heart to have brought the rest so far. He supposed a great deal of his change of mood could be laid at Pahu's feet. Seeing what the young monk could do, Jamba had found a faith he had never had before. He believed in Pahu.

Unable to cross the swamp in a single day, they made camp on a patch of dry ground, first cautiously prodding the closest ponds with long sticks to ensure no crocodiles were lurking nearby. Their rations were running low, Jamba noticed wistfully, chewing on some cheese and a biscuit and wondering if he ought to eat anything else. Big Brenda had brought stacks of rations from her bazaar for the villagers, but even her bounty was beginning to dry up. They crowded around a small fire built to battle the night's cold as darkness fell, all eyes on Pahu as he took out his drum. Some heard the first Sleeper howl of the night as the moon rose, but after that all were transported to distant dreams they had once had, impelled by the power of the monk's music.

Jamba heard the young man's grief in the song, clear as the stars popping out in the sky. The tune, *Gone Brother Gone,* was ancient, well-known as the moon, and, with lumps in their throats and cracking voices, many of the villagers joined in when Pahu started to sing in unusually deep, doleful tones. Even duppy started to gather around the monk, shining ethereal silver in the moonlight. The song told the tale of a brother gone to war, a bitter lament of battles and death tolls.

Mumbling the words, Jamba reflected on his coming home from conscription. He had returned from his mandatory time in the army to find his parents slain by a plague and their estate in shambles. He had not known how to run the estate. All he had known the previous two years was how to swing a sword and how to play knucklebones. His life had been a jarring juxtaposition of long stretches of boredom interspersed here and there with exciting but terrifying near-death encounters with pirates, Goblins and criminals.

He had won several sword tourneys upon his return and earned hundreds of doubloons and the attention of many a fine young woman. A young wastrel, he had blown through his riches in no time with his chosen lady and blown through funds he did not have when she died. There were not enough sword tourneys in the world to keep him in pocket, and the more he drank and the less he trained, the slower he became, until he could scarcely win a duel. He had tried to keep the estate by gambling what little he did have, but his luck had turned against him. To his astonishment, he felt tears trickle down his fuzzy cheeks for the first time in years. Glancing around, he saw that he was not the only one. There was nary a dry eye in sight.

The song was too melodious, though. Jamba was so lost in phantasmagoric recollections that he almost forgot about the Sleepers. Fortunately, Pahu did not. The beasts were almost upon them when the monk switched up his tune, jolting his listeners with a series of dissonant beats. The skitterers yowled and retreated back into the night. Pahu played all night, but inconsistently. He toyed with the Sleepers, inviting death by repeating a few riffs and then banishing it with a sudden shift in tempo. The Sleepers ebbed and flowed like a dark tide, surging closer to the island of humans by the fire only to fall away again. Jamba had never imagined such mastery over the monsters. He slept fitfully, dreaming of all he had lost, startled awake now and then by a particularly cacophonous chord.

The next day, after a short snooze under the rising sun, the smugglers set forth with a spring in their step, more and more confident the closer they came to the edge of the Bog that the devil was either not in residence or was giving them a wide berth. Jamba wondered where he could have gone as he swished through the hibiscuses in the shade of the unruly mangrove trees, startling a woodpecker. The trees fell away around noon, and the smugglers let out sighs of relief as they breathed in the sweet scents of the jacaranda-filled meadows unfurling before them, the Blueschist Belt hazy in the distance to the south. The sun scorched them as they strolled through the meadows, Lug Thorm and the village children picking flowers and chasing butterflies and one another.

"He truly is a sweet soul," Pahu remarked as Jamba chuckled at Lug's antics.

"That he is," agreed Jamba. "Perhaps, if you become Lullabyer, you can help change attitudes towards the lagahoo. As you can see, he's just a big baby."

Pahu raised an eyebrow and said, "If?"

Jamba smiled. "When."

Pahu nodded. "Prejudices are difficult to shift, but I will try."

Jamba's heart glowed in his breast. He cleared his throat. "Ahem. D'you mind if I ask you how you do … what you do? With the Sleepers?"

Pahu shook his head. "I don't mind, but I don't know if I can explain it. Once I attune to the Sleepers' nature through my song, I can … speak to them, after a fashion. I don't know how else to describe it. It's … intuitive."

Jamba nodded thoughtfully. "Well, I'm just grateful you *can* do what you do. We'd have all been six feet under long ago if not for you, Pahu. You save all our lives night after night. Look at these people. They'd do anything for you. They revere you like a God and love you like a friend. I think … I think you'll make a great Lullabyer, Pahu."

Pahu smiled a little. "Thank you, Jamba. That means a lot."

"He shouldn't be doing what he's doing at all," Magnuz Opherio snapped, materialising by their side in ethereal form. *"He should be singing the Lullaby, so that he can send all the Sleepers to sleep, not attuning to their nature and treating them as pets!"*

Pahu started, then said stiffly, "You have not finished teaching me the Lullaby yet, father, so how can I play it? I am doing what I can to keep us all safe."

"Well, we'll fix that soon enough!" said the Lullabyer, drawing himself up.

Jamba left them alone to learn the famous song, quickening his pace to walk with Ruffle Feathers in the vanguard. "D'you think he can do it, Ruffle? D'you think he can learn the Lullaby *and* save us from the crusaders, too?"

Ruffle did not hesitate. He waved a hand, painting letters of fire in the air, 'I do.'

"Me, too," said Jamba, surprising himself with his own conviction. "We just have to make sure we keep him alive long enough for that to happen."

Ruffle nodded. 'That's the trouble.'

"Well, at least we haven't seen any more Justiquans since Dos Rios," said Jamba. "Perhaps that means they only landed at Oldport and Dos Rios north of the Belt. Perhaps we've already scourged half the country."

'I think it likely. The west coast is uninviting to say the least.'

They set a faster pace when they realised they might not reach the Belt by dark and arrived at the blue-hued, colonnaded façade of the fortress dug into the mountain range with little time to spare, breathlessly banging on the portcullis and shouting the witches within. Once more, Jamba studied the scuffed sculpture carved into the cliff wall above the doorway, identical to that on the other side, depicting a Lullabyer playing a damaru and singing, the force of his music pushing back the Sleepers – or perhaps directing them? Watching the sun edge over the horizon inch by inch, already more than half gone, he felt his gut clench in fear, despite his faith in Pahu's skills. It would only take a single small mistake on the monk's part for the Sleepers to slip past his sonic guard and wreak devastation among the villagers.

"Can't you magic it open like the witch did?" Jamba asked Ruffle, only to be subjected to a scowl.

Pahu started to tap his drum and sing *Bluenecks and Brigands,* the tale of the Belt and the two warring factions whom it had served in times long gone. After just one rendition, he switched to playing uncomfortable, discordant notes to repel the crepuscular creatures he knew would be surfacing.

Vivian Malakbet opened the door and poked her head out. "What happened to the divine music?" she cried.

"This is Pahu, the Lullabyer's son," Jamba explained hurriedly. "He has to play such bad music to keep the Sleepers at bay, because he can't sing them to sleep yet. Please, just let us in before we all end up as Sleeper fodder!"

Vivian pursed her lips. "Is that so?" She nodded. "Very well. But tell him to cease that caterwauling once he's within the walls."

She waved a hand, and the portcullis flew up. The smugglers beckoned the villagers inside, and the portcullis slammed down again in their wake.

"Who was it then?" came the airy voice of Violet Malakbet once all were inside and Pahu had put an end to his tuneless melody.

"That lovely singing came from the *syrinx* of our young friend, Pahu here, the future Lullabyer," Vivian told her, turning a coy smile on the monk.

Pahu squirmed, and Jamba realised with a start that the young man was likely a virgin, unused to attention from the opposite sex.

"Oh, no," murmured the smuggler, seeing the predatory look in the witches' eyes. "What is it about musicians that makes women so wet?"

"Wet?" quizzed Lug, brow furrowed.

"Never mind," said Jamba quickly, while Kofi and Wagnar snorted.

"I guess you don't have any kids, Lug?" asked Kofi snidely.

Jamba punched him on the arm, while Lug just looked confused and said, "No."

Chuckling and rubbing his arm, Kofi said, "I've never had any myself either. What about you, Wagnar?"

"I had a daughter … in Dos Rios …"

"I'm sorry, my friend," said Kofi, patting the man on the shoulder. "I'm sure she's frolicking free of cares in the Sunset Isles, though."

Wagnar nodded, wiping away tears, his voice thick. "Thank you. It pleases me to imagine such a thing."

"I would have had a son had my wife not died in childbirth," said Jamba unexpectedly.

They turned to him with shocked expressions.

"You were married?"

"You had a wife?"

'Mnana was pregnant?' asked Ruffle Feathers, wide-eyed. 'You never told me that.'

Jamba nodded, eyes blurring. "He would have been about Pahu's age."

"What happened?" asked Lug softly.

“Just a wasting sickness, the healers said,” replied Jamba, shrugging with a lump in his throat. “There was nothing that could have been done. Ahem, excuse me, I have to go sate the snake.”

In Jamba’s absence, the witches soon had Pahu under their spell, giggling and purring and stroking him, fluttering their eyelashes and flipping their hair and complimenting him on how handsome and amazing he was and what a beautiful voice he had. By the time he returned, his eyes dry once more, the monk was putty in their hands. When they suggested that Pahu – and by extension, everyone else – stay longer than a single night, Jamba immediately leaped down their throats. To his surprise, though, Magnuz appeared at that moment to contradict him, saying that perhaps Pahu ought to use this time while they were ensconced safely in the fortress to finish learning the Lullaby.

“One extra day won’t make a difference,” said the Lullabyer’s spirit.

Jamba rolled his eyes when Pahu agreed to stay.

37

Foreign Memories

Jeremias Colcott dreamwalked through memories not his own, scarcely able to remember his own name.

He snapped out of a dream within a dream when Waddi-waddi said, "Concentrate! Do you feel the bones' energy?"

He had unearthed an entire skeleton along with the skull now, digging at Jinglespur's black earth with his bare hands. Holding up the skull to the hazy scarlet horizon, he sent his mind inside it, faintly sensing the minute traces of energy left over from its time in the land of the living.

"I ... sense it," he said.

"Good," purred the age-old necromancer. "Now, in order to reanimate the corpse, you must flood its energy with your own, remembering at all times that the corpse must call you master. Repeat it over and over to yourself as you begin to send out your energy. I am its master, you say to yourself. I am its master, I am its master."

Jeremias tried, almost bursting a phantom blood vessel. "I ... do not know how to send it my energy."

"Oh." Waddi-waddi blinked. "I forget sometimes that you had little knowledge of the great art before you met me. You have come so far in such a short time. Not many could have survived out there beyond the walls."

"I wouldn't have had to if you hadn't abandoned me out there!" Jeremias growled, anger swamping him at the recollection.

Waddi-waddi shrugged. "It was necessary. You needed to be jolted from your comfort zone, forced into new territory to learn new skills."

Swallowing spite, the seneschal said, "It is done now. What did you mean by the 'great art' anyway?"

Waddi-waddi smiled. "Why, obeah, of course. Come now, try again."

Jeremias nodded and fixed his eyes on the skull once more. Something akin to rain dappled it. He sank through the eye sockets into an abyss.

He came to in a deafening cacophony, blinded by dust and yowling in agony. Squinting through the plumes, he could make out a ring of obeahmen all around him, casting fire and lightning at him from their fingertips. Sucked down into the ground as if he stood in quicksand, his body turning to stone, his arms chipping away, he screamed, "I am Waddi-waddi, you fools, and I will never die!"

Abruptly, he was back in Jinglespur with the skull in his hand.

Waddi-waddi was shaking him by the shoulder and shouting, "Where have you gone, Jeremias? Jeremias! Run, you fool! Back to your body! The marshal comes!"

The seneschal scrambled to his feet and took off running, glancing over his shoulder to see Marshal Clauss striking at Waddi-waddi with a blazing white blade and shrieking, "Get out of my way, damn you! Come back, Colcott, you coward!"

Waddi-waddi defended himself with a shining staff of white energy and hollered, "Run, Jeremias! I'll hold him off!"

Jeremias flew through the citadel wall, hunted through the labyrinthine corridors for a short while and then put his soul back in his body like a key in a lock.

He juddered awake, ice in his veins, and eyed the giant crystal by which he had been meditating in the bowels of the citadel.

"Who am I?" he asked softly.

As he performed Waddi-waddi's regimen of stretches, he saw again the battle against the obeahmen in his mind's eye, wondering where the memory had come from, for it was not his own. Had he been trapped in the necromancer's dream? He wasn't sure.

He sidled past the mad mob running riot inside the citadel, chanting gibberish with as much fervour as zealots. When he exited the citadel to check on the curved wall and its defenders, he saw that the wall had more pockmarks than ever before, half its sunlit battlements shattered by the boulders flung from the Justiquans catapults, half its fighters gone. Every day made a difference now.

Jeremias thought the crusaders could have focussed their aim on a single spot in the wall and likely infiltrated the necropolis by now if they so chose, but guessed they were content to whittle down the defences from without a while longer, for all the boulders and bolts from the catapults and ballistae were aimed squarely at the defenders on the rampart. Boulders crashed into the wall again and again like the beating of war drums, and bolts thrummed through the air to transform men into corpses in the blink of an eye. The suriving Chilpaean soldiers struggled to protect the entire length of the wall now, haring back and forth as breaches sprang up like molehills. Every time the soldiers quashed one group of crusaders surmounting the wall, another was ready to take its place further along. The Chilpaeans were being run ragged, Jeremias saw with a pang.

"Siege towers!" bellowed General Malone hoarsely, bobbing and weaving, his scimitar whirling through the air to slaughter a slew of knights so that he could reach the ladder they had climbed.

Jeremias' eyes popped out of his skull as he beheld the first siege tower hove into view, a behemoth construction of wood and metal – a tower on wheels able to be pushed and pulled all the way up to the wall.

"Kill the haulers!" Malone yelled, but it was hopeless.

The Chilpaeans had long since exhausted their arrows. A few lobbed spears and swords down at those hauling the siege towers toward the wall on ropes, but few hit their mark and the towers inched closer bit by dreadful bit. There was no stopping them. Jeremias stood rooted to the spot, watching in terror, until finally the towers crunched against the wall and the log doors built into the upper halves dropped down to form ramps onto the rampart. Justiquan knights and soldiers swarmed out of the towers like bees from a hive and swamped the wall in moments.

General Malone, Dreyfuss Alamoigne and a squad of Chilpaean soldiers fought desperately to stem the flow from one such tower, standing at the bottom of the ramp and killing anyone who ran down it. Jeremias saw Malone in the eye of the storm, blocking a blow from a Justiquan broadsword before grabbing his attacker by the throat and swinging him into another of the crusaders, sending both toppling even as he parried a blow from another foe. Pushing the sword crossed on his own up and away, he gave himself a moment to slice open the crusader's side by his armour straps. Blood gushed from the wound, and the man cried out and fell to be trampled by his comrades. As they stepped over him, the general took a heartbeat to spear both of the knights he had thrown to the ground as they struggled to rise, weighed down by their armour. By his side, Dreyfuss twirled his spear like a stave, batting back the enemy battalion one by one, occasionally sweeping one or more off the wall with a single swipe.

A hundred paces along the wall, Zov Lorr and his troops from Jawduck fought valiantly in the face of the flood of foes pouring from a second siege tower, but they were falling like flies, outnumbered and out-armoured. Jeremias winced as he saw the Justiquans use their armour to their advantage time and again, barging men aside and clobbering them with gauntlets and vambraces, greaves and even helmets. The seneschal witnessed one unfortunate Chilpaean's skull bashed in by a headbutting crusader and sent up a prayer to the Ferrymen to care for the man's soul. Zov Lorr saw the armoured Knights' tactics, though, and nulled them with agility, dodging their blows and then ducking low to sweep out their legs from beneath them, bringing them toppling down one after another with a series of cymbal-like clangs as their steel plates hit stone. The crusaders could not halt their rush out of the tower, propelled on by those behind them blind to the peril, and so a swathe of them tripped and fell over their prone comrades, giving Zov and his men a chance to even the odds a little. They stabbed and slashed mercilessly at the men on the ground until the ramp and rampart ran red with blood, glistening in the afternoon sun.

Still, they could not plug the flow of foes. As Zov and his warriors were pushed back step by step away from the tower, allowing more and more Justiquans to flock onto the wall, Jeremias glanced still further down the wall to where Wam Guir strove with all his might to blockade another tower with his bloated body and butterfly-bladed axe. Crusaders dogpiled onto him, bedecking him in wounds, but he threw them off with a roar and a display of muscle hidden beneath his rolls. His axe arced as inexorably as the moon, knocking aside swords, severing heads and denting helmets.

Taking Jeremias and the Justiquans by surprise, he leaped up onto the ramp then and charged into the tower, bulling soldiers aside with sheer brawn until he reached the staircase inside allowing Justiquans to rise up from the ground. His men were hot on his heels, dispatching all those he had bowled over in his mad dash. Soon, they held the inside of the tower against the crusaders, who were funnelled into the narrow staircase so that no more than one or two of them could assault Wam and his men at once.

"Wam!" shouted one of his men still on the wall. "Zov's in trouble!"

Wam Guir came barrelling back out of the siege tower and gambolled along the wall toward his friend, shouting over his shoulder, "Hold that tower, lads!"

Like a war ship, he hove into the crusaders ganging up on Zov Lorr, reminding Jeremias of a mad ram the way he butted them left and right with haft and blade, sending soldiers tumbling over the wall. In no time, he had torn his way through the press to reach Zov's side and the two captains battled back to back, shamshir and axe gouging bloody holes in the enemy ranks as Justiquans continued to pour out of the closest siege tower. Though they could hold their ground, Jeremias saw, they could make no headway against the sheer number of enemies mounting the rampart. Some crusaders even started to hop down from the wall, descending the stone steps until they stood inside Jinglespur, the first outsiders to do so in centuries.

Those inside the necropolis easily spotted the unarmed seneschal standing and gawping among the tombstones close by the wall and rushed towards him with foreign war cries on their tongues, blades held high, glittering in the scorching sunlight.

"Let me help you, Jeremias," said a familiar voice in his ear, and the seneschal spun to see the duppy of Waddi-waddi standing beside him, silvery and ephemeral as the reflection of the moon in water.

"Waddi-waddi?" he gasped.

The spirit nodded, a smile haunting its lips. *"It is I. We are attuned now, you and I. Let me help you and I can wipe out these crusaders as easily as brushing bugs off a table."*

"How?" asked Jeremias desperately, watching the crusaders lope closer out of the corner of his eye.

"All you have to do is agree, Jeremias."

Jeremias hesitated, but saw no other way. If he did not do something, Jinglespur would surely fall by day's end.

"Very well. I agree. Help me."

As the words departed his lips, his soul departed his body. He watched himself move as if in a dream from outside his own flesh. His arms rose without any conscious volition, and streams of crackling, whooshing fire flew from his fingertips to engulf the invaders, setting their very skin ablaze in an instant. Screeching in torment, they writhed on the ground for a while in vain before they died, their flesh charred, their armour blackened. Jeremias watched himself climb the steps to the rampart and approach the siege tower about to overwhelm Wam Guir and Zov Lorr. Once more, his hands rose and wildfire gushed from his fingers, wreathing the Justiquan soldiers in flames and setting the entire tower ablaze in mere seconds. The tower crumbled like a sodden biscuit and collapsed, the men inside and at the base screaming as it crushed them.

While Wam Guir and Zov Lorr finished off the crusaders atop the rampart, Jeremias turned his attention to the siege tower Wam had abandoned, where his men had been pushed back and crusaders once more proliferated on top of the wall. Flames flowed from the seneschal's fingers like incarnadine rivers, torching the tower in an instant so that a pillar of fire pricked the sky. The crusaders fared no better, withering on the spot under the whooshing inferno, transformed into ash statues of themselves as they screamed. Finally, Jeremias burned down the tower haranguing General Malone and Dreyfuss Alamoigne. Careful not to incinerate any Chilpaeans, who were more than happy to step out of the way, Jeremias strolled the length of the wall, sanitising it with his occult blaze.

Justiquans hurled themselves off the rampart to escape him, knowing there was more chance of surviving the fall than the flames. Once the wall was clear, the seneschal finally turned to General Malone, who had been following him and demanding to know what in the name of the Gods was going on.

"You may have your body back," he said, and from outside his body, Jeremias was yanked back inside in a heartbeat.

As his old prison of flesh closed around him, Jeremias felt weary beyond wonds, his legs wooden, his eyelids leaden and his tongue tied. He crumpled to the floor at Malone's feet, and the general hollered for healers to help him even as he watched the Justiquan army hightail it back across the meadow of wild petunias outside the wall toward the stockade to the southwest, evidently petrified of the man whose fingers bloomed fire.

38

Devil Doll

Prying open his eyes and tearing himself from the blanketed straw pallet in which he had slept the past two nights, Jamba Klach arose, stretching and yawning, determined to depart the Belt within the hour. He had advised Pahu Opherio against staying an extra day, but the fortress' safety and the promise of two decent nights' sleep were hard to argue against. So, they had stayed. Jamba had meant to check if the monk was sleeping alone high in the Belt in one of the officers' rooms, but, exhausted, he kipped till late morning both days, thrilled just to have a soft place to rest and time to sleep.

On their first morning in the Belt, the broad grin on the monk's face had told him he should have checked. Pahu had spent most of that day with Magnuz Opherio, learning the Lullaby, and when the evening had rolled around once more, when all were taking their supper in the bare-walled mess hall, he had played ballads for the witches and the villagers, his sugar-sweet voice lifting them high above their troubles.

Jamba had cleared his throat at the end of a rendition of *My Tattered Heart*, shattering the safe and comfortable atmosphere by saying gruffly, "We should head for Jinglespur in the morning, Pahu."

Pahu had glanced at him, almost as if he had entirely forgotten the existence of the smuggler and his quest. Jamba had not been surprised – hormones were a tyrant.

"He's right, Pahu," Magnuz had added, much to the smuggler's relief. *"We have dawdled enough. I am loath to give these crusaders even an extra heartbeat in our country. We must cast them out at once. You said Colcott and Malone were holed up in the necropolis, Kofi, yes?"*

Kofi Touluz had nodded. "I did. I know not if they yet live, however. I know only that I received a messenger rook from Jinglespur a couple of weeks ago, giving me the job of recovering the Lullabyer crystal."

"How was the pay?" Jamba had asked sarcastically.

"It was good," Kofi had replied, straight-faced. "Ten thousand doubloons."

"Ten thousand doubloons?" Jamba had exploded. "There's no way Jeremias has access to that much since the treasury was captured. I think you've been lied to, my friend."

Kofi had looked thoughtful for a moment and then nodded. "Come to think of it, you might be right." He smiled. "I am glad I did not kill you."

Jamba had chuckled ruefully. "Me, too."

"How are we to cast out the crusaders anyway?" Pahu had asked then, looking to his ethereal father.

Magnuz had frowned. *"What do you mean? We cast them out, boy!"*

Pahu's brow had wrinkled. "Yes, but how? Surely if the army were capable of casting them out, they would have done so by now."

Magnuz had opened his mouth to retort and then shut it again. *"We'll find a way,"* he snapped after a moment. *"We must, therefore we will. First things first, let's just get to the necropolis."*

"But how do we even get inside if the place is besieged?" Jamba had put in, Pahu's concerns solidifying into dreadful premonitions in his mind. "Your son makes a good point."

Magnuz had turned his stern gaze on the smuggler. *"We will find a way, damn your eyes!"*

The following morning, the monk, assassin, deserter, Goddess, smugglers and villagers broke their fast with the witches in the mess hall, cramming porridge and dumplings graciously provided from the Belt's pantry down their throats as if starved, knowing they needed to be on the road before the sun rose too high. Already, its light was beaming in through the windows, gradually illuminating the world in shades of gold. Jamba felt refreshed. He could not remember the last time he had slept in a bed. Once they had eaten their fill, their chairs scraped as they rose from the table, one by one bidding the witches adieu. The villagers filed out as the smugglers made their final farewells.

"Are you truly leaving us?" Vivian Malakbet asked Pahu when it came the young monk's turn, cupping his face in her hands and pouting.

The monk nodded. "I must. But I will never forget you. Goodbye, Malakbets."

Vivian had turned cold, releasing him and spinning away. "Fine, then. Go. You go to your death out there, monk!"

Pahu sighed. "I do wish you were coming with us, but you have made your intentions clear."

He turned to leave, but Violet Malakbet snarled, "You're not going anywhere!"

Walls of spitting, crackling green witch-fire roared into existence in both the doorways, blocking off all exits from the room save the windows. Jamba eyed them, but did not fancy falling to his death. The mess hall was situated high up in the Belt, as were most of its more serviceable rooms. The lower floors housed the barracks and armouries, where he and the other smugglers had slept, while the monk and villagers had taken the nicer rooms upstairs. Kofi, Wagnar, Mama D'lo and the villagers, now trapped outside the mess hall, called out in alarm. All eyes fixed on Violet, whose wide, bow-legged stance and tensed, clawed hands marked her as the spell caster.

"We thought you'd change your mind by now," Violet rasped as her sister took a step back to stand by her side. "When you agreed to stay for one more day, we figured you'd stay for a second, and a third, just as scared of leaving these walls as we are – as you should be! We will not let you leave, only to get yourself killed! Vivian!"

Vivian took a tightly bound straw doll from one pocket and a needle from the other and poised to poke the doll. "I'm sure you recognise this," she purred. "It is a devil doll, bound with *your* hair, Pahu! Anything that happens to the doll happens to *you!"*

So saying, she viciously jabbed the doll in the midriff with the needle, digging it in and twisting it. Pahu cocked his head, confused.

Violet, on the other hand, doubled over with a scream and screeched, "Stop it!"

Vivian yanked out the needle in horror as the witch-fire masking the exits winked out and the shrilling ceased to be replaced by a weird cackle emanating from Ruffle Feathers' tongueless mouth.

The old man waved a hand, grinning as words of fire took form in mid-air. 'I did a little snooping around last night and discovered your devil doll, girls. It took me quite a long time to carefully extricate Pahu's hairs and replace them with Violet's. You have no hold over Pahu now. Let us leave.'

They all gaped at the obeahman.

"Curse you, old man!" Violet shrieked, flinging a small ball of sizzling green witch-fire from her palm at the trickster.

Fortunately, Ruffle had anticipated such a response and threw up a golden bubble of crackling, wavering golden energy around the smugglers and the monk, against which the witch-fire spluttered out as if it had hit water. Violet threw several more fireballs for good measure, none of which availed her anything save to vent her rage. Vivian drew a straight steel dagger from a sheath secreted at the back of her belt and launched herself forward. She flew through the bubble intended only to keep magical attacks at bay and raised her dagger high to bring it arcing down towards Pahu's throat. Jamba caught her arm and threw her back out of the bubble. She snarled and raised the dagger again.

"Enough!" Pahu's mellifluous voice cracked like a whip, freezing everyone in place. "I need no protection."

So saying, he took a few steps forwards to stand immediately before the witches, outside the bubble. Jamba wanted to stop him, but somehow he could not. A man had to do certain things alone, he knew.

"If you want to kill me," said Pahu, spreading his arms and dropping his damaru on the floor with a bang and a gasp from Magnuz, "here I am."

Vivian raised the dagger a few more inches, a strangely plaintive look on her face, and Jamba's breath caught. He pictured Pahu sprawled on the floor, his throat slit, and knew he would tear the witches limb from limb if that happened. Nothing on Maradoum would stop him.

Vivian slowly lowered the dagger, though, and Violet relaxed her posture, both transforming in that moment from powerful witches to scared little girls.

"We gave ourselves to you, hoping that would be enough to convince you to stay," Vivian sobbed, her eyes welling. "We only made the devil doll as a last resort. We didn't think you'd truly be foolish enough to leave. But you don't want to stay … you don't want us … you want only to leave. Don't we mean anything to you?"

"On the contrary," said Pahu softly, "you mean everything to me, but so does Chilpaea. And we cannot be together if the country is no more. I asked you to come with me last night, but you told me you were too frightened and I said I understood." His voice hardened. "Now, I give you no choice. You *are* coming with me, because I need your help. Chilpaea needs your help. You've seen what the Sleepers can do. You know your mother was wrong. And you know I'm the only one who can stop them. You sit alone in here, selfishly serving your own needs. It is time to change. You *can* change. Help me save our country, our people, and you will no longer have anything to fear, I promise you. You have the power to make a difference in the fight to come. Chilpaea will be lost without you – as will I."

"Who are you to give us orders?" Vivian snapped, eyes blazing.

Pahu drew himself up. "I am your Lullabyer."

39

The Lullaby

Jamba Klach was speechless when the witches agreed to accompany them. He'd have sooner believed he'd have had to fight his way out of the Belt. He had dreaded the idea of battling the lindworm, but it proved that the beast had gone hunting in the mountains. Now, it was Pahu who seemed to cast the spell. The witches fawned over him, walking by his sides, hanging on his every word and even brushing crumbs from his lips when he ate a biscuit later that day. Their fast broken, the smugglers and villagers, the monk, the Goddess, the assassin, the deserter and the witches all set out of the south face of the Belt towards the witchwood and, eventually, Jinglespur Necropolis, where Kofi Touluz had told them they would find the seneschal and the remnants of the Chilpaean army.

"We should visit Nirby this time, no?" Jamba said to Ruffle Feathers as they hiked across an untended farm, the wheat wilting in the heat.

Ruffle wiped sweat from his forehead with the back of his hand, glowered up at the smothering summer sun scudding through the clear blue sky for a moment, and then flicked his fingers. 'You are thinking we might be able to recruit more help?'

Jamba nodded. "Recruit more help and save more people – if they yet live. Chances are Nirby is a ruin, just like Dos Rios."

Ruffle nodded, a smile haunting his lips as he puffed on his pipe and blew bluish plumes. 'You have become quite the noble saviour of Chilpaea.'

Jamba punched him on the bony arm affectionately. "Someone's got to save this godforsaken country."

"It is *not* godforsaken," Mama D'lo pointed out, seeming to materialise by the smuggler's side. "But these crusaders are powerful beyond your ken." She glanced towards the young monk, walking a short way behind with the shade of his father. "Pahu is the only one who can stop them now." She returned her gaze to the smugglers. "Unless you can summon a demon big enough to destroy the entire Justiquan army and its sorcerous commanders, Ruffle?" The obeahman scowled at her, and she smirked. "I didn't think so."

"I never really believed in the Gods before I met you," blurted Wagnar, colouring when Mama D'lo transfixed him with an icy glare. "I mean no offence. I just thought you were, you know, made up stories for children."

"Even if we are *made up,*" she scolded him, "that does not make us any less real! Who do you think made *you* up?"

Wagnar shuffled his feet like a chastised child, saying in a small voice,

"I believe now, though."

"I have always believed in the Gods," said Kofi Touluz. "I dedicate each and every kill to the God of Blood, Galush-Kagen."

"Ugh, that numpty," scoffed Mama D'lo.

Kofi made no reply.

"I always believed, too," added Lug, nodding seriously. "My ma taught me you have to respect the Gods, or else they'll come and snatch you away and make you eat nothing but vegetables all day long."

Jamba and the others burst into laughter, their peals echoing out over the fields, while Lug looked on, perplexed.

When his sides stopped cramping, Jamba shouted over his shoulder, "Pahu, we're heading towards Nirby to see if there are any there to join our cause."

Pahu paused in his attempt at singing a verse of the Lullaby and nodded. "Sounds smart. We'll need all the help we can get."

"That's perfect," said the magenta and aquamarine shade of his father when he finished repeating the verse. *"Tell me, Pahu, what do you know of the Lullaby?"*

Taken aback, Pahu stammered, "Er, well, it's .... It's the Lullaby, isn't it? It's the song that puts the Sleepers to sleep."

Magnuz rolled his eyes. *"It is a sixty-beats-per-minute ballad-style song in the melodic minor scale. It is the gift given to us by the Gods. It is our island's salvation, passed down from father to son for generations. It is a song that only the Opherios, blessed with syrinxes like the greatest singers of all time, the birds, can sing. It is our legacy and our purpose. It was my life's meaning, Pahu, and now it is yours. What I just taught you was the last verse. You now know the Lullaby in its entirery, my son. It is a grave responsibility and a sacred bounty all rolled up in one. You must never forget it, and you must pratise it every night. And when the time comes, you must teach it to your son just as I have taught it to you. For now you truly are the last living Lullabyer."*

"That's it?" Pahu squawked in surprise. "The whole thing?"

Magnuz nodded. *"Indeed it is. A powerful piece of music. Use it wisely, Pahu. Now, all that remains is to test it."*

"Thank you, father," said Pahu, meeting the spirit's gaze. "I'm honoured."

Between them and the witchwood, the small town of Nirby lay tucked in a verdant valley, surrounded by undulating farmland. As in the north, many of the farmhouses the travellers passed had been put to the torch. Wandering down a dirt road winding its way between farms and mango groves to the valley, watched over by tweeting thrushes and kingbirds, the smugglers in the vanguard signalled those behind them to halt with raised fists when they heard the faint jingling of harnesses and the clopping of hooves coming from behind a screen of mangoes around noon.

It was impossible to hide all the villagers, so Jamba signalled for the woman and children to wait and beckoned the warriors, drawing his scimitars. A contingent of pale-skinned infantrymen in leather armour, fifty strong, rounded the corner ahead of them and let out yells at the sight of them, unsheathing steel. The man in the lead, clad in steel plate with a plumed helm glinting in the light of the blistering sun, jabbed his sabre at the sky, cried out in his home tongue and then they were all kicking up dust as they charged headlong at the smugglers and villagers. Jamba, Lug, Kofi, Wagnar and a few more brave warriors formed a line across the road to protect Ruffle Feathers and the rest of the villagers.

Before the galloping horses could reach them, however, Ruffle had ripped asunder the fabric of the world, slashing open the veil between realms to create a ghastly, odious green portal directly in the path of the careening crusaders. Several men skidded straight into the rift with dwindling screams, never to be heard from again, while the rest frantically pulled back or steered wide of it as strange spider-like creatures the size of bloodhounds started to skitter out, their insides protected by spiky exoskeletons, their mandibles clacking.

The spider demons pounced yards through the air towards their foes, landing with almost unerring accuracy on the men they targeted, clinging on with their eight legs and greedily sinking their mandibles into hot flesh. A score scurried through the rift before it snapped shut, and between them they shredded the obeahman's enemies with the ease of spiders gorging on webbed flies. Jamba watched a couple of the crab demons miss their mark, flying through the air, but most found a target. He watched in horror as soldier after soldier was borne down by the leapfrogging fiends, screaming as the mandibles dug in.

Only a few escaped the demons' wrath – those on the flanks, who rounded the rift even as it spawned. Those few crashed into the wall of warriors, only for their legs to be scythed out from beneath them by Jamba's sweeping scimitars. Jamba felt no mercy for the men he maimed. Besides, he told himself, he put them out of their misery a mere second later. As he sidestepped and slashed, wincing at the whinny of pain he caused, he saw Lug and Wagnar shouldered aside by two burly galloping Justiquan soldiers and prayed they were not severely injured.

A Justiquan charged him, broadsword arcing down. Jamba blocked it and tripped him, using the man's own momentum to send him sprawling. As the smuggler turned to cut the man's throat, another crusader almost caught him in the back with a stab of his sword. Kofi parried the blow, however, and grabbed the attacker's arm as he did so, yanking him off-balance with a grunt.

The man hit the floor with a thump, eyes popping, and Kofi stamped on his face until his skull split. Jamba nodded his thanks to the assassin as he finished off the tripped Justiquan and saw that Vivian and Violet Malakbet had torched the other two burly crusaders who had made it past the demons. Their corpses flickered with arcane lime fire, flat on the ground. Up the road, the spider demons were happily picking the rest of the crusaders' skeletons clean of flesh.

"Not one wound among us," Jamba said, smiling broadly and bowing to the obeahman and the witches in turn. "Our thanks!"

Vivian and Violet turned up their noses. Ruffle grinned and bowed theatrically, before waving a hand to reopen the hideous, fetid green rift. Jamba watched in amusement as the spider demons were torn unwillingly from the carcasses on which they were feeding, pulled as if by a vortex back into the ghastly green gash, screeching in dismay all the way.

The rift closed with a *pop* once all had been sucked through, and the smugglers, villagers, witches, Goddess, assassin and deserter stepped over the skeletons of their foes and continued on down the road, wrinkling their noses at the bitter attar and humming along with the age-old Lullaby emanating from the throat of the young monk. Though the tune was exactly as Jamba remembered, familiar as his mother's face, something was off … like a flat note, save all the notes were perfect. Jamba could not put a finger on it, but he sensed it all the same.

40

The Battle of Nirby

As soon as the smugglers topped a hill and gazed down on the town of Nirby, it was clear it was no ruin – not yet. By the purple glow of twilight, they beheld pale-skinned, armoured Justiquans patrolling the paved streets in droves, the few dark-skinned folk present cringing in their presence as if expecting a whipping. Though clouds shrouded the dying sun, the smugglers could see that most of the timber-built houses had been savaged by the Sleepers. Roofs had been torn off, doors had been ripped from hinges, and walls had been clawed open. Two stone structures yet stood predominantly intact in the centre of the town, however – the town hall and the adjacent open air Temple of El Vandu, God of Luck. Jamba scowled at the temple as he snorted some witch-spice and felt the familiar tingle of energy rushing through his body once more. He had once believed the God of Luck to be his own personal patron God in his gambling days, but now he knew better. Luck had deserted him long ago.

"What do we do?" asked Lug, fidgeting and then sniffing a few spice seeds when offered.

"We take back our country," said Pahu firmly, striding forward with damaru in hand, the witches by his side.

The smugglers looked at one another in surprise, then Jamba shrugged and followed the monk.

"The Justiquan commander will be in the town hall if he's smart," Jamba said as he caught up. "That's where we want to be. It looks like the only viable structure in which to spend the night. So, we need to find a way to oust him and his men and get in there. My guess is they'll have all the entryways barricaded save for a small side entrance. We don't have long. We'll have to be fast."

Magnuz Opherio, his body formed of blue and purple light, translucent as smoke and glittering like the stars at night, overtook them. *"You had better let the warriors and obeahman take the vanguard, Pahu, unless you plan on slaying the Justiquans with your music. What you have been doing is abominable. What you did to Ol' Higue was unforgivable. Your gifts were not meant to be abused in this way, Pahu. You are the Lullabyer. You are meant to sing the Sleepers to sleep, not join them!"*

"I know, father," Pahu ground out through gritted teeth. "I am doing my best to keep us all alive night after night."

"You leave him alone!" snapped Vivian Malakbet.

"Go on, shoo!" added her sister, Violet, flapping a dismissive hand.

Magnuz scowled. *"I will not be shooed by a couple of gold-digging whores! Pahu is my son."*

"Ooh, you're lucky I can't slap that beard off your face!" Vivian fumed, fists clenched.

Jamba chuckled and shook his head at the ongoing bickering between the witches and the Lullabyer. His smile faded when they were spotted by the Justiquans in town. There was no means of masking their approach down the hill; the town had clear sightlines. A legion of shield-bearing knights in steel plate banded together and moseyed out of town to meet them across a farm torn and trampled to shreds by the Sleepers. Pahu and the witches hung back, and Ruffle Feathers whirled his arms in arcane gestures and a magenta scar rent the air with a whoosh and crackle. Jamba gagged on its perfidious perfume as wings from within flapped the sulphuric smoke in his face. In a flash of fuchsia flames, the void-plumed demon bird, Izulu, swooped out of the rift, cawing and snapping its sharp silver beak.

"Kakaw! Greetings, human!" it squawked in Traveller's Tongue. "Once more, Djhuty sends me in his place. He is far too busy right now with matters in his own realm to help the likes of you, but *I* am hungry. *Kakaw! I* have come for a feast, so you had better provide me something to eat if you do not wish your own gizzards to be my supper! What would you have of me, *master?"*

Jamba had not thought birds could sneer, but he was sure it sneered the last word.

Ruffle Feathers waved a hand as the crusaders took out their weapons and started to advance more purposefully up the hill towards the magic so clearly taking place. Jamba could make out their startled expressions when the rift fastened itself shut with a popping sound and a whoosh of violet fire.

Words limned in fire burned in mid-air. 'Not to worry, I have a feast and a half for you, Izulu. Behold the town in the valley, plagued by the foreign crusaders. If you would serve me, slay my pale-skinned foes but leave my brethren of darker complexion be.'

Izulu bobbed its head, laying eyes on the bounty that awaited it and shrilling gleefully, "As you wish!"

So saying, the demon flapped its wings and disappeared up into the dark cloudbank overhead in a blink. Jamba wondered if it had abandoned them for a moment, but then it pierced the clouds once more, dropping like a rock on the advancing soldiers and clawing open jugulars with its talons, gouging out eyeballs with its beak and jabbing its venomous scorpion-like tail wherever it could reach. Feeling sick, Jamba watched those stabbed by the tail immediately swell up like inflated pig's bladders only to pop in an eruption of gore.

"Charge!" he bellowed, brandishing his scimitars and pelting towards the surviving soldiers, who had been thrown into disarray by the demon's antics.

He had to admire their bravery as he hurtled towards the crusaders; not one of them fled. All held their ground, hefting shields high and swiping at the demon bird. Hearing the smugglers' pounding footsteps on the sun-baked earth, they turned just in time to bring their swords and shields to bear. Roaring like a bear and sprouting fur like one too, Lug dented one of the knights' shields with a single swing of his warhammer. Then, he was inside the knight's guard, smacking the man back with the haft to create room to swing the heavy head again. The warhammer hit the man's helmet with a gonging sound, crushing the skull within. Beside the lagahoo, Jamba leaped high and kicked at a shield, sending the man holding it reeling back with a grunt, his composure lost. Jamba landed lightly, batted aside the poorly positioned shield with one scimitar and skewered its wielder through the neck with the other. The man's eyes widened, and he coughed blood as he slid off the blade that had killed him.

Kofi deftly struck high with one sword, forcing his foe to raise his shield, and then ducked, spun and cut the knight's ankle out from beneath him, making the man squeal like a stuck pig. Kofi kicked aside the shield, knocked aside the man's sword and slit his throat when he fell. Wagnar brought his standard issue iron battleaxe, complete with a single heavy crescent blade, slamming down two-handed onto another of the knight's shields, but his foe was wily enough to angle his shield so that the blow glanced off. The knight's broadsword snuck out as Wagnar staggered, slicing along the deserter's ribs and making him gasp at the welling of searing ice cold pain.

Glimpsing the deserter's plight from the corner of his eye, Kofi parried his own foe's sword away for a moment so that he could lash out with his second blade at the knight about to impale Wagnar, catching the man in the gap between cuirass and helmet with a spray of blood and sending him spinning to the floor to trip those behind him. Wagnar tried to heft his battleaxe, but could not lift it above his waist with one arm, nor with two. Sweating and hissing in pain, he backed away. A couple of knights made to chase after him, but – either through beneficence or happenstance – Izulu chanced to burn those knights to a crisp with a blast of its crimson lightning breath.

Between them, the smugglers, the assassin, a couple of the villagers with stolen Justiquan swords and the demon bird made short work of the knights, staining the flowers in the untended field red with their blood. A few Justiquans fled across the farm, but the witches brought them down with tossed balls of sizzling green witch-fire. Jamba winced at the sound of the men's screams as they burned in the eldritch flames. A few fled back towards the town, but Izulu gave pursuit and soon crushed their skulls in his beak. Not one escaped.

More soldiers were pouring out of the town now, predominantly clad in leather armour with only a handful of knights remaining. Izulu fell on them with a wrath that Jamba could only call demonic, incinerating them in swathes as it flew back and forth overhead with incarnadine lightning crackling from its maw. Screaming men soon transformed to living torches and then to blackened husks as the demon bird's energies burned them to the bone. Those fortunate enough to escape the fiend's fury had only a skirmish with the smugglers and witches to look forward to, though. Panicked and out of formation, they made easy pickings for both witch-fire and blade.

Seeing only the sun's bloody stump on the horizon as he swung around a blow, Jamba grew impatient and tried to bring his swordfight to an end, dodging a blow when he should have parried in order to more easily find his next attack. He gritted his teeth when he felt his opponent's sword slice a line of fire across his belly and knew how close he had come to being disembowelled. His sword found its mark in the soldier's skull, but the smuggler knew he shouldn't have taken the risk. He did not want to be caught battling the Justiquans when the sun set, however. Still, he forced himself to fight on with a modicum more care, taking his time and awaiting the perfect opportunity to strike.

One soldier, more skilled than the rest, kept him waiting far longer than he would have liked, forcing him into a deadly dance of advancing and retreating, stabbing and dodging, slashing and ducking, parrying and riposting. Jamba lost count of the number of times he thought he had killed the man, only to quickly learn he had failed yet again to pierce the wily soldier's leather armour. Finally, the red-bearded man caught Jamba out, punching him in the face when they crossed blades and sending him reeling. By the time the smuggler's eyes cleared, the man's broadsword was arcing towards his neck. Jamba threw himself aside, landing unceremoniously on the ground and scrabbling back to his feet just in time to knock the soldier's sword away as it came for him again.

Jamba was stuck on the back foot then, retreating and blocking, bobbing and weaving as the soldier's sword sought him out over and over, humming like the warm wind as it scythed through the air mere inches from the smuggler's flesh. Witnessing one of the Chilpaean villagers fall to a crusader's broadsword, his heart pieced, Jamba cursed aloud. The man had fought alongside the smugglers every night since they had left Bessaroca, and it panged Jamba to see him torn down. What panged him worse was the sight of the man's killer eyeing him up like as if he were a pigeon perfectly sized to fit the crusader's plate. He knew he had to bring his current skirmish to an end fast lest he be forced to fight two foes at once.

He threw himself at his opponent like a feral cat, twin scimitars flashing out left and right to hypnotise the crusader and lull him into a false sense of security with a series of rapidly executed but simple and easy to block attack patterns. Once the soldier had the measure of the pattern, blocking every blow and growing confident enough to retaliate here and there, Jamba switched it up. Suddenly, his looping slashes became lightning-fast lunges that his opponent was unprepared for. Backing away and parrying frantically, the soldier brought Jamba into contact with the second soldier who had slain the villager. Cursing inwardly as he parried the second man's attacks, Jamba tried desperately to continue his assault on the first soldier who was on the back foot, but could do so now with only one scimitar.

Praying that his inevitable death would be swift and painless, for he knew his odds against two skilled and armoured foes, Jamba blinked in surprise when the first soldier tripped on a hump of grass and fell flat on his back with a thud. Caught gawping too long at his good luck, Jamba was almost impaled by the second crusader. Spinning around the thrust intended to disembowel him, however, he found enough space to take a split second to ram his scimitar down into the fallen crusader's chest, the tip of the weapon easily puncturing leather and flesh to cleave into his lungs. Jamba withdrew his sword in a red spray and faced his remaining foe with blood dripping from one blade. To his surprise, the man turned and ran away, arms pumping.

Staggering and gazing around, Jamba bore shocked witness to all the remaining soldiers fleeing over the fields. Some of the villagers were giving chase, as was Izulu.

The sun had almost set, however, casting the world in a vermillion haze, so Jamba shouted, "Let them go! Just get to the town hall! The Sleepers will deal with them."

So, ignoring those hightailing it out of the valley, the smugglers made a beeline for the town hall. More Justiquans – leather-bound soldiers and clerks in brown robes – streamed out of the side of the large stone building as they approached, hollering in fear and running for the hills.

"How nice of them to vacate the place for us," Jamba commented wryly, well understanding any man's unwillingness to stand against such an unholy foe as Izulu.

The smugglers and villagers piled into the town hall through the side entrance, which proved – as Jamba had suspected – to be the only entryway not blockaded with boards, chains, bedframes, wardrobes, dressers and tables and chairs. It looked as though the Justiquans and Chilpaeans had all been penned up there every night. Blankets covered the floor. As the sun was about to set, the townsfolk gathered hopefully around the town hall, having been hiding during the conflict, now pleading for entry. Pahu ushered them in graciously. It was a tight fit. Jamba dreaded to imagine how tight it must have been when the crusaders had been in residence. People would have been piled on top of each other, he was sure. He was pleased so many had survived the Sleeper attacks, though.

When asked how they usually defended the side entrance at night, the townsfolk answered with barricades and with shields and steel. Loath though he was to touch such a cowardly instrument, Jamba helped gather the dead crusaders' shields by the last rays of day, just in case of emergency. A chill coursed down his spine when shadow found him outside and he heard the first howls of the night as Sleepers somewhere emerged from their warrens. He and the others scuttled back inside on the instant and started piling some of the furniture in the side entry, where the door had long since been torn clear.

They were just in time. The Sleeper horde descended on them like a baying storm, shaking the entire hall with their attack, clambering all over it and clawing at the doors, the slate roof, the barricades and the walls. The people inside cried out as a small hole in the roof was slowly but surely enlarged by gouging Sleeper claws and bits of detritus fell on their heads. The barricades by all the doors looked suddenly flimsy, in fact, thought Ruffle Feathers as he closed his eyes to concentrate on the energy required to maintain Izulu's presence in the realm.

Pahu started tapping his drums and singing the strange whistling Lullaby he had learned from his father. All remembered the tune, having heard it almost every night of their lives – if only distantly. They recognised it as easily as the backs of their own hands and relaxed a jot in the knowledge that the monsters they faced were about to pass out. The monk sang the melody perfectly. But it had no effect on the Sleepers. The slavering beasts did not seem to even register the music, but snarled and howled and snapped their eerie jaws just as viciously as ever. The villagers stared at Pahu with wide, frightened eyes, wondering why the Lullaby could not save them, and the monk returned their gaze with his own uncertain stare, fear for Chilpaea bleeding his heart.

"Why isn't it working?" he whispered.

By the side entry, Jamba, Lug and Kofi took the brunt of the assault with armed villagers behind them ready to take their place. Wagnar had sullenly agreed to sit out while his wounded side healed. Jamba's stomach stung where it had been slashed open at first, but fortunately it was a shallow wound and he soon forgot it in the heady melee, all his being devoted to swordplay. Though battling the Sleepers was no duel of finesse, it yet required utmost concentration and careful timing. Anticipation was key. He had learned through experience now to predict the monsters' movements from their posture and the bunching of their muscles before a leap.

He felt as though he had finally found the flow of the fight, as though he were dancing to the Sleepers' rhythm and thus timing his executions perfectly. He did not allow himself to grow overconfident, however, nor did he try to rush as he had done outside. A beast could still catch him unawares now and then; it was the nature of combat against so many that at any time a random foe could catch him off-balance and he would have to adjust in the blink of an eye or be mauled. His arms ached as his scimitars hummed through the air, a thrumming accompaniment to Pahu's drum as the monk switched tunes and began to play grating, discordant music.

Jamba saw the difference in the Sleepers at once. They howled as if pained and gave up their assault on the instant, turning and skittering off into the shadows with their tails between their legs. Izulu gave chase, torching the monsters to smithereens with jets of vermillion lightning squawked from its beak. Exhausted, though he had fought for but minutes, Jamba nodded gratefully to Pahu, who nodded back even as his fingers continued to tap the damaru.

41

Return to the Witchwood

By morning, the townsfolk of Nirby had pledged to follow Pahu Opherio wherever he led, having borne witness to his power. They were especially grateful to be able to find closure with their friends and relatives who had been slaughtered by the crusaders. The resident duppy in town took form before their eyes by the light of dawn under the sway of the young monk's soulful tunes, only to then be banished to the Sunset Isles after a teary farewell. The spirits vanished in heartwarming twinklings of light.

The monk, smugglers, townsfolk, villagers, witches, Goddess, assassin and deserter departed early that morning, sleeping only a little after sunrise, for most had grown used to sleeping through the weird jarring music Pahu played to keep the beasts at bay by now and they had a long way to go to reach the witchwood. The townsfolk and villagers had second thoughts about following the young monk when they heard they would be passing through the witchwood, but their loyalty won out. Many still muttered about Pahu's inability to render a functioning Lullaby, though. The monk had no answer for them. Nor did his father.

"You must have sung it wrong," Magnuz Opherio asserted when confronted. *"Just practise and try it again. It will work."*

So, Pahu practised with his father all day as they walked. Bumbling through the bee-ridden meadow of golden orchids fringing the witchwood that afternoon, Jamba Klach could recognise the tune the monk sang as the eerie faraway song he had heard almost every night of his life, but something about it still did not sit right with him somehow. Pahu was close to perfecting the Lullaby, he knew, but something was missing. Normally, eyelids drooped upon hearing the first note of the arcane song. Adults struggled to remain awake through its length, and it was practically impossible for children. When Pahu sang it, though, the Lullaby did not make Jamba sleepy, and it certainly did not make the Sleepers sleepy. Lug and the children danced through the sunny meadow to the melody, unmindful of its intended purpose, merely enjoying the rhythm.

"So, you truly met Papa Bwa?" Wagnar Long asked again, wiping sweat from his brow.

"Yes!" replied Jamba, tugging at his beard in exasperation.

Wagnar shook his head with a smile. "I don't believe you."

"Believe what you like," said Jamba, itching at his bandaged midriff. "You'll see for yourself soon enough."

The witchwood, visible in the distance as a white scar, marched closer all afternoon until it reared before them, its colourless boughs painted gold by the sunset. The smugglers, assassin, deserter, monk, Goddess, witches, villagers from Bessaroca and townsfolk from Nirby all strolled into the protective umbra of the wood with time to spare before dusk – though only the smugglers saw it that way, having passed through before, safe from the Sleepers. The villagers and townsfolk were jittery as kittens.

Feeling his blood freeze the same as they did, Jamba could well understand the shivers he saw rippling through his countrymen as they entered the shadow of the wood. The sounds from outside, the chittering of the peewees and warblers and the buzz of the bees and mosquitos, drifted away like forgotten dreams until they lingered only on the edge of hearing. Jamba saw heads twitch this way and that, trying to track the ephemeral movement they caught in the corners of their eyes, and he knew they were peeking through the veil, glimpsing the hundreds of duppy lost in the woods. He could see them himself, almost, just on the edge of vision, like a forgotten word on the tip of the tongue.

"I know it is an unpleasant sensation," he tried to reassure his countrymen, "but we are safe in here, I promise. No harm will come to you in the witchwood – not from the Sleepers, anyway. Avoid the deeper parts of the swamp and you should be fine."

Far from reassured and muttering among themselves, the Chilpaeans yet followed Pahu as he ploughed purposefully through the witchwood, putting their fate in the young monk's hands. Some of the children cried, sensing the eldritch atmosphere, but were quickly shushed by their parents.

The outer rim of solid land and white-barked, slightly furry trees soon gave onto a slope beckoning the travellers down to a steamy swamp that shone the colour of dried blood in the perishing light thanks to the sun-tinted rushes and reddish sedge growing by the shores of the many stagnant pools littering the area, their surfaces black as mould with algae. Jamba and the others tried their best to find paths through the morass that gave the largest ponds a wide berth, occasionally resorting to sprinting between ponds when there seemed no way around. Jamba's heart pounded in his throat at such moments, his hair slick on his sweaty scalp – and for good reason.

Jamba led the way, testing the paths, and so it was his duty to make the first run between the ponds. Taking a deep breath and hurtling between two dips in the land filled with brackish water and red sedge, he yelped when the water on his left burst up into the air to shower down on him as a thirty-foot-long Chilpaean crocodile shot up out of the pond like a toothed arrow, its massive jaws gnashing shut less than a foot from the terrified smuggler's backside.

"Find a way around! Find a way around!" he shrieked, running away.

The other smugglers and the villagers nodded and, seeking a way to skirt the huge ponds, set off in the opposite direction from Jamba while he yipped and hopped around amid the rushes, trying to escape the chasing crocodile's hunger.

He rejoined them later in the day, stippled in dirt and sweat, breathing heavily and glancing over his shoulder again and again. "I lost it … I think."

Lug tried calling for Papa Bwa, but got no reply. By the time twilight eclipsed the world and the Sleepers' howls broke the night air, they had seen no sign of any living creature, only wafting phantoms in the steam rising from the pools. Bivouacked down among the trees on solid ground as far from the pools as they could get, they listened to the faraway howls and gradually, when the sounds never grew closer and the Sleepers did not fall upon them, the villagers and townsfolk reluctantly came to accept that they were safe within the witchwood, despite the peculiar sensations it provoked and the duppy haunting their every step.

Freed from the need to create discord to rebuff the beasts, Pahu played and sang the Lullaby that night. It made no difference that anyone could tell; the Sleepers still sent up their own howling chorus in accompaniment. When Pahu tired of the Lullaby, he played Pacho's favourite songs with a sombre smile, all of them roof raisers that washed away the people's fear, warmed their hearts and lifted them high on a wave of sonic nirvana.

Clapping and singing along, Jamba grinned to see Papa Bwa sat beside him, puffing on a baui pipe carved in the shape of a dragon and clapping and singing along just as enthusiastically to a rendition of *Lost In The Woods*. The father of the forest was just as the smuggler remembered him, a short, ebon-skinned, hunched old fellow with the upper body of a man and the hairy legs and cloven hooves of a billy goat. Two small horns sprouted from the lion's mane of dark hair framing his grandfatherly face, and his beard was slick and black as algae. His witchwood cane lay by his side. Jamba wondered when he had appeared there.

When the song came to an end, Jamba cleared his throat and said, "We have a visitor."

All eyes turned toward him, but hooked instead on Papa Bwa, and mouths fell agape, for none could look into the evergreen eyes of the father of the forest and not recognise him for what he was – an ancient and powerful entity beyond their ken.

"Blessings, my children," said Papa Bwa in a voice like the crunch of gravel under a cart wheel. "It is good to see you again, Jamba, Ruffle, Lug. You too, Mama D'lo. It has been a long time."

Mama D'lo sniffed. "Not long enough. Your stink still offends me."

Papa Bwa chuckled. "And your scent is still perfume to mine nostrils."

"Oh, shut up, you old flatterer," said Mama D'lo, flapping a hand and blushing. "We're going to work together to save the country from those blasted crusaders. Fine. But I don't have to like you."

"You don't *have* to," agreed Papa Bwa, "but it would make the experience a great deal more enjoyable for all of us."

"And who said I cared anything about that?" Mama D'lo snapped.

Bwa sighed. "Same old mother of rivers, I see."

Mama D'lo clucked her tongue. "Same old father of forests, I see. Look at yourself, Bwa. You're a mess. And you're getting old!"

"No more than are you, my love."

"I'm not your love. I put an end to that nonsense long ago."

Papa Bwa nodded, hand on his chest. "And broke my heart in two."

"You broke *my* heart!" Mama D'lo snapped, and no more was said on the subject.

Jamba longed to know what had happened, but was too afraid to ask. He guessed everybody else felt the same. It did not feel right, as a mortal, to pry into the goings on of Gods. What right had he?

"Your music is beautiful," said Papa Bwa to Pahu after a drawn out silence, clumsily changing the subject. "You will make a fine Lullabyer – if you master the Lullaby in time."

"Thank you, Papa Bwa," said Pahu in his soft, melodious voice, dipping his dreadlocked head. "Will you come with us to help buy us the time you speak of, or will you let the country fall?"

Jamba gaped. He could not believe the monk had been so abrupt and accusatory to the God. He half-expected Bwa to smite Pahu down then and there.

Instead, Papa Bwa laughed uproariously. "Ah, I like you, young man. I don't know what use I'll be in a battle outside my forest – but yes, I'll come with you."

Pahu bowed his head again. "I thank you, father of forests, on behalf of all Chilpaea."

42

Hatbrim

The town of Hatbrim on the shore of the Agua Alta River, sandwiched between Jinglespur and the witchwood, had been completely taken over.

Watching the pale-skinned Justiquans patrolling the sun-gilded streets and moseying in and out of the rich merchants' houses from the shadows of a stand of limes and palms on the far side of the bridge leading into town, Jamba muttered, "Thanks for nothing, El Vandu," before turning around and traipsing back down a slight slope to where Pahu, his fellow smugglers, the assassin, the deserter, the witches, the Gods of river and forest, the townsfolk from Nirby and the villagers from Bessaroca were hidden by the lay of the land.

"The place is chock-full of the pale-skinned wretches," he said bluntly. "I didn't see a single one of our countrymen among them. I don't know whether they evacuated or met the Justiquans' blades, but they are all gone, I am sure of it."

Pahu clenched his hands, but surprised the smuggler by growling, "Let's make camp here. No fires. I don't want to give away our position."

"Wait here?" Jamba blurted. "But, with Ruffle's help, we could clear out the town before sunset and take shelter from the Sleepers and the elements in Agrissimo's Temple or the merchants' mansions – those are the only structures left standing. They look a little worse for wear after all the Sleeper attacks, but they should hold another night."

Pahu shook his head, jaw set. "No. We make camp here and attack during the night. I have an idea for how to banish these parasitic Justiquans without shedding a single drop of Chilpaean blood."

"I know what you are thinking, my son," said Magnuz Opherio in a deep, faraway voice, materialising beside the monk in a flash of blue-and-purple light. *"But this is not the way. The Sleepers are not a weapon to be wielded. They are creatures of Maradoum – just like you and I. It is not right to use your powers this way, Pahu."*

"Who's to say what's right?" Pahu snarled, rounding on his father. "The Justiquans and Sleepers are monsters plaguing our land, bringing death and destruction. Why shouldn't I lay waste to them to them if I can? Why not let them slaughter each other like sheep?"

Magnuz crossed his arms and shook his head. *"It is not about them. It is about you. You are staining your soul with all this blood on your hands. The Justiquans are not –"*

"I don't care!" burst out Pahu, throwing his arms up. "As long as

Chilpaea is safe, I don't give a rat's ass about me. This is the only way I can protect my people."

Magnuz's expression softened a little. *"I care."*

Pahu snorted. "That's why you sent me to the furthest corner of Chilpaea to be as far away from you as possible."

"I knew you would be safe there," said Magnuz softly, but Pahu did not hear him.

The monk had already walked away. The Lullabyer sighed and melted from sight, pondering how best to get through to his son.

Darkness fell. They did not witness a single Justiquan patrolling outside the town and guessed they had gotten lucky with their timing. Likely, the last patrols had been well before sunset, thought Jamba – and if they knew anything about Chilpaea, they would have no reason to expect an attack from the witchwood. Though legends spoke of the awful ends met by those who ventured inside, none spoke of the witchwood coming after anyone. Jamba shuddered at the thought, then realised it was now true, after a fashion. The witchwood marched with them in the form of old Papa Bwa. The rivers accompanied them in the form of Mama D'lo. The thought warmed Jamba' heart. Once, he had feared the witchwood above all things. He had encountered new horrors since then.

As soon as the sky purpled to black, the howls began to sound, both faraway and close by. The townsfolk and villagers cringed and huddled together in the midst of the farmer's field in which they lurked. The smugglers, assassin and deserter drew their weapons, peering into the abyss of night with slitted eyes. Papa Bwa and Mama D'lo looked on placidly. Pahu picked up his drum and started to play. He did not even attempt the Lullaby. Dark, angry melodies sprang from the drum, from his fingertips and his soul, fast and fricative and somehow jarringly rhythmic, as though the monk had found the perfect middle ground between creating discord and melody. Jamba could almost bob along to parts of it, while others made him recoil.

The music thumped out into the night, and the Sleepers danced to its tune. Jamba and the others watched in slack-jawed amazement as the beasts rampaged towards them by the thousand, half-lit by the silvery glow of the moon and stars, only to skitter past them on all sides, flowing around them like a river around a rock and continuing on towards Hatbrim. Jamba gawped, hearing the town light up with screams. The torches around the temple and the stone-built mansions flared with the whoosh of the movement of so many Sleepers, before winking out one by one as the beasts snapped the poles on which they were mounted.

Pahu's dire melody mounted, almost drowning out the crusaders' shrieks as thousands of Sleepers converged on Hatbrim with a single purpose in mind – destruction. Though they had evidently failed to penetrate the

Justiquans' defences thus far, when driven by Pahu's music like bees of a hive mind, they concentrated on the town in numbers the crusaders had never seen and soon ripped through the solid stone temple's barricades and the mansions' slate roofs and planked up windows. Jamba watched them scurry inside the buildings in horror, watched blood spurt from the windows. A few Justiquans made it out of the doors of the mansions, trying to flee with wails on their lips. They made it only a couple of paces before they were borne to the ground and shredded by Sleeper claws.

Jamba heard crying and turned to see mothers shielding their tearful children's eyes with their hands to protect them from the sight. Some turned their children around and covered their ears. Jamba's own eyes welled unexpectedly. He wasn't sure how it was different from Ruffle Feathers annihilating the Justiquans with the help of his demons, but it felt different. Ruffle knew he toyed with dark forces. He had come to terms with the risks. Pahu, on the other hand, had been so innocent when Jamba had met him. The smuggler hated the way the world had tainted the young man. By the time the town fell silent but for the Sleepers' victorious howls, Jamba felt sick to his stomach.

The witches appeared to have the opposite reaction, unconsciously stroking themselves and rubbing up on Pahu like cats. "Such power," they purred in his ears, "such tremendous power! More! Show us more!"

"Enough!" Magnuz snapped, winking into existence in front of the monk playing the damaru. *"You have done more than enough, Pahu. Now, stop this madness!"*

"Madness?" Pahu growled, a wild glint in his eye. "This is not madness, father. It is *power!* The power of the Gods! Behold my work, father, and rejoice, for Chilpaea will finally be free!"

Magnuz spun in horror when he heard the Sleepers yowling and yipping in pain, his eyes going wide at the indistinct sight of the shaggy beasts mauling one another to pieces by the silvery moonlight, staining the waters of the Agua Alta red with their blood. Pahu's music raged into the night, fast and furious, dark and deadly, and the monsters responded like puppets on strings.

"No, no!" Magnuz moaned. *"You must stop this, my son! You must stop this! It is our responsibility to look after all the men and beasts of Chilpaea, not massacre them, not turn them on one another! Stop this at once, else they are not the monsters, Pahu – you are!"*

Pahu's manic laughter echoed out over the ruins of Hatbrim.

43

Breach

Jeremias Colcott had resolved never to dreamwalk again.

His waking hours were plagued with dreams now, of memories not his own, so that he scarcely knew who he was or what he was doing half the time. He did not know exactly what had happened when he had burned down the siege towers, but he suspected that Waddi-waddi had somehow possessed him, like a demon from the old stories. He did not want to lose himself. The thought of being stuck outside of his body forever as a duppy unable to pass on to the Sunset Isles terrified him. So, he avowed never to dreamwalk again.

The problem was he was not sure he *could* stop. He had to sleep, and he did not know how to avoid the dreams that came. He did not know how to avoid Waddi-waddi. Every night when he closed his eyes, the necromancer was there, awaiting him with a broad smile. Jeremias tried running from him, tried hiding, but the necromancer followed. The necromancer always found him. And it was not only Waddi-waddi who awaited him in his dreams but Marshal Clauss too, seeking every night to slit the seneschal's spirit's throat with his blistering white energy sword. There was no escape. Jeremias slept less and less, unwilling to give in for too long, and so his waking hours became even more befuddled until he could hardly tell the difference between dreams and reality. He tried to fly through the citadel walls once while awake and banged his head sorely.

He was not the only one losing his grip on sanity either. Every day, more and more people succumbed to mania or lost themselves in a never-ending trance, staring at the citadel's ancient black walls. People danced and sang around the seneschal with hysterical glee one moment, only to collapse into weeping balls the next. So many people had committed suicide that the soldiers had been forced to confiscate all the weapons they could lay their hands on, anything sharp. So, when Jeremias bumped his head on the wall, the closest soldiers glanced at him suspiciously, thinking he was trying to bash his brains out.

General Malone was at a loss, confused as a fish on land. Jeremias refused to tell him, to tell anyone, anything, but he suspected Dreyfuss Alamoigne must have informed the general of what little he knew – namely that the seneschal had been communing with the giant *Kun-Yao-Lin* crystal in the basement. Malone had little time for the mystery, however, occupied every waking hour with conducting the necropolis' defences. So, Jeremias was left to his own devices, left to wander the hinterland between life and death known as the dreamworld.

The Justiquans did not build more siege towers, but returned to the tried and true tactic of throwing ladders up against the wall. The day after Jeremias had burned down the towers, they had attacked with comic anxiety, climbing slowly up the ladders with dread written on their pale faces. When no one had set them ablaze, however, they had scrambled up onto the wall as eagerly as ever to cross blades with the defenders.

Now, the catapults had finally begun to aim all their boulders at a single section of the wall, seeking to crack it open, and Jeremias knew the Justiquans were in the final phase of their conquest. They were ready to storm the necropolis as soon as the wall fell. Their army formed up each day under the sweltering sun in the blue-flowered meadow, but never committed the entirety of their force. Jeremias knew they were waiting for the wall to shatter. He was surprised it had not fallen already. It had taken some time for the catapults to adjust their aim, but now boulders crashed into the same spot again and again, making the structure creak and groan like an old man. Jeremias was impressed by the strain it had endured, but it was weakening, its stones crumbling day by day.

Abruptly, four days after the bombardment began, under a withering noon sun, the targeted section of wall came crashing down with a roar like the Gods were rowing that quaked the ground for a league. Losing his footing, Jeremias worried the citadel might slip off the cliff into the sea, but the ancient structure thankfully held its ground. On his rear end, coughing and wiping watery eyes, Jeremias peered through the golden clouds of rock powder to see that the wall had been split in two, and a large gap now yawned open, littered with rubble.

He heard the war horns blast and felt the aftershock of the Justiquan army's advance outside the walls. The crusaders were moving in for the kill, he thought, scrambling to his feet.

General Malone knew it, too. "Soldiers, to the breach!" he roared over the furore of confusion, sword held high as he led his men down from the now useless wall towards the breach.

Jeremias watched the Chilpaean warriors array themselves alongside the general in front of the gaping jagged-edged hole in the wall, an urge to bite his fingernails welling up in his chest. He needed to do something. If he did not, they were all doomed. He counted just a few hundred Chilpaean warriors and knew Marshal Clauss commanded thousands. Once more, the silvery ethereal duppy of Waddi-waddi materialised by his side. Jeremias sensed him and saw him out of the corner of his eye, but refused to acknowledge him.

"Let me help you again, Jeremias," said the necromancer. *"I may never have managed to teach you how to raise a zombie army of your own, but* I *can do it – if you lend me your body once more."*

Jeremias ignored him, eyes fixed on the steel-plate-clad Justiquan knights glittering in the blaring sunlight as they surged through the breach in the wall with blades bared and shields held before them, bellowing foreign war cries.

As they slowly and carefully traversed the rubble in the gap, General Malone yelled, "Forward!" and he and his men met them head on as soon as they cleared the strewn masonry.

Steel skirled on steel, blood splattered the cobbles, and the shrieks of the dying and wounded reverberated out over the necropolis, the echoes bouncing back off the black buildings like the endless laments of the duppy. The Chilpaeans managed to stand their ground at first, for the knights had to spread out and tread carefully to avoid tripping on all the loose bits of stone, and so the natives had the advantage of solid footing. General Malone engaged some of the keenest Justiquan frontrunners with a speed that belied his age, his scimitar flashing through the air to clang time and again against a broadsword that would otherwise have taken off his head.

Guessing the frontrunners were the rashest of the troops, he lured them in with the simplest of feints and deceptions, mock-stumbling or pretending blindness or indeed blinding his own enemies with the reflection of the sun on his sword. The first few fighters fell for the bait, thinking the general a weak old man, easy prey, and lunging forward with little care for defence. Malone's scimitar whipped past shields and greaves to cut deep into the major arteries in their inner thighs, or slit them from ear to ear between helmet and cuirass before they could even say a last prayer.

Those behind the frontrunners paid the general the respect he was due, having witnessed his victories, advancing on him cautiously with heater shields held before them, swords pointed over the top.

The general grinned and slapped his blade on his palm, shouting in Kwi patois, "Come on, you yellow-bellied lackwits! Come at me!"

The crusaders closed in on him like a pack of ravening coyotes, bashing him this way and that with their shields so that he bobbed about as if lost at sea, frantically parrying their sword thrusts inches wide of his body over and over, spinning like a top. Jeremias lost sight of him amid the melee for a moment and feared he had gone down. A moment later, as two crusaders collapsed, he realised the wily general must have ducked low to take their legs out from under them, opening a gap in their defences into which he sprang. His scimitar licked out left and right once he was past the shields' defences, and he laid two men low in as many heartbeats before retreating to stand once more by the side of his steadfast companion, Dreyfuss Alamoigne.

Dreyfuss feinted with his spear at his foes, making them lift or dip their shields and then responding accordingly, pronging them in the thigh or the neck where there was a break in their armour. In this manner, he was able to tackle foes one on one and armoured bodies began to pile up at his feet, flies immediately buzzing around them interestedly. As more and more poured through the gap in the wall, however, even his blurring spear proved incapable of keeping them at bay.

Bashing him with numerous shields and slashing at him with multiple swords, the crusaders soon snapped his spear as he sought to block them. Still, Dreyfuss jabbed the spear point into one of the men's eyes through his visor, making him scream and fall back with blood spurting. Dreyfuss tried to win free of the circle of foes, whacking at them manically with his broken spear haft, but they smacked him back with their steel heater shields and impaled him on two broadswords. Jeremias felt winter settle over his heart at the sight of the soldier sagging to the ground.

Further along the disintegrating line of defence, Wam Guir and Zov Lorr skirmished shoulder to shoulder like long lost brothers, axe and shamshir working in tandem to shred their foes, their respective regiments heavily depleted. By now, both had grown used to the other's stratagems and idiosyncracies. Zov knew Wam would be off-balance after a hefty swing and so always made sure to be ready to divert any blades seeking to take advantage. Likewise, Wam knew Zov had a tendency to lose himself in a one-on-one duel and occasionally missed figures in his periphery, so he kept an eye on his friends' foes as well as his own lest one of them should effectively sneak up on the single-minded man.

It was like they were two halves of a whole, thought Jeremias, watching in admiration of their skill. Though he had always thought Zov Lorr the better fighter, he saw now that Wam's talent was in dealing with crowds, while Zov's was in annihilating a single foe. Wam's axe hummed through the air to keep back those the two were not ready to deal with, while Zov's shamshir beckoned those they were. Once in their range, a Justiquan did not stand a chance and was soon beaten and slashed to a pulp at their feet, where corpses had begun to accrete into a small hill.

The Justiquans trampled their fallen, however, and advanced in such numbers that even Wam's thrumming axe and Zov's whistling sword could not stem their flow. Jeremias' heart panged as he witnessed the foreshadowing of their demise in General Malone's stumble, and again when he saw those closest to Wam and Zov go down under the crusader onslaught, leaving the two captains vulnerable to flanking manoeuvres. The Justiquans had them hemmed in like sheep in a pen in a blink, growling like sheepdogs as they circled the two back to back warriors.

"Bring it on, you vermin!" Wam roared in Kwi, spittle flying, speckling his beard. He brandished his butterfly-bladed axe. "Show me what you've got! I'll send you crying home all the way to your mamas!"

"Chilpaea will not forget our names," Zov assured them, shaven face composed as he flourished his shamshir, "but she will surely forget yours."

Jeremias had no idea how they lasted so long against such a slew of foes. He thought they might even break free of the confines of the ever-thickening ring of crusaders surrounding them when Wam took two knights down with a single swing of his glittering axe and Zov leapt into the gap, slashing this way and that with lightning speed with his shamshir and laying another three low in as many blinks, but then the crusaders dogpiled on them and they were lost to the seneschal's sight. Tears blurred Jeremias' eyes. What an ignoble way to die, he thought, buried under a mound of your enemies. Wiping away his tears, he resolved that they would not be forgotten.

"Lend me your body, Jeremias!" Waddi-waddi was insisting by the seneschal's side. *"Let me help you or we are all doomed! The crusaders will roll across Chilpaea like an iron wave, wiping out our communities and our people, our towns and villages, our proverbial sons and daughters. These are my people, too, you know, Jeremias. All I want is to help! I don't understand why you won't let me. It is simple. Lend me your body and I can do anything! I can slay them with fire as I did the siege towers, or beckon the undead to do my bidding! Just lend me your body."*

"Lend?" Jeremias snarled, turning on the spirit, unable to still his tongue any longer. "I know what you're doing, Waddi-waddi. You told me all along, and I should have listened. Nothing matters to you except finding a way to return to the land of the living, right? Even if you have to displace a soul to do it. *That's* what you're trying to do, isn't it? That was the entire point of dreamwalking, wasn't it? That was the entire point of the stretches and exercises, too. Not to attune my mind to the dreamworld but to attune my mind to *yours,* so that you could possess my body, take it as your own and thus return to the land of the living. Admit it, damn you!"

A smile slow as syrup split open Waddi-waddi's spectral face, and he spread his hands. *"You found me out. You're smarter than I thought. The only question now is – how much do you want to save your country, Jeremias? Because without me, it will fall."*

Jeremias returned his gaze to the fracas, which was drawing nearer to him by the second as the Chilpaeans were forced back step by reluctant step. The further they retreated, the more room the Justiquans had to pass unhindered through the hole in the wall. Once the necropolis' defenders had retreated far enough, there was nothing to stop the Justiquans from flanking them, encircling them and slaughtering them from all sides. Seeing it begin to happen, the Chilpaean warriors on the flanks being overwhelmed by the massed crusaders there, Jeremias turned back to Waddi-waddi, tears brimming in his eyes, his heart aching.

"Do what you have to do," he sobbed. "Take my body. But save Chilpaea, I beg you. As you said, these are your people, too."

Waddi-waddi bowed his head solemnly. *"Thank you, Jeremias. I will save them, I promise you. And I will not displace your soul. I have become too fond of you. We'll simply ... share ... your skull. It will not be comfortable by any means, but neither will you be gone."*

Jeremias gasped as he felt an inundation of energy into his frame, and a moment later he was not alone inside his own mind. He could feel Waddi-waddi slithering in like a serpent, crowding his skull, but he could still see through his own eyes. He felt the necromancer extend tendrils of power into his arms and legs to take control of his body. The necromancer did not have complete control, though. Jeremias could not find the words to describe the eerie sensation, but it was just as Waddi-waddi had said. They were somehow *sharing* his skull, sharing his body, each as in control as the other.

"Don't worry, Jeremias," the necromancer said with the seneschal's own lips. "We'll take care of Chilpaea together."

Then, he turned on the invaders and stalked towards them purposefully, the air around him crackling with latent power. As he strode, he cast his arms out wide and chanted an alien fricative incantation unlike anything Jeremias had ever heard in a deep and powerful voice most unlike the seneschal's, with a double timbre as if he spoke with two voices overlapping. Jeremias recognised the second voice as his own with a start.

Jinglespur responded to his words of power. The cracked, sun-baked earth split apart, and from the thousand graves inside the necropolis rose one by one an army of putrefying corpses and fleshless skeletons. Waddi-waddi's infamous zombie army, thought Jeremias, dumbfounded by the display of power. The zombies moaned as they emerged into the golden glow of the afternoon sun, stretching desiccated arms and legs. Flies buzzed around them, trying to lay maggots in the decaying flesh so that their young would have plenty of fodder. Jeremias saw one woman with tatters of flesh moulting off her naked body and felt sick.

He felt sicker still when he witnessed the zombies fall upon the Justiquans, tottering straight past the Chilpaeans as if they didn't exist. The zombies had no fear of death nor pain, so they ran headlong into the knights' blades for the most part – only for the knights to then realise in horror that they were not dead. Or rather, they were as dead as they could be. They were the undead, and a broadsword in the belly was nothing but a mild irritation to them. They did not even bleed.

Beheaded, disembowelled and mutilated, the zombies staggered on, slowly but surely overwhelming the Justiquans inside the walls with sheer numbers and eventually bearing them down to the ground to have their throats ripped out with undead teeth. Jeremias watched a dead man tear a crusader's helmet from his head and rip a bloody chunk out of his cheek with a bestial roar, making the man scream. The dead man moved on to its next victim, and the man with the bitten cheek choked to death on his own blood, unable to move as the undead poison spread through his body. Not long later, he rose once more to join the undead army, his eyes glassy and his flesh greying as zombification set in.

Now, the thousand zombies outnumbered the few hundred crusaders within the walls and, slaughtering all those within reach and thus increasing their numbers yet further, the undead stumbled over the debris and out of the breach in the wall to meet the rest of the Justiquan army in the meadow beyond.

Jeremias watched in horror, hearing himself say softly in a double timbre, “Go, my pretties, go.”

44

Zombies

"What's happening to him?" Jamba Klach asked Ruffle Feathers the next day as they traipsed through a sun-soaked meadow of wild petunias in the late afternoon, exhausted after a sleepless night of listening to Pahu's wrathful rhythms.

Smoking baui from a pipe shaped like a dragon and exhaling aromatic clouds through his nostrils like the great beast of legend, the obeahman replied with letters of flame carved into the air small enough that no other but Jamba and Lug Thorm could read them. 'Pahu has become wayward with the stress of our journey. The pressure placed on his shoulders would take a toll on any man, and he is still so young. Either the strain will break his mind, or he will overcome it and find a path to inner peace.'

Jamba wanted to scoff at such a pompous sentiment as inner peace, but he knew Ruffle was right, after a fashion. The monk needed to come to peace with himself. And his father wasn't helping. Magnuz was mid-lecture as they strode across the meadows forming a half ring around Jinglespur Necropolis, the land long left to fallow as it had been near the witchwood. Here, as there, people feared to tread, feared to grow crops lest they be tainted by the dark deeds haunting the place or lest they disturb the duppy said to have roamed here since before even the Time of Witches, since the time of Waddi-waddi.

"D'you think any of the rumours about Jinglespur are true?" Lug asked nervously, twiddling his thumbs. "They can't be if the seneschal and our people are holed up safely in there, right?"

Jamba nodded thoughtfully. "Maybe. But we don't know they're holed up in there safely anymore. It's been weeks since Kofi heard from the seneschal."

"You think the duppy might have gotten them?" Lug asked, eyes wide.

Jamba shrugged. "Or the crusaders. Let's just pray they haven't been overrun yet."

As Jinglespur Necropolis slowly hove into view on the purpling horizon, the smugglers' brows furrowed at what they beheld, not understanding at first. As they came closer, it became clear that the Justiquans had been surrounding the necropolis – presumably besieging it, Jamba thought, spotting the charred remnants of siege towers and abandoned catapults and ballistae among the flowers. Now, though, every one of the crusaders was hightailing it away from the necropolis, running west as fast as their legs could carry them, armour clanking, shrills on their tongues. Jamba squinted at the warriors throwing off the Justiquan yolk. Not only were they pouring through a gap in the wall in their hundreds, but they were also leaping fearlessly off the fifty-foot-high walls to plummet down on the Justiquans from above. Jamba could not believe his eyes. Surely no living man would be so brave, so foolish?

The deceptions of distance faded away as the smugglers drew near, and their eyes popped out of their skulls as they witnessed the true nature of Jinglespur's saviours. Dead men harried the crusaders. Women, too. Zombies risen from their graves stalked the gloaming, some still with threads of cloth attached, some with vestiges of flesh, others mere skeletons, all bent on the utter destruction of the Justiquan war machine. The smugglers watched in dread fascination as the zombies hurled themselves from the walls or pounced on the fleeing Justiquans from the ground, clawing, punching, kicking and biting to claim their first kill and then scooping up their victims' weapons if they succeeded to make the next a little easier. Those who were bitten died only to be reborn as zombies themselves.

"What in the name of the Gods is going on here?" Jamba asked softly.

Venturing anxiously closer alongside the Lullabyer's glowing shade and wondering if they too would end up zombie fodder before the day was done, the smugglers saw a figure waving at them from the wall, beckoning them. Padding closer still, the zombies parting before them so that a path opened up through the throng, they made out the cocoa-coloured face of Jeremias Colcott.

The seneschal's eyes flickered with purple flames. "Welcome back, Magnuz! It is good to see you again, my old friend. What think you of my new army?"

While the zombies ravaged the Justiquan army and screams pealed out over the meadows, the smugglers, witches, Gods, assassin, deserter, Lullabyer, monk, townsfolk from Nirby and villagers from Bessaroca strolled straight through the undead horde and into the necropolis through the gap in the curving wall to find Seneschal Jeremias Colcott and General Raoul Malone waiting to meet them. Piles of upturned dirt here, there and everywhere spoke of the origins of the undead, and the air stank of sorcery. Jeremias' eyes no longer blazed, but a flicker of fuchsia fire remained.

"Welcome to Jinglespur," he said, throwing his arms wide, his reedy voice thicker than the Lullabyer remembered, as if it had a double timbre, like two voices speaking at once.

He also seemed more self-assured than Magnuz recalled.

"It is good to see you again, Jeremias, and you too, Raoul," Magnuz said, *"even in this form. I had to dissuade your assassin from bringing me back prematurely, Jeremias. The Skinner was most helpful in reuniting me*

with my son, however, so thank you for that."

"It does my heart wonders to clap eyes on you once more, Lullabyer," said General Malone thickly, saluting.

Jeremias' brow crinkled. "You *wanted* to go with them?"

"Well, no, not initially, but then I persuaded them to help me reach Pahu and they did what no other could – delivered me safely, there and back."

Jeremias blew out his cheeks. "Wow. I must say I'm surprised, but I'm pleased you were able to reunite with your son. Of course, that made the most sense under the circumstances. But you have not yet taught him the Lullaby? We have endured Sleeper attacks every night since the palace fell."

"He has yet to master it," said the Lullabyer with a severe glance towards his son. *"But he is close."*

"Excellent," beamed the seneschal. "With my zombie army and the Lullaby, we should be able to take back our country once and for all!"

"That is the plan. What happened to you, Jeremias? How do you now control a zombie army? Last time I saw you, you could barely control a quill."

Jeremias laughed in a manner the Lullabyer had never heard before – rich full laughter from the belly. "Yes, a lot has changed these past days. After Cocoba Bay fell, Raoul and I led the survivors here and called for an evacuation of Hatbrim, Jawduck and Nirby to reinforce us. I'm not sure what happened to Nirby, but Hatbrim and Jawduck showed up in their entirety, every living man, woman and child, so we had to take them in, of course. I've had to shoulder a great deal of responsibility, but the biggest change was meeting the spirit of Waddi-waddi."

"Waddi-waddi?" the Lullabyer exclaimed, while the smugglers looked on, slack-jawed.

"Yes," said Jeremias. "Not unlike yourself, he trapped his own duppy in a *Kun-Yao-Lin* crystal the size of a house. I found it one night while exploring and explained to him the predicament the country faced. Quoting patriotism as his cause, he agreed to help me by teaching me some of his ancient arcane knowledge. I have learned to dreamwalk in the spirit plane, how to fight with my mind, and, of course, how to reanimate corpses to do my bidding. Suh knowledge, Magnuz, such knowledge as I have never known ..." His faraway eyes glinted purple in the sun.

The Lullabyer was awed, and a little afraid. *"You should be careful, Jeremias. Waddi-waddi is the greatest of deceivers, the inventor of lies."*

Jeremias' brow crinkled, and he spoke in a voice unlike his own, a deep powerful voice. "Oh, you'd like him to believe that, wouldn't you?"

Magnuz blanched at the look in the seneschal's eyes and the strange power he felt radiating from the man, but then Jeremias shook his head as if clearing it of thoughts and was himself again.

"I am being careful, Magnuz," he said in his own voice, albeit with the strange double timbre still in effect. “I am only doing what I must for Chilpaea. I did not know if you were coming back.” He turned to the smugglers. “And it’s good to see you again too, Ruffle Feathers, under the circumstances. Thank you for bringing back the Lullabyer and his son. You are a true patriot.”

Ruffle grinned and bowed, flicking a hand. ‘You’re welcome. It is amazing to see what you have become, what you can do now.’

Jeremias returned the grin. “Yes, so don’t test me again!”

“Jamba Klach,” said General Malone, striding forward and offering his hand, “thank you for your service, old boy. Remarkable job. Remarkable.”

“Thank you, general,” said Jamba proudly, puffing out his chest, “and I think we can shed some light on what happened to Nirby, seneschal. We have the remnants of the town with us. It had been taken over by Justiquans when we passed by on our way back from the Monastery Calliope, so we slew them and freed the residents. They chose to come with us, to follow Pahu. As did the villagers of Bessaroca in the north. We didn’t find any more of our countrymen than that, I’m afraid …”

“Well, that’s one mystery solved,” said Jeremias. “You did well saving those you could. Thank you, Jabba.”

“Jamba.”

“Jamba.” The seneschal switched his gaze to the monk. “And you must be the famous Pahu Opherio.”

“I am,” said Pahu, stepping forwards.

“And who are your lovely companions?” asked Jeremias, eyeing the witches.

“This is Vivian and Violet Malakbet.”

“The witch’s daughters?”

“Yes, but they do not hold the same views as their mother. They’re here to help, seneschal, just like the rest of us.”

Jeremias nodded, though he did not look convinced. “If you say so. How close are you to learning the Lullaby, Pahu?”

Pahu forced a smile. “Very close. But in the meantime, there are other things I can do – like bring the entire Sleeper horde down on the crusaders’ heads in Cocoba Bay.”

Jeremias blinked. “You can do that?”

“I can.”

The seneschal nodded thoughtfully, a smile growing across his visage. “I like the way you think. First things first, though, we have to deal with these Justiquan scum before we can get to Cocoba Bay. Come up to the rampart with me and we’ll see what they’re cooking up, the meddlesome swine. My people will show the folks from Nirby and Bessaroca into the citadel.”

While the villagers from Bessaroca and townsfolk from Nirby were led to the questionable safety of the haunted citadel, the smugglers, witches, Gods, Lullabyer, monk, assassin and deserter all followed the seneschal and general up a set of stone steps to the rampart, where they could spy on the havoc wreaked by the undead from an elevated vantage point. The crusaders surrounding Jinglespur had fallen back to regroup with the rest of their forces encamped in a log-built stockade on the edge of the cliff overlooking the Dragon Sea to the southwest. As they tried to cram too many men into too tight a space all at once and jammed in the entryway, however, the zombies hounded their heels, tearing them down from behind. The zombies were none too smart – Jamba thought he saw one wrestle with a knight for several long minutes, trying to bite and stab his armour, before finally ripping off his helmet and finding his throat with its teeth – but they got the job done eventually. He could not argue with the results. The Justiquans were facing a mass culling, their numbers being gnawed to the bone, like their bodies. The soldiers behind the palisade tried to shut the log-built gates in their comrades' faces, but those outside would not allow it. So, the gates remained open and the zombies snuck in and the entire stockade became a crimson-lit bloodbath dancing to the music of screams by the eerie light of sunset.

It was difficult to tell, but the seneschal suspected some of the crusaders fled southwest back towards Cocoba Bay. Regardless, none of them assailed the necropolis walls again that night.

"Can you believe it?" Jamba asked Ruffle Feathers in quiet, reverential tones as the solid stone doors of the citadel slammed shut behind them. "Not long ago, we were simple smugglers. Now, we're standing in the legendary Jinglespur Necropolis, surrounded on all sides by Chilpaean royalty and the armed forces, on a quest to save the country from Sleepers and invaders. Life is wild."

The obeahman waved a hand, and words of fire swam into existence in mid-air. 'It truly is.' He gave his friend a sly look. 'Should I raise the issue of our payment with Pahu while we're here?'

Jamba smiled ruefully and shook his head. "No, don't mention it."

Lug gawped wordlessly up at the cobwebbed black walls and the moonlight streaming in through the high, thin windows. A Sleeper snarled at one of the windows, trying in vain to squeeze through the small aperture and making the lagahoo jump. The beasts' howls echoed faintly around the citadel as they emerged from their warrens to prowl the surface.

"I guess we're stuck in this offal hole for the time being, away from forest and river," Papa Bwa said wistfully, glancing askance at Mama D'lo. "D'you want to snuggle up together like old times?"

Mama D'lo snorted. "Fat chance."

"D'you know much of Jinglespur?" Pahu asked his father.

"No," replied Magnuz. *"Little is known of the place, save what has*

been transcribed from the etchings on the walls. All we know for certain is that this was once the capital of the country, the seat of the Lullabyer and his family – until the accursed necromancer, Waddi-waddi, conquered it at the head of a zombie army not unlike the one we just witnessed. Many theorise that he kept the Lullabyer alive to continue to sing the Lullaby, while taking over rulership of the country in all other ways. I worry, seeing the undead outside, that Jeremias Colcott may not be the Jeremias we once knew."

Pahu frowned. "You think he is possessed?"

Magnuz bobbed his ephemeral head. *"It is possible. I have heard of such things."*

"It is said that powerful duppy can possess the living, displacing a body's soul," added Vivian Malakbet.

"It seems easiest for them to possess family members," said her sister, Violet, "or those with whom they share a close connection."

"What should we do?" asked Pahu, fidgeting with his drum.

"We should keep an eye on him," said Magnuz, watching the seneschal out of the corner of his eye.

"I don't know how I'm going to sleep in here, surrounded by duppy," Kofi Touluz confided in Wagnar Long. "I can practically hear their wails."

Wagnar clapped the assassin on the shoulder and grinned. "I, on the other hand, intend to sleep like a baby fat on its mother's milk. No duppy's going to disturb me, let me tell you."

Kofi shook his head. "You're mad. I daren't even blink."

Wagnar chuckled. "The infamous Skinner – scared of a few wee spirits?"

Kofi frowned. "Do not make light of the duppy. They are the spirits of our ancestors, and they hold power we do not understand."

Despite his concerns, Kofi was soon fast asleep along with the rest of his companions, sure in the safety of the citadel's stout doors if nothing else.

Jeremias Colcott meditated deep into the night, until finally he lay down to sleep.

As soon as his head touched his makeshift pillow of old clothes, he rose once more in spectral form, flying through the citadel ceiling and up into the air in the dreamworld to hover over a dark echo of the necropolis in skies of wool rimmed by blood as if the horizon was wounded. Faint ephemeral rain pitter-pattered his head, making the shadowy streets glisten.

He did not have to wait long. Soon, a speck resolved in the sky, soaring towards him at speed from beyond the wall.

"Jeremias Colcott," Marshal Clauss sneered in Traveller's Tongue once he was within range, snakelike face contorted into an expression of disgust as if he smelled something foul. "I don't know where you found the knowledge or the power to raise an army of the dead, but I tell you this – you

will regret it! You may think you have won, but you faced only a finger of the Justiquan army – only a limb of the mighty war beast that is the crusaders! There are thousands more of us, Colcott. You have not won. You cannot win. All you have done is delay the inevitable. Zombies or no zombies, we will destroy you. In fact, I'm going to destroy you right now! What's the matter? No necromancer saviour tonight? Are you not going to perform your disappearing act again?"

He was just as Jeremias remembered him from the parley, save paler of complexion without the sunburn and now translucent as steam. His short, ivory hair gleamed in the dark scarlet radiance that suffused the dreamworld and his steel-plate armour glinted dully, but his broadsword shone with bright white fire.

The seneschal shook his head. "I'm tired of running, and there is no one to save me but myself. I'm not afraid of you anymore, Clauss. It's time we put an end to this."

"Good," purred the marshal, "because I too was tiring of your running. Now, hold still while I kill you for what you did to my army!"

Jeremias no longer felt slow, or old. He understood the dreamworld now, understood that his energy was as boundless as his imagination. So, when the marshal came spearing through the air towards him, Jeremias calmly imagined a scimitar like the general's in his grip and used the blade to block Clauss' attack, the peal of the crossing apocryphal swords ringing out over the phantomscape. The marshal tried to circle him, but Jeremias imagined vultures hemming him in. He tried to stab at the seneschal, but Jeremias imagined boas binding his arms. He tried to kick the seneschal, but Jeremias imagined Chilpaean crocodiles biting off his legs. He tried to spit at the seneschal, but Jeremias imagined him coughing up cockroaches instead. Constricted by boas while crocodiles gnawed on his leg stumps, Clauss tried to curse the seneschal with a mouthful of bugs, but Jeremias ran him through with his blazing pearlescent scimitar.

"That is for Magnuz and Dajuan!" Jeremias hissed, watching with satisfaction as the crusader's spirit melted away.

45

Traitor

Pahu Opherio gazed down on Cocoba Bay from the hilltop to the east, the tumbled down city cast in ethereal light by the full moon sailing through clear starry skies. The city itself lay dark and lifeless, save where the ribbon of the Agua Alta River glittered like molten steel in the moonlight, cutting the city in twain. The only lights burning were the torches up on the western promontory on the other side of the city, where Maawu Palace had once stood. Pahu breathed in deep and detected a faint bitter whiff of smoke. The city was still burning, he thought angrily. Then, he noticed Ruffle Feathers puffing on a baui pipe nearby and rolled his eyes at his own imagination. The anger was still real, though, pounding through his veins, compelled by the chaotic current kicked up by the rapid beating of his aching heart.

"I know what you're thinking, my son," said the shade of Magnuz Opherio, standing by his son's side. *"Don't do it, I beg you. It is not the Justiquans' souls I care about. It is yours."*

The howls of the Sleepers were growing louder by the second.

Pahu set his jaw. "There is no other way, father. We do not have enough men to do this on our own. You've seen it for yourself. I don't know what else you would have me do. You told me I must take back the country, save it from crusaders and Sleepers, and that is what I intend to do. Can I never do anything right in your eyes? Will you never be proud of me?"

He had meant the last words to be caustic and sarcastic, but they burst out of him pathetically, sobbing like a plea, and he cursed inwardly.

"Son, I will always be proud of you," said Magnuz softly, moving to lay a hand on the young man's shoulder and then remembering that he could not with a wince, *"but –"*

"Argh, there's always a but!" Pahu growled, flinging himself down on the grass to more easily play his damaru. "Just let me do what I have to do, Magnuz!"

Magnuz flinched as though struck. His son had never addressed him by name before.

"Very well," he said stiffly, before vanishing in a flash and a burst of blue-purple sparks, *"but you will regret it."*

Mad and melancholy music flowed easily from Pahu's fingertips then, the drum coming alive with a frenzied booming melody that echoed out over the land to be heard for leagues, alerting almost every Sleeper on the entire island to lay siege to Cocoba Bay on the monk's behalf. The Sleepers came in swarms, howling and hooting, coating the land like a shaggy black carpet and skittering straight past the monk, the smugglers, the witches, General Malone, the Chilpaean military and the seneschal and his undead army as if they did not exist. Impelled by Pahu's manic music, thousands of beasts swept down on Cocoba Bay in a great skittering rush that seemed destined to wipe the crusaders off the face of the map. They hurtled through the city unimpeded and beelined for the promontory, hurdling wrecked buildings, egged on by the tumultuous tune drumming in their ears.

Victory seemed imminent. What could possibly stand against such a force of monsters? Jamba thought, watching with bated breath.

A second song, a tolling of bells, pealed out from the headland with such power that it almost booted Pahu's tune from the ears. Jamba Klach winced at the keening, unmelodious racket. The Sleepers, previously converging on the promontory as one like beasts of a hive mind, now sent up a pitiful wail and scattered like cockroaches, caught between the hammer of Pahu's melody and the anvil of the second song.

"What is happening?" Jamba yelled over the cacophony.

"It is the Justiquans," replied Pahu, his mellifluous voice drifting easily on the wind to be heard by all close by. "They've learned the magic of discord. That's how they've survived against the Sleepers for so long – the same way we have, by caterwauling something awful so that the Sleepers will stay away. I cannot believe it, but … their music is standing up to mine. I cannot compel the Sleepers to attack."

"Keep trying!" Magnuz snapped, reappearing. *"Now that you've committed us to this folly, we cannot fail. Their obeah ought to be nothing compared to yours, Pahu! We were given our gifts by the Gods themselves!"*

Sweating with the speed at which his blistered fingers flicked the drums, Pahu panted, "I will try, father."

Hours later, the sun bloomed into view and all the young monk had managed was to keep the Sleepers from their own throats. The beasts retreated to their warrens, their last howls lingering in the air, and Pahu brought his song to an abrupt end, blowing and sucking on his fingers. The second song trailed off a moment later, its last tolls reverberating in the air mockingly.

"I told you it wouldn't work," said Magnuz smugly.

"Grr, there's no pleasing you!" Pahu snarled, throwing down his damaru. "And you didn't tell me it wouldn't work. You told me I'd regret it if I tried it."

"And do you regret it?"

"No! It was worth a try."

"So, what are you going to do now, Pahu?" the shade of the Lullabyer asked condescendingly.

Pahu jerked his chin towards Jeremias Colcott. "Not me. Him. It's your turn, seneschal."

Under the blistering summer sun and accompanied by a swarm of flies, the zombie army descended on the Chilpaean capital like a skin of scum on an unclaimed corner of a stinky stagnant pond, slowly spreading over the countryside in their thousands. With the dead walked the smugglers, the witches, Pahu Opherio, the spirit of Magnuz, the assassin, the deserter, the Gods of River and Forest, the seneschal, the general and what remained of the Chilpaean army, minus a contingent left in Jinglespur Necropolis to look after all the displaced folk still in the citadel.

"How are the ribs, Wagnar?" asked Jamba Klach, plugging his nose whenever a particularly pungent putrefying mass of skin and bones walked past, but still amazed and thankful that the zombies were not snacking on his brains like they did in the stories. They did not even seem to notice him.

Wagnar Long winced as he lifted his left arm and grunted, "They still sting, but I don't think they're broken. I'll be able to crack a few skulls, I reckon."

"I'm not sure we'll even be needed," joked Kofi Touluz. "Look at all these cursed things!" He gestured at the moaning zombies, one of whom chanced to stumble and fall, crack open its head on a rock, and then get up and stagger on with a dull groan. "There's thousands of them! Maybe they'll wipe out the crusaders for us."

"I hope so," put in Lug, sweating in the heat of the sun and the close proximity to so many abominations of nature.

'They are mindless walking bags of skin and bones held together by magic,' said Ruffle Feathers in letters of flame. 'I think it likely our aid will be required.'

Kofi pouted. "Damn. I thought I'd finally get the day off."

As Jamba and Lug sniffed the last of their witch-spice, Ruffle frowned and waved a hand. 'Is that wise? You'll kill yourselves with the amount you've been taking.'

Jamba grinned ruefully and shrugged. "It's true. My lungs are aching. But I figure we're probably about to die anyway."

Entering Cocoba Bay in the midst of the undead, the smugglers found the city deserted, half the buildings burned to the ground. Not a soul wandered the streets. A warm wind moaned up and down empty boulevards between blackened husks of houses, rippling the sluggish waters of the Agua Alta. Jamba felt a chill course up his spine despite the heat as he stalked down the street beside the river and wondered what had happened to the thousands of his countrymen who had called this place home. They could not all have been annihilated when the crusaders invaded … could they?

They finally encountered resistance when they found the last standing bridge crossing the river, the slow-moving waters beneath glittering in the blinding light of the morning sun. On the far side of the stone bridge, made up of several elegant arches dipping their toes in the water, thousands of sweating, pale-skinned Justiquan soldiers in leather armour awaited them, accompanied by a few knights in steel plate. Their leader, standing astride the bridge, was a man Ruffle Feathers, the Lullabyer and Jeremias Colcott knew only too well. Hot fury clawed at their hearts at the sight of Councillor Chup Morton, his fat frame bedecked in evidently purpose-built, gold-trimmed armour consisting of steel plate discs strapped together to protect the majority of his ample upper body. He carried a gold-trimmed steel helmet under his arm wide enough to fit his dark-skinned, flabby moustached face.

"Morton!" the Lullabyer exploded in outrage. *"How dare you side with the Justiquans against your own countrymen? I pray you die of shame on the spot!"*

Councillor Morton smirked. "I haven't a speck of guilt, I'll have you know, Magnuz, and I sleep like a log in a soft bed every night. I chose the winning side, because that's the only thing that makes sense."

"You faithless traitor!"

"Yes, yes," replied Morton in Kwi in a rolling baritone, flapping a dismissive thick-fingered hand. "Just give up already so I can get back to my comfy bed, would you? Did you know they have the finest grapes in the world in Justiqua? They're delicious as they are and even better in wine."

"We're not giving up," ground out Pahu in the same tongue, stepping foot on the bridge. "Get out of the way, Morton. You have not chosen the winning side. From here on out, your name will be a byword for treachery, synonymous with betrayal, a smudge on the otherwise noble history of the brave people of Chilpaea! Now, stand aside!"

The councillor blanched at this, but quickly recovered himself. "Listen here, you snotty little brat, I am the most powerful demon-summoner in all of Chilpaea – even more powerful than that old hooligan, Ruffle Feathers! So, watch your tongue, or I'll have one of my *friends* tear it out!"

Unbeknownst to anyone, Mama D'lo had long since slipped into the Agua Alta. Now, her voice bubbled up from the river to ask in gurgling tones, "Oh yes? You and what army?"

With that, the river seemed to become sentient and decide it really wasn't too fond of having Justiquans anywhere in its proximity. So, awakening, it sprang up out of its bed and pounced on the unsuspecting throng of soldiers packed tightly together, washing them all away down the street with a whoosh. Some were swept into the river, never to be seen again.

Councillor Morton gawped for a long moment, before recovering and barking a series of ululating alien words that made Jamba's eyeballs itch and told the smuggler he was casting a spell. The fabric of space and time tore asunder with an audible ripping noise, and a mighty red rift opened up by the councillor's side, gushing flames and odious smoke. A ten-foot-tall demon the likes of which Pahu had never seen squeezed through the rift a moment later. Horned, clawed and winged, with scales the colour of blood and claws as long as knives, it was a nightmare given life.

"What would you have of me, master?" it boomed in Traveller's in tombstone tones as the rift snapped shut at its back.

Morton pointed at the zombie army and said in the same tongue, "Kill them all, Chongo."

The river sprang up again and tried to deluge the demon, but Chongo batted it aside without even touching it, its claw seeming to send the water spraying back with an unseen shockwave.

Ruffle tugged urgently on Jamba's arm, waving a hand to form words of flame. 'Quick! We must call Djhuty! He is the only one with the power to stand up to such a foe.'

He squeezed shut his eyes and started whirling his arms in eldritch patterns known only to those who practised the ancient arts of obeah to summon demons from other worlds. Chongo was already halfway across the bridge and prowling closer by the second, flames marking its footfalls. To Jamba's relief, a purple rift split open the curtain between realms within seconds, puffing out pungent purple smoke and a magenta blaze.

Ruffle nodded to Jamba and the smuggler took a deep breath and shouted in Traveller's, "Djhuty the Diabolical! Hear our call in our hour of need! We need you! Please, help us!"

Spidery blue-black fingers curled around the edge of the fiery rift as they would any other physical threshold, and a moment later an androgynously handsome indigo face popped through, contrasted by a tuft of stark white hair. Eyes burning with unholy infernos took in the tableau before it, before the purple-flame-rimmed body emerged, clad only in a dark loincloth and a cloak of what appeared to be raven feathers, a bone staff topped with a horse-like skull clutched in one hand. A black-plumed bird the size of an ape swooped through the rift after the demon to perch on its shoulder and scour the bridge with a blood-red glare. The rift stitched itself shut behind them.

"We meet once more, *shivath previk,"* Djhuty the Diabolical purred in sophisticated Traveller's Tongue, adding unknown syllables that made Jamba's hairs stand on end.

Words in Traveller's Tongue wreathed in flame winked into existence before the demon's eyes. 'Please, Djhuty, we need your help! We are in dire need. This is our final battle to reclaim our homeland. We must cross this bridge, but a demon stands in our path.'

"And what do I gain by doing so? *Medhja ruuk."* Djhuty gave the demon approaching along the length of the long bridge a disinterested glance and then inspected his obsidian fingernails.

Ruffle waved a hand towards the Justiquans regaining their feet, spitting out river water. 'You may feast on all the pale-skinned crusaders you please.'

Djhuty weighed this for a long moment while the bridge shook to the dirge of Chongo's tread and then drew in a breath and said resignedly, "Very well. But there are barely enough of them for both Izulu and I."

'More will be coming!'

"Well, that is good news," said Djhuty with the ghost of a smile. "Now, be a good fellow and stand back, would you? *Horzik muur.*"

Djhuty twirled his staff in his hands as he advanced towards Morton's demon and spoke alien words in his home tongue. Chongo grunted a response, and then the two clashed like forces of nature, shaking the sky with their arcane arts. Djhuty hurled a blistering array of black spells at the scarlet-skinned fiend, but Chongo seemed to soak them all up like a sponge. It ate Djhuty's dark shockwave in one bite, and even when abyssal tentacles enwrapped it, Chongo shrugged them off and somehow won free. Izulu blasted it with vermillion lightning, but Chongo seemed to absorb the energy without flinching. Watching, Ruffle Feathers started to suspect with a sinking feeling that Morton's fiend could command no spells itself but was immune to magic.

Coming to the same conclusion, Djhuty conjured an ephemeral morningstar into existence in his spare hand and remarked calmly in Traveller's, "Slippery git, aren't you?"

With that, he blurred towards his foe like an arrow in flight and the bridge shook beneath them as the two demons came to blows, clawing, whacking, biting and sending purple ichor spraying through the air amid a chorus of grunts and yelps. Chongo wrapped its enormous red hand around the smaller demon's neck and bore Djhuty easily high up into the air with a few beats of its powerful wings. Once high enough, Chongo dropped him to his death.

What Chongo did not realise – indeed nor did Ruffle – was that Djhuty's exceptional mastery of obeah granted him the ability to levitate. When Chongo dropped him, he allowed himself to fall a few feet before coming to a halt, hovering high above the bridge in the big blue bowl alongside Izulu. Roaring in fury at the development, Chongo dropped on the smaller demon like a preying falcon, claws rending, and the battle was continued in mid-air. Izulu squawked and propelled itself at Chongo, gouging with talons and tearing with beak. Drops of dark blood pitter-pattered on the bridge and in the water. The Chilpaeans and Justiquans gazed up in awe at the demons' fracas for some time before their gazes dropped and they eyed one another across an empty expanse of stone.

"Charge!" roared Morton.

46

Zogartha of the Void

“Take the bridge!” yelled Jeremias Colcott at the top of his lungs.

Where he pointed, the zombie army strode – or staggered, stumbled and ambled at any rate. Some with putrefying muscles on their legs managed to run. Soon, the bridge was swarming with soldiers in leather armour and skeletal zombies. The song of battle rang out, the scuffle of footsteps, the skirl of steel on steel, the shrieks of the dying and the staccato thudding of blades finding flesh.

Councillor Chup Morton retreated behind his front lines, calling out, “When I heard of your ability to cast spells without your tongue, Ruffle Feathers, I was inspired to learn the trick for myself. Now, I can cast two spells at once!”

Ruffle ground his teeth in jealousy as Morton waved his arms in occult patterns and then raised his arms above his head, palms to the sunny blue sky. With a crack of thunder in the firmament and a flash not unlike lightning, what appeared to be two clay pots materialised in the councillor’s hands. Morton laughed maniacally and tossed them both over the heads of his own soldiers, aiming them to come crashing down on Pahu, Papa Bwa, Jeremias, Malone, Kofi, Wagnar, the smugglers and the witches. He raised his arms to the sky again, and a clap of thunder granted him more pots, which he also flung.

Ruffle Feathers watched the pots sailing towards him gloomily, knowing he could not move fast enough to escape the blast. He recognised the spell. The pots were not made of clay but of obeah. They glittered like starlight as they arced through the sky above him. He knew when they landed, they would explode, releasing a burst of compressed energy potent enough to vaporise anyone within a radius of several feet. He could cast neither defensive spell nor counterattack while concentrating on keeping Djhuty in the realm, so he watched his doom drop towards him wordlessly, praying to the Twins for sweet dreams.

A golden sheen obscured his view. The magical pots smashed against it, exploding a foot above the old obeahman’s head and making him flinch. Not an ounce of the explosion had made it through to him, though, he quickly realised, patting himself down to make sure he was all there. The zombies outside the barrier were not so lucky. A handful of them popped like touch-me-nots, fountaining gore up into the air. Ruffle looked up in time to witness another pot sail through the blood and burst on the golden sheen, and another, and another as Morton kept conjuring and throwing them. Zombies burst apart into charred chunks mere feet from the obeahman, spraying him with blood.

Ruffle looked around to behold Vivian Malakbet standing beside Pahu, her arm raised above her head, a determined look on her face. She glowed with power, just like her shield, which formed a bubble around them all capable of repelling all spiritual assaults. Physical objects could pass through unhindered, however, Ruffle was reminded as he spat out cold zombie brains. Not one pot made it through her eldritch barrier, but Ruffle could see Vivian was starting to sweat. She could not keep it up forever, he knew.

Witnessing their predicament, pinned down by magic pots, Mama D'lo seized control of the river once more, forcing it to flow against its nature high up into the air to come cascading down on Morton and the Justiquans once more. As she hurtled down towards them, however, a magical poisoned dart shot from the almost intact rooftop of a nearby ruined house speared through the water and found her in its midst, piercing her heart. The water flopped down lifelessly on the crusaders without enough force to wash them away, for its soul was gone.

Sensing her demise, Papa Bwa roared in rage. "Damballah!"

A fogbank swept in from nowhere, obscuring the bridge in a blink. Soldiers cried out in concern. The zombies just moaned. A few heartbeats later, it swept on, coalescing as it did so into the form of a giant white snake. Nobody realised Papa Bwa was missing until they saw the God riding on Damballah's back, soaring straight across the bridge towards the roof of the ruined house from which the dart had been shot.

When he laid eyes on the culprit, Bwa thundered, "Bazil, you spineless wretch! How dare you lay low the river queen? You are less than half the God she is – and you have chosen the wrong side. You have betrayed your country! There is no punishment more fitting for you than death save pain, so I sentence you to both!"

Panicking, Bazil the forest devil brought his blowpipe to his lips and launched another dart. Damballah vanished in a puff of mist and the dart flew harmlessly through the vapour, but – borne by momentum – Papa Bwa flew through the air to land on Bazil before the devil could blow another dart. Borne down, Bazil reached out a hand and a nearby tree leaned over to smack Papa Bwa. In a blink, though, Papa Bwa had torn a branch from the tree and rammed its jagged end through the forest devil's heart. The tree stood straight again as Bazil breathed his last breath.

"*I* am the father of the forest," growled Papa Bwa, "and I tolerate no devils."

Above him in the sky, Djhuty finally managed to sneak a tentacle down Chongo's throat and eviscerate the crimson demon's insides, hollowing it like a woodpecker. Its body made a great splash when it landed in the river and sank like a stone. Crying out in rage, Morton intoned a new incantation, his deep voice echoing out eerily over the city and making Jamba's flesh crawl.

'Stop him!' signed Ruffle Feathers.

While her sister maintained the eldritch bubble, Violet poked her head out of the magical construct and spewed witch-fire from her palms at the councillor. He was too far away, though, and all she achieved was incinerating a swathe of groaning zombies.

"Hey!" barked Jeremias indignantly.

Violet ignored him. "I can't stop him from here!"

Fortunately, Papa Bwa and Djhuty the Diabolical, both floating in mid-air above the brawling soldiers and zombies, converged on Morton then and the councillor's mantra dwindled away in the face of their stern glares.

"I know what you are thinking," Djhuty warned in Traveller's. "Don't do it. It will be the death of you."

"You're as bad as Bazil," proclaimed Papa Bwa in Kwi, turning his nose up. "A traitor to your own people. You deserve no better fate than he."

"Accept your demise with dignity, human," Djhuty advised, drifting closer. "Go quietly and we will make your end painless."

Morton looked frantically from the demon to the God, hesitated and then screamed, "I will not go quietly! Zogartha of the Void, aid me now!"

Djhuty blanched and backed away as a thunderous clap heralded the opening of a titanic rift, murmuring, "No!"

This rift did not gush flames or smoke. It sucked at heat and light like a vortex, blacker than Jamba had known black could be, and through it stepped a horror of epic scale torn straight from the darkest of gulfs, the deepest of nightmares. Djhuty's fuchsia eyes bugged as they beheld the entry of Zogartha of the Void into the realm. It stalked into the Agua Alta River on a hundred long tendrils, each ending in a crab-like pincer, its jagged body reminding Jamba a little of a sea urchin, held high above the water's surface. The massive rift that had birthed it sealed itself with a loud *pop*, and the river washed the banks with displaced water.

Mustering his courage, Djhuty soared towards the leviathan, Izulu at his side, the pair of them blasting the larger fiend with lightning the colour of blood and dark shockwaves powerful enough to kill swathes of Sleepers. Zogartha let out an ear-splitting keening noise, making all the Justiquan soldiers clap their hands to their heads in pain and thus leaving them vulnerable to the zombies, who did not care one iota about their rupturing eardrums but ploughed on regardless, leaping on the soldiers, bearing them down and stabbing or biting them with lustful moans.

Zogartha turned three huge reptilian yellow eyes on the demons, and its tendrils splashed and lashed out faster than Jamba could blink, seeking to swat or enwrap. Djhuty and Izulu zigzagged through the scorching sky like flies irritating a horse, dodging the dripping wet tentacles and attached pincers by a hair's breadth again and again, dire energies pouring from their fingertips and beak to rend at Zogartha's lightless hide. Though the leviathan shrilled, though, the attacks seemed to have about as much effect as a bee sting.

Eventually, Zogartha caught Izulu with a glancing blow, sending the avian demon plummeting ignominiously into the river. Then, it snatched Djhuty out of the air in one long arm, brought the hollering demon to its round, fang-lined maw and tossed the smaller demon inside despite Djhuty's roars and incantations and the black spells with which he burned the bigger beast's gullet. Watching for several seconds, Ruffle Feathers expected Djhuty to burst free of Zogartha's throat or stomach like a maggot eating the larger demon from the inside out, but after a few long seconds, the truth slowly dawned on him. Djhuty the Diabolical was gone. He sensed the end of the demon's life, the weight of the spell keeping him and Izulu in Maradoum abruptly lifting off the obeahman's chest.

His hands over his ears to muffle Zogartha's screech of victory, Ruffle beheld Councillor Chup Morton grinning and prancing on the spot despite the blood trickling from his ears. Zogartha bent to lower its alien visage towards the councillor, who was clearly shouting in glee, though Ruffle could not hear his words thanks to the ringing in his ears. Morton jabbed a finger towards the old smuggler, clearly ordering Zogartha to wipe him and his friends out. Zogartha opened wide its horrific maw and, with a great whoosh, sucked the surprised councillor down its throat in an instant. Ruffle winced as he witnessed the man disappear down the gullet. Then, Zogartha's great eyes were turning on him, and the blood froze in his veins. He had never felt so small, powerless and insignificant as he did in that moment, under the gaze of an ancient being a hundred times his size. He could see death, plain as day, in the slitted pupils.

He turned to Jamba and hastily waved his arms to form arcane symbols in the air, almost messing them up thanks to his trembling fingers. 'Look after the others, Jamba, my friend, and keep them out of the way. There is nothing else for it. I must summon Shazarad.'

Jamba gaped. "But you once told me that demon almost killed you, that you cannot control it – just as Morton could not control Zogartha! Don't do this, Ruffle! It will be the death of you!"

Ruffle nodded, a tear in his eye. 'And yet I must. You must buy me all the time you can, for this is no easy enchantment.'

He waved his arms again and felt obeah flow through his veins like lava, torching the fear and rewarming his blood. He poured energy into the summoning until he pulsed with power, glowing from the inside. An eldritch wind whipped his dreadlocks about his lined, cocoa face, and the very air around him crackled with energy. Before Zogartha could reach him, Damballah the hissing snake God slithered through the air in a blur to careen into the black fiend's spiky body. Reeling back a single step, Zogartha snagged the snake out of the air with one of its long tendrils and started to crush it. Bwa flung himself off the serpent's back to land on the demon's spiky face with a roar, hacking at it with a Justiquan broadsword he had picked up and spilling purplish blood.

The demon was about to consume the snake when Damballah dissolved into a fine mist and drifted away. So, it turned its attention instead on the God, plucking him off its face with a pincer as a man might pluck a bug. Papa Bwa roared in anger and pain as he was squeezed until he was blue in the face, and then the pincers snipped and the two halves of his body, severed at the midriff, plummeted into the river with twin splashes, staining the water red for a moment.

Jamba glanced this way and that frantically, fear welling in his heart, unsure how he was to slow down the colossus where even a God could not. His desperate eyes alighted on Jeremias and the witches.

"You have to do something!" he yelled at them desperately, barely audible over Zogartha's shrilling. "You're the only ones with the power to slow that thing down until Ruffle is ready!"

The witches shook their heads at once, visibly shaken. "We cannot stand up to such a beast," said Vivian, a tremor in her normally strong voice. She appeared drained, and she had let her arcane bubble fade away. "Its power eclipses ours like the moon before the sun!"

"Combined, we have enough power to fight this fiend!" said Waddi-waddi in Jeremias' mind.

Jeremias suddenly stood straighter, not so hunched, and his voice, when he spoke, resonated more deeply and powerfully than usual, reinforced by the strange double timbre.

"I am the sun," he said, stepping out of the protective golden aegis.

By force of will, the seneschal-turned-necromancer floated up into the air and began to bombard the leviathan with jagged cords of crackling lightning, great balls of whooshing flame and spears of red-hot energy. All spluttered out on contact with the demon's black hide with no discernible effect save to enrage the beast, so that it keened and lashed out with its tendrils, trying to snag the irksome seneschal. Jeremias flitted this way and that in the air to avoid the swiping tentacles, fast as a dragonfly, pantaloons and shirt billowing. He cast icicles sharp as razors at the demon, golden stars capable of shredding metal, humming green discs that could cleave through stone and a beam of roaring violet energy that would have pulverised almost anything on Maradoum. The demon withstood it all, though the beam plainly hurt it, pushing it back and redoubling its wails. The river sloshed around it as it staggered.

Encouraged, Jeremias continued the beam, trying to bore into the fiend. He held still a heartbeat too long, however, and a tentacle came for him. Seeing it rise up out of the water from the corner of his eye, he tried to dart aside, but the pincer at the end of the abyssal tendril caught his leg. Jeremias screamed at the searing white spike of pain he felt as his left leg was severed from his body in a single snip. Losing concentration in an instant, he dropped out of the sky to splash into the river.

"Jeremias!" cried out the Lullabyer's spirit in angst.

Zogartha turned its reptilian eyes on Ruffle Feathers just in time to witness a massive rift spawn by the obeahman's side, a slash in the air redder than blood, coughing vermillion flames and odious smoke.

Words of fire flashed before Jamba's eyes. 'Call Shazarad the Terrible!'

Feeling as though he would soon regret it, the smuggler cried out in a parched, cracking voice, "Shazarad the Terrible, we summon you!"

The earth shook as a demon taller than the tallest building in the city stepped through the rift into the river, sending up plumes of steam amid a great hissing and casting a crimson haze over the entire city as if the sun was setting in a sea of fire. The temperature on the bridge rose several notches in a heartbeat in its proximity, for the demon's entire vaguely humanoid body blazed, lava coursing down its length. It sucked in air through the slits it used for nostrils and breathed out smoke through its gash of a mouth, baring dagger-like teeth. Its eyes lit up the bridge like lanterns where it looked. It flexed sharp claws and laughed uproariously.

"Who dares to summon Shazarad the Terrible?" it boomed in a voice fit to cow a thunderstorm, sweeping the bridge with its luminous gaze until its eyes came to rest on Ruffle Feathers. Ignoring the obeahman's words of fire, it thundered, "You! You're the one who dared summon my Children. It is because of you that one of them now lies slain! And for that … you will suffer."

It reached down to scoop up the puny human with fiery talons, but huge pit-black tentacles encircled its body before it could grab him, pulling the demon away. Roaring in frustration, Shazarad the Terrible spun to lock eyes with Zogartha of the Void, and the battle of the behemoths began. Jamba thought the entire island must have shaken when the two beings from other worlds collided, squeezing and punching and kicking and biting. Zogartha reeled under the weight of its foe's punches, and Shazarad brayed in pain whenever pincers snipped its fiery skin. More and more tendrils wrapped around Shazarad until the flame-wreathed fiend was forced down to one knee under the pressure. Its flames roared and reared, flickering higher and higher, but Zogartha did not seem to mind.

Ruffle Feathers thought his demon was doomed, but then he saw Shazarad wrap its arms around some of the tentacles, grasping them tight. It pushed up hard and reared out of the river with a hiss and a cloud of steam, rising to its feet once more and manhandling – or demonhandling – Zogartha back until it slammed the tentacled demon against the bridge, rocking the whole structure and sending bits of shattered stone splashing into the river. The zombies collapsed to a man as the bridge juddered, and the Justiquans – many also falling but swifter to rise – took the opportunity to lay into the prone undead, maiming scores of them so that they could never rise again, no matter how much they flapped their leg and arm stumps.

Looming over them, Shazarad started to rip off Zogartha' limbs one by one with its long, sharp teeth, while the demon of the Void shrieked and flailed, trying to wrench the other off it or gouge out the fire demon's eyes with its pincers to no avail. Shazarad had it pinned now and showed no signs of letting it go. Biting off enough tentacles to clear a path, Shazarad lunged forward and bit deep into Zogartha's body, ripping free urchin-like spikes between its teeth and spitting them into the river, before biting again, and again. Zogartha's blood stained the river purple as it slowly slumped down in Shazarad's grip. Finally, when Shazarad had chewed deep enough, its tendrils loosened their grip and the leviathan sank beneath the surface of the water, never to see daylight again. With Zogartha gone, Shazarad sucked in a deep breath and, staggering, almost lost his balance. Lava poured from dozens of wounds on its nightmarish face and body as the demon leaned on the groaning bridge, sending cracks shooting along its length as it struggled to bear the fiend's weight.

"That," panted the demon, turning towards Ruffle Feathers, "was a good fight. Whence did that beast originate, human?"

Ruffle pointed to the headland where Maawu Palace had once stood, where people could be seen scurrying around in the distance, the sun in the blood-red sky glinting off their armour.

"Hmm," Shazarad purred deep in its throat, "a good fight."

With that, the demon pushed itself up, further fracturing the bridge, and began to plod methodically towards the promontory, crushing houses under heel and leaving craterous fiery footprints in the streets when it left the river behind. Ruffle considered sending words of flame chasing after it, but it was already on a collision course with the crusaders and he did not want to once more invoke the demon's wrath or remind it that he had summoned its Children to do his bidding in Oldport, resulting in the death of one of its offspring. So, he watched it go and prayed it would reduce the Justiquan army on the headland to smithereens.

Switching his gaze back to the bridge, the obeahman saw that, thanks to their fearless, painless zeal, the zombies had at last wiped out the crusaders blocking the way. Some of the last soldiers were now fleeing southwest towards the promontory, paralleling the demon's route.

"I don't know what you did," said Pahu to Ruffle, stepping forward, "but I'm glad you did it. Can you control that thing?"

Ruffle shrugged, exhausted.

Pahu nodded as if expecting as much. "Very well. We'll just have to pray it's on our side, then. We should get moving. With luck, we can oust the crusaders by sunset."

47

Musical Warfare

With Jeremias Colcott gone, the zombies had no one to lead them. Since they took their orders solely from the seneschal, without him they simply wandered off in all directions, following whatever took their fancy. Pahu Opherio supposed he should be grateful that the undead were not trying to eat the Chilpaeans, but frustration gnawed at him behind the eyes nevertheless. One of his most powerful tools, a near immortal zombie army, had been snatched from his hands at the hour of victory, and he rankled at the fact. He had grown to like Jeremias too over the last few days, so he prayed the seneschal yet lived, even while knowing it unlikely.

So, marching uphill without the undead towards Maawu Palace on the promontory overlooking the bowl of the bay from the west, Pahu and the remnants of the Chilpaean military finally found the invaders hiding behind a stone wall crossing the width of the narrow headland. The afternoon sun pounded on their temples. Blinking sweat out of his eyes, Jamba Klach thought he recognised some of the wall's masonry from the palace, of which there was no sign. Reaching it ahead of the smugglers, Shazarad shattered the wall with a single blow of its fist, sending men and stones flying. Jamba would have cheered at the sight if he was sure the demon was not about to do the same to them.

Watching from behind the demon with the others, he observed a lone figure sauntering through the debris of the broken wall and, through clouds of dust, recognised the Knight-Commander, Godfrey Saint-Marcente. Though Shazarad was busy obliterating the surrounding crusaders with its pounding fists and lava spittle, for some reason it could not destroy their commander. Its hands and saliva rebounded off a semi-transparent glowing green bubble of crackling energy surrounding the man, unable to penetrate it. Roaring in vexation, the demon redoubled its assault, bringing both hands hammering down as one on the man and trying to drown him in drool.

Jamba watched open-mouthed as Godfrey calmly took out his wide, curved sword – which the smuggler noticed had nine jangling bells attached to the blunt edge. A nine-ring sword, he thought wonderingly, having heard of such a phenomenon but never seen one. This one had been fashioned to hold bells in place of the rings, however, which Jamba had never heard tell of before. The Knight-Commander swished the sword through the air, and in response the bells clanged against the blade, producing a metallic sonic shockwave that buffeted the gargantuan demon back a couple of paces. Jamba could not believe his eyes.

Then, Godfrey was advancing, lashing his sword vengefully left and right to swipe at nothingness. Though his blade did not touch the demon, it nevertheless brutalised it, for every swing created a sonic shockwave sharper than a razor. Growing larger as they went, these shockwaves pulsed out from the Knight-Commander over and over, each savaging the gigantic demon a little more, scything open its fiery skin and spilling its lava-like blood on the cobbles, where it burned through to the earth beneath. Reeling and roaring in agony, Shazarad tried once more to clobber its tiny foe, but in vain. Shockwaves severed its hands at the wrists one by one, and then brought it to its knees by cutting out its ankles from beneath it.

As the demon flopped down to its knees with a bellow, Godfrey leaped impossibly high in the air and gave his sword one final, decisive slash. Shazarad's outcries were cut short when its head toppled off its shoulders to come crashing down on the ground and roll unceremoniously, bouncing, back downhill towards the bay. The demon's neck stump erupted with lava like a volcano, and its body collapsed to one side, toppling off the cliff edge to land with a great splash in the ocean far below. Godfrey alighted lightly on his feet and took in the monk, assassin, deserter, seneschal, general, smugglers, witches, soldiers and zombies with a dull glance. Behind him, the mauled Justiquan army formed ranks, ready to advance past the lava left in Shazarad's wake.

Godfrey squinted at the spirit of the Lullabyer, recognising him despite his ethereal state. "Is that the best you've got?" he demanded haughtily in cultured Traveller's Tongue, his voice carrying across the few hundred yards between them easily despite the laughing sea wind. "How many times do I have to kill you, Magnuz, before you stop being a thorn in my side? Although perhaps I ought to be thanking you really, for bringing the last of the resistance in this Prophet-forsaken country to my doorstep so that I can wipe you all out in one fell swoop. Who is that by your side? I sense his power, so it must be the younger son you shipped off to the monastery in the north, right? Pablo, was it?"

"My name is Pahu Opherio," said the monk loudly, stepping forward, "and this is *my* country. Return my sister, Patma, to me, get on your ships and leave, or you will regret it."

Godfrey smirked. "You did well at Jinglespur to defeat Marshal Clauss, I'll say that. But you aren't on my level, boy. I've been training as a witch-hunter all my life. Even your demon could not stop me. And as for Patma – she's my daughter now. You have my word that I'll give her every care when raising her in Justiqua after I wipe out you and your friends. She'll never know about any of this nastiness. She'll never even know your names."

Pahu felt his blood boil, his temples pounding, and before he knew it, he was striding purposefully forward, his hands unconsciously smacking the damaru in his hands, rapping out a malevolent beat full of hatred and bile. The smugglers and witches darted forward to restrain him, but were buffeted back by the sonic shockwaves emanating from the drum like palpable ripples in the air. They could none of them get near him. All they could do was follow nervously at a distance, praying that he knew what he was doing. Magnuz was the only one who could keep up with him, since he had no physical frame.

"This is not the way, Pahu!" he yelled, standing in front of his son to block him.

Pahu walked straight through him, making Magnuz shudder.

The Lullabyer pursued the monk, shouting, *"The power in our music comes not from fear or hate but from peace and love, Pahu! You will never master the Lullaby until you learn to master your mind! You cannot fight fire with fire! You cannot quench hate with hate! Please, Pahu, I'm begging you – stop! You go to your grave!"*

Ignoring his father, his hands moving faster and faster on the drum until an interminable tattoo thrummed in the air, Pahu walked on. Swishing his sword left and right and sending out sonic shockwaves of his own, Godfrey strode to meet the monk. Rebuffed by the crusader's shockwaves, the smugglers and witches fell even further behind Pahu and called out after him in concern. He paid them no heed, seeming unaffected by the commander's nine-bell sword. The jangle of the bells and the pounding of the drum clashed in a discordant cacophony that set Jamba's teeth on edge and made his head ache.

He could barely even watch the two musicians as they advanced on one another, both now bending into the shockwaves they could finally feel emanating from the other, looking as though they were struggling uphill against a gale. His eyes watered as he beheld Godfrey staggering back, overwhelmed by Pahu's music. The commander managed to plant his feet once more, though, and began whirling his nine-bell sword around and around in circles. The blade whirred faster and faster until it became a blur, and then the circle it sketched seemed to take on a life of its own, like a maelstrom in mid-air, sucking at Pahu and absorbing the shockwaves from his drum without allowing them to affect the Justiquan.

Drawn in by the vortex, Pahu tried to dig in his heels and backpedal, but he could not. He was caught as surely as a fly in a web, and each second saw him slide closer and closer to the blurring blade. He rapped out a desperate powerful riff on the drum that staggered the Knight-Commander, but the blade never stopped spinning and a moment later, Pahu was trapped in the middle of it. Jamba had to avert his eyes, for the maelstrom broke his brain, but when he looked back, the nine-bell sword had stopped spinning and Pahu lay dead on the floor with a great gash across his chest, his unseeing eyes staring up at the onset of sunset.

"No!" screamed Magnuz and the witches.

48

War for Chilpaea

Jamba Klach's heart stopped at the sight of Pahu sprawled in the wide sloping street, rouged by the red rays of the setting sun, and he felt hollow, numb. A chill swept through him despite the day's warmth. How could they possibly free Chilpaea now? The last of the Opherios was dead, and there was no one to stop the Sleepers now – no one but Godfrey Saint-Marcente and his nine-bell sword. Jamba wondered for a moment whether they ought to keep the Knight-Commander alive so that he could protect the country, but then he sneered at himself inwardly. Chilpaea did not need the protection of an outsider. He would rather perish at the paws of the Sleepers than live in servitude to the knights.

With that thought, he hefted his scimitars and charged, determined to at least reclaim the corpse of the fallen monk. Lug Thorm, Kofi Touluz, Wagnar Long, General Raoul Malone and the Chilpaean army were hot on his heels, bellowing war cries. Vivian and Violet Malakbet, Ruffle Feathers and the shade of Magnuz Opherio were by Pahu's side in an instant, checking his pulse and wailing when they found nothing.

Brimming with tears, Violet rose and turned her furious gaze on the Knight-Commander while her sister continued to sob wretchedly beside her. She wished she had cast a protective bubble around Pahu, but she had been unable to concentrate enough to do so thanks to the constant shockwaves. Now, though, she could at least avenge the monk's death. Conjuring a glimmering dagger comprised of humming jade energy in both hands, Violet flew at the Knight-Commander, imbuing her limbs with preternatural strength so that she blew past the smugglers and soldiers in a trice, taking the lead before anyone could stop her.

"There must be something you can do!" Magnuz pleaded the obeahman, hands clasped before him, ghostly tears trickling down his cheeks. *"Please, Ruffle, help him, I beg you!"*

Ruffle Feathers hesitated, then waved a hand. 'I do know one spell that may be able to save him, but it requires a tremendous amount of energy and I have never successfully pulled it off before.'

"I'll do whatever it takes, just save him!"

Deaf to the world, Vivian looked up just in time to see her sister crash into Godfrey Saint-Marcente, daggers stabbing fast as lightning at the commander's unprotected face and the weak points in his armour. Godfrey parried her every blow with blistering speed, taking her by surprise, for her eldritch daggers ought to have been able to cut clean through ordinary steel.

She knew then that the nine-bell sword must be heavily enchanted. Not only that but whenever it swung, it propelled her back with a peal from the bells. Vivian rose to support her sister, vengeance in her heart, but Magnuz stood before her in a flash, hands raised to stop her.

"Wait!" he said urgently, pressing his hands together. *"We can salvage this! We can bring him back – you and I and Ruffle together! Please, Vivian, if you love him – help me!"*

Vivian hesitated. The urge to bury her fingernails in Godfrey's eye sockets burned deep in her soul, but she forced herself to swallow her spite and remember Pahu as he had been – kind, clever, innocent, and powerful as a tempest. In that moment, she forgot her hate and her shoulder slumped.

"Tell me what I must do," she said.

"We must give Ruffle Feathers our energies," said Magnuz, *"but be careful – give him too much and you will lose yourself, your very soul."*

Prancing in circles around the dead monk in an arrhythmic jig, Ruffle painted ancient occult symbols of power in the air in tongues of flickering fire in a language known to none present but Vivian. The witch closed her eyes and focussed on transmitting her energies to the capering obeahman, knowing the duppy dance had begun. She had heard of such a piece of obeah, but never seen it performed. Perhaps, she thought, if she had known such a trick, she could have brought back her mother. As Magnuz siphoned his energies to the obeahman, unseen by all, the Lullabyer crystal in Ruffle's satchel began to shrink.

Meanwhile, Violet was battling Godfrey alone, while the smugglers and Chilpaean soldiers strove to catch up with her. Behind Saint-Marcente, the Justiquan legions advanced to meet the Chilpaean forces. Lean and lithe as a palm swaying in a strong gust, Violet swayed this way and that to dodge the Knight-Commander's sword and retaliated with a viciously fast series of stabs and cuts that would have shorn an unpractised man to pieces. Godfrey was far from unpractised, though. A consummate swordsman, he caught every swipe on his own blade and pushed the witch back with a combination of muscle and shockwaves.

Allowing herself to be shoved back, Violet moved with the momentum, gaining space to hurl her jade daggers at the Knight-Commander. As soon as she had done so, two new daggers materialised in a flash of green in her hands, and she lobbed those, too. His sword swinging faster than she would have believed possible, Godfrey swatted the knives out of the air. Grinding her teeth, Violet threw more and more but to no avail. The Knight-Commander knocked them all out of the air, advancing a step at a time until he was once more close enough to launch an attack. Springing high and flipping over his head, hoping to skewer him in the back, Violet never landed. She coughed up blood, suspended in mid-air, impaled on the nine-bell sword, which the crusader had reversed and stabbed backwards.

The smugglers cried out in horror at the sight, but Vivian did not hear them, intent on saving the monk. Seeing that the Chilpaeans would reach him before his own forces did, Godfrey cast aside the witch's corpse and quickly retreated behind his own lines then, much to Jamba's vexation. Out in front of the others, the smuggler had been hoping to avenge the witch with a single stroke of his sword. Now, though, he locked eyes on a different target in the front line of the Justiquan army, a target wielding dual blades. It was a target Magnuz Opherio recognised all too well from the night Maawu Palace had collapsed, for the piggy face had been the last sight he had seen as he breathed his last breath. Jamba pointed one of his scimitars at Major Ortega, singling the armoured man out, and the two swordsmen beelined for one another like moths to flame.

Their four swords scraped together in a great spray of sparks, and then skirled apart only to slam together again with enough force to jar Jamba's wrists. All around them, Chilpaeans clashed with Justiquans in a furore, shouting and wailing, hollering war cries and letting out death screams. The discordant song of steel on steel, brittle and clanging, echoed out over the city. Lost in the rhythm of battle, Jamba's world tunnelled down to his one foe. Nothing else existed to him in those moments except Ortega and his blades.

His eyes tracking the crusader's every shift in stance, every flick of the wrist, every flicker of the eyes, Jamba was able to anticipate the man's moves and catch them with lightning reflexes, sometimes surprising himself with the speed at which he swung his scimitars. Time and again, he thought he was about to feel cold steel in his flesh, only to avert it by a gnat's breadth with a sweep of one of his swords. Ortega was younger – and probably fitter, thought Jamba – but the smuggler held his own, fuelled by a bottomless wrath sucking at his insides. These crusaders had taken his country, his friends, and now the only hope he had for retaking the capital.

Blind fury egged him on, and he whirled his swords in wilder and wilder attack patterns when the basics did not serve, leaping and pirouetting, feinting and attacking high and low to try to catch Ortega out. Ortega was too skilled and too fast, though. Everything Jamba tried, the major turned aside, retaliating with his own series of unknown, unpredictable attack patterns that had Jamba on the back foot as he sought to find and analyse the methods being used against him. Ortega favoured a swift, far more practicable style than Jamba's own flamboyant moves, never turning his back on the smuggler, but always keeping his swords moving, jabbing, jabbing, jabbing, and then slicing unexpectedly, trying to take out the smuggler's knees. Jamba leaped out of the way, leaping and spinning and wishing he could circle his foe, for the man's style was very stationary. He knew he could not, though, with so many other foes so close by. He had to find a way through Ortega's guard rather than around it.

Feeling his strength start to wane and knowing the younger man would have the greater stamina, Jamba knew he had to do it sooner rather than later, too. Even when he managed to land a blow, it only ever glanced off the major's steel plate armour. He decided on a risky gambit. He needed to wait for his opportunity to strike, and he knew if he missed by even an inch, he would die. Ortega did not give him the opportunity easily, however. He raised one of his swords above his head time and again, but always the second blade was perfectly positioned to protect his weak spot and, more often than not, Jamba was off-balance from the last blow and in no positon to take advantage of the pose. He waited, biding his time, parrying and riposting, parrying and riposting.

Each blow was still aimed to kill, just in case he got lucky, but he knew he would need to try an unusual move to catch Ortega off-guard, for he had the major's measure now and, loath though he was to admit it, Ortega was one of the finest swordsmen he had ever fought. Tricks as old as the book were used against Jamba again and again, tricks he had only ever seen one or two other men master. He could hardly believe it when Ortega switched one blade to reverse grip mid-attack, the move almost ending the fight then and there as the reversed sword split the skin on Jamba's left shoulder, failing to go deep as the smuggler danced back but still making him gasp at the torturously icy sensation.

Ortega followed up with both swords in reverse, using an attack pattern Jamba had never seen and which he had to defend on the fly, figuring it out as he went. The smuggler parried wildly with his right blade, trying not to use the other unless absolutely necessary, his left arm burning with welling blood. He could not retreat far to gain space either, for Chilpaean soldiers stood at his back, awaiting their turn in the vanguard. So, he swayed this way and that, bobbing and weaving and even jumping over Ortega's blades here and there when the dastardly Justiquan attempted a low blow. Landing awkwardly after one such jump, his weight all on one foot, he had a split-second decision to make. Forwards or back?

He could spring either way, but he had to choose one or the other before he overbalanced. He knew in the back of his mind he would have chosen to hop back on a sensible day, but he was feeling far from sensible. Burning anger was all he felt, and he sprang forward before he even made a conscious decision, his desire for vengeance grabbing him by the collar.

Luckily, Ortega reacted exactly as he had hoped, lifting one blade high for a chop while warding the smuggler off with the second. Jamba barely managed to bat the blocking blade aside as he leaped, and the sword sliced his side. He did not care, hardly noticed in fact, as his own right-hand scimitar buried itself deep in the major's exposed armpit, under his armour, cleaving through his ribs and skewering his heart and lungs. Ortega grunted and coughed blood, before his eyes crossed and he slumped off the smuggler's blade to fall to the ground with a clang.

Retreating and allowing a Chilpaean soldier to take his place, Jamba looked around, breathing heavily. Though the Justiquans had the better tactics and strategy with their close formation and shield-wall, the Chilpaeans had passion on their side. The smuggler saw one Chilpaean disembowelled but refusing to submit to death's grip until he had taken his killer with him. Another stood over the injured body of his friend, flailing two swords to keep the crusaders at bay. Another leaped fiercely into the fight as soon as he was given the chance, pushing back the Justiquans and giving his waning comrades a chance to catch their breath at the cost of his life. Jamba saw General Malone strike down six enemies in quick succession with his scimitar before a slice to the leg staggered him and he too retreated to allow another to take his place.

Big Brenda from Bessaroca was giving a good account of herself in the melee, Jamba saw, hacking at steel-clad soldiers with more zeal than skill, but still managing to slide her stolen Justiquan sword between steel plates now and then to bring down a foe. The fighters eddied, and the burly woman was lost to sight for a moment. The smuggler's heart broke when he glimpsed Big Brenda's body on the ground a few seconds later, her throat slit.

He craned his neck to peer over his rapidly dwindling countrymen's heads and look behind him towards the dead monk. Witnessing Ruffle Feathers dancing and shining like a beacon, eldritch energies coruscating around him, the smuggler's brow furrowed and he started to sidle backwards through the ranks of warriors alongside the grievously wounded, eventually popping out of the back of the pack of serried soldiers and loping over to the obeahman. Lug, Kofi and Wagnar had evidently had the same idea, for they joined him from the fracas a moment later.

"What's going on?" asked Lug, his furry face worried.

Ruffle did not reply, but kept jigging with a mania plain to see. The witch and the Lullabyer's shade appeared entranced, their hands on Pahu's chest.

"I think … I think they're trying to bring him back," whispered Jamba in awe, a spark of hope flaring in his heart as the sun sank closer to the horizon.

49

Duppy

Pahu Opherio awoke from what seemed a long and deep sleep and gazed up into the face of Vivian Malakbet silhouetted against the rose petals of sunset, who kissed him deeply with tears on her lips, and the ghostly face of his father, who smiled down at him with more warmth than Pahu had ever witnessed on his stern old visage.

"Oh, Pahu, thank the Gods you're alright!" Vivian sobbed.

As Pahu sat up, Magnuz Opherio inclined his head. *"Welcome back, Pahu."*

"What happened?" asked the monk, scratching his head.

"You died," Vivian told him in a small voice. "And so did Violet."

"But Ruffle Feathers brought you back," added Magnuz.

'How are you feeling?' asked the obeahman in letters of flame.

Pahu gaped. "I feel fine. You saved me? I don't know what to say … Thank you, Ruffle."

Ruffle waved a dismissive hand. 'You're welcome.' He grinned as he picked up the monk's dropped damaru and offered it to him. 'Now, save our country, Pahu.'

Pahu smiled wearily and nodded. "I had the strangest dream, in which mother Calliope showed me two futures. In one, I ravaged the world at the head of a Sleeper army with a scowl on my face, alone but for beasts. In the other, I was surrounded by you. By my friends and family. And I played the Lullaby with a smile on my lips and the Sleepers slept. I know which future I choose. I understand now what you were trying to tell me, father. I know now the reason the Lullaby did not work. I cannot play the Lullaby with anger in my heart. I must do it with love."

He took his drum from the obeahman and started to play.

The smugglers, the spirit of the Lullabyer and the witch fell back in shock as he rose smoothly to his feet. Though blood still stained his simple brown monk's robe, they could see through the slash in his garments that his chest was healed. No scar now marred his flesh. His music pealed out, sad and slow, calling clouds to cast the day in shade. A faint drizzle began when he started singing the words to *Gone Brother Gone.*

Hearing the soulful tune ring out over the skirling song of battle and laying eyes on the resurrected monk, Godfrey Saint-Marcente growled angrily and shoved past his men until he stood in the vanguard of the Justiquan army, facing the Chilpaeans. There, he whipped his nine-bell sword this way and that, and once more razor-sharp shockwaves sprang from the whistling blade to cull his foes by the dozen. Where the sword swung, a slew of men died in great bloody sprays, many torn in twain at the midriff. Seeing this, Jamba wondered why the Knight-Commander had not used such skills against Violet Malakbet and guessed he must have been drained from his fight with Shazarad, or he had simply thought the witch not worth the effort.

Now, though, whether he had recouped his energies or decided it was worth his while to slay Pahu all over again, Godfrey was clearly trying to slaughter a path through the Chilpaean army straight towards the monk. With just a few swipes of his sword, he succeeded, obliterating the Chilpaean army with shockwave after shockwave so that the cobbles ran red with their blood. He prowled alone towards the monk down a corpse-choked street then, stepping over the bodies of the dead and dying and ignoring their groans. His soldiers appeared too frightened of him to follow. Jamba could not blame them.

Godfrey drew up to the smugglers, who had formed a defensive line between him and the monk still playing rapturous music, and pointed his nine-bell sword at them. "You have seen what I can do," he barked over the melody in Traveller's. "Stand aside or I'll tear you limb from limb."

He said it in such an understated way that Jamba knew it to be true.

Still, the smuggler shook his head. "I'm not going anywhere."

"Nor I," echoed Lug.

"Nor I," echoed Kofi.

"Nor I," echoed Wagnar.

"Nor I," echoed Vivian.

Drained, Ruffle Feathers was the one sprawled on the ground now, breathing but utterly exhausted. Magnuz stood in line with the smugglers, though he provided no physical obstacle.

"Then, you'll die!" Godfrey snarled and whipped his sword across his body, slashing the air at waist height.

Lug was struck down where he stood, shorn in half at the midriff by the shockwave emanating from the blade, so that both halves of his hirsute body toppled to the ground while the top half moaned piteously. Kofi and Wagnar sought to dodge, catching only the tail end of the shockwave where its power diminished. Both were hurled to the ground, winded and bruised, while Pahu seemed entirely unaffected. Anticipating the shockwave emanating from the blade, Jamba leaped as high as he could in the air and felt the whoosh of the deadly wave of energy pass beneath his boots. He landed, rolled beneath the next wave and came up just a couple of feet away from the Knight-Commander, catching him unawares and slashing at his throat with both scimitars, missing by a mere inch as Godfrey leaned back and hitting only the steel cuirass, knocking the Justiquan back a step. He followed up the attack with leonine speed, scimitars flashing in a fast and complex attack pattern with which Godfrey could not keep up, off-balance as he was.

"You will not take my country!" Jamba roared, spitting with fury, his scimitars skirling against the steel breastpate again and again.

The Knight-Commander reeled in the face of the onslaught, but finally found his footing and caught the smuggler's blades, one on his own sword and one in his gauntlet.

Jamba's eyes widened as Godfrey panted, "You're a worthy fighter, smuggler. I see now how you were able to take the crystal all the way across the island and back. I can always use talented warriors by my side. You should join me. I can offer you wealth and adventure beyond your wildest dreams – women, wine, baui, gold, anything your heart desires!"

It was Jamba's turn to reel as images of life as a rich man flooded his mind.

He shook his head to clear it. "Chilpaea is my mother and I am her son, and I will not abandon my brothers and sisters to die at the hands of scum like you! Lug will be avenged!"

So saying, he broke contact with the nine-bell sword and sought to take off the Knight-Commander's head with a single swipe. Godfrey swayed back and tried to spin the smuggler by twisting the sword in his gauntlet, but Jamba released it and leaned into his blow, the tip of his scimitar flicking across the crusader's cheek and drawing a thin line of blood. Instinctively, as he would have done in any ordinary duel, he backed up a step, expecting a riposte, forgetting for a split-second that his foe was capable of ripostes far beyond his ken. By the time he remembered, it was too late. He tried to jump the next shockwave too late and screamed at the splitting pain as both his legs were severed at the thigh. He hit the ground hard, shrieking again at the agony of his leg stumps striking the cobbles. He felt an invisible ice-cold hand on his cheek. It was strangely soothing. He recalled the last time he had felt such a sensation – in Dos Rios, in the mayor's wine cellar.

His breath seemed to desert him fast. He was cold. He lay there wheezing and wondering where all the duppy had come from. They stood beside him on all sides, Chilpaean men, women and children, faint at first but pulsing brighter and brighter with every beat of the monk's drum.

He saw Lug's upper half lying close by and crawled towards it, grabbing the lagahoo's hand and whispering, "You did good, Lug. Rest now. I will see you in the Sunset Isles, my friend."

Lug smiled weakly before the light in his eyes winked out and Jamba's heart cramped in his chest. He could scarcely see anything in the shade of the dark rain clouds – nothing but the unnatural luminosity of the duppy all around him, hundreds of them. He rolled his head over and saw Godfrey advancing on Pahu, bent double as if pushing against a strong wind, clearly trying his utmost to reach the monk but struggling. Pahu's music grew louder and louder, *Gone Brothers Gone* reverberating out over the land for leagues, and the duppy shone brighter and brighter, seeming almost to take solid form.

Godfrey finally took notice of the spirits when they grabbed hold of him, bodily restraining him and hauling him away from the monk playing the damaru. The Knight-Commander broke free of their grasp for a moment and slashed at them wildly, his face contorted in fear. The duppy took no notice, the nine-bell sword and its shockwaves passing through them as if they did not exist. In a matter of moments, they had the Knight-Commander restrained once more, his legs and arms pinned. Jamba saw one duppy stride forward then, an ornate longsword in his hands, and recognised the Lullabyer's oldest son, Dajuan Opherio. Dajuan plunged the sword into Godfrey's screaming mouth and the ephemeral blade popped out of the Justiquan's nape, dripping real blood. Snarling, Dajuan twisted the sword viciously so that the Knight-Commander spat blood, before yanking it back out and allowing the corpse to fall to the ground. Then, the spirit of the Lullabyer's heir turned and bowed to Pahu, who bowed solemnly in return, still tapping the drum.

As Pahu strode past Jamba, sparing him a lingering glance, Jamba felt as if the monk were singing to him and him alone, the lament soothing. "I come at last, Mnana," Jamba murmured, laying his head back. "Ferrymen, take me to blessed sleep."

Pahu's music empowering them, the duppy rolled over the crusaders like a silver wave, led by Dajuan Opherio. Though the Justiquans' blades passed through the spirits as if they didn't exist, the duppy's own ghostly weapons sank deep into the crusaders' flesh, drawing real blood. When the sun teetered on the brink, the Justiquans volubly surrendered and offered up baby Patma. Pahu altered his music, pulled back the duppy and strode to meet the Justiquan army himself to retrieve his little sister.

A young officer met him alone in the shadow of the ruined wall and handed him the babe. "Here, Lullabyer," said the man in a trembling tenor. "I am Captain Riktoff Garquon, the most senior living officer in the Justiquan army. I am authorised to return to you what was wrongfully taken."

Backed by duppy, Pahu took his sister, resisting the urge to coo and croon. She appeared unharmed. The sight of her chubby smiling face made his heart sing. He glared at the officer.

Captain Garquon shrivelled under his gaze and the withering gaze of the hundreds of spirits like a chastised child. "What now, Lullabyer?" he finally squawked nervously. "You have accepted our surrender. Will you grant us safe passafe to our ships that we may leave your shores before the sun sets and the Sleepers find us out in the open with no music to defend ourselves?"

Pahu glowered at the man for a moment more. Then, he grunted. "If you hurry, you might just make it to the docks in time. Leave our shores, Garquon, and never return, you hear me?"

The captain nodded ardently. "I hear you. Thank you, Lullabyer, thank you for your clemency!"

The spirits escorted the crusaders to their ships docked in Cocoba Bay, and then Pahu, Patma, Magnuz, Ruffle Feathers, Vivian, Kofi, Wagnar, General Malone and the tattered remnants of the Chilpaean army watched the Justiquans sail off into the sunset. Jeremias Colcott found them there as night fell, having washed up by the ocean when he had fallen in the river.

"How are you alive, old boy?" asked General Malone in astonishment as he helped haul the seneschal out of the water up onto the beach by the piers.

Sodden, teeth-chattering, Jeremias indicated his leg stump, which had stopped bleeding. "Lucky for me, obeah is meant for healing."

Magnuz Opherio sighed, his heart swelling at the sight of both his sons standing side by side, one flesh and blood, one spectral as smoke. *"You will make a great Lullabyer, Pahu,"* he said. *"I only wish I could be around to see it."*

"What do you mean?" Pahu asked. "Where are you going, father?"

"My energies are drained. The crystal in which I stored my soul is about to disappear. It is time for me to pass on to the Sunset Isles, my son." He laid a hand on Dajuan's shoulder. *"And you're coming with me. It is time to let go of your hate, Dajuan. It is time to go."*

Dajuan nodded, smiling.

Tears trickling down his face, Pahu sobbed, "I don't want to lose you, father."

Magnuz smiled, trying and failing to wipe away a tear with a phantom finger. *"You won't. I will always be with you, my son, watching over you. On that you may rely. I love you, Pahu. Sing us on our way, would you?"*

Pahu nodded and began to tap the drum, eyes welling. The Lullaby rang out clear and true then, and the Sleepers slept and the duppy vanished like mist under the morning sun.

50

Epilogue

A year later, Pahu Opherio returned to the headland west of Cocoba Bay where Maawu Palace had once stood, gazing at the rolling reflections of the sunset in a sea of fire. Out upon the gilded waves, slowly drifting closer, was a fleet of galleys.

"The Justiquans haunt our shores once more," observed Vivian Opherio, linking arms with him.

"I knew they'd be back," grunted Wagnar Long, spitting on the grass.

"Invasion is in their nature," said Kofi Touluz.

"I'm sure they're just using the current to sail past us on a trading mission," said Jeremias Colcott, leaning on a crutch. "They wouldn't dare try to conquer us again after what happened last time."

Raoul Malone snorted. "Not likely. That'd be a strange route for them to take. They're here for us, Jeremias."

"If they land, we'll be ready for them," said Pahu.

Ruffle Feathers puffed on a baui pipe carved in the shape of a dragon and waved a hand, inscribing words of fire in the air. 'I know I will.'

Pahu took Patma from his wife's arms, smiling, but sadly, like the sun half cast in shade. "Hello, baby sister." He kissed her on the head, and she stared up at him with big innocent eyes. "Sorry about all the kerfuffle." She giggled and he smiled. "D'you recognise your family? This is Seneschal Jeremias Colcott, this is General Malone, and this is my advisor, Ruffle Feathers. These are my bodyguards, Kofi Touluz and Wagnar Long. And this is my wife, Vivian. Isn't she beautiful? As for my parents, my brother and all those who died so that we can stand here now … I'll tell you all about them when you're older. For now, I need to sing the Lullaby. Will you help me?"

Patma gurgled happily as Pahu began to sing. The Sleepers did not rise that night, nor any other night while Pahu Opherio reigned.

"Long live the Lullabyer," murmured Kofi.

Out now …

The Night Comes Alive: A Gothic Fantasy Novel

If you enjoyed the book, leaving a review would go a long way to showing your appreciation and would in turn be much appreciated. Thanks!

Check out the Convent Series or more from the Chronicles of Maradoum Series at www.rosshughes.biz

Follow my Facebook page: Ross Hughes, Author